The Moon A

By Frances M.

Second Edition: Published December 2022

ALL RIGHTS RESERVED

This book is licensed for your personal enjoyment only. It may not be resold or given away to others to sell it, and it contains material protected under International Copyright Laws and Treaties. This book or any portion of it may not be reproduced, copied, or used in any manner whatsoever without the express written permission of the author or publisher, except for the use of brief quotations in a review.

Thank you for respecting and supporting the author's work.

Copyright © Frances M. Thompson

For Bobbins,

Thank you for being a wonderful friend for over twenty years. And thank you for being just as hilarious as Jake, but at least 80% less bitchy.

And for the women and youth of Iran,

May your fight for freedom and love prevail.

Introduction

The following contains possible spoilers but will ensure a safe and enjoyable reading experience for all.

The Moon Also Rises is a spicy romcom and as such you should expect some detailed love scenes and more than a few opportunities to laugh. But as with the best comedies, this book also touches on serious and difficult topics. This includes the characters talking about parental neglect, family estrangement, the death of parents (by illness and by suicide), credit card debt and money problems, homophobia, and being in a cult. There is also a conversation between two characters about struggling to conceive and there is very brief on-page biphobia/panphobia in one scene. This book is also intended for an 18+ audience as it contains graphic sexual content. And please be advised that there is endless swearing throughout, a medium-sized pansexual panic, and more than a few gay flaps. Please also note that "Mom" is not a typo as that's what brilliant Brummies call their brilliant moms.

Add this book to your Goodreads shelves: https://geni.us/TheMoonGoodreads.
And if you like listening to book playlists, go to Spotify and search for the playlist "The Moon Also Rises" and if you see one by 'frankiebird' you've found the right one! There's also another playlist mentioned in this book that Jake's love interest has made and that's also available on Spotify if you search "DJ Lunar Soul Chillout".

"We are all like the bright Moon; we still have our darker side."

Khalil Gibran

"The Moon is a friend for the lonesome to talk to."

Carl Sandburg

"Be both soft and wild. Just like the Moon."

Victoria Erickson

Prologue

Fifteen Years Ago
New Year's Eve, Sydney

Jake

Somebody's bollocks should get pickled for this.

Like, seriously. It's a shambles. The sound is off, the lighting is giving me a headache, and don't even get me started on the potential health and safety implications of the over-crowding situation we have thanks to a photobooth far too close to the main entrance to the dance floor. But what do I know? I'm just a lowly under-employed assistant manager of a hotel restaurant gate-crashing the New Year's Eve dance event in the hotel's top floor nightclub because he shamefully didn't get a better offer. The only thing making up for the evidently poor organisation are the views of the harbour from up here. And the music. I crane my neck to try and get a better look at the DJ, because whoever it is, they're kicking out some stonking tunes.

"Yeah, it's banging," Steveo shouts back. *Oh, did I say that out loud?*

"Want another drink?" he asks me while his mouth is close to my ear.

"Sure," I say and knock back the last slug of beer in my bottle. Before I can ask him to get me a white wine spritzer instead of another beer that will make me bloat even more than that first one did, he's off, heading to the bar. I find my eyes naturally fall to his backside. It's still just as pert as I remember from last night. And still just as married to a woman.

"When will you learn?" I ask myself out loud, turning my head back to face the front stage. The crowd is as busy and as much of a fire hazard as it was a moment ago and again, the poor lighting set-up means that all I can see of the stage are flashes of light so I still can't identify who's DJing. I probably should have read the set list in advance, but it was a rash decision to come, mostly prompted by Steveo's late announcement that he would be in Sydney for a few days, thanks to his wife getting a last-minute deal on a girls' holiday in Bali. The greatest surprise of all had come when he announced he wanted to go out rather than watch the fireworks from my apartment. Steveo hardly ever wants to be seen out in public with me. However, 'public' is sort of stretching where we are now considering it's a dark nightclub overpopulated with people at least ten years his junior. Kind of like I am.

"Seriously, Jake," I mutter to myself again. "When will you stop being someone's bit on the side?"

I should never have called him when he left his phone number on the back of his receipt that evening he dined in the restaurant a few months ago. But it seemed so… romantic? That just goes to show how low the bar is when it comes to me and romance.

Regardless, I should have done what I always promise myself I'm going to do; wait and meet a nice man who doesn't hide me away. A man who is proud of who he is, and proud of who I am. I mean, I would like to be proud of who I am too, but I know better than to ask for too much.

I sigh and try to think of Steveo's redeeming features, besides the one in his trousers. We do have fun, I think to myself as I watch him walk back balancing four drinks. Wait. Four drinks?

"Got us a little shot to keep our beers company," he shouts at me as he spills drops of all four drinks on my shoes. Shoes I polished for half an hour this afternoon, like the idiot I am for thinking he'd notice. That *someone* would notice.

"Great. Thanks," I say with gritted teeth as I take my drinks.

Steveo nods at me to down the shot and begrudgingly, I do, wincing as the vodka burns my throat and churns my stomach. I've barely rearranged my facial features back into something normal when Steveo nudges my arm with his surprisingly pointy and hard elbow.

"Come on, let's dance!" he yells.

I'm not entirely sure why I agree, but I do. I let him take me to the dance floor and for the first few tracks we dance like awkward straight white men, our drinks being thrust out into the air in various directions, more often off the beat than on it. But after ten minutes, Steveo spins me around and lines up his chest against my back. His arms don't circle around me but I feel the warmth of his body, and the outline of one particular part of his anatomy, push up against my backside. I lean back against it, and him.

The music has an air of seventies disco to it and I sway my hips to the rhythm. It's the kind of song I feel I should know and it's easy to close my eyes and feel the music pump through my body, my veins, my mind as I start to forget all the many problems with Steveo. Maybe tonight will turn out alright. Maybe tonight will mark the beginning of a better, brighter year.

Encouraged, I turn around and slide my thighs around Steveo's leg, interlocking our groins closer together. He straightens up a little, pulls back and I watch him glance around the dance floor. I ignore how that elongates my spine and makes my jaw clench. I need to help him forget. If he just dances with me like this a little more, rocks that beautiful big cock into me a little, and maybe, brings his arm around my waist and…

"What are you doing?" I hear him shout in my ear just before he pushes me away, a hand on my chest.

I step back, a little dazed and very confused. Except I'm not. Not at all. I know exactly what's going on. And I've had enough of being treated like this.

Pushing my hand against Steveo's chest and moving him back, I turn and storm off the dance floor.

"Jake! Wait up!" I hear him call out, even over the music and noise from other revellers, people who probably aren't with someone who's ashamed of dancing with them.

I pick up my pace and the music changes to match this, leaving that soulful swinging disco beat behind for a hard thump of an EDM rhythm, my least favourite kind of music. Good. I'm ready to go home now.

I pause briefly when I realise we haven't even seen the new year in yet, and I glance at my watch. Thirty minutes to go.

Rolling my eyes at nobody, I start walking again when I realise how pissing perfect it will be that I see the new year in while walking home completely alone.

How bloody brilliant it will be that the world-famous fireworks will paint the sky hundreds of different colours as I am slipping into my PJs. How fucking fantastic it will be that when I call my sister to wish her a happy new year, she will only just be starting to get ready for her own celebrations.

Jesus. When did my life become such a tragedy?

But before I dive headfirst into this wallowing, I need a piss.

Not wanting to risk seeing Steveo in the nightclub toilets, I dig in my wallet for my staff pass and head to the personnel-only doors near the stage that lead to the backstage rooms and the facilities. I keep my head down as I walk past people rushing around some of them drunk, others anything but – all clipboards and headsets and stressed shouting – and I go to the gents' toilets.

Inside, I quickly relieve myself at a urinal and then wash my hands and splash my face with cold water before taking a good look at my reflection.

I don't hate what I see – I have a nicely put-together face and a jawline many would be jealous of – but I don't love what I see either. My chestnut eyes reveal the sadness and dejection I feel, my dark blond hair is no longer holding the same shape I spent far too long putting it in earlier, and my cheeks look a little hollow, no doubt because I didn't eat a decent meal all day in order to fit in the Armani jeans I stupidly bought on sale and a size too small.

"Jesus, Forester. You're too good for this," I say to myself.

"Yeah, you are," a voice says and then I hear a toilet flush. I hear the click of a lock opening on the nearest cubicle and a striking man walks out. He's tall – roughly the same height as my five feet eleven – and he's wearing black trousers and a black woollen turtleneck, which I find mind-boggling considering it's been 30 degrees for the last few days. He must be crew and here with one of the DJs on some whistle-stop tour.

"Sorry," I say to him via the mirror as he comes to wash his hands. "I talk to myself too much."

He gives me a side smile before bending down to wash his hands, like really washing his hands with soap and water and lots of scrubbing. Maybe he's hotel staff. I should keep my eye out for him, I think as I take in his light brown skin, dark hair, and sexy stubble.

"Most people don't talk to themselves enough," he says with a smile that has my eyes glued on him. That's when I see the colour of his eyes, a grey so light and ethereal it's practically silver. I have to blink to remember to speak but still I can't find words worthy of a witty reply, which is not like me at all.

"Ha," I say eventually and quite pathetically. "Maybe."

He starts to rinse off the soap's bubbles. "Well, whatever it is, or whoever they are, I hope they don't ruin your night," he says and that's when I realise he's from England, like me. There's even the soft lull of a West Midlands accent.

"Oh, it's too late for that," I say.

"The night is yet young." He steps around me to reach for paper towels. "And so are you, bab."

He looks up and down my body then, a very open assessment. His lack of subtlety prompts me to be just as direct.

"Are you accosting me?" I ask, putting a hand on my hip.

"God, no," he says with a grin that would suggest otherwise, or maybe that's the godawful shot I just did blurring my vision and interpretation of curious looks.

"Don't sound so horrified!" I put my other hand on my other hip. He scrunches the paper towel into a ball and we both watch as he throws it towards the bin and it lands.

"I'm not horrified, but let's just say I'm probably not the answer to your problems." He folds his arms across his chest. A nicely solid chest, I believe.

"You're from the UK." I deliberately change the subject away from my problems. I'm quite good at that.

"Birmingham. You?"

"Surrey, originally. Now a citizen of the world."

"Yeah, me too, I guess," he says, and I have to look away from those eyes again.

I hear a buzzing, and I move to put my hand on my phone but there's no vibration. Of course, Steveo isn't even trying to contact me.

The man in front of me is looking at the screen of an expensive-looking smartphone by the time I look back at him.

"That's my cue to leave," he says. "Got a plane to catch, unfortunately." As he looks at the phone's screen I see him cringe, very noticeably.

"Whatever it is, or whoever they are, I hope they don't ruin your night," I repeat his words to him, nodding at his phone.

He looks up. "The night is yet young for that," he says with that mirthful smile again. "Goodbye, handsome stranger."

"Ha!" I can't help my laugh. "Goodbye, man who is very inappropriately dressed for an Australian summer."

"You're not wrong." He pulls at the neck of his jumper. "And hey?"

"Yeah?"

"Nice shoes," he says with a lingering look at my feet, and then he's gone.

PART ONE – NEW MOON

"Don't worry if you're making waves just by being yourself. The Moon does it all the time."

Scott Stabile

Chapter One

Present Day, London

Jake

"You do this for me and I will pay for Dolly's grooming for a whole year," I say into the phone.

"A year? You can't afford that," Derek immediately counters.

I shrug. "What are credit cards for?"

"You're that desperate?"

"I am *that* desperate," I groan into the phone.

Lionel's wedding has come out of nowhere, and when I mean nowhere, I mean I have successfully ignored the invitation for their whirlwind wedding for the last three months but now the date is just five weeks away and I am still dateless. Did I do that because I didn't actually expect them to get married? Possibly, and apparently stupidly, yes.

"Why do you need a date so badly?" Derek asks and I swear I can hear the soft scratch of a nail file doing its thing in the background.

"Because..." I begin even though I really don't want to dig up this sorry story again. "Because he's the one that got away."

"Oh Jakey, you're breaking my heart," Derek says and I really can't tell if he's being sarcastic or genuine. It's a fine line with most of my social circle, myself included. Because it serves me better, I choose to interpret his tone as one of real concern.

"So you'll come?" As I shift in my chair with excitement, I notice my assistant Sharon walking into my office, carrying a laptop. She's talking to a man who follows her in. A man who is carrying a bundle of envelopes and other post, including my *Homes & Garden*, *Lonely Planet* and *BBC Travel* magazines. He must be the new post guy.

"God, no. I can't pretend to be your boyfriend. That's way too weird." Derek snaps me back to our conversation. I put a finger up to Sharon to show her I'm busy talking.

"Derek, you literally blew me once a week for a year when we were at uni!"

Derek sighs loudly. "I also studied geography and used Superdrug hair gel. Mistakes were made, Jake. Mistakes were made."

"What do I have to do?" I'd like to say Derek's the first person I've begged but he's not. In fact, he's the fourth friend I've asked to do this favour for me and it looks like he's going to be the fourth to turn me down. I am running out of both time and friends.

"Nothing will convince me, Jake. I have plans that weekend and I'm not changing them."

"I hardly think watching Eurovision finals with your Chihuahua-Pomeranian mix dog constitutes plans," I say but then adjust my tone. "Listen, I'll give you the afternoon to think about it. I'm tied up running through our upcoming schedule with our newbie events manager who will no doubt be as bossy, boring, and buttoned up as the last one..."

"Oh, yes. What was her name again?"

"Tasha. I forgot you met her at our Christmas do when you came with me last year. See you did that for me, Dezza. Why won't you step up again and—"

Sharon clears her throat, making a noise that isn't dissimilar from a flushing plane toilet.

"Yes, Sharon?" I pull my phone away from my ear slightly and then see the postman is trying to catch my eye and opening his mouth to say something, but I save him the trouble. "Oh, thank you for the post. Pop it down over there on the table if you don't mind."

He opens his mouth to respond but seems to change his mind as he turns and places the pile down. I take in his appearance and realise while his clothes are all black, they do seem to fit his slim physique well, and while his shaved head is a little predictable and unimaginative, it does suit his chiselled dark features. "I have to say, you're very smartly dressed for the post room staff," I comment.

"Thank you, I—" he begins but I don't hear what he says next because Derek is threatening to hang up on me.

"Jake, I've got to go. You've gone from begging me to do you a solid to ignoring me completely which is not good for my mental health…"

"*Your* mental health?" I declare, gripping the phone close to my ear again. "I'm the one feeling dejected. I have a good mind to send you and all my lousy friends an invoice for the emotional damage all this rejection is going to cause. I see some very poor decision-making on my horizon, especially in relation to my credit card, or worse, my Grindr tags—"

I'm unable to finish my sentence because my phone is snatched out of my hand and away from my ear.

"Sharon!" I exclaim. "Give me that back!"

Sharon's voice booms like only Sharon's voice can, a perfect match for her solid physique and her short jet-black hair with its gravity-defying spikes. "Jake, I'd like to introduce you to Rami Kazimi. Our new Head of Events."

She nods at the postman as she says that which means… he's not the postman at all.

"Oh," I say, eyes widening. I'm about to apologise but then I see the time on the clock behind his head. "But you're two hours early for our meeting."

"Yes, well, funny story," he begins, smiling in a way that is nervous and jolly and I have time for neither.

As if detecting this, Sharon jumps in, "Rami's going to be working from your office today, and tomorrow too."

"What?" My jaw drops.

"Maybe next week as well," she adds quickly as she scratches at the back of her pixie-cut. I swear I see her lips curl with glee as she watches for my reaction, her dark eyes sparkling a little.

"Here? Why isn't he getting Tasha's old office?"

"No can do. Tony nabbed that before her stiletto heel marks had been buffered out of the marble floor. Rami was supposed to be moving into *his* old office."

"Oh, God, the dungeon," I say before I can stop myself, glancing at Rami whose smile looks like it could be slipping. Shame, it's quite a nice smile full of bright white teeth and framed with dusty pink lips that don't seem to thin out even when stretched into his awkward grin.

Sharon flashes an unconvincing smile up at Rami as she stretches her short, round body to put my phone on my desk.

"It's not really a dungeon, but it does indeed need better internet apparently, and there's not even a working phoneline connection down there so maintenance is going to address all the above as soon as is humanly possible. But it will be fine you, Rami, working here for the foreseeable, won't it Jake?"

Uh oh. She's using *that* voice with me.

"Can't he share your office?" I try one more time.

"I don't have an office, I have a corridor." Sharon's thunderous look tells me exactly what she thinks about that.

"But I literally just got my own private office for the first time in well, ever. Do you know how long I've waited and how hard I've worked to get to a place where I can just fart in peace?"

"You think I don't hear some of those rippers? Now, quit your moaning. It won't be for long. Just as soon as maintenance can drill some big holes and poke pipes down channels or something."

"Now I know I'm really angry because I don't even want to play with the blatant innuendo you just served me on a silver platter!" I cross my arms like the cranky toddler I apparently am.

"Should I go?" Rami points to the door. "I could always work in Reception. In fact, maybe that would be better..."

Sharon holds up her hand to him. "No, Rami. Jake is mid-way through his gay flap so just five more minutes and it will all be over."

"*Gay* flap? How very dare you, Sharon? I'll report you to HR for homophobia." I point my finger at her.

"Homophobia? I'm a gold-card-carrying lesbian, and you know it, you nimcompoop," Sharon says with a dismissive eye roll. "You play Words with Friends with my wife, for crying out loud."

"Ugh." I grunt but reach for my phone in the next breath. "That reminds me, it's my turn. And actually, what is Daniel doing the last weekend in May? He'd make a lovely looking date for this blasted wedding."

"There's no way you're taking my son anywhere. Poor boy is still recovering from when you came over and plucked his eyebrows last week," Sharon mutters. "Besides, he's twenty-three, hardly an appropriate age for your date."

"Tell that to my sister," I mumble referring to Jenna's partner Marty who is many years her junior. "Anyway, he should be thanking me. Those brows added real definition to his face, which has sadly acquired your substandard bone structure."

Sharon points a stubby finger at me. "You may be turning forty this year, Jake Forester, but you're not too old to go over my knee and—"

Rami coughs again, much louder this time. His smile has completely vanished too. "I think I'm going to go and get a coffee, or something. Anything that will take me somewhere else—"

"You stay right here. Look there's already a desk for you—" Sharon grabs hold of his arm and practically hurls him towards my table.

"That's my meeting table for important meetings with important people!" I stand up.

"No, it's not. It's where you store all the paperwork you should have shredded or filed already and where you have your lunch reading Mail Online and eating cheese and pickle sandwiches. And you can do that at your desk."

I gasp with a hand on my chest. "And get grated cheese in the cracks of my keyboard? You savage, Sharon."

"Me a savage? I'm not the one giving our new colleague the worst possible welcome."

I close my eyes then and when I open them, I make sure I have a smile on my face. I turn to Rami.

"Yes, my apologies. I shouldn't have made... assumptions. Of course, you can work in here, for however long you need to."

It literally pains me to say such nice things. Am I really becoming this grumpy in my middle age?

"Apology accepted, Jake," he says with a returning smile so warm some of its heat reaches me, loosening a little of the tension in my shoulders. It's as we share eye contact that I notice the colour of his eyes, a light, bright grey that seems to sparkle in the artificial lighting. God, how lucky do some people get having eyes that unusual, that captivating? No wonder he doesn't seem to feel the need to make much of an effort with sparkling conversation. He doesn't need to.

"Well, that's very decent of you." Sharon gives me a very self-satisfied look. "Let's make you some space over here."

She reaches over and grabs the post and all the other stacks of paperwork. She scoops it all up and then strides over to my desk. There she dumps all the papers on what little space remains.

"You bitch," I say, pulling harder on my pout so I don't show even a hint of a grin.

"Dateless desperado," she says back before she walks to the door. Her tone becomes sunnier as she turns to the man who will now be sharing my office. "Good luck, Rami!"

Sharon is gone before Rami replies, and he swallows whatever words he was mumbling. I move to sit back at my desk, sighing again when I see the mess of papers covering it

"Sharon seems... interesting," Rami ventures as he goes to the table and pulls out a chair.

"Sharon is a ruthless and insensitive battle-axe, but she's the best personal assistant I've ever had, and I love her dearly," I say finding all those words suddenly exhausting. I can't believe I now have to summon the energy for small talk with this stranger. While he's certainly easy on the eye, he's already gone some way to show me he has the personality of a cucumber so I can't even enjoy a little banter.

"That makes complete sense," he mumbles as he sits and opens his laptop. My top lip curls in a sneer when I notice it's a newer model than mine, and with a screen two inches bigger. The bastard.

"Who did you have to blow to get that?" I demand.

He practically gets whiplash from looking up at me so quickly. "Pardon?"

"Fancy laptop." I waggle my finger at the device. "How did you get the job anyway? I don't remember you coming in for an interview. I sat in on some of them." I know I would remember seeing those eyes recently.

Rami takes a moment to think on his answer, lips closed flat. "I didn't exactly go through the usual recruitment process," he says, and I wait for more information but he closes his mouth again and turns back to the laptop.

"Are you friends with Bill, or Simeon?" I ask, referring to the two owners of the company we work for, Status Hotels & Venues. When I see his shoulders rise, I know my answer even though he doesn't speak.

"It's both, isn't it?" I ask and again his silence and tense upper body are confirmation.

Shit. If he's friends with them then not only do I have zero opportunity for banter but I also have to be on my best behaviour. In fact, I probably need to do more than that to undo the damage of the mistaken identity and the admittedly ridiculous gay-or-otherwise flap I just had.

Resisting the urge to groan and hang my head in my hands – because knowing my luck, this man has eyes in the back of his head as well as a much better laptop than me – I instead move the papers Sharon dumped on my desk to the floor and get back to work. And by work, I mean continuing to go through my contact list to find a suitable date for Lionel's wedding.

Chapter Two

Rami

He thinks I got this job because I'm friends with the owners.

Technically he's not wrong – I was offered the job without an interview – but saying we're friends is stretching the truth to elastic proportions. I wouldn't call them more than acquaintances. I don't really have any friends. Not anymore.

In fact, one of my motivations for taking this role was to hopefully meet some new people and change that. I should have done it sooner – it has been nearly two years since I left LA after all – but making new social contacts is practically impossible when you're forty-three, more than a little mistrusting of people, and have a rather unpleasant recent past you find difficult to talk about.

I suppose it's a good thing, therefore, that I can strike this guy off my list of potential new friends. Jake Forester is making it abundantly clear he doesn't want to have anything to do with me, even in a work sense, let alone a social setting. I'd like to say I'm relieved, but I'm not. I may even be a little disappointed. He's funny, quick-witted and although it's only appeared once or twice, he has an almost addictive smile that teeters between cheeky and wicked perfectly. He has some of the best banter I've ever heard and has exactly the kind of sardonic, dry sense of humour I love, and yet the sharp look in his light brown eyes is making it very clear what he thinks about my getting here on an easy ride.

And he's not wrong. Getting this job was relatively easy. But everything else until that point was a long, bumpy, and at times horrendously difficult ride, which is probably why I feel defensive enough to open my mouth many long minutes after he last speaks.

"I'm not here on a freebie. I have a job to do, and I'm going to do it." I don't like how stern I sound, nor that I can't seem to follow it up with a smile, but I need him to take me seriously. He seems to absorb what I'm saying, the only movement on his face the raising of both eyebrows as he looks up from his phone.

I continue to explain, "I met Bill and Simeon at an event, years ago. We stayed in touch on and off, and when they heard through some other mutual acquaintances that I was looking for a new opportunity, they approached me with this role. But they expect me to work, and I expect to be held accountable for that work."

"You have nothing to prove to me." Jake holds up his hands. "I'm just being bitchy because your laptop is nicer than mine. I am very, very good at being a bitch, FYI. But I'm also excellent at my job so I'm afraid you'll have to put up with one to get the other, especially if you're sharing my office for a few days."

I smile despite myself. "I can cope with that. Are you a gossip as well as a bitch?"

"That depends. If the subject of gossip is more attractive than me then they're fair game." Jake leans back in his chair and I feel like he's finally looking at me properly for the first time, his eyes wandering a little over my face.

"Well, at the risk of having my ego trampled on again—" I begin but he interrupts.

"Again? You mean the postman thing? Oh, that's a compliment. Most of the post room are gym rats who are also volunteer fire fighters. They're the best looking *and* most decent humans in the whole building."

I chuckle at this, unsure if it's true.

"Well, could I ask you to not tell anyone else about how I got the job here? I'd like people to base their opinions on my work rather than whatever tenuous connections I have."

Jake narrows his eyes at me. "I'm detecting an accent. What is it?"

I swallow around the lump that automatically pops up in my throat. I spent ten years in California, getting an accent was never my plan but I suspect it happened regardless.

"I used to live in the States," I say, hoping my vagueness isn't an invitation for more questions.

"No, no, that's not it. Where did you grow up?"

"Oh," I say, taken aback. "Birmingham. Is that what you're hearing?"

"Yes!" Jake claps his hands together. "That's it! It's almost adorable. Listen, your secret is safe with me if you can do me a favour." Jake pauses as I nod. "I really need to find a date for this wedding in just over a month and I'm failing miserably. I am going to spend the next hour or so making some phone calls. You mind putting up with that?"

"I can put up with that."

"Good. And can you listen to them judgment-free, please?"

"I never talk or think badly about people more attractive than me," I say, surprising myself.

"Ha! You're smooth. But it won't work on me. I know you're only trying to butter me up so I keep your nepotistic connections to BS on the down-low."

"BS... Shit!" His eyes widen in shock. "That's what you call Bill and Simeon?"

"Sharon started it!" Jake points at the door she walked out of earlier.

"It never seems to be your fault, does it?" I joke. I can't help but laugh, even though that makes the pink flush of his cheeks turn scarlet.

"Ugh, you're annoying me now." He tuts before looking at his phone again.

His dismissal of me, albeit possibly in jest, rubs on a nerve I didn't know was so raw.

"Haven't you got phone calls to make?" I say, defensiveness rising in me.

"Don't remind me." Jake groans then rubs at his forehead.

"Why can't you just go to the wedding by yourself?"

"It's my ex's wedding," he says, his gaze back on something outside.

"Your ex invited you to their wedding?"

"Well, I suppose calling him my ex is a bit of a reach. We're former... ugh, what's the word..."

"Lovers?"

"God, that sounds like we're in an Edwardian novel."

"You've just shagged, then?"

"No, it was... It was a bit more than that." Jake's gaze drifts to an undefinable spot in the room.

"And now you want to show up with someone on your arm to show him you're not bitter. That you moved on. That you're doing fine without him."

"Yes, yes and yes. I have all those untruths to prove to him."

"Ever thought you could do that just as well showing up alone? With a smile on your face, a tailored suit on your body and a well-chosen gift in your hands?"

"God, you have no clue who you're talking to, do you? You think I'm that level-headed and self-confident?" Jake swipes around on his phone. "Listen closely, Mr Events. You're about to learn that I am the very opposite. And ugh, I hadn't even thought about what I'm going to wear. I suppose I have to go shopping now too."

"What's your size? My sister is a tailor, she could maybe help you out. It's tight on the timing but I could twist her arm."

"Your sister is a tailor? For men?"

"Yes, why is that so unusual?" My skin prickles as I think about Radia.

"Not unusual at all. Just..." Jake pauses. "She's a lesbian, surely?"

I blink at him. "She is but I'm not sure what that's got to do with anything..."

"Only that, annoyingly, many gay women wear masc clothes better than most men, so I was just trying to fit the missing puzzle pieces together."

There's a compliment in there somewhere, but even so I don't like the idea of him trying to fit together puzzle pieces relating to my sister. Not that she's got any secrets. It's my puzzle pieces I don't want him getting anywhere near.

"Shall I call her?" I ask, digging in my trouser pocket for my phone.

"Is she expensive?" Jake leans forward a little. "I hate to ask but I'm on a bit of a budget for this wedding and haven't even factored in the total bribery cost yet."

"She'll do mates' rates," I say and the word "mates" sticks to the roof of my mouth.

Mates. Maybe Jake and I could be friends still. Maybe this will help him see I can be a good friend. Or maybe I could do something else.

I suck in a breath and speak before I can stop myself.

"Listen. If you can't find someone, I could go with you. As the job title suggests, I know exactly how to navigate gatherings and have worked at a few weddings in my time."

"I'm sure I won't be that desperate," he says, not even looking up from his phone, which stings as much as his words.

"Thanks." I huff out a laugh, but it doesn't ease the nausea that follows the lurch of my stomach.

"I didn't mean it like that," Jake says but still doesn't look up. "But I do have other friends I can try and blackmail into coming with me."

"I'm sure one of them will go with you." I sound just as sour as I briefly feel.

Jake makes his phone calls and while I may be listening judgement-free I am still listening, and within minutes of each conversation it's clear Jake is no closer to finding a date. I try not to listen too closely, but it's hard not to. Every other sentence Jake says is a punchline for some amusing joke or witty retort. I feel almost dizzy about how quick his mind works, and his energy... his energy is like a firework that never fades. While I manage to get my email working, find the company intranet and start working through some of the training material I was tasked to read, I still find my attention being pulled towards Jake and this mission he's on. He's on call number five and getting increasingly frustrated with his friend Harry, who apparently would rather go to Bicester Village outlet shopping with his mother than be Jake's fake date.

"Really, Harry? You're choosing Mildred over me. No, no it's not for Jenna's wedding. They're not getting married... Are you saying that you would come if it was for Jenna's wedding but not for the man who broke my heart?" Jake switches the phone to his other ear all the while he carefully applies lip balm to his pout like it's an expensive lipstick. "Fine, maybe I broke his, but he got pretty close. As close as any man has. So please come. Please... No, I will not *pay* you to be my date... Seriously? Does our winter of fucking mean nothing to you? Okay, half a winter... Look, it's going to be incredible. One groom's family is Jamaican and the other is Italian, so the food is going to be off the charts... Oh, for fuck's sake, Harry, you're not really doing that diet again... No, I'm not buying you a new suit... It's just one day... Okay, how much do you *want* to come with me?"

It's at this point that I'm so tempted to do exactly what Sharon did and reach over and grab his phone and save him from himself, but instead, I clench my fists and glance at the time on my laptop. This gives me an excuse to cough loudly and when Jake looks up at me from under heavy brows, I indicate I need to talk to him.

"Just a second, Harry." Jake moves the phone away from his ear. He gives me an impatient scowl. "Yes?"

"Our meeting starts in six minutes," I say.

Jake doesn't even try to hide his eye roll as he goes back to speaking to Harry.

"Have a think, Harry. Let me know if you can do it. Or tell me how much it would... cost me."

I cough again. I can't stop myself because I don't like hearing what he's saying. I don't know the man, but I don't like the idea of Jake having to pay anyone to be his date, to be a good friend to him.

After Jake hangs up, he stares at his phone for a few seconds, his expression holding onto a slightly sad-looking blankness, and then he blinks, and all his features jump into action again. He combs back some of the loose strands of the ash blond hair that flops onto his forehead and his mouth pulls into a pout that doesn't do his soft pink lips any favours but it still doesn't look out of place either. His pale white skin still has a little colour in it, and I'm not surprised considering how much effort he just put into trying to convince his friends to be his date for this wedding. He pulls down on his shirt sleeves and I see then that his navy suit fits his narrow frame well, and for some reason my eyes then roll down his body even though the desk obscures most of it.

"So, do we want coffee for this meeting? Or tea?" he asks as he goes about moving a few more papers from his desk to the floor. With his downcast expression I can't see the warm hazel shade of his eyes, but I can see how long and elegant his eyelashes are, which is a very weird thing to notice about a new colleague.

"I'll have a cup of tea." I stand, abruptly wanting to move. "I'll go make it."

"You'll do no such thing. Only Sharon knows exactly how I like it. When it comes to tea, I mean." He winks at me before raising his voice. "Shazza! Two teas please!"

I'm pretty sure I hear a grunt or a groan but Jake ignores it, so I decide to as well. A moment later Sharon is stood at the door.

"How do you like your tea, Rami?" she asks.

"Black, no sugar," I reply with a smile.

"Righty-oh. One no-fun tea for you and one pretentious oat milk tea in which the bag has to be squeezed ten times and stirring is only permissible in a counter clockwise direction for madam over there." Sharon sharpens her gaze on Jake, but I swear there's the ghost of a smile on her lips.

"Thank you, Sharon, you old wench." Jake unplugs his laptop and brings it to the table. "So, shall we get started?"

"Sure," I say and I open up the corporate calendar in one tab and alongside it a clean page in the Notepad app of my laptop.

Jake takes a moment to look at the chair next to me and then the one on the corner of the table. When he opts for the latter, I sense it's because it's slightly further away and I try hard to not take it personally. Quickly, he launches into a big speech about how he and I are supposed to work together. There are no surprises. It's my job to plan events, budget for them and execute them, and it's his job to ensure the company's venues provide everything we need, within his budget and on time.

"It's going to mean a lot of open communication." Jake leans back in his chair. "Your predecessor was good at that, I'll admit, but she didn't make it much fun. I am much more amenable and accommodating when someone can ask me things with an appropriate emoji. I'm talking smiley faces, not aubergines, just to clarify. And I can be quite partial to an amusing GIF or two on a Friday."

"Noted," I say, biting back a grin.

"So, this is where both our teams will have visibility on projects," Jake says, and he quickly opens up an app that is completely new to me. There are rectangular boxes and text all over the screen. He starts opening more tabs within it as he talks about staff, facilities, catering, and other words I lose. I'm about to ask him to slow down a little when Sharon returns with two steaming mugs of tea.

"Here you go, you lazy man-children," Sharon mutters as she somehow manages to bang both mugs on the table with a thump and yet not spill a drop.

"Thanks so much," I say and try to catch her eye with my smile.

"Yes, ta muchly, tea bitch," Jake says, still focused on the laptop in front of him.

Sharon folds her arms as she stares at Jake. "Need anything else? Your pimples popping? Your arse wiping?"

I frown at Sharon's words, but Jake doesn't even blink.

"No, thank you. Go back to your cross-stitch sub-Reddit and leave us be," he dismisses her and I'm starting to think Sharon is playing her part perfectly when she tuts and marches out of the room.

"So, just to rewind," I say. "What's this app called? I don't think I've used it before—" I lean closer to Jake hoping that will stop him skimming through text I'm trying to read. It doesn't work. What does pull his hand off the laptop's trackpad is his phone ringing. He retrieves it out of his pocket in a rush.

"It's Harry! I knew he'd see sense. Pathetic empathetic Pisces that he is," Jake answers the phone in his next breath. "Hazza! Are you going to put me out of my misery and come to this wedding after all? ... What do you mean— ... I thought you were calling to— ... No, I don't want to talk about that right now... I know it's my fortieth but really who cares? ... Well, *I* don't care. Tomorrow? If I agree to this, will you come to the wedding with me? ... Oh fuck Bicester Village and Mildred! ... Sorry, Harry. I didn't mean that. You know I love Mildred and outlet prices on designer brands as much as the next guy... Fine. Let's do lunch and discuss... They all want to come too? Jesus. Funny how you all want a free party for my birthday but won't take the one on offer at this wedding... Yes, I am bitter... Whatever... Yes, ugh, see you tomorrow. Love you, hate you."

After hanging up Jake throws his phone onto the table and we both watch it slide away from us.

"Still no luck?"

Jake's lips are clamped shut for so long that I speak again.

"You know, I really don't mind going with you," I offer again even though I'm not sure I want him to say yes.

"You don't know me. And we work together. Two good reasons for me to again say, no."

I nod and realise I did want him to say yes. I wanted to have something to look forward to because starting this new job was the thing I'd been looking forward to for the last few months and well, now it's happening, it hasn't proved to be as successful or exciting as I imagined.

Jake sighs loudly and I'm surprised this conversation isn't over. "The third good reason is because... I don't need just a date. I need someone to be my boyfriend."

"Boyfriend?"

"Yes. My date needs to pretend to be madly, deeply and ridiculously in love with me." Jake's eyes finally land on mine. "I think we can both agree that's a tall order for anyone."

I open my mouth to speak but I don't feel qualified to say what I want to say. As it happens, Jake hasn't finished talking.

"I'm sure you're excellent at putting on a three-day wellness convention for five thousand people but I can imagine pretending to be gay with a high-maintenance boyfriend you have to support while he experiences emotional trauma watching the one who got away get married is a stretch too far."

I let his words land and realise very quickly the easiest thing is to agree. "You're probably right."

"Funnily enough, that was my next top tip for us working together," Jake says with a few swift shakes of his head and shoulders, as if he's unleashing something that was weighing him down. "I am nearly always right about everything. And when I'm not, I will still pretend I am."

"Good to know."

"Now, about this app. You've never used Share before?" he asks as he reaches for his lip balm again.

I shake my head.

The aggravation I feel when I watch Jake's eyes roll again is akin to how foolish I feel for thinking we could be friends.

"Pay attention. I'll talk you through everything but I'm not going to repeat myself. I have a three-thirty appointment with the gym's elliptical trainer and need to save all my energy for that." He smacks his lips after re-applying lip balm.

"Fine with me," I say wishing I had an ounce of his quick wit to have an equally amusing response.

But I don't. All I have is feeling foolish, feeling rejected and feeling like maybe this job isn't going to be the answer to all my problems like I thought it could be.

Chapter Three

Jake

"So, how's your week been, Jake?"

Every other week my therapist Anita asks me the same question, and every other week I lie.

"Fine. Good. Great."

"How was work?" she asks, laying her pen in the middle of the open notebook in her lap.

"Fine. Mostly."

"Anything happen you want to talk about today?"

"Not really."

"Anything in general that is playing on your mind?"

Oh, only the fact I owe most of the banks in the UK and half the department stores thousands upon thousands of pounds. Let's also not forget how I haven't gotten laid since December last year. And while we're at it, should we talk again about my mother who committed suicide when I was twelve years old, and I still can't quite make sense of that.

"No, nothing."

"Okay." Anita draws in a breath as she looks down at her notes. "Then let's talk about your father. Did you talk to him by any chance?"

"No," I say. *As if*, I think.

"Did you think about calling him?"

Yes, practically every day.

"Not much," I mutter.

"Did you try reaching out to him?"

Every single time I thought about him. Even picked up the phone a few times.

"Not really," I mumble.

And every other week, eventually Anita figures out I'm holding out on her. "Why didn't you call him, Jake?"

Time to start telling the truth because I'm running out of excuses. "Because it's his turn to contact me? Nothing but a happy birthday text for a year. You'd think he'd at least like to know if I'm alive."

"Are you regretting not going up to visit at Christmas last year?" Anita asks, her soft calm voice a sharp contrast with my acidic tone.

"He didn't invite me," I snap back.

"That's not exactly what I asked," Anita says in that careful air of hers that somehow both placates and irritates me.

"Fine. I am regretting it. Sort of. But I didn't want to go without Jenna." I shrug. "And it was nice being in Dublin with her and Marty, and his family."

It really had been. Almost too nice. How was it that being with my sister's partner's family felt better than most of the days I've spent with my father in recent years?

"Why do you think your father doesn't get in touch much?" Anita asks, and not for the first time. After many long months of therapy, we've reached a stage where she often wants me to do my own psychoanalysing, which begs the question why I pay her hundreds of pounds I can ill afford every month. But I do know why she does it and arguably that is evidence enough that these sessions are going somewhere, if rather slowly and expensively. Anita wants me to remind myself that my father and I are not wired the same. She wants me to admit that if I want a relationship with my father, it's possible I'm going to have to put in more effort than he does. And if I don't want to do that, well, then I have to let that dream die and find some peace with it.

Just like I have to make peace with the fact I will die in debt, single and alone, and always, always wondering if there was more I could have done to save my mother.

Hmm. Time to change the subject.

"You know, something interesting did happen at work," I say crossing my legs in the opposite direction.

Anita's face freezes for a split second before it relaxes into a kind smile.

"What's that?" She indulges me.

"We've got a new Head of Events. Rami, his name is. He's been sharing my office for just over a week now, much to my dismay, but I'm trying to be civil and accommodating. He just never has anything amusing or interesting to add to a conversation, and he thinks too much before he speaks, which as you can probably imagine I am both envious of and enraged by. But anyway, funny story, he offered to be my plus one for Lionel's wedding. Isn't that ridiculous?"

"Lionel as in your ex-lover?" Anita asks, as sharp-eyed as ever.

"No, Lionel as in Lionel Richie," I reply. I figure I pay her enough for her to forgive my sarcasm. "Did you not know we were long-lost friends?"

Anita's smile is brief and tight.

"Yes, Lionel, my err... ex, I suppose," I concede.

"How are we feeling today about Lionel getting married?"

I wince. I hate when she phrases things in the first-person plural. It's terrifying to think of there being more than one me.

It's my turn to indulge her. "We're feeling... a little dejected, a bit sad and very regretful."

"Regretful, why?"

"Because I often wonder if he was my..." I pause when I realise how wet and hot my eyes have become. "I often think about how I was wrong to push him away in the way that I did."

Anita waits as a couple of tears spill over and she watches me as I wipe them away before they get very far.

"Do we think going to Lionel's wedding is a good idea?" she asks.

No, we do not but I can't bail now. I've promised him I'll be there, and I don't want to break my promise. I owe him that much.

"I actually think it would help bring me closure." I toss another lie in Anita's direction.

"I'm curious. What was it about your relationship with Lionel that makes you think it could have possibly worked out otherwise?" Anita asks in her silky voice.

"Oh, I didn't say that it would have worked out in the long run. I don't even *think* that. Of course, we wouldn't have worked out. It would have failed eventually."

"You say that like it's a foregone conclusion."

"Because it is. Or rather it was. And I proved this when I slept with someone else, didn't it?" I say a little self-righteously but a second later I'm cringing as I recall the way Lionel's face fell when I'd told him what I'd done. Pain lances my insides as I remember how the light in his eyes was snuffed out and his mouth shrank as if to stop any words from ever escaping. At the time, I'd thought telling him was the decent thing to do – we were never an official couple, after all – but there was nothing decent in how either of us felt when I dug up whatever seed of a thing we had and threw it away.

"I seem to recall you saying Lionel was willing to work through it. Have you had any more thoughts about why you didn't want to do that?"

I groan at the reminder and it zaps me of the energy I need to lie. "Because I would have just been delaying the inevitable." I shake my head and straighten up in my chair. People leave me. That's just what happens. Especially people like Lionel. "Lionel was always too good for me. Too pure. Too innocent."

Anita levels me one of her most serious looks. "So, what does that make you?"

After a quick tut, I can't stop my hands coming along for the ride as I try to stop this line of questioning. I know exactly what she's doing.

"Look, I know I'm not inherently bad. I know I am enough just as I am, that I'm worthy of love and all that rubbish, but trust me, Lionel is made of different stuff. He's sweet. He's kind. He would never sleep with the random Greek man who delivered our cold meats and cheeses no matter how sinewy his forearms."

"Jake—"

"Look, I'm kidding, okay? I know that although I did a bad thing, that doesn't make me bad. And I know that Lionel has moved on from it all. I mean it was two years ago and he's getting married now. Married! He really couldn't have moved further past it. And I want to show him that I've done the same by going to his wedding."

"And you'll go with this new friend of yours?"

"Friend? Which new friend?" I lean forward to lift my glass of water and take a sip.

Anita consults her notes. "Rami."

Jesus, why did she write his name down? He's hardly a big deal.

"He's not my new friend. He's just someone I work with." I almost add *"whose presence gets on my nerves a lot"* but then realise that would be unfair, and possibly untrue. "Well, I did say no to his offer, but considering none of my friends are stepping up, he may be my only option. I mean, on paper it even looks like a good idea. He works in events, has probably planned thousands of flashy weddings so he'll know exactly what is expected of the whole day. And he mentioned that he doesn't drink either so I don't even have to worry about him ending up in a bush with a member of the wedding party, or face-planting in the chocolate fountain like some of my lightweight friends probably would. And he'll look ever so smart in a tux. It actually could be win-win."

"Jake, are you telling me this because you would like this to maybe result in a… romantic relationship with Rami?"

"God, no!" I splutter, horrified at the thought of even trying to flirt with such a two-dimensional man. "No, I'm telling you because I want to check if it's a smart thing to do, going to Lionel's wedding or if it's yet another chapter in my self-sabotage story."

Anita takes a moment to consider this. "Of course, it's more important what *you* think but I don't think you need to worry about self-sabotage. Perhaps he can also support you as your friend through it. It actually sounds like a great opportunity to be vulnerable with someone."

"Right. It's not like I'd be dragging Rami there in order to pretend he's my new boyfriend who I'm madly in love with, just to maybe try and reassure Lionel that I too have moved on. No, it's not like I'm doing that."

Anita's face folds in a frown. "Jake, you're not planning on doing that, are you?"

"No." I wave a hand at her and hear a light wheeze in my laugh. "Of course not. I was just trying to make you laugh."

"We've talked about this, Jake. You don't come here to make me laugh." Anita's eyes lift to the clock behind my head. "Or to talk about made-up scenarios that we both know you're sensible enough to avoid."

"Right," I mutter and ignore the heat climbing up my neck. "Anyway, Daddy Issues, huh?"

Chapter Four

Rami

When my working in Jake's office rolled into its second week – the discovery of asbestos in "the dungeon" meaning I wouldn't be relocating there for months potentially – I started going on walks to give us both space from one another. It hasn't been a huge hardship. My body has appreciated the regular exercise and if I time it right, I can get back shortly after Jake's disappeared to the company gym, meaning we then only have to brave a couple of hours sharing the same breathing space before I leave around six o'clock.

It's also helped me feel more for this gigantic city that seems to have no end and no beginning. Yes, LA was big, but it wasn't like London. In Los Angeles, you drove everywhere and the centre of the city, rightly or wrongly, was an area you avoided, not the heart of its metropolis like it is in London. That being said, it's the perfect city to walk in. There is always so much to see, so much to observe and discover. And as I walk, I jump in on group calls with my team who I am slowly starting to trust myself leading, and I also dictate emails and communications for my remote assistant Rebecca to type up and send. It suits me, working like this. I have never worked a job where I had to sit behind a desk all day, every day, and I was relieved when Bill and Simeon said that I didn't need to in this role either. They just care that I get the work done, and right now, that's all I care about too. I've started to tell myself if I can keep working like this, I may begin to enjoy the work a bit more too.

I wouldn't say I'm going on these walks to avoid Jake, but it's become clear over the last week or so that we're definitely not going to be friends. Despite my zealous use of emojis in all my emails to him, far too many minutes spent researching funny GIFs for Fridays, and the way I bring him a coconut milk double shot latte most mornings, he hasn't exactly mellowed to my presence in the office.

His tone changes whenever he speaks to me, and he's even stopped making jokes at my expense, something that shouldn't depress me at all, but it does. I lived a fairly banter-free existence for the last six or seven years, and I crave the kind of sense of humour Jake has.

There's something about being near him when he's bantering with Sharon or someone on the phone that wakes me up, excites me almost. I get this sense that what you see is what you get with Jake and considering my past, that's very reassuring. But it's not there when he talks directly *to* me.

It's not like on my first day I expected to walk into a room of people willing to be my best friends, but I did think I'd have made a few friends by now. But to most people I work with, I'm their boss and to those on a similar level to me – like Jake – they don't come to work to make friends. They already have countless friends, as well as their own families and busy lives away from work. They just want to do their work and then go home. They don't want to have coffee for more than fifteen minutes. They don't want to go grab something to eat after the working day is done. Sure, Bill and Simeon have both invited me out for a dinner, but so far I've refused. Becoming closer to the company's owners would do little to improve my popularity with everyone else.

Jake clearly has more than enough friends and I dare say the rest is true about everyone else roughly the same age as me. It's not like *they* spent a number of years deliberately cutting everyone they loved out of their life.

Maybe that's why today's walk has a specific destination and I've timed it so I'll hopefully get there at a good time. If not, I'll sit and wait until she's free. I just really need to see somebody who cares about me.

A bell rings as I open the door, and my sister is the first person behind the long glass counter to look up and see me. Dressed in a three-piece suit made from purple and yellow tweed with a matching lilac hijab, a smile beams out of her face as she approaches me.

"Rami!" she says before I pull her into a big hug. "This is a surprise."

"Yeah," I say and release her. "I was in the area so thought I'd pop in. You got time for a quick break?"

Radia glances at the man at the far end of the counter, who I assume is her boss, Giles. His name does not match his short, stocky body, nor his impressive, curled moustache. He's wearing tailored suit trousers with a waistcoat, both in a royal blue pinstripe. Muscles bulge out of his white shirt, and I know my eyes linger on them a little too long because my sister subtly knocks her elbow into me as she asks him if she can take a break.

"Go ahead, take as long as you want," Giles says as he stops folding fabric to walk over and shake my hand. I don't know if it's his physique or the firm grip of his hand but my body heats as he pulls away. "Heard all about you, man. It's a real honour to finally meet you. I couldn't believe it when Radia told me who you were."

I flash a quick glare at my sister. "Well, thanks. All a long time ago now," I say, my stomach swirling in on itself with something nauseating. Nostalgia? Regret? Shame?

"Come on," Radia says and she leans over the counter to grab her phone and a set of keys, clipping them onto her belt hoop with a carabiner. "Lunch is on you!"

Once we are outside and a decent distance away from the shop, I return the nudge that Radia gave me, but it's a little harder than hers was. "You told him about me. Do you tell everyone?"

"No, but he's my boss and my friend. I've been working there for a long time. He was there for me when..." she trails off.

"When I came back from the dead," I finish for her.

"I was more thinking when your brain started working again." She leans her arm against mine and I know she wants me to look at her, so I do. Her silvery eyes – the same narrow shape and shimmering grey shade as mine – twinkle in the early summer sunshine. It's good to see her.

"Whatever it was, I'm glad it happened," I say, and despite it all, I really am.

"Me too," she says, and we walk together in silence for a few seconds before she speaks again. "How's work going? Still a refugee in the diva's office?"

"I did not call him a diva!" I protest. "And I'm pretty sure you shouldn't call me a refugee considering our parents were *actual* refugees."

"Dark humour is my speciality, and you can't take that away from me." Radia points a finger at me. "Fancy some falafel? There's a place around the corner and it's heavenly."

"Sounds perfect. Show me the way," I say.

"Anyway. You didn't call him a diva, but you definitely said he was being a bit 'diva-ish'. Remember? You were telling us about this whole wedding date drama he's having."

"Oh, did I tell you about that?" I know I talked a lot about my new job with Mom, Radia and my youngest sister Roxana on Sunday because they'd almost been more excited about me starting it than I had been myself. I wanted to reassure them it had all gone well, even if that wasn't quite true.

"Sounded like he annoys you a bit," Radia continues.

"You could say that."

"Just because he's a bit... camp?" Radia is filling in the blanks but is doing so perfectly. "That's not like you to hold that against someone."

I sigh and am glad when I look up and see what I assume is the falafel place, a Lebanese deli a few doors away. "That's not why he annoys me. He... No, *the situation* annoys me because it's hard work sharing an office with someone who doesn't like you very much."

"I doubt he doesn't like you. He probably just doesn't know you yet."

"Well, he's hardly trying to get to know me. I actually offered to do him a big favour – be his plus one to that wedding he's going to, the plus one he's apparently so desperate to find – and he declined, so I think that does actually mean he doesn't like me."

"Not at all. It means he thinks it's a bit weird going to a wedding with a complete stranger, and I would go some way to agree with him."

"That's possible." My shoulders sink as I concede this point. "He also made it clear that he wanted the wedding date to be a bit more than just a buddy thing. The wedding is for his ex, so he's actually looking for someone to pretend to be his boyfriend."

"And you offered to do that for him? He's a complete stranger to you too."

"I felt sorry for him. And I also thought that was what friends did for one another."

"But you're not..." Radia pauses, her hands in her pockets, and she rocks on her heels like she's always done when thinking something over. "You *want* to be his friend."

"*Wanted*. I think that ship has sailed. And it's probably for the best," I add.

"Right," she says but she doesn't sound certain at all. "Come on, let's go eat our body weight in chickpeas."

We go in and after my sister is greeted by the staff like a long-lost family member, we place our orders and take fresh mint teas to a small table. Radia quickly starts telling me a story about a customer who just placed an order for wedding suits, and how she managed to convince them to go for a teal silk blend rather than the traditional black morning suits they came in for. It's so brilliantly Radia. Despite her dark sense of humour, she lives life in technicolour and tries to encourage everyone to do the same.

"That reminds me," I say, after waiting for a good moment to interrupt. "I told Jake you may be able to do a suit for him, for this wedding. I reckon he'd be very up for something colourful and loud. Could you do it mates' rates?"

"When's the wedding?"

"Three and a bit weeks, I think."

"Are you high? Three weeks? I haven't even fitted him yet."

"His proportions are pretty standard. Similar to mine actually. Maybe you have something off-the-rack you could tailor to him?"

"You've noticed his proportions, hey?" Her eyebrows bounce.

"Radia," I warn just as our food is placed in front of us, smelling and looking delicious.

She holds her hands up. "If Jake really doesn't mind something off-the-rack, tell him to pop in but soon. Like yesterday. And yes, I can do mates' rates. I think if Giles knows it's for a friend of yours, he'll practically pay for it himself."

"Thank you."

"Oh, listen, I'm not going to be coming up on Sunday now," she says as she breaks off a chunk of pita and starts scooping up hummus, falafel and pickles.

"Really? Why?"

"I have a date," she says with a smile that would be smug if it also didn't make her eyes sparkle.

"With Barista Babe?" I lean forward.

"Yes! I asked her out yesterday morning and she said yes! We're going to Somerset House for an exhibition."

Something slices into the excitement I feel for my sister. It's an ugly-shaped feeling and I know its name immediately: jealousy. I'm jealous my sister was brave enough to ask someone out. I'm jealous she was confident enough to put her heart on the line like that. And I'm also jealous of Barista Babe for getting my sister's time. Because I'm terrified too. Terrified if Radia does enter into a new relationship with this woman, that will mean I lose time with her. My sisters and my mother have been more than my rock the last few years. They've pulled me out of the darkest place and I will never be able to express how grateful I am for their loving, warm, caring presence in my life. Grateful and undeserving.

"You're so grown-up," I tease instead of even hinting at the unwelcome sick feeling swirling my stomach.

"Rami, I'm thirty-five. I'm ancient."

That's the thing about living away from home for so long. You think people stay the same age as when you left, when you last saw them. But as I look at Radia now, with the gentle creases at the corners of her eyes and laughter lines that frame her smile, just like I have, I see how wrong that is and how much I have missed with her and even more so with Roxie.

"So, what's her real name?" I ask.

Radia opens her mouth to answer, but we are interrupted by a shrill ringing noise. I wait for her to pull her phone out and answer it but she doesn't move, she just looks at me.

"Aren't you going to answer that?" I ask her.

"Aren't *you*?" Her forehead furrows and there's a puzzled look on her face.

"Oh, shit, it's my phone!" I bring my hand up to the jacket pocket where my phone is and am still surprised it's ringing as I pull it out. It's a number I don't recognise.

"Hello?" I answer.

"Rami, hi." I hear Jake say over a lot of background noise that suggests he's outside and surrounded by traffic.

"Jake? Is everything okay? I'm just having some lunch and then I'll be back in the office," I say, unsure why I feel the need to explain where I am as if that will ease the shiver of peculiar and totally unnecessary panic running through my veins. Why would Jake call me? And from a different mobile number? I was pretty sure I had his number saved.

"Good God, I'm not your mother checking up on you. I couldn't give a chimpanzee's testicle where you are. But I just wanted to quickly ask you something while we were both out of the office."

"Okay, go ahead," I say and then I mouth the words 'Jake' and 'work' to my sister, and she nods but doesn't stop watching me.

"Well, you know your first day in the office and how hilariously disastrous that was," he says with a half-hearted laugh.

"When you mistook me for postal staff? Yes, I remember that." I catch Radia pulling a face.

"Oh, well, if you're going to just throw all my mistakes back in my face, we may as well stop this conversation right now because we'll both be old and grey by the time you're finished," Jake rushes out.

"Jake, wait. I'm sorry. I was trying to make a joke," I say.

"Well, I don't have time for your weak attempts at humour, Rami. Neither of us are getting any younger."

"I guess that's true. So what's up?"

The phone rattles as he sucks in a breath. "I need to ask you a favour."

"I'm listening."

"On that first day, you…" Jake pauses, and I wait. "You offered to be my plus one for my friend Lionel's wedding."

"I did," I say and I find Radia's eyes again. She's studying me with a small smile, one that I know I'm returning now, although I don't really know why. I have no reason to smile, do I?

Jake sighs before he speaks again. "Well, is that offer still open?"

Chapter Five

Jake

As I sit and look at the menu, I feel my throat constrict. The prices are extortionate. Maybe if we spend ten minutes or so talking about the upcoming architecture convention that our Manchester hotel is going to host, we can expense it. I certainly don't expect Rami to pay for it when I'm about to ask him to do such a big favour for me.

Pulling out my wallet I glance quickly at the credit cards I have in there and I mentally try to recall which ones still have some credit available on them. Just as I'm remembering with considerable relief that I paid off an extra three hundred quid on one of my MasterCards last month, I see Rami approaching my table.

Dressing in all black doesn't normally do anything for me – I've long stipulated to anyone listening that it's only for funerals, kinksters, and goths – but there is something about this uniform of his that suits him. Not that that's really a compliment. Black personalities are basically as unappealing as head-to-toe black clothing. But I must concede his black trousers fit him well, keeping a nice shape to them when he walks, and his black T-shirts are always a little more than a basic cotton tee, like the one he wears today which has a slightly higher neck than usual and looks like it's made from a heavy jersey material. His black denim jacket is also deceptively smart, almost edgy in fact, with its matte black buttons and all-black stitching, and I make a note to try asking him the label to see if it's a brand I can maybe afford. On credit, of course.

"Hey," Rami says as he sits down opposite me.

"Hi." I force a smile out. I hope it's one of my better ones.

"Nice place," Rami says looking around. "Not sure why we couldn't walk here together though."

My smile morphs into a pouted scowl before I can hold it back. "Apart from hungover Burger King dates with Sharon, I never go to lunch with anyone from work. If we had left the building together, it would have been all over Share's gossip channel before the end of the day."

Rami's eyes widen. "There's a gossip channel on Share? Why didn't you show me that?"

"Because you're still new, so you *are* our gossip. Anyway, trust me. You don't want people thinking anything romantic is happening between you and me. You're already on shaky ground with your morose clothing choices and very limited banter. You really don't want people thinking we're shagging as well."

Rami flashes me an unexpectedly quick and wry smile. "But isn't that exactly what you want *Lionel* to think?"

I flutter my eyelashes as I swallow. "Yes, about that. I suppose we should discuss it as that's why we're here."

"It is," Rami says, and he seems to relax a little, leaning back in his chair. Our eyes lock in together and I am momentarily lost for words, stupidly adrift in the iridescent silver of his eyes and it feels like he does me a favour when he looks away and picks up his menu.

"Shall we maybe order first?" he asks.

"Sure," I say, closing my eyes for a moment longer than a blink as if that will erase what they just did.

After studying the menu in silence for a minute or so a server comes over to take our order.

"And would you like anything from the wine list?" he asks after we give him our food choices.

"Oh, no, thank you," I say.

"You can if you want," Rami offers.

Not at these prices, no way.

"I'm fine with water, thank you," I say ignoring how tempting a glass of pinot grigio is right now. My throat is still inexplicably dry.

"So, the big day is just under two weeks away," Rami begins. "Are you excited? Nervous?"

"I'm... something," I say. *Everything*, I think.

"My sister told me you didn't call for a fitting. I think it's getting a bit late now for her to—"

"Oh yes, that. I wanted to thank you for your kind offer, but I already have a tux that is perfectly adequate. It cost far too much two years ago so I should definitely get some more wear out of it. Also, wait until you see my arse in it. It may actually turn you."

"Well, that's..." Rami begins.

I plough on, suddenly worried I've overlooked a key detail. "You do have a tux, don't you? Did I mention it was black tie? I mean, it's a little over the top, I know, but it is a gay wedding at a country estate and Luigi works in Fashion PR so I suppose it's somewhat to be expected."

"Luigi, that's Lionel's fiancé?" Rami asks.

"Yes, unbelievable name, isn't it? Who knew Italians were actually called that? I thought it was a made-up Italian name just for Japanese computer games and pizza take-aways."

"You know that could sound a little offensive," Rami says in a gentle voice.

I feel all my features fall. "You're right. I'm sorry. I'm not normally such a dickhead. A bit of a bitch sometimes, yes, but I do try my best not to be a racist twat."

"I don't think you're a dickhead or a racist twat," Rami says as he reaches for his water.

"But you don't like me very much, do you?" I ask and my face still feels loose, like everything is a bit empty.

As it annoyingly often does, it takes a moment for Rami to close his mouth and formulate a reply. "I don't dislike you, Jake," he says, and I wait for him to elaborate, to offer some further reassurance perhaps, but he doesn't. I shrug it off.

"Well, I suppose that's good enough for what we have to do. I mean, don't worry, I won't insist we kiss or cuddle up for photos or anything. I just need you to look like you might like me."

"Jake—"

"And you won't have to put up with me all night. I'll be busy being the social butterfly I am after two glasses of champagne. So don't take it personally if I disappear now and then. Just promise me—" I pause. "God, this feels really cheeky."

"Go on," Rami says leaning forward.

"Just don't cop off with one of the bridesmaids or anything, okay? The last thing I need is Lionel's pity over being dumped by my boyfriend on his wedding day."

Rami lays both of his hands flat on the table. "Jake, I promise you I won't dump you on their wedding day."

"I appreciate it," I say, and I hope it shows in my face which finally feels a bit more like my own again. We both lean back as some servers bring over our food.

"I do have one request myself," Rami says as they walk away.

I roll my eyes with deliberate emphasis and hope the sarcasm I am summoning is audible. "Gosh, you're so demanding!"

Rami flashes me a quick smile of acknowledgement before rushing out his next words. "Can we have fun? I mean, at the wedding. It's been a while since I was a guest at a wedding – I've worked a fair few, of course – but it would be fun to be a guest with you and just enjoy a day out. Together."

I'm not sure what I was expecting him to ask but it certainly wasn't that. After flicking out my serviette and laying it on my lap, I pick up my knife and fork while looking at Rami. I observe how his smile tilts up a little more on one side than the other, and how his thick eyebrows really do hold the most perfect arch. And those eyes, looking at them feels like witnessing the moonlight lighting up the darkest night. I bite back my own smile before I speak. He is going to look very handsome in a tux on my arm, or rather, somewhere close to the vicinity of my arm.

"I suppose we can try," I say and then start to eat the world's most expensive tortellini.

*****

With most of the wedding day's logistics discussed and agreed upon, we're drinking coffee after our meal when Rami asks me the last question I expect from him.

"Did you meet up with your friends to talk about your fortieth birthday party? I heard you talking about it on the phone the other day."

My top lip curls involuntarily. "Sadly, yes."

"And?"

"I've agreed to have a party. They left me no choice. Said I would be banished from our bi-monthly spin and bitch meet-ups if I didn't do something."

"When is your birthday?"

"The third of September, so just over three months to come up with an excuse to get out of it or if that fails, plenty of time to try to get hit by a double-decker bus."

"I know big social events can be daunting..." Rami sips from his cup and I don't know why my eyes stay focused on his lips as he licks them afterwards.

"Oh, no, I love big social events. You'll see the way I work a room at this wedding. I just don't want it to be a room full of people who want to celebrate me."

"Why not?"

Because I'm not worth celebrating. The thought punches into my brain without warning. *Ouch.*

"Because I don't feel great turning forty, to be honest," I say, and I am being exactly that. Honest. "I feel like I haven't done as much with my life as I wanted to by this stage."

Rami squints at me and leans back in his chair. I wish I didn't notice how attractive he looks in that relaxed, confident way some men have just simply sitting in a chair. I wish I hadn't noticed how attractive he looks, full stop.

"Really? In what way?" he asks.

"How old are you?" I say, deliberately avoiding his question. I brace myself for the answer.

"Forty-three," he says, and I nearly choke on the bite of macaroon I just took.

"Really?" I ask. "But you look... younger."

Rami shrugs. "Light brown don't frown, I guess?"

A surprised laugh darts out of me.

"You know, none of my friends were around to celebrate my fortieth and I really missed them," Rami says.

"Why, where were they?"

"Oh, I was living in California and most of my best friends were over here." Rami talks in an unusually rushed way. "Flights are expensive, you know. Some of them have kids. It wasn't easy for them to come over."

"Yeah, but you could have come home."

"I could have, but... I didn't." He clears his throat before continuing, "My point is, have the party. Let your friends celebrate you. Do you have family too?"

"My sister, Jenna. She's also my best friend. She used to live in London but is in Dublin now with her partner, Marty. Irony of ironies, I moved to live here a year after she left."

"You must miss her," he says

"Yeah, I do," I admit.

"Where were you living before that?"

"Marrakech, for a year. Managing one of Bill and Simeon's resorts, actually. That's how we met. Before that I was in Crete for five years, managing a family-owned high-end resort. That was where I met Lionel..." My thoughts threaten to wander away but I quickly reel them back in. "And prior to that, I was all over. Did seasons in nearly all corners of Europe, and a couple in Egypt and Tunisia too."

"Ahh, Egypt. Beautiful country."

"Is that where your descendants are from? I'm hesitant to make assumptions but you called your sister *shaqiqti* on the phone the other day, which I know is Arabic."

"Well, I'm impressed you know some Arabic. My parents are first-generation immigrants from Iran, but my mother's family was originally from Lebanon, so she also spoke Arabic and a bit of French with us as well as Farsi. Mom and Dad moved here shortly after the Revolution in 1979. They had me when they were both just twenty, so I was a baby when we arrived, and my sisters were born here later."

"So, you can speak Arabic, Farsi, French, and English? Wow."

"They're all a bit rusty, but *naeam, bale, oui* and yes." He smiles and I realise that was another attempt at a joke. It was terrible, but in an admittedly cute sort of way.

"That's lucky. My mother was Spanish but sadly never taught us. I've tried to learn since but it's quite limited now." I pray he doesn't ask more questions about my mother.

"Learning new things gets harder the older we get," Rami says, his eyes so steadily on me again, I have to look away.

"What are your sisters' names?" I ask.

"Radia and Roxana, or Roxie."

"And which one works as a tailor?"

"Radia. Roxie was a happy but very big surprise when my parents thought they were long done with child-rearing. She's only nineteen and lives at home, still in Birmingham."

"Wow, that's a big age difference,"

"It is," Rami agrees and for a minute I think he's going to say more but he doesn't.

"Are you all close?"

This brings another tentative smile to his face. "We are. Sort of. I go home every Sunday to spend the day with them."

"You see your parents every week?"

Rami swallows before he replies, "Actually, it's just my mom. Baba, my dad, died four years ago."

"Oh, shit. I'm sorry to hear that."

"Thanks," he says and his smile wavers until he nods at me. "What about you? How often do you see your parents?"

"I'm also in the one living parent club. Terrible membership benefits, aren't they?" I smile weakly. "My mum died when I was younger. A lot younger. It's just my dad now but he lives up in Scotland, so I don't see him that much." I deliberately don't find Rami's eyes and then take a big drink of my coffee, finishing it. "You know, I should probably head back to the office. Will you wait ten minutes before you come back?"

Shaking his head, Rami chuckles in a way which could be laughing at me or laughing *with* me and it annoys me that I can't tell the difference. "Sure," he agrees.

"I'll get everything organised before the big day. I've told them about your vegan meal choices. I'll hire a car, get a gift, and will tell Lionel my amazing new boyfriend Rami is coming. Oh, and I've already confirmed with the venue that we're in a room with two single beds, so you don't need to worry about one of my wayward homosexual limbs groping you in the middle of the night."

I swear Rami's cheeks turn a little pinker. *God, straight men are such over-reactors.*

"Okay, thanks," he says.

"You are going to be alright with this, aren't you? I may have to touch you now and then to keep up the pretence. But I promise to be appropriate."

His brow lowers when he catches my eye. "I am totally okay with this, Jake. Don't worry. I'm happy to help."

I'm about to find the server to get the death sentence that will be our bill when I see a waiter already on the approach with a phone in his hand.

"I'm so sorry to interrupt but I see you've finished now—" he asks.

"Yes, we'd like the bill when you're ready," I say and move to gather my belongings, but the server keeps talking, looking at Rami.

"Could I get a photo?" he asks.

"You want to take a photo of us?" I say, confused.

The server looks at me as if I've just grown an extra head. "No, I want a photo of—"

"It's fine, let's do a selfie, shall we?" Rami pushes up to stand beside the server and their faces both adopt wide smiles as the server holds his phone out and takes the photo.

I'm still slack-jawed and blinking as Rami sits back down.

"What on God's green Earth was that?"

Rami smiles but doesn't meet my eyes. "Oh, it's the funniest thing... I sometimes get mistaken for this famous Persian actor. I don't have the heart to tell people I'm not who they think I am."

"Really?" I tilt my head to the side as I study him. "What's his name?"

"Oh, you wouldn't know him. Iranian guy. Very talented. Super sexy too, obviously." Rami waves a hand up and down his torso and boasts a smile that I haven't seen before. A smile I quite like.

My laughter stalls in my throat for a second before it blasts out of me. "That was almost amusing, Mr Events."

"Almost?"

"Still room for improvement, but you know, maybe I'll rub off on you. Maybe by the end of this fake wedding date you'll have a sense of humour."

And maybe Rami's right. Maybe it will be a fun day together.

Chapter Six

Rami

My apartment is too big for me. With 160 square metres spread over one large living space, one master bedroom, one guest room and two bathrooms, whenever I'm here alone it feels too big. Too empty. And I'm always here alone.

Before I moved in four months ago, I was living at my mom's house – my childhood home – for nearly two years while I got a grip on my life again, and prior to that I was in LA for ten years. Ten long years where I was hardly ever alone.

Initially, that was because I was living the bachelor lifestyle that meant I had staff to take on my domestic chores, a team to help me manage my schedule and workload, and a rotating door of loose acquaintances wanting to be in my company... or rather dine out or party at my expense. Then I met Michelle and within a year we were living together in a beautiful mid-century Santa Monica bungalow we bought and turned into a home over three years, and then... Then there were four years of living somewhere very different. Somewhere I try not to let myself return to mentally.

That's why it's Friday night and rather than sit at home completely alone with my memories in a too big, too empty apartment, I'm playing MarioKart virtually with my two sisters.

"Oh no, you didn't!" Roxana squeals in my headphones when I throw an ink bomb in her direction.

"Ha! Gotcha!" I laugh gleefully.

"That's not playing fair," Roxie bemoans but I check the map and see her fast on the approach behind me regardless.

"His days are numbered, Rox, I'm coming at him from the front," Radia says over our shared call.

"I don't know why I agreed for you both to be on the same team," I tut as I try to loop back and head in a new direction away from them both.

"Because you owe us," Radia replies. "You abandoned us for a giant sandpit and a white woman with a kaftan addiction."

"Pah! He didn't abandon us for RemiX and Michelle," Roxie is quicker than I am to respond. "He abandoned us way before that, for international superstardom."

"Well, at least he occasionally answered text messages and called us while he was busy being famous and touring the world. RemiX was what cut him off completely," Radia adds. "Must have been all that beige linen. Earth shades do look good on our skin tone."

"It can't have been the raw vegan food," Roxie adds. "I tried some beetroot carpaccio the other day. Yuk. Gross."

"You know I am still here?" I say, my voice shaky. Objectively, I know it's a good sign that my sisters like to banter about my past, but it's one thing to know how royally you fucked up and quite another to make a joke about it, especially with those you hurt most.

"That's precisely why we're still banging on about it," Radia clarifies. "Can't have you even thinking about doing anything similar ever again."

"Like I would," I say with a shudder but it's not because the possibility horrifies me, it's because I fear that the part of me that did join RemiX, that cut off my family still lives inside me.

"He can't," Roxie pipes up. "He's thrown out all his linen. They wouldn't let him back in."

"That's right. He's back in his Steve Jobs era," Radia adds.

"Steve Jobs?" I ask, frowning as I side-step both Radia and Roxie's players.

"Only ever wearing black. Partial to a roll-neck for special occasions."

"I've always liked black and roll-neck jumpers," I say defensively.

"Not something to be proud of," Radia replies.

"Oh, piss off."

"Rads, he's going to come right around the side of—" Roxie warns our sister.

"Oh, yeah, I got him!" Radia says gleefully.

"Nope. Not this time." I steer Toad away at the very last second to avoid Radia's Daisy.

"Let's try and corner him next," Roxie says.

"Seriously? Can't you just let me win one round?"

"My answer is the same." Radia's voice turns menacing. "You owe us."

I groan. "How long do I have to pay my dues for it all?" Not that I care what the answer is because I already plan on showing my sisters and mother how sorry I am for the rest of my days.

"At least another five years. What do you think Roxie?"

"To be honest, I've nearly forgotten all about it. I just like how he's back now," Roxana replies, and her words warm my gut in a way that feels almost overwhelming and certainly overly generous.

"Yeah, it's kind of nice," Radia says. "Oh, just let me get you, Toad! I have to go in a minute anyway."

"Oh, yes, dinner with the Queer Eyes," I say referring to Radia's friends, mostly fellow graduates from the fashion course that she did at Central St Martins.

"Yep. I need help deciding what to wear for Saturday." Radia's voice suddenly gets louder. "FOR MY THIRD DATE WITH THE POSSIBLE LOVE OF MY LIFE!"

"Love your optimism," I half-laugh, half-mumble as I somehow side-step Roxie's Yoshi for the second time in as many seconds.

"I don't think you know how I feel about her," Radia says. "Like I wake up smiling. She makes me smile before I even open my eyes. And you both know how much I hate mornings."

"Ugh, don't remind me," I agree.

"Oh, you didn't even see her at her worst," Roxie chimes in. "When you were out in the desert hanging out in your cult, it was my job to bang pots and pans outside her door to wake her up whenever she came to stay and would sleep past ten o'clock."

Radia is quick to disagree with her sister but I'm not listening. I'm too busy reeling from Roxie's words, or rather one specific word. *Cult*. I still have a problem with that word. Not because it's not true. RemiX was a cult, I know that now. But knowing that doesn't make it hurt any less.

"Yeah, I'm sorry about that," I mutter.

"Oh, Rami, you need to stop being sorry," Radia says. "Grovelling is not a good look."

"But you just said I have to pay my dues for five years!" I protest while also trying to keep the conversation as jokey as possible.

"Yes, by letting us capture your mushroom head and throwing you in jail... Yes! Like that!" Radia yells as she finally grabs me with her piranha plant.

"Boom!" Roxie's celebrations fill my ears.

I'm not surprised. My attention began wavering not long after they began casually discussing my absence from their lives.

"Okay, that's my cue to go," Radia says. "You should also both go do something else that isn't hanging out online at eight o'clock on a Friday night."

"Ugh, but that would mean talking to people," Roxana groans.

"Yeah, people suck," I agree but it sounds much weaker because it's not true. I don't hate people at all. I just don't *know* any people in London, at least not anyone who is unfamiliar with how I spent the last six years of my life. And honestly, I don't want to see anyone who does know. The questions I would have to answer. The explanations I would have to have. It's still beyond me.

I know that a lot of this is because I didn't finish the rehab I joined after I left RemiX. Barely one week in, I left and fled to the UK to see my family. At the time nothing would have stopped me doing that, because it was in rehab that I found out my father had died.

Did I think my father would live forever? Honestly, yes, part of me did and this brings me some illogical reassurance. Because if I really thought that then it can go some distance to excuse how I cut my family off. Maybe I always intended to return to them? Maybe I always assumed there would be time to do that? But in the next breath, I am quick to self-correct. I didn't cut my family off with the intention of rebuilding that connection at a later date. When I was in RemiX, I was all in. I believed in what Gee and Michelle were saying.

I believed in Gee, my one-time best friend, and I believed in Michelle, my one-time girlfriend. I believed in them until I realised it was starting to cost me my sanity.

"You want to keep playing? Rami?" Roxana's voice slices into my thoughts. I realise Radia has already gone and I'm not even sure I said goodbye.

"I don't mind. Do you?" It would be very helpful if she did. I really don't want to be alone with my thoughts right now.

"Not really. I'm tired and tomorrow's Saturday so I have to be up early to work," Roxie says with all her trademark honesty and directness, a quality that took me a little time to adjust to when I returned from LA, but now I love it. I envy her it, in fact.

"Then go get an early night," I say, trying to ignore the stab of disappointment I feel that I now have more hours alone to kill.

"Are you sure?" Roxie asks in a quiet voice. "I hear what you're saying to me and I want to believe it. Like, that's what my brain is telling me to do, but Mom was telling me the other day how you sometimes say things just to make us think you're doing better than you really are, so maybe I'm missing a cue or something."

The fact my nineteen-year-old sister is trying so hard to figure out if I'm okay is not just upsetting, it's downright depressing.

"Go get ready for bed, Roxie, I promise you I'm fine. I'm tired from work and tomorrow I'm going to do a long run and maybe sort out my records, so I should get an early night too."

"Oh, the records part sounds fun, but I'd rather stick toothpicks in my eyeballs than do the running part."

I smile to myself thinking how it's the other way round for me.

"Goodbye, Roxie. Big hugs to Mom."

"Bye, Rami. See you Sunday."

"See you Sunday," I say back and let a small smile land on my lips. The weekend is not completely empty. I will return to my family home on Sunday like I do every week. It may not count for much considering my previous actions, but I do hope travelling back up to Birmingham to see my mother and Roxie, sometimes accompanied by Radia, is appreciated.

After shutting down the games console, switching the TV off and sliding my headphones off my head, I stand up and walk to the guest room. I open the door and stand there for a long time just taking in the view of countless stacks of cardboard boxes, each one filled with vinyl I amassed over the years, starting with the not insignificant collection my father used to DJ with.

Fun fact. Staring at boxes does not unpack them.

Unpack. Ugh. I hate that word. It was thrown around far too frequently during my time in RemiX and while I didn't dislike it much at first, by the time I started hearing it again at rehab I had an almost physiological response to it.

And yet I know I do still need to unpack. Both the small mountain of boxes that practically fill my spare room and everything that happened over the last four years I was in California.

But where do I start? Or rather which one do I start unpacking first? The boxes or the mental load?

Neither is an appealing prospect and both will demand energy from me I'm not sure I have, despite having plenty of time. But do I want to spend that time sifting through too painful memories? Do I want to pass that time recalling just how much I miss DJing? Do I want to spend hours touching records my father used to play, many of them ones I would hand to him when I used to accompany him on his DJ gigs in our local pub? Do I want to dive into that endless well of grief?

It's not even a question of if I want to. It's a question of if I'm capable of doing it. And I have an easy answer to the question. No. I am not capable of doing that. Not yet. So, I turn around and close the door behind me. I'll find something else to fill the time with. Something that doesn't hurt as much. Something that doesn't remind me of the mistakes I made, and all the things I lost. It's only a little disconcerting that the first thing that springs to mind is getting my tux out to take to the dry cleaners tomorrow so it's ready for this wedding I'm going with Jake.

It's only a little puzzling that this event, happening next weekend, prompts an excited twist in my stomach and a little energy to go and polish my shoes. It's only a little strange that whenever the dark memories threaten to return as my lonely evening progresses, I remind myself of next weekend and it makes me feel a little bit better.

PART TWO – FIRST QUARTER

"The Moon is beautiful only when the mind is seeking beauty and the heart is loving."

Debasish Mridha

Chapter Seven

Jake

It's everything I would want, I think, as I drive up the winding driveway towards a grand sandstone stately home. On either side of the road, rolling green fields stretch as far as the eye can see, interrupted only by trees and fences. A very late blessing of spring blossom decorates the trees that line the last stretch of driveway and under a bright blue sky, cloudy pink petals fall all around us. Several land on the hire car's window screen and many of them stick to the glass, almost like they want to taunt me. They slightly hamper our view of the house itself which is a vast property built in Stuart style with a flat roof, perfectly symmetrical windows stretching out over two wings on either side of the main building and a Palladian-style terrace that looks out over the expansive grounds.

"Wow," Rami says as if to rub salt in my wounds. He sees it too. He sees how beautiful it is. And how it's not my wedding.

"I mean, it's okay…"

"Okay? This is like driving into the set of a BBC Austen adaption."

"Wow, you really have been gone from the UK for an age. Didn't you get *Bridgerton* in the US?"

I feel Rami's eyes on me. "Jake, I hope you're not going to snap at me every time you feel a teeny bit jealous of Lionel and Luigi. It will make today twice as long, and half as fun."

I switch on the window screen spray and wipers at full blast, shoving away the blossom petals, possibly a little aggressively.

"It's just a bit extra, isn't it? This venue, the black-tie dress code. No doubt they've probably got a string quartet welcoming guests and a hamper of white doves to be released after the ceremony. It's just so over the top, it's so…"

"You," Rami says, and I feel his eyes on me. But I don't turn to look at him. I spray the window screen spray again.

"Bastard blossom," I mutter.

"It's exactly what you would want, isn't it? If you were to get married?" Rami continues because apparently, he likes to cause me emotional distress.

When I turn quickly to look at him, I instantly regret it. Although his words feel taunting, his expression is not. His eyes are darker than usual but not in a threatening way, rather in a warm and searching way, and his mouth is stretched into a soft and very sympathetic smile. He has what can only be described as a kind expression on his face.

"It's not what—" I begin to protest.

"It's okay to want that. It's always okay to want things, even if they're currently out of reach." He shifts in his seat.

I open my mouth to disagree, that being my default mode for most of our drive here, but I suddenly don't want to. His words bring me a gentle wave of peace, a light sprinkling of ease, so I choose not to bat them away.

"That's sort of comforting," I mutter.

"You're welcome," he says.

"I didn't actually thank you," I point out.

"No, but you will have to at some point today and I am so looking forward to it," Rami replies, and all that kindness has been replaced by a sneering facetiousness. It's frustrating that both looks suit his dark, handsome features so well.

"I don't suppose they want us to park in front of the front door," I say returning to the task in hand.

"Best not. Ah, look, there's a sign for the car park there." Rami points to a wooden sign in the shape of an arrow with *Car Park* written on it in looping calligraphy. Under the words is a crest with two Ls in it.

"Really? They have their own fucking crest?" I bite out.

Rami chuckles into his fist as I tut another three times, all the while we follow the road that takes us around to the rear of the property, the *huge* property.

"How on Earth could they afford this place?" I think out loud. Being Lionel's boss for five out of the last seven years means I know exactly what his salary has been recently, and I have a fair idea of what he's earning at his current role, which is managing a luxury hostel near King's Cross. My conclusion is that Fashion PR must be a lot more lucrative than I imagined. Or maybe Luigi comes from money. That would be the cherry on top of this shit sandwich.

"Maybe he knows the owner? Did Lionel contact you about maybe using one of Status' venues?" Rami asks.

I feel heat in my cheeks. "Not exactly. Lionel and I… We haven't talked very much over the last few years."

"But you are still invited to the wedding? Because if not, we just made a very pointless three-hour-journey."

"Oh, I'm invited. We are sort of in touch. I mean, we text a bit. We like each other's Instagram posts. We both send very amusing GIFs to the same WhatsApp groups we're in. But we haven't spoken one on one in a long time."

"Oh. Is that his doing or yours?"

I think about all the missed calls. I think about the voicemails he left. I think about the emails he sent me that I never replied to.

"A bit of both," I answer in a quiet voice.

After I park, we take our bags out of the boot of the car and spot another wooden – and ugh, crested – sign for Reception where we need to check-in. Because of course this venue is big enough to have rooms for all the guests. We dutifully follow it as it leads us through an archway in the high sandstone wall that surrounds the property.

"Wow," Rami says again as he steps into the grounds, the grounds being a stretch of beautifully designed, immaculately kept, and lusciously lush gardens. It's exactly what I would describe as a typical English country garden, comprised of various intricate arrangements of flower beds all boasting a wide variety of flowers, shrubs and plants. There are colourful beds of roses criss-crossing with banks of lavender, begonia and gardenia, and in the middle there's a small water fountain and circular pond. A little further down the garden, away from the house,

I see high-rise bushes that could be a maze, and gravel paths zig zag through the greenery inviting you to stroll around the gardens and enjoy it all.

"Wow indeed," I say although I sound a lot less impressed than Rami. A fizzy warmth lands in my nostrils. "Come on, it's a recipe for death by hay fever out here."

I march off along the gravel path ahead without waiting for Rami to follow and I'm just rounding the pond's edge when I see a couple on the opposite side of the water, sitting on a bench and locked in an embrace.

"Oh, for fuck's sake," I say under my breath. At least I thought it was under my breath but when their heads pull away from each other and turn towards us I suspect it was louder than I intended.

"Jake!" Lionel's voice hasn't changed, still warm, soft and lyrical. And he looks exactly the same even if his facial hair is styled a different way – a goatee – and his glasses are new, their fashionable frames highlighting his big brown eyes perfectly. A part of me wants to rush forward and hug him. Another part of me wants to turn and run away. And a smaller, more insane part of me wants to rugby tackle him to the ground and beg him to marry me instead.

But then I see Luigi stand up after him, and I know the chances of him considering such an offer are non-existent. A tall man with a slim but defined physique, Luigi couldn't look more Italian if he tried, nor could he be more attractive. He's dark-eyed, olive-skinned and has a goatee that looks annoyingly identical to Lionel's. His smile is broad and appears genuine as he comes to stand next to Lionel who is waving me over to them.

"That's the happy couple?" Rami leans closer to my ear to ask.

"Unfortunately, yes," I say through a smile that is all gritted teeth. "Of course, we bump into them before I've had a chance to pluck my eyebrows and exfoliate."

Rami doesn't reply but he does nudge me as he moves past me to approach them.

"So lovely to meet you," I hear him say, his hand out-stretched. "Congratulations to you both."

Not unlike a disobedient puppy, I follow behind him.

"I'm Rami..." he continues as he shakes their hands in turn. I open my mouth to speak but it promptly slams shut when Rami adds: "Jake's boyfriend."

As shocked as I am hearing him say that – with no prompting, no instruction – more than that, I feel relief. I know it's a complete lie, but it helps ground me in some silly, stupid way. It especially helps as I watch Luigi slide his hand over Lionel's shoulders and it comes to rest on the back of his neck, a neck I've kissed before, a neck I may have even grabbed hold of in the throes of passion. Maybe that's what prompts me to grab Rami's hand with mine and I am flooded with more relief when Rami doesn't pull away. In fact, he doesn't even look at me. He doesn't do anything but hold my hand back in return.

"Lionel, it's good to see you. Thank you again for the invitation. And my goodness, what a stunning venue you found for the wedding," I say, relatively easily.

"It's so great to see *you*," Lionel says and before I know what's happening, he steps forward and pulls me into a hug that rips my hand out of Rami's. I eventually return his embrace and am proud of myself that I wait a few seconds before I inhale deeply. He still smells the same. Like freshly washed linen on a spring day. I allow myself half a second to savour it with closed eyes.

"This is Luigi," Lionel says as he pulls back. His face glows with pride as he turns to his husband-to-be.

"Yes." I hold out my hand to this handsome man who I now see is irritatingly well-built, his body filling out his shirt and narrow trousers perfectly. I shudder at how good he is going to look in a tux later and start praying there's a well-stocked minibar in our room so I can soften the blow in advance. "Lovely to finally meet you, Luigi. And congratulations. You got a good one here."

As I say that last sentence, my eyes are pulled to Lionel and I hate what I see. He returns my gaze, looking happy, grateful, and proud. I don't know who exactly he's proud of but I'm going to pretend it's me.

"It's a real pleasure to meet you," Luigi says, sounding more like English aristocracy than native Italian. "Lionel talks about you so much. I feel like I already know you."

"If it was anyone else, I would tell you not to believe a word he says, but as it's Lionel – the world's kindest human – I'm going to say lovely to meet you too."

Light laughter bounces between us but when it peters out, silence falls. It makes me panic a little, which is why I ask my next question.

"Isn't it bad luck for you to see each other before the wedding?"

"I know. We're being a bit risky, aren't we? A pair of dangerous Debbies!" Lionel declares.

"Oh, *mi amore*, that's all nonsense. You know what our counsellor said about traditions like that, and that what really decides a lasting marriage is how we communicate, keep checking in with each other. Which is what we are doing." Luigi strokes the back of Lionel's head as he turns to us. "She recommended we have quiet moments this weekend, just us, so we can stay connected. That's what we were doing before we get ready and the ceremony begins. Jeannette is fantastic, by the way, if you ever need a couples' counsellor," Luigi adds in earnest.

I don't hide my surprise. "You're having therapy already? Surely that's for later down the road when one of you doesn't pick up your socks and the other never takes the bins out?"

"Oh, no, a healthy relationship always needs help and so we're using it to deepen our bond," Lionel says.

"Of course you are," I mumble, possibly a little tartly.

"I think it's very romantic," Rami says loud enough to cover my words but then silence falls again.

And it lingers long enough for me to notice the way Lionel and Luigi look at each other and how they instinctively lean towards the other, their arms touching. I am busy observing their intimacy, feeling all manner of prickly and unpleasant feelings, when Rami breaks the silence.

"This venue really is incredible. How did you find it?"

I may be a little surprised he speaks first, but I am completely shocked that he does so while slipping his hand back into mine and giving my fingers a quick squeeze, hard enough that it makes me turn to look at him. It could be my imagination, but he gives me exactly the same kind of look Luigi and Lionel just shared – chin dipped, eyes boring into me, unblinking – and I smile back at him, another wave of relief washing over me.

Fuck, I really am going to have to thank him for today, aren't I?

"Isn't it stunning? It's owned by one of Luigi's clients and they practically insisted we use it, didn't they, darling?"

"They did indeed, *mi amore*," Luigi replies, and I hear again his perfect Italian pronunciation. Brilliant. He's fucking bilingual.

"Have you seen inside yet? Shall we give you a quick tour?" Lionel asks. "Oh, silly sausage me. I haven't even asked you how your journey was?"

"It was fine," Rami replies. "At least it was for me. Jake drove so I was able to relax a bit. He's good to me."

I wish I didn't see the way Lionel recoils at this, as if he's surprised.

"You know," Luigi narrows his stare on Rami. "You look ever so familiar. Do you work in fashion? Modelling?"

"Him? Modelling? Ha!" I exclaim and only regret it when I see how horrified Lionel and Luigi look. I'd forgotten how Lionel has a different sense of humour to me.

"I work in events," Rami says, smoothing over my blunder.

"He's our new Head of Events," I add.

"Oh, you work together?" Lionel says. "That's… nice."

My stomach drops when I realise where this stilted reaction has come from. When Lionel and I were hooking up together I frequently used our working together as a reason we could never be an official couple. At the time I did think it was the right thing to say, to do, and ironically, I still think that way – Rami and I are a fake relationship after all – but I can hardly explain that now.

"It's a funny story, actually," Rami begins. "I had to move into Jake's office on my first day as mine wasn't ready – still isn't, in fact – and so we were literally sort of forced together. He couldn't escape me."

"I wouldn't call that a funny story, at all." I wrinkle my nose.

The silence returns and I am about to curse my own dry sense of humour when I feel Rami's body shake with chuckles.

"You can be such a sarcastic bitch sometimes," he says, nudging into me. "You're lucky that it's one of the things I like about you."

As if it's an invitation to laugh with him, Lionel and Luigi join in.

"So, about that tour?" Lionel then says.

"Yes, we can take you to your room first and then show you everything else. We have to keep some of the details of the ceremony a secret, of course, but I think we can show you where everything is happening," Luigi adds.

"Oh, we don't want to put you out," I say quickly. The thought of a pre-wedding preview is nauseating. "We'll just check-in and go to our room..."

"Jake can barely keep his hands off me," Rami says, leaning forward. The words – and the implied meaning – are so foreign in his deep, serious voice, I am momentarily stunned while he keeps talking. "You know what it's like, the early stages of a new relationship."

"Oh, we do," Lionel says, and a blush of colour darkens his brown cheeks. He gazes up at Luigi as he speaks. "Do you remember that one time you locked your front door and hid the key so you could keep me all to yourself for a weekend? And then you went and forgot where you hid the key, so on Monday morning we had to practically turn your place inside out to find it." Lionel turns back to us. "And do you know where the key was?"

There's a pause before we realise he's actually waiting for an answer.

"Oh, no idea," I say, somehow sounding very interested even though that's the last thing I am.

"In the microwave! Such a sneaky snake!" Lionel declares as he places his hand on Luigi's chest, a stretch of pectoral muscles that could be described as sculpted, if I was feeling generous, which I really am not.

"And rather dangerous too!" Luigi adds with something I think one could label a guffaw.

"You're a wild one!" I say and I know Rami picks up my sarcasm when he squeezes my hand again. I'd almost forgotten our fingers were still linked.

"I still double-check the microwave when I go to make my morning porridge," Lionel says with more of his sing-song laughter.

"I can imagine," I say, but there's no sarcasm there now. Just fondness. And a sinking reminder that this man is too good, much too good for me.

"Anyway, all joking aside," Rami says. "I want to take Jake up to our room to chill out for a bit before we get ready."

"Of course, but before you go, do you have a few minutes, Jake?" Lionel asks with eagerness, shuffling forward slightly. "Luigi is about to go and get ready with his groomsmen, but I have a bit of time now."

My body tenses from my hair follicles to my toenails. I'm trying to search for an alternative excuse when Rami's voice fills my ears.

"Lionel, if it's all the same to you, I think for the next few hours I'm going to be hiding our room key in the minibar, if you catch my drift," Rami says with a wink that pulls on every one of his features. "Because I'm assuming there's no microwave in our room."

"You assume right, my friend, you assume right." Luigi guffaws again as he slaps Rami on his arm in camaraderie. I swear stopping myself from rolling my eyes actually burns up a handful of calories.

"I suppose we'll see you later at the ceremony," Lionel says looking at me as if to confirm. He doesn't look sad, exactly, just a little forlorn or disappointed. It's a painful reminder of the way he looked at me when I told him I slept with a man whose name I can't even remember now.

"Come on, Lover Boy." Rami starts to walk off, leading me back to the path that will take us to the reception. Without looking back at Lionel and Luigi, I walk a little behind him, this time like an embarrassed puppy who just rolled around in their own shit.

We are out of the gardens and approaching a side entrance for the house when Rami's warm palm pulls away from mine.

"I guess it's safe now," he explains.

I stare down at my hand for a moment. It feels bare and emptier than it should. "I suppose so."

"Are you okay?" Rami stops and turns to me. "That was a bit… intense."

"By intense do you mean incredibly awkward and terribly embarrassing for me?"

"Something along those lines."

"Well, then it won't surprise you at all to know that no, I'm not okay, and actually I'd suddenly rather drink a carafe of my own urine than go to this wedding." I feel my shoulders sink, and not because of the weight of my bag which is full of far too many lotions and potions that are not going to turn back the hands of time in two hours, no matter their price tag.

"You definitely don't want to drink your own piss, trust me," Rami says with a wonky grin, but he leaves me no time to question his comment. "If it makes you feel better, I think they're completely convinced that we're an item."

A surprise of a smile pulls at my lips. "You're right. We did good. Or rather you did. Do you have a secret performing arts degree you haven't told anyone about?"

"Why would I keep that a secret? I'd be proud of that!" Rami says as we start walking up the steps and into the building.

Half a giggle falls out of my mouth before I clamp my hand over my lips. "Oh, God, you just made me laugh. I really am rubbing off on you!"

*****

Following the directions the receptionist gave us for our room, I am about to try and lift my left hand and check my watch but the bag I'm carrying is too heavy, so I have to swing my arm to get some momentum behind it. In doing so I feel a momentary freedom from the weight that was in the bag. Except it's not momentary. I look down and see I'm still holding the straps of my Longchamp weekend bag, but they are no longer connected to the royal blue canvas they were attached to a moment ago.

"Are you fucking kidding me?" I say to my bag that is slumped on the floor. "You cost more than two hundred quid!"

With his own bag on his back, Rami circles back and bends to scoop up the handle-less bag. Holding it against his chest, he straightens out and smiles at me in a way that could be trying to comfort me but could also be a little mocking.

"Nothing some superglue won't fix," he says.

"Well, guess what 'Lover Boy'," I say with spiteful emphasis as I start to follow him down the corridor again. "I didn't pack superglue. My skincare routine is quite desperate these days, it's true, but I've not yet resorted to those sorts of measures. Besides, I doubt superglue is going to fix the rest of the disaster that is the following twelve hours. Did you even see how fucking attractive and bloody charming and pissing friendly Luigi is?"

"God, yeah, absolute wanker," Rami says. He's getting better at sarcasm.

"And he's clearly stinkingly, offensively rich. That accent cost more money in school fees than I'll earn in seven lifetimes."

"He could just pride himself on good elocution," Rami says but I ignore him.

"And what's with them going to therapy already? Why can't they just wait until they hate each other like a normal couple?" I continue, waving around the straps in my hand, even though I'm facing Rami's back.

"I think it's one of the most sensible things I've ever heard of," he says and if he was closer, I think I would thump him, or step on his toe at least. "Very romantic too."

"Yes, that's why I hate it. I hate all the romance that's here today. Why can't they just have a registry office wedding with some lukewarm supermarket Cava? Why do they need to flaunt their love in our faces?"

Rami stops at a door and puts both of our bags down in front of him. He rummages in his pocket for the key we were given.

"Jake, you do know what weddings are for, right?"

"I know, I know. Celebrating love. The best day of their lives, blah-di-blah-blah-blah. But why, oh why does the best day of their lives have to be the worst day of mine?"

Rami puts the key in the door and pushes down on the handle. Before he opens the door, he looks back at me. "This is not going to be the worst day of your life; can you trust me on that?"

I'm pouting when I reply, "Fine. It won't be the worst day of my life. It will just be in the top ten of worst days of my life."

"I can work with that," Rami says, and he pushes open the door, before bending down to grab the bags. He steps to the side. "After you, Lover Boy."

Loosening the grip on my pout a little, I walk into the room thinking how I have a couple of hours to try and calm down. Beautifying myself and dancing to Wham!'s greatest hits should do the trick, two things that are instant serotonin boosters for me. Maybe Rami's right, maybe it won't be the—

"Fucking worst day of my life!" I yell as I stare at a beautifully made king-size bed, the only bed in the room.

Chapter Eight

Rami

Jake practically pirouettes on his heels to turn and leave the room, charging down the corridor.

"I'm going to fix this mess!" He yells out to me and I am about to call after him to say there's really no need, but he's already turned a corner and is out of sight.

Going into the room, I seize the opportunity to be alone, possibly for only a few minutes. I dump our bags on the desk and sit on the floor cross-legged with my back resting against the bed. I pull out my phone, find the app I need and set the timer for five minutes. It makes no sense that I find it easy to slip into a languid emptiness in my mind after the chaotic few hours I've just spent with Jake, but I do. And I treasure it. I don't even think about RemiX or Michelle or Gee or my dad or anything that curdles my insides.

The timer goes off quicker than I expect, and I slowly come out of my meditation, wriggling my toes and stretching out my fingers, before shaking out my limbs and getting up. I move to stand at the window on the far side of the room, noticing we have a view of the gardens we just walked through. They stretch out much further than you realise on the ground, and from up here I also see a large oval-shaped lake at the very end of the grounds, before rolling hills and woodlands claim the horizon. Taking in all the greenery, I'm struck by how beautiful and peaceful it is, and how good it feels to get out of the city.

This sense of open calm is uncomfortably familiar. It's how I felt when we moved out to the Mojave Desert four years ago. The wide endless skies and views for miles and miles held such promise back then, and while I learnt that they were false promises, I wonder if maybe there is still peace to be found in the countryside for me one day.

But probably not today.

After meeting Lionel and Luigi, I can understand a little better why Jake is so worked up about today. They make a striking couple – handsome, gentle-natured and clearly besotted with each other – and it seems like it's not just surface-deep. At the same time, it was palpable that Lionel and Jake share history, that there is possibly still unfinished business there, something that Lionel seems ready and keen to resolve, while Jake is only determined to run away from it.

Whatever it is, I feel the need to remind myself it's not my problem. I agreed to come and be Jake's plus one, to put on a good show as his fake boyfriend. I did not agree to help him confront his past. Indeed, to do so would be hypocritical when I am still running from my own.

Jake is gone so long I decide to at least unpack my suit and hang it up to prevent any creasing. I then look in Jake's bag and do the same for his because I figure regardless of where we sleep tonight, he'll also not want a crumpled suit and shirt. Hanging them in the wardrobe, I feel a foreign pang looking at the suit bags hanging side by side. It feels peculiarly intimate, our clothes sharing this small space together. Bizarrely, I don't ever remember feeling this when Michelle and I shared a closet space, but then again that 'closet' was a room, not a small wooden wardrobe. Even in the desert she made sure there was plenty of room for her clothes and shoe collection.

Eager to push this memory away, I stick my head out of the door to see if Jake is on his way back. When all I see is an empty corridor, I pull my phone out of my pocket and go to call him, but I get distracted when I see several text messages from Radia.

<How's it going Fake Boyfriend?>

<P.S. Just chatted with Mama and she says it's fine you skip tomorrow. I told her you were at a wedding with your new friend from work – did not mention the fake boyfriend farce – and she was so delighted. I think it would make her happy if you skipped tomorrow because you were having fun.>

<P.P.S. That was an extraordinarily long P.S. Sorry.>

<P.P.P.S Is it cheesy if I buy Barista Babe a single red rose for our date tomorrow?>

<P.P.P.P.S. I'm done now.>

Smiling as I read each one, I sit on the end of the bed to reply.

<It's going okay. Jake's blood pressure may not survive the day, but I will. The couple getting married are very nice. I will be there tomorrow to see Mom and Roxie. I promised them I'd be there, so I will be.>

<P.S. The rose is a lovely idea. Do it.>

<P.P.S. I'm done now too.>

I'm just returning my phone to my pocket when there is a series of loud bangs on the door. Opening it, I see a very flustered Jake standing with his hands on his hips.

"Fucking Lionel!" he barks in my face. "He saw that we were assigned a room with single beds and swapped us into this room."

"Ah, that's so sweet of him," I say as Jake barges past me and throws the straps from his bag onto the bed. He must have had them this whole time. I don't know why but this makes me want to laugh a little but seeing Jake's thunderous expression, I manage to contain it.

"Oh yeah, a real fucking sweetheart," he spits out.

"Jake," I begin. "It's not a big deal. The bed is plenty big enough, and we'll no doubt be going to bed late anyway. It's just to sleep in."

"Of course, it's just for sleeping in! Jesus, did you think I was going to try and seduce you?"

"That's not what I—"

Jake ignores me as he collapses onto the end of the bed, sitting in roughly the same spot I just was. "It's just very annoying when I planned this to be as easy as possible for you. I am aware how much I'm asking of you, coming here and pretending to be gay and my boyfriend. And I do not say that lightly or easily. I'm not good at praising straight people."

"Err, why?" I ask, suddenly bewildered.

"Because life is already easy enough for you," Jake says with a small shrug. "Life-threateningly boring, of course, but easy too."

"Jake, what if I—" I start to explain.

Still, he interrupts, "Here's what we can do. We can top and tail? Or put pillows down the middle? Or if we have enough spare bedding one of us could sleep in the bath? Wait—" He stands up and rushes to the door of the ensuite bathroom. "Yes, there is a bath. Good. We have options."

I lift my hands up to grab his attention when he turns back around. "Jake, I really don't care if we share a bed. You're actually coming across as kind of homophobic yourself right now getting all worked up about this."

Jake's face turns a brighter shade of red and I notice a vein throbbing in his neck. "I am not getting worked up!" He points a finger in my direction but then looks down at it for a moment before lowering it, his voice also dropping. "Okay, maybe I am getting a bit worked up."

I hesitate for just a moment before I walk over to him and grip his upper arms. "Sit down," I say and lead him back to the end of the bed. "I'm going to run you a nice hot bath, find you a glass of something alcoholic and then I'm going to play you one of my chillout playlists that never fail."

"You make playlists? How very nineties of you," Jake mutters and I can't decide if he's being sarcastic or genuine. Regardless, it reassures me that he won't assume it's one of the playlists I created when I was once an award-winning DJ.

I glance at my watch. "We have exactly two hours before we have to be downstairs for the welcome drinks, so that's plenty of time to calm down and get ready. I mean, it's more than enough time for me. Is it enough time for you?"

"Haha, Lover Boy," Jake sneers, his eyes narrowing as he looks up at me. "Believe it or not, I can go from gargoyle to goddess in thirty minutes flat."

It's then I notice for the first time that Jake has a thin strip of freckles decorating the bridge of his nose and under his eyes. They're so light they're barely noticeable but the sunshine filtering through the window makes them pop and it also makes the hazel in his eyes more golden, like pools of liquid honey.

"I'm sure you'll look amazing," I find myself saying. It would appear Jake is as stunned as I am by my words and he doesn't say anything, not even a quick scathing retort.

Blinking and stepping back, I go to my bag and find the Bluetooth speaker I packed on a whim. I put it on the desk opposite the bed and then get out my phone. Once the two devices are connected, I find my Soul Chillout playlist and hit play. I then take the speaker into the bathroom, put it on the windowsill above the bath, and adjust the volume so it can still be heard over the rushing of the water as the tub fills. I'm grateful that the provided toiletries are of decent quality, and I pour half of the bubble bath into the tub.

"You really are running me a bath?" Jake appears in the doorway carrying two quite large bags of what I assume are his toiletries. "That's sort of nice."

"Well, it's in my interest to lower your flapping levels." I shrug as I move to leave the room. I can't stop myself searching for his freckles again as I walk past him.

"Thank you," Jake says so quietly I'm not sure he wants me to hear it, so I don't respond. I just close the door behind me after I leave.

*****

Jake stays in the bathroom for well over an hour and I set about getting myself ready in the bedroom. I would have liked to have had a shower before changing into my tux but I know Jake needs the time alone more. I'm relieved when my suit still fits me seeing as I lost a lot of weight while I was in RemiX, but I know time at home when I returned from California did help me gain some of it back. There really is no better cooking than my mother's, and it was her cooking – her careful adapting of her best dishes to still be vegan for me – her comfort and her company that helped get me back to a place where I felt ready to live again. It took many long months, but I got there, all thanks to her. Thinking about this, I reach for my phone and send her a quick text.

<Looking forward to seeing you tomorrow, Mama.>

I don't expect her to text back for a while, so I go to my messages with my youngest sister Roxie and send her one too.

<Get Mario Kart ready for tomorrow, nerd. I'm going to kick your butt.>

As predicted, Roxie texts back immediately.

<That's what you think, Old Man. But hope you're ready to lose hard because I am charging the controllers as I type. BTW, aren't you at a wedding with a new boyfriend?>

I roll my eyes. *Thanks, Radia.*

<Not a boyfriend. A new friend. Maybe.>

<If you're suffering through a white people's wedding with bad food and drunk people, he must be at least a friend.>

I laugh at Roxie's take-no-prisoner's sense of humour and a strange thought blasts into my mind. Jake and my little sister would get on like a house on fire.

<One of the grooms is Black so am hopeful the food will at least be seasoned!>

<Mom just got your text. She says you can miss tomorrow if you're too tired.>

I hold my breath as I type back.

<I will be there. I promise.>

<I've told her. She's smiling.>

And that's exactly why I'm going. To make my mother smile. To make her happy. Because for a long time, too long, I didn't do that.

<Admit you're smiling too.> I reply.

<Only because I'm going to ruin you tomorrow, Toad.>

<Whatever, Yoshi.>

When I put my phone away I realise that I can hear Jake humming along to D'Angelo. After being momentarily surprised he knows the song, I find myself smiling at how his voice is a little flat and breaks on the higher notes. It makes me smile so much that I have an irrational urge to leave the room.

I tell myself it's because a walk before the ceremony would be nice. I tell myself it's because Jake will need space to get dressed in the bedroom and probably doesn't want an audience. I tell myself it's because it may be the last chance I get ten minutes to myself before the end of the day. But really, I know it's because I can't stop thinking about Jake's freckles, how nice it felt when we held hands in the garden, and how something like hope or maybe even desire bloomed inside me when he leaned his bodyweight against mine as we stood chatting to Lionel and Luigi. I know it was all for show, so it frustrates me I'm still thinking about it now.

"Jake!" I call out through the door.

"Yes, Lover Boy," he replies in a high-pitched voice.

"Going for a quick walk and to find that drink I promised you," I say, applauding myself for coming up with the perfect excuse.

"Oh, no minibar?" Jake asks and he sounds disappointed.

I quickly look around the room, searching. "Not that I can see."

"Well, thank you," he says and the authenticity in his tone makes me pause for a moment outside the bathroom before I turn and leave.

*****

Following more crested signs to the bar, I am surprised to see Luigi – looking incredibly smart and handsome in a cream tux with black details – on his phone pacing back and forth in front of the long wooden bar where three waistcoated servers are arranging glasses. I ask one of them if they could pour me a glass of whisky and soda with two ice cubes. While I wait, I realise Luigi is talking in Italian but even if I don't understand a word, I can tell that he's not happy with whoever he is talking to. I'm being handed my drink when Luigi's call ends.

"Curses!" He stares at his phone.

"Problem?" I ask.

"Oh, hi. Sorry, I didn't see you there, Rami."

"Looked like you were busy with something."

"Yes, terrible news. My cousin's wife has just gone into labour," he says with sinking shoulders.

"That's terrible news?"

Luigi shakes his head. "No, of course not. But the thing is, he's our DJ. Or he was supposed to be. Have you heard of Maximiliano?"

"Maximiliano is your cousin?" Maxi's a young DJ from Milan that had a huge summer hit about eight years ago. Although his techno-influenced brand of EDM isn't my cup of tea, I've read some articles about him and respected how he managed his quick rise to fame when he was only in his late teens. I suppose he must be approaching thirty now. Funny how quickly time goes by, especially when you're locked away from the rest of the world in the desert.

"Second cousin, technically, but yes. He was going to be DJing later but now he can't. So, we are down a DJ. I'm pretty sure I could pay the band to stay for another hour or two, but all our pals were so looking forward to busting out some mega moves with Maxi."

I press my lips together to ensure I don't laugh at Luigi. I can only imagine what he and his pals look like busting out those mega moves.

"How long do you need a DJ for?" My back straightens as I ask, the words feeling like a risk.

"Well, if the band can take us through to midnight, I suppose just two hours. Everything needs to be shut down by two o'clock anyway."

I pull in a deep breath before I reply. "I could do it,"

"You? But you're not a DJ. Are you?"

Not anymore. "Not exactly, but I do have some experience."

Luigi cocks an eyebrow as he studies me and I wonder for a second if he sees through my lies, or worse, he recognises me. He did say I looked familiar in the garden, after all. "Would you really not mind? What about Jake?"

"Oh, he'll be bored of me by then." It amuses me that Luigi thinks I'm joking when I'm telling the most truthful thing yet. "He's already warned me he's going to be social butterflying all day and night."

"Ha! Yes, Lionel says he can work a room like no other. You know, I hope you don't find it awkward us inviting you both when Lionel and Jake have… you know, history. We thought it would be the best possible way to break the ice, so to speak. Lionel was so happy when Jake told him he'd met someone, you!"

"Was he?" I try to ignore how I feel at this shift in the conversation. It feels wrong to talk about Jake when he's not here.

"Oh, yes. Lionel really doesn't want any bad feelings." Luigi's eyes are dark and serious again.

"I think Jake feels the same way," I say even though none of this is adding up quite right in my mind.

"Well, hopefully, we can put it all behind us soon. Considering we all live in London, it would be fabulous to be chums."

Chums. I've never had a chum who used the word chum before. I smile thinking how I should repeat this joke back to Jake later.

"That would be nice," I say before realising the full implications of what Luigi is suggesting. Us all being friends in London would mean Jake and I continuing to pretend to be boyfriends. What's more terrifying than the prospect itself is how it doesn't completely terrify me. It almost excites me.

"So, what do you need to know or look at before your set?"

"My set?" I frown. I haven't heard those words in a long time.

"DJing for us? Later?"

"Oh, right. Yes. Well, do you have the gear set up already? I can just have a look at it, and I have my laptop with lots of music on it with me so that should be all I need to bring."

Luigi points to some double doors leading off the bar and I reach for Jake's drink. As we walk in that direction, I feel Luigi's large hand clap me on my upper back, jolting me forward.

"Jake's a very lucky man, Rami," he says.

"He's something," I reply, completely clueless as to what exactly that is.

Chapter Nine

Jake

I'm standing in front of the mirror at the desk, adjusting my bowtie and edging closer and closer to losing the will to live. Again. If it wasn't Dolce & Gabbana and matching both my socks and the bright pink with red polka dots silk handkerchief I plan on having folded in my jacket, I would throw it away because it's taken almost fifteen minutes to tie up and it's damn well nearly undone all the de-stressing I just did in the bath while listening to Rami's undeniably very calming playlist.

When I hear the key turn in the door, I absent-mindedly smooth out my eyebrows, wondering if they also need a little gel to be tamed.

"Got you that drink," Rami says as he approaches me and I turn to take it. My mouth is open ready to thank him for the drink, for the bath, for the playlist, but when my eyes land on him, my words evaporate. So does my next breath.

I already knew Rami was an attractive man. He has been blessed with high cheekbones and a poker-straight, dominant nose, and those silver eyes are not ones anybody would forget in a hurry, especially when you recall how perfectly framed they are by those thick, black eyebrows. And although I don't think he's a vain person who spends hours man-scaping, there's something about that grey-black stubble which is always at the perfect five o'clock shadow length that makes me wonder if he does care more about his appearance than I originally suspected. All this I can comment on objectively, but what feels very subjective and very real is how I am reacting to him wearing a tux. He looks more than striking; he looks arresting. My breaths are being arrested. My thoughts are being detained. And my cock is beginning to think it's being cuffed as it fills out my underwear.

"Jake." I hear him say. "Your drink."

My hand, thankfully, moves to take the glass because there's possibly not enough blood in my brain to send any more complicated messages than that.

"Thank you," I manage to utter as I can't stop my eyes diving down to take in the full length of him.

"Looks like I'm going to be wearing a tux a lot more often in our office," he says as he fiddles with the cufflinks at his wrists.

"Pardon?" I barely hear what he says because I'm so busy looking at how his trousers taper to the length and breadth of his legs perfectly. It has me assuming it must be bespoke, possibly even couture, and I had no idea he had such a narrow waist or broad shoulders. It's almost impossible to pull my eyes away from his patent dress shoes that are so perfectly polished they reflect the gleam of the ceiling light.

"I've never seen you so quiet," Rami says in a gentle voice.

"You look—" I say because I feel it's only fair to compliment him, even just a little bit. "You look good."

It's so inadequate it's almost a lie, but when Rami looks down at the floor and chews on his smile, I know I'm right to hold back. He wants to laugh at me and how flabbergasted I am over him in a tuxedo. I'm such an idiot. An idiot who hasn't had a shag in far too long.

"You don't look so bad yourself," he says when his eyes look up again.

"Your shoes are so shiny," I say, determined not to read too much into his compliment.

"*Too* shiny?" he asks and I see the worry in his frown.

"No such thing," I say and take a much-needed sip of my drink. It helps melt some of the tension in my throat and hopefully will also go some way to redistributing the blood flow in my body.

"So, funny story," Rami says. "Luigi and Lionel's DJ has cancelled on them…"

The witch in me wants to rejoice, but I manage to rein in my cackle.

"So, I'm going to step in for them."

"What!?" I turn to face him. "But you're not a DJ?"

Rami clears his throat. "Well, not exactly, but I have done some DJing in the past. You know, doing events, festivals and the like. And my father was a DJ."

"Was he?" I ask looking at Rami's pensive smile.

"Yeah, DJ Moonlight."

"That's an... interesting name."

Rami chuckles to himself. "Someone told him once that he was moonlighting as a DJ, because he was doing it on the side of his normal job. And he just liked the sound of it. His English was always excellent, but sometimes he didn't get some of the idioms or subtleties of the language. So yeah, DJ Moonlight."

"It has a nice ring to it. Was he very successful?"

"God, no. I mean not in any global or monetary sense. But he did pubs and clubs all over the West Midlands for nearly twenty years and he was truly loved, so in that respect, you could call him very successful, yes."

"Sounds like a great guy," I say. When I look at Rami again his eyes – and clearly thoughts – have drifted somewhere else.

"He was the best," he says. Not wanting to interrupt this moment of Rami's, I step to the side and open the wardrobe to retrieve my suit jacket. When I close the wardrobe door, Rami is there gesturing for me to hand it to him.

"Allow me," he says, and I pass it over.

As he holds it up and I slide my arms into it, I catch a hint of his smell, a spiced musk that has a fresh air tone to it, almost like a layer of mint. I don't hate it, at all, and I instantly wish I'd never smelt it. When the jacket is on, I feel his hands come to rest on my shoulders, brushing off whatever he sees there.

"Looking good, Forester," he says behind me and my eyes bolt open with how sexy his voice sounds saying those words, saying my surname, with his mouth so close to my ear. I glance quickly at the drink I just placed on the desk. How strong is it?

"We have about ten more minutes until everything starts downstairs," Rami says. I turn to find him sitting on the bed, opening up his laptop. "I just want to find a few things on here to help me later."

"Oh, yes. Mr DJ," I say as I reach for the handkerchief and start folding it.

"You don't mind?" Rami looks up at me. "I suppose I should have checked. It will only be for two hours, from midnight, so maybe you'll have a whole army of new friends by then to hang out with."

"Midnight? I'll hopefully already be in bed asleep by then. Or passed out in the water fountain outside, trying and no doubt failing to end it all. But seriously, it's fine. I'm sure Lionel and Luigi will be very grateful."

"Which will make you look good to them," Rami says.

"How?"

"By having a boyfriend who saves the wedding, or at least the dancing part of the wedding."

"Hmm, you're right. Just no other grand gestures or big favours please, they'll end up liking you more than me, which is not something my ego can take today," I say as I place the handkerchief in my pocket and faff around with it a bit more, tutting when the top point keeps falling to one side.

"Here." Rami comes to stand opposite me. His hands and eyes are on the handkerchief in my breast pocket, meaning I can take in his face at my liberty. And fuck, if I don't catch another whiff of that delicious smell.

Jesus, do I fancy Rami? I roll my eyes again, this time solely for my own benefit. Of course, I probably do. That's literally the only thing missing from this already disastrous day – falling for an unavailable straight man. *How very vintage Jake.*

"It's fine," I say reaching up to move his hands away from me, suddenly finding his proximity agitating. I manage to make it look less aggressive when I then reach for the lip balm in my jacket's inside pocket.

"I'm sorry we're not matching," he says pointing to his black tie which is velvet, a nice sophisticated touch.

"I'm not, only losers have matching bowties," I say as I click the lip balm's lid back on after applying it to my lips. "Right. Let's go face the music, shall we?"

*****

Lionel and Luigi don't just have matching fucking bowties, they're wearing matching fucking cream tuxes. And there's a string fucking quartet serenading guests as they sip welcome bellinis out on the terrace overlooking the gardens. I would also put what little money I have in my bank account on there also being a hamper of poor suffocating doves somewhere around here waiting to be released on Lionel and Luigi's first kiss as husband and husband.

Ugh, this wedding is insufferably perfect.

Circulating alone and greeting guests, I notice Lionel trying to catch my attention multiple times. I avoid his approaches until I see the moment he gives up, his shoulders dropping and his eyes lingering on the floor for a few seconds. To help ease the sting his evident disappointment brings me, I search the crowd for a server with drinks and make my way over to the nearest one.

"I probably should have checked how well you can handle your drink," Rami says as I grab my second flute of champagne.

"I can handle my drink," I insist. When I hear just how snappy it sounds, I lower my voice and slow it down to appear a bit calmer. "Sorry, I'm a little on edge."

"Really? I hadn't noticed." Rami says and I hate how well he's managing to do sarcasm now.

"I really can handle my drink. Unless of course, I start removing clothing or looking for a microphone at some point. And as the DJ you are under strict instructions to ignore me should I request It's Raining Men."

"Understood," Rami says with a closed-lip smile as he tucks his hands in his pockets.

"Shit, you don't have a drink. Shall we go get you a juice from the bar or something?"

"I'm fine, Jake. But thank you," he says, looking out over the gardens. "They couldn't have gotten luckier with the weather."

I follow his gaze and take in the cloudless blue skies and bright sunshine. There's the gentlest of breezes which carries the sweet and soft scent of roses up to us, something I can actually enjoy because I am dosed up on antihistamines for my hay fever. I inhale the smell deeply, grateful for it filling my nostrils rather than catching another inhale of Rami's scent. I now suspect the reason why I don't recognise it is because it must be a horrifically expensive cologne. And I reassure myself that that's also the reason why I like it so much; I've always had expensive tastes. It's got nothing to do with the man wearing it.

Pulling my eyes back to our fellow guests, I quickly survey the people nearest us.

"Jesus Christ it's like a Tom Ford convention here. They either look like Tom Ford models or like Tom Ford him-fucking-self," I mutter.

Rami's laughter is hearty and loud. "You're not wrong. Do you know anybody here?"

"Not a soul besides you and the happy couple," I reply. "Lionel and I were closest when we worked in Crete together and his family never visited, sadly. He always spent winters with his parents in Devon, so I never met them."

I don't want to add how they probably wouldn't have wanted to meet me considering how I treated their son, which is another reason why I'm avoiding anyone who looks vaguely like Lionel as well as the man himself.

"But they both live in London now, right? Luigi was saying how he would like us to all hang out," Rami says.

"Ha! I am pretty sure by the time today is over they will likely want nothing of the sort. Even if we manage to pull off this pantomime of a relationship—" I am promptly cut off by a warm hand on my arm.

"Are you Jake?" I follow a manicured brown hand up a shapely arm and to the beautiful face of a woman who has Lionel's big dark eyes and impossibly wide and warm smile. Shit. It's almost certainly Lionel's mother. And judging by her colourful outfit and make-up she is twice as vivacious and vibrant as her son told me she was. I know I'm going to like her instantly.

"Who wants to know? Are you the tax authorities?" I say, jumping straight into the role I can perform only too well.

"Haha! It is you!" she says with a loud, melodious laugh. "Lionel said you'd be the funniest man at the wedding."

"Lionel is right about a lot of things," I retort. "I've always said that."

She laughs again before holding out her hand. "I'm Melanie, Lionel's mother."

After shaking her hand, I put my palm on my cocked hip. "Mother? I was certain I was talking to his sister!"

Melanie lightly pats my arm. "Lionel doesn't have a sister, and you know it! But I'll take that compliment and put it in my purse for later. And who is this young man with you?" She turns to Rami.

"Oh, this is Rami." I watch them shake hands.

"I'm Jake's boyfriend," Rami adds, and I don't know why I feel another shot of pride hearing those words again, or in the way Rami's hand finds mine after he shakes Melanie's extended palm. I decide to put it all down to necking my first glass of champagne in record time. "A pleasure to meet you, Melanie. Your son and Luigi look very happy."

"Oh, they are. And we are all so happy for them. We adore Luigi. And Lionel deserves it, right, Jake? You probably know how lost he was when he came back from Crete after that last season. It was awful. Do you remember?"

"I... uh, yeah," I sputter clumsily, praying the guilt I feel isn't manifesting as a scarlet blush on my cheeks or neck despite how alarmingly hot I feel.

"I wanted to thank you, actually," Melanie continues. "That's why I hunted you down. You were such good friends for five years in that resort he loved, and he always said you were the best boss he's ever had. Lionel had never worked abroad before so it was always a comfort to me knowing he had you there keeping an eye on him."

By the time Melanie finishes talking, my guilt has turned into a dizzying shame-filled nausea. It's only when Rami's fingers squeeze mine that I find it possible to talk.

"I really didn't do anything. It was a pleasure to work with him. Lionel was such a good team member," I say. *So good, I never should have taken advantage of him*, I don't add but I am thinking it, thinking it so hard a headache is now joining my nausea.

"I know, which is why it was so disappointing when he had that breakdown, but you were so good to let him go when he needed to. It took him months to get back on track, but he did it. And look at him now. He's got a great job and a truly fantastic man. And this wedding... I mean, can you believe we're even standing in a place like this? I keep thinking Colin Firth is going to walk up through the garden drenched from a dip in the lake!"

"That's exactly what I said this place looked like! Like *Pride and Prejudice!*" Rami says with an enthusiasm that shouldn't annoy me, but it does.

"Oh, surely you're too young to remember that series," Melanie says. "Got yourself a toyboy, hey Jake?"

I have to take a moment before I can play along with this charade. Does she really think Rami is younger than me?

"Actually, Jake is younger than me." Rami leans forward. "I'm forty-three and he turns forty later this year."

"You are not!" Melanie exclaims and it's Rami's turn to get a pat, this time on his chest. "Oh, my, and you're very toned under that suit, aren't you? Do you work out?"

"Well, I don't—" Rami begins but my frown is threatening to break through my plastered-on smile, so I interrupt.

"Melanie, it's such a pleasure to meet you, really it is. But we were just going to get Rami a drink from the bar. Would you like us to get you something?"

"Oh, no thank you. I'm fine with this bubbly stuff. But that's ever so sweet of you." She touches my arm again and I wish I couldn't see Lionel's smile on her face.

"Oh, I'm not sweet. It's a free bar! Why else would there be so many people here?" My joke takes a second to land but thank God it does as her laughter fills my ears.

"You are a hoot!"

"That's me!" I say, pulling on Rami's hand in the direction of the bar.

Considering the good weather, I'm not surprised there isn't anyone inside the bar and we are able to order Rami a tonic water in no time at all.

"Jesus, still half an hour before this thing gets started," I say after checking my watch.

"Melanie was lovely," Rami says. "I think it's going to be a great wedding."

"Oh, sure, it's going to be the fucking wedding of the fucking millennium," I say with jazz hands and no holding back on the acid in my tone.

"Jake, please, can we talk?" A voice interrupts my performance.

Shit. Lionel.

I glance at Rami who nods at me very slowly and very deliberately. When his hand comes to squeeze the top of my arm, I nearly beg him not to leave me but even I have some standards and I'm going to do my best to hold onto them before they're taken away from me by the copious amounts of champagne I am now promising myself as Rami walks away and Lionel steps in to take his place in front of me.

"Lionel, we really don't have to do this now. You're about to get married for Christ's sake. You should be with your family or doing stretches or having a nervous poo or just doing something... else," I say, calling on every facet of my wit to get me out of this conversation.

"It's actually really important to me we talk before I get married," Lionel says, still solemn.

"What on Earth could be that important?" I huff out a laugh.

"I want to apologise."

I pause letting his words sink in. "*You* want to apologise? *To me*?" My voice is practically a squeak.

"Yes." Lionel nods. I realise that he's wearing contacts. The lack of glasses has the illusion of enlarging his features and somehow bringing his face closer to mine. "The way we ended... how things ended in Crete. It was such a mess."

When I realise how serious he is, as inexplicable as that is, I drop my facade.

"Yes, it was, but Lionel, it was *my* mess. Me. Mine. *I* made it a mess."

"But I just left." Lionel leans a little closer. "I didn't even hand in my resignation properly. Didn't even print it off and sign it. I just emailed it to HR, with you cc-ed. Cc-ed, Jake! How terrible is that?"

"Could have been worse. You could have bcc-ed me."

"You were my manager!"

"And you were my employee, which is why everything that happened," I put my hand firmly on my chest and make sure I meet his eyes, "it was all my fault, and I'm truly, truly sorry. I should never have started a sexual relationship with you, and after I did, I never should have let it get to where it... got. And then I should never have slept with the Greek man who delivered our sausages. I made a huge mess of a friendship I sincerely valued, and I will always be sorry for that."

Lines form in Lionel's forehead and his chin wobbles once, twice, and I am almost certain he's about to cry, when his features do an about-turn, and his face stretches into a wide, genuine smile.

"Well, I'm still sorry for leaving like I did. I'm also sorry I pushed you so hard about us maybe being official. I see now how impossible that would have been. I realise now that you were trying to protect me by not getting more serious, and I'm grateful for that."

My stomach sinks with Lionel's generosity in interpreting the situation this way, the wrong way, but I don't correct him. I don't dare tell him that the reason we were never official is because of my deep-rooted commitment and abandonment issues.

"Lionel, please don't blame yourself for any of what happened between us. I know you have far more important vows to make today, but could you make me that one small promise?"

Lionel's eyes are misty when he nods at me. "I can do that. Can we hug now?"

And we do. We hug in a way that I'm quite certain absolves a lot of the shitty feelings that have been plaguing me since I woke up that morning in Crete and discovered he'd gone. I want to poke myself in the eye for not trying to instigate this sooner. Yet another thing I judged wrong. *Idiot.*

"I figure it's different for you and Rami," Lionel says into my ear before he pulls back. "You're more colleagues, right? You're not his boss. That's why you're more comfortable being with him."

As we pull apart, I will never know if my smile is more like the grimace it feels like. "Something like that."

"I'm so happy you met Rami. I know you said it's early days but you make such a good-looking couple," Lionel says.

"We do?" I say, my eyes involuntarily searching for Rami.

"Yes, and the way he smiles at you. It reminds me of the way Luigi looks at me. That's another thing I must thank you for, Jake. I never would have met Luigi had it not been for you."

"I'm not sure that's true," I begin, my eyes back on Lionel.

"Oh, it is. And it's a really good story, in fact. The day I met Luigi I was actually on my way to your work. It was not long after you'd started your new role. You'd not replied to my calls and texts, so I just decided I was going to show up to try clear the air, and honestly, I also maybe wanted to see if you wanted to try again, have a real relationship. But do you know what happened?"

I shake my head, feeling a little dizzy.

Lionel continues, "I got on the Tube going the wrong way – silly country bumpkin that I am – and when I realised, I rushed for the doors but they closed on me and my jacket got caught in them. And can you guess who stepped up to help me get free?"

"Luigi," I say with a tight jaw.

"Yes, we started talking and didn't stop. Before I knew it I was ten stops away from your work, and I had swapped numbers with..."

"Luigi," I say again, and I really hope Lionel doesn't see the speck of spittle that flies out of my mouth.

"Isn't it funny how life turns out?" he asks.

"Isn't it?" I look away because I can't take another second of his dazzling warm smile. When my eyes find Rami, leaning against the back of a chair and watching me, his forehead pushed forward, it's like feeling my anchor go down and I can stop swimming. I'm not here alone. He's not who everyone thinks he is to me, but maybe I can also pretend he really is here for me. No matter how devastating it is to hear Lionel was on his way to maybe try and start a relationship with me, Luigi did us both a favour by meeting him that day. There's no doubt in my mind Lionel will be much, much happier with Luigi than with me. This should bring me some comfort.

"Maybe you and Rami will get married one day," Lionel says beside me, no doubt watching me looking at my fake boyfriend.

I'm about to laugh at the suggestion but then Rami's lips move to make two letters: *O.K?* I nod at him and find myself returning the smile he gives me.

"Maybe," I say to Lionel because I know he wants to think it and it's the least I can give him in this moment.

"Oh, butterknives, I need to go. Jake, thank you for this chat. I can't wait to have a drink with you later. With my husband! Argh! Can you believe it?"

"I'm starting to," I say honestly and reach for his arm, squeezing it through his tuxedo jacket. "Go be despicably happy, Lionel. You deserve it."

There is next to no time between when Lionel leaves my side and Rami is there. And I'm grateful for it. There's too much going on in my head for me to process it all and if Rami is there annoying me, making silly, pointless small talk, and handily standing by my side looking very aesthetically pleasing, I can push my conversation with Lionel to one side and hopefully get through this day.

And if that fails, there's always champagne.

Chapter Ten

Rami

Jake's even cuter when he doesn't talk, which is exactly how he is for many minutes after we return to the terrace from the bar. This leads me to chat briefly with fellow guests as the string quartet plays Vivaldi's *Spring* and we all comment on the same things: the wonderful weather, the stunning location, the happy couple.

What starts to make Jake look a little less cute is when he begins hunting down drink after drink and I am eventually forced to excuse myself from a conversation with Luigi's aunt and uncle so I can try to lead Jake away from another server who walks by with a tray, but I'm not quick enough. A few minutes later Jake gives me a look that is anything but cute when I swap his fourth glass of champagne for my glass of sparkling water, but I stand by this decision. We're barely one hour into a wedding that hasn't even officially started yet and he's already swaying on his feet.

"God, you're so boringly sober," he says but downs the glass of water.

"Are you pissed off I don't drink now?"

"No, not really. I'm secretly jealous. I have a lot of respect and admiration for sober people. My sister's partner is sober and is the life and soul of the party. I wish I could do that." He sulks.

"Jake, you could do that. Easily."

"Well, not today," he says as everyone's head turns to one of the Tom Ford clones tapping his glass with a teaspoon.

"Ladies, gentlemen and non-binary finery," he calls out in a Town Crier-esque voice. "The ceremony is about to begin. Please take your seats in the orangery."

"Orangery? Of course, they're getting married in a fucking orangery," Jake mutters as he hands me back the now empty glass and sets off, dragging me behind him because somehow we're holding hands again.

A tall and spacious Victorian greenhouse, the orangery immediately reminds me of the glasshouse in Kew Botanical Gardens which we would visit about once a year with my parents when we would go to see our cousins in West London. With a row of orange trees down each side, the central area has been cleared for rows of chairs, all of which face a small stage which is also framed with two orange trees, which like all the others, are in blossom. The sharp, floral scent fills the warm air, and the lush green leaves and pure white petals contrast beautifully with the bright blue sky that persists through the glass roof overhead.

"I wish I was blind," Jake says to me as he takes it all in. He breathes in deeply. "And had sensory issues so I couldn't smell either."

"No, you don't," I say as I hand our glasses to a server collecting empties. I briefly press the side of my arm against Jake as I speak. "Just because they are having a day like this, doesn't mean you won't one day in the future. Come on, let's take a seat."

Jake insists we take two chairs in the final row, and I don't have the energy to argue with him. After we are seated, I peruse the ceremony programme that was left on my chair, and I choose not to comment on how Jake sat on his without picking it up.

"You okay after talking to Lionel?" I ask. I would like to say I'm not curious about what they talked about, but I am.

"Oh, yes, fine. Completely fine. He apologised to me for doing absolutely nothing wrong, and then I discovered he was on his way to confess his undying love to me when he first met Luigi. So, you could say I feel utterly let down by fate right now, but otherwise, I am absolutely fine and dandy."

"That must have been hard to hear."

Jake seems surprised by my response as he turns to study me. "It was, thank you for saying that, Rami," he says before lifting his hand and waving around us. "And thanks for all this. For keeping me company. For running me that bath earlier. And for—"

"Moderating your alcohol intake?" I offer.

"I feel less grateful for that but considering I'm possibly seeing twice as many orange trees as everyone else, I suppose I should be."

"You're welcome, Forester."

Jake flashes me a strange look but it fades quickly. He drops his eyes as he shifts in his seat and re-crosses his legs.

"Do *you* think I look older than you?" he asks a beat later. "Do I really look that haggard?"

"Jake, that sounds like it could be a dig at me but I'm going to ignore it and instead insist that you don't need to worry, you look fine," I say carefully.

"Fine? Fine is an adjective for the weather!"

I suck in a deep breath. "Jake, you look good. You are a handsome man. And this suit really does look fantastic on you."

Jake blinks at me and we are both silent again for a moment. I almost start to think that the air feels more charged, loaded, but then Jake finally talks with pouted lips and that makes it dissipate. "That's better. Wasn't so hard, was it, Lover Boy?" He nudges his elbow against my side, and I don't know why but that makes me smile.

A moment later, the ceremony begins and it is beautiful. There are sophisticated choices of music and readings. Their vows are poetic and heartfelt. And they both cry at various moments, as do most of the guests. When I see Jake wiping under his eyes, I reach inside my jacket's inner pocket and pull out one of the tissues I placed there earlier. A few moments later, when I hear Jake sniff, I twitch to reach over and squeeze his knee, but I don't. It's not that it would feel inappropriate, it's actually more that it would weirdly feel very appropriate to do so and I have no clue where that has come from. It strikes me then how much I am not hating pretending to be Jake's boyfriend. Mercifully, I am pulled away from this stark realisation when I hear sudden applause. I look up and see Lionel and Luigi kissing – their first kiss as husband and husband. When I hear a throaty choking sound come from Jake, who is applauding nonetheless, I let myself reach over and squeeze his leg, just above his knee.

While I am stunned by how solid and warm he feels, Jake himself is startled enough by my touch that he stops clapping and stares at my hand. I remove it quickly and go back to applauding the happy couple, somewhat relieved when everyone else in front of us is standing so I can do the same. After a second or two, Jake joins me but I keep my eyes facing forward at the happy couple.

Minutes later Luigi and Lionel walk back down the aisle hand in hand while we all listen to a sweeping and moving operatic version of *I Will Always Love You* in Italian being sung by a woman who serenaded them with a similar interpretation of *Unchained Melody* when they walked into the ceremony. As they approach us, I see Lionel spot Jake and somehow his already broad grin stretches further. I nod at Luigi who looks like he's won the lottery in multiple countries, and then I quickly turn my attention back to Jake who has sat back down and is finally looking at the program, his fingers stroking the black-and-white photo of Lionel and Luigi on the front page.

Much to my surprise he doesn't look like the emotional wreck I am expecting. He's even smiling to himself.

"That was a beautiful ceremony," he says without looking up. I sit next to him and wait for a 'but' or a punchline, but it doesn't come.

"It really was," I agree.

"I think I needed that... To see them get married, I mean. To know that they're meant to be together and that we, Lionel and I, we really are in the past, and maybe there doesn't need to be any hard feelings. Maybe we can be friends again, he and I, and me and Luigi too."

I nod immediately very aware of how my name is missing from that sentence. To try and distract myself from this uncomfortable feeling, I focus on how people are starting to file out of the orangery.

"I could even stop being a bitch about their wedding," Jake adds.

"Really?" I say, my disbelief intentionally audible.

"Well, I can try."

"It's good to have ambition in life."

"You know your sarcasm has come on leaps and bounds today." Jake taps my leg and when his hand lifts we both look at it before he places it on his own thigh.

"I have, have I?" I smirk.

"Yes, and I take full credit, of course."

I nudge him before I move to stand. "Come on, Forester. I think you're allowed another glass of champagne now."

"Fair wedding guests!" The Town Crier's voice calls out from behind us. "Your presence is required on the terrace once more as we release twenty-eight white doves into the air, the number signifying today's date."

"Oh, for fucking fuckity fuck's sake," Jake drawls barely under his breath and I almost give myself an injury with how quickly I spin to give him an admonishing look. He holds his hands up and his smile is full of mischief and playfulness.

"Okay, starting now!"

*****

As it happens, when we're back on the terrace Jake doesn't reach for another glass of champagne and instead joins me in drinking orange juice. He also surprises me when the light scoff he makes as the doves are released and fly high in the sky isn't accompanied by a sharp-edged comment. And when we are encouraged to mingle once more with the guests, all while we sporadically watch Lionel and Luigi have their photos taken in the gardens below, Jake is indeed the social butterfly he promised he would be.

When it's time for a group photo, everyone is invited to stand at the bottom of the stone steps. When I see couples all around me holding hands or wrapping their arms around their partners, I speak into Jake's ear.

"I'm going to put my arm around you, Lover Boy," I say. "Just for the photo."

Jake's groan is too loud to be genuine revulsion, at least that's what I tell myself. "If you must," he sighs. But when it comes time for the photo to be taken I feel a bit more of his weight lean against me. I turn and see his smile is broad and bright. I suspect mine is too, because I like having my arm draped around his back a bit too much. As the photographer barks a few more orders for people to make adjustments to their positions, I reassure myself I only feel this way because in recent years I've been so starved of intimacy, companionship, or anything remotely representing affection or fondness with someone I'm not related to by blood.

However, I'm questioning this again an hour or so later when we're eating dinner and talking with the couple next to us. Marco and Salvatore are from Sorrento where Luigi has one of his summer houses, the plurality of his holiday accommodations not missing an eye roll from Jake. Marco tells us all a story about Luigi at university and after he delivers the – frankly uninspired – punchline and we all laugh, Salvatore covers his husband's hand on the table. It's while I watch their joined hands that I feel a warmth cover mine. I can't stop myself turning to Jake to see if he did it because he wants something, but he's still laughing – albeit in an undeniably forced way – and his eyebrows quickly bounce once in a way that is almost warning. *Right, don't draw attention to it.* Instead, I flip my hand over so I can hold his hand properly, interlocking our fingers.

I don't know how long we hold hands for, but I know by the time Lionel is giving his speech, my right hand is free again for me to go into my jacket pocket and retrieve another tissue for Jake.

"God, that was so sweet," he says, his voice cracking in more than one place as he wipes at his eyes. "This wedding is turning me into a puddle. Thank God I opted not to wear mascara today."

After the speeches, we are invited to vacate the ballroom and go to the bar. I accompany Jake to the bar where he orders a glass of wine, and possibly flirts a little with the bartender. I indicate a free table for us to sit at but Jake has another idea.

"Let's go outside, it's far too noisy in here with all these annoyingly attractive people enjoying themselves."

Once out on the terrace, I follow Jake to stand close to the stone balustrade wall that looks out over the gardens. I take a few moments to close my eyes and tap into all of my senses. I feel the same warm air on my skin. I hear the murmurings of chatter all around us. I taste the zing from the orange juice I just sipped. I smell the same floral scents I did earlier as we walked through the garden, and there's also something else, something a little citrusy, a little airy or earthy and possibly even fruity too. It takes me a moment to realise what I'm smelling, what I'm actively breathing in deeply to inhale more of, is Jake. My eyes are not yet open when Jake asks the one question I hoped he'd never ask.

"So, California, huh? What exactly were you doing out there?"

I'm grateful my eyes are already closed. It gives me a moment to compose myself before I reply, or rather, before I stretch the truth to its absolute limits.

"I moved out there for work, mostly."

"Doing the same job? Events?"

"Sort of." I turn so I can rest my back on the stone wall and avoid looking at his curious expression.

Jake doesn't miss anything. "Hmm. You're being cagey. That makes me think there's some big dark secret about California you're trying to keep from me."

"It's not like that," I say, I put my drink down on the stone wall and tuck my hands in my pockets. "It's more like... Well, the thing is... I had a bad break-up."

"In California?"

"Yes."

"Is that why you left?"

"Yes," I say, and it does feel good not to lie, even if it's not the whole truth.

"I'm sorry to hear that," Jake says. "Break-ups suck."

"This one really did," I admit. "We still don't speak. I find that hard."

"You broke up with her?"

"Yeah," I say.

There's a beat of silence in which Jake plays with his lips in his mouth and I can't read his thoughts.

"How long did you live over there?" he asks eventually.

"Nearly ten years in total, but before then I travelled a lot for work, so until two years ago, I hadn't really lived in the UK for nearly twenty years."

"That's a long time," Jake says. "Wait, that must mean you didn't see your youngest sister growing up?"

"No, not really," I say both saddened by my confession but also touched by the way he remembered Roxie's age.

"Your family must be happy to have you back. Are you really going to go up to Birmingham tomorrow to see them?"

"Taxi to the train station is booked for seven o'clock."

"Jesus, I hope you don't expect me to be conscious to wave you off."

"Wouldn't dream of it." I smile.

"It's good that you're making up for lost time. With your sister, I mean." His words sound heartfelt and that makes them all the heavier to hear.

"Yeah," I say, and I can feel how heavily my features have fallen. "I'm trying to do what I can."

"Oh, I get it now," Jake says like something has just clicked. I turn to look at him because I don't know what he's referring to. A shard of icy panic straightens my back as I wonder if he's finally figured out who I really am or what my real story is. The possibility is utterly terrifying.

"You also said that your dad died," Jake says, his eyes fixed on mine. "Four years ago. So, you weren't here, when he died?"

You don't know the half of it, I want to say. But I don't.

"That's right," I say instead.

"That sucks too."

"Yep, it really, really does." I focus so hard on one particular window on the back of the stately home that I start to see two of them. But at least I don't cry.

Chapter Eleven

Jake

In my humble-ish opinion, I do really well during the meal and during the drinks in the bar as they set up the ballroom for the band and dancing. I would even go so far as to say I transform into my most social self once we return to the ballroom and a live band starts playing a range of soul and disco songs from the last five decades. Rami and I stick to the outskirts of the dance floor, chatting with some of the guests we got to know at our table during dinner and I'm about to give Marco and Salvatore tips for their upcoming visit to Marrakech when I am grabbed by Melanie and swept into the growing number of dancers. It doesn't take long for my feet to find the beat, for my hips to sway, and for me to start enthusiastically singing the lyrics at Lionel's mother who returns the favour.

A moment later, Lionel is dancing with us both. It delights me an irrational amount when Luigi steps into our small circle and starts dancing with all the grace and rhythm of a drunk sloth, and in response I concentrate a little harder on busting out some of my best Britney, Beyoncé and Madonna-inspired moves; I like to have something for everyone.

By the time a thin layer of sweat covers my whole body, I realise what's happening. I'm having fun. I don't know why this makes me look up and search for Rami, but when I do eventually spot him, I see him standing against the wall on one side of the room, staring down at his phone and occasionally touching the screen. I look away and dance some more, this time swinging Melanie around. A couple of songs later, I look over at Rami again and see he's doing exactly the same thing. Indicating to my dancing companions that I need a drink, I walk over to him.

"You know, you've been on your phone so much people will start thinking you've got a bit on the side," I say as I sidle up to him.

"Yeah, sorry." Rami pockets his phone. "I've been making a note of the songs people have enjoyed the most and trying to find others similar that will work for my set later."

"Set, hey? Are we taking it a bit seriously?"

"Probably." He shrugs in a way that I instantly think is adorable. Just as promptly, I blame that reaction on the champagne.

"So, you like music," I say.

"Love it," he replies and his face lights up again.

"But you can't dance?"

"Well, it's not that I *can't*. It's more that I *don't*. At least not very often. Only on very special occasions. I prefer to watch other people dance, have fun, enjoy themselves."

"Hmm." I consider this but I don't know why. It's hardly riveting information.

"*You're* a great dancer," Rami says.

"I know," I say and pretend to throw long hair over my shoulder. "There's a reason my mum called me John Travolta growing up."

"Did she really?" Rami chuckles. "That's very cute."

I'm not sure if it's the reference to my mother, or the softness in Rami's eyes, but I feel a prickly heat climb my neck and I want to abandon this topic of conversation.

"Okay, you're boring me now. I'm going to go dance again. Make sure you watch me with a love-glazed expression." I wink at him.

And it's exactly what I do. I dance until I've discarded my jacket and bowtie and undone the top two buttons on my shirt. I dance until my feet scream with pain, and I grow slightly concerned I've sweated enough that my nipples are visible through my shirt. I dance until I absolutely have to go to the bathroom or I will risk a UTI.

On my way, I look again for Rami, who is in the same part of the ballroom, but he's now sitting. And he's not looking at his phone. He's looking at me, tracking me as I walk across the room towards the toilets.

"I need a slash!" I shout and I know he's heard me when, smiling, he shakes his head and gives me a thumbs up.

When I return, bladder empty and nipples in check, I head straight for Rami but I see he's not alone. The bartender I was possibly flirting with earlier is talking to him as he collects glasses.

"It's so cool," the young man is saying. "Wait till I tell my mates. I didn't even know you were—"

"Jake!" Rami says, standing up.

"Hello," I say a bit baffled by the alarm in his voice and face. "Am I interrupting?"

"Nope, no, not at all." Rami moves to grab my elbow and weave us out to the dance floor. "Let's dance!"

"Oh, *now* you want to dance?"

"They're playing Stevie Wonder! I can never say no to Stevie."

It takes only a few beats for me to realise that Rami can dance, really, really well. His moves are subtle and small, but they're always in time with the music – Stevie Wonder's *Sir Duke* – frighteningly so. He also sings along, his hands shaking out a different beat to his feet. Just as I'm admiring his movement, he grabs hold of my hand and spins me around. He keeps hold of me as he leads me through all sorts of spins, dips, twirls and slides. I can barely keep up, but it doesn't seem to matter. Rami is there to stop me, catch me, hold me. I shouldn't like being thrown around a dance floor this much, but my God, I do.

The song ends far too quickly, and then the band quickly announce the next will be their last song. I'm rolling up my sleeves ready to be tossed around by Rami again when I realise this next song is not like the last. The tempo is slow, the melody a little sombre and while I know it's Stevie Wonder again, it's his much slower, much more romantic song, *As*, which I know well because of George Michael's cover.

I stop rolling my sleeves and look at Rami. Also standing still, his eyes find mine and he tilts his head slightly. I know what he's asking before I see his arms open. It's only after I step into them that I realise I just as quickly knew my answer.

It would be a stretch to say we're dancing. We're not. We're really only swaying but at least we're doing so in rhythm, thanks mostly to Rami's steady hold on me. I don't think I'm drunk. I've not had a drink in hours, and I surely sweated off most of what I drank earlier, but suddenly I feel light-headed. Is it the way Rami's hands are on my waist? Is it the warmth of his chest which isn't exactly pressed against my body but is still close enough to pass heat to mine? Or is it how on my neck I can feel the vibration of his humming along to the song? Is this light-headedness because of... Rami?

"You two!" I hear a familiar voice and turn my head to see Lionel and Luigi dance beside us. "So cute you give me toothache!"

"Adorable," Luigi agrees with his husband before they waltz on by.

"If they only knew." I pull my head back to look at Rami.

"That we can barely share an office without giving each other headaches?" he finishes.

"And I thought I hid my ibuprofen-popping so well," I say with a side smile.

"You are never subtle, Forester. Not about anything." Rami has his own little grin.

I realise I'm not in the mood for banter, nor am I in the mood to argue with him. Instead, I move closer again and press my cheek against the side of his head. It feels like a test, but I know I've passed when Rami applies a little pressure back in my direction.

"But don't ever change, okay?" I hear him say and it halts my breath. Once I'm able to inhale again, I open my mouth to ask him what he means by that, but I hear another voice.

"Rami, I hear you're doing a DJ set?" It's Melanie, Lionel's mum. I turn my head to see she's dancing with a man who has the same closely cropped afro and wide brown eyes as Lionel. The same man who gave the most heartfelt speech about his son.

"Did you meet my husband, Bobby, yet?" Melanie asks and we both nod at Bobby as he gives us each a wink.

"This is Jake, Bobs. You know, Lionel's boss in Crete. The one who looked after him all those years," Melanie tells her husband as my cheeks blush red. I suppose it's partly true. Until it wasn't. "And this is his boyfriend, Rami."

"Pleasure to meet you both. You make a very handsome couple," Bobby says and there's more heat in my cheeks, but this time for a very different reason.

"Rami's obviously punching above his weight, but thank you, Bobby," I joke, and Rami's gentle chuckles are a relief.

"Ha! They do keep us on our toes, don't they!" I hear a booming voice call out. Lionel's father may look like his son but his voice is ten times lower and louder. "Nothing like having a younger partner, hey Jake?"

It's impossible to stop my jaw dropping.

"Oh, shush. Jake is younger than Rami!" Melanie declares, swiping at her husband's chest.

I don't know why it hits me so hard. I don't know why it rains so heavily on my parade. I don't know why my stomach sinks like I've just received bad news. Maybe I am simply too tired to tell myself it doesn't matter, but I suddenly need to be somewhere else. I smile weakly, mutter something about getting some fresh air, and step out of Rami's embrace. I walk away to an empty table on the periphery of the dance floor and put my hands down and lean over it.

"Jake, he didn't..." Rami is only two steps behind me.

"I don't care." I hold up my hand to stop him talking. "I mean of course I care. I feel as bruised as a fucking peach in a tumble dryer. But the point is, I know I *shouldn't* care."

Rami steps closer to me, almost as close as when we were dancing.

"I have to go start my DJ set in five minutes, but I don't want to leave you like this," he says.

"I'm fine," I say. "I should probably go to bed anyway. It's been a long day."

When Rami's eyes blink in rapid succession and his lips fall open, I see disappointment. "Of course," he says.

"No, wait, I want to watch you." It really is the least I can do after everything he's done for me today. I think momentarily about the bath, the tissues, the hand squeezes. Recalling all of it suddenly makes me want to cry, which is utterly ridiculous.

"Jake, you don't have to."

"I want to," I say, and unexpectedly, I do.

"Okay, well, I just need to run up to the room and grab my laptop. You need anything from there?"

"My trainers, please," I say, dropping my gaze to my shoes. "These are killing me."

"Yes, boss," Rami says, and he turns and walks away.

After finding my jacket, I sink into the nearest chair and give myself permission to indulge my morose mood, which is easy to do as I survey the couples who are lost in each other on the dance floor. My eyes linger on Luigi and Lionel. After a while, I realise what I feel is not jealousy of either of them specifically, but rather envy for what they have. It's not like I'd reached a point where I'd given up on love, but for a long time now I've been so used to accepting it's never going to happen, I don't even consider it a possibility. This is why the comments about my age – and the whole drama about having a fortieth birthday party – hit me so hard.

A long time ago, I'd always assumed it would happen by the time I was forty, if it was going to happen at all. It doesn't help at all that faking a relationship today – having a hand to hold, a body to slow dance with, a man to make snarky comments about people's outfits with – it's all given me a taste of honey. It's given me a hint at what I'm missing and likely going to miss for the rest of my life. It's reminded me that even if I have adjusted to the idea that it's never going to happen – because I must, it's basic self-preservation – part of me still doesn't want that as my future. Part of me still wants what I will almost certainly never have. And that hurts.

"Are you okay?" Rami is back in front of me. A little breathless and holding his laptop, he drops my trainers to the floor by my feet.

I wave my hands at him before bending to pick up my shoes. "I'm fine. Just sulking about being called old again."

Rami's brow furrows but he doesn't say anything.

"Go, Mr DJ." I encourage him as I start to swap shoes. "And please don't be a total disaster. I'm too fragile to be shown up. I've been embarrassed enough today."

He smiles at this. "I'll do my best. Any requests?"

"You choose something for me," I say with a smile that slips as quickly as it arrives because I really am so tired.

A few minutes later Rami's set has begun. For his first song, he chooses an extended version of Sylvester's *You Make Me Feel Mighty Real* and as the song gradually builds, the dancers multiply. He's certainly judged the crowd perfectly as I see members of both families dancing with the countless Tom Ford lookalikes and models. Watching them is fun, but after a while my eyes are pulled back to Rami and I see him focus intently on what he's doing. I assume he's getting to grips with whatever equipment he has in the small booth that stands off to the side of the stage but I'm impressed how comfortable he looks. He pops headphones on and nods his head with the beat. The frown across his forehead is one of concentration and I start to trust that maybe he knows what he's doing.

The man can dance. The man can DJ. The man is a master of small talk with fellow wedding guests. The man knows when to hold my hand. And he's slowly, slowly learning the art of sarcasm. Maybe I have misjudged Rami Kazimi.

He blends Sylvester perfectly into a more upbeat dance track from a decade or so ago and several members of the crowd roar with approval when they recognise what it is. My foot starts tapping and a little of the weight I was feeling a moment ago lifts. I consider getting up to dance, but my feet still hurt so I don't move. Instead, I go back to watching Rami, which also makes me feel a bit better.

After a few songs, he looks up and catches my eye. He smiles and nods at the dance floor and gestures for me to dance. I shake my head. Honestly, I'd rather just watch him. He looks so at peace, so intentional and content. It's quite nice to see him looking happy and relaxed. He stares at me for a beat longer but then shrugs and goes back to work.

I watch him and occasionally the crowd for a few more moments before I realise what else would make me feel better. I pull out my phone and message my sister, Jenna.

<Sorry I've been ignoring your texts. Wanted to get through today and avoid moaning at you too much. But thank you for thinking of me. Rami and I had fun.Xx>

Much to my surprise, she replies less than a minute later.

<WHEN WILL I GET TO MEET RAMI?>

Yes, I also told my sister I was seeing Rami. What's one more lie when you've told countless others? Besides, it was worth it to hear how happy Jenna was for me. Ever since she found love with Marty, she's been desperate for me to find the same thing with someone. I haven't got the heart to tell her it's unlikely to ever happen.

<What are you doing up? It's gone midnight.>

<Waiting for Marty to finish his shift. I may or may not be wearing lingerie that I could also use to slice cheese.>

I shudder. <You're testing my ability to keep down the very high-quality meal and champagne I've consumed today.>

<Can you send me a photo of you and Rami in your tuxes? I've only asked 20 times already. I WANT TO SEE HIS FACE!>

<Maybe later. Plot twist. He's currently DJing at the wedding.>

<Serious?! What a legend.>

She's right. He really kind of is. And I've been such an arsehole to him. Ugh. Something else to feel shit about.

<Wish you were here.> I type back before I can stop myself.

<Wish I was there too, just possibly wearing something a lot less revealing and wedgie-inducing.>

<Vom.> I laugh and sniff. This is helping me feel a bit better at least.

<I'll get you one in your size for Rami to enjoy.>

<Double vom.>

<Go dance to your DJ boyfriend.>

<Bossy. Love you.x>

<Love you more.x>

I put my phone down and am about to loosen the laces on my trainers because my feet are still throbbing when I hear a voice, Rami's voice, boom out of the speakers.

"The next song is a special dedication. Very special indeed, because it's for my boyfriend, Jake Forester. Yes, him sitting over there in the corner. It's Michael Jackson's *P.Y.T.* and I'm playing this for him because that's exactly what he is, a Pretty Young Thing."

As the song's opening bars play, every single wedding guest turns to look at me and many start gesturing for me to join them on the dance floor, but I'm frozen. Frozen in shock at what Rami just said, and at the song he chose for me. I stay frozen as I watch Rami leave his booth and start walking up the side of the dance floor towards me, a microphone in his hand.

"Seeing as he refuses to dance, I'll have to be a bit more persuasive," Rami is saying before he hands over the mic to Lionel who just happens to be standing close by.

Immediately at the start of the first verse, Rami starts lip-synching every word and dancing, expertly dancing. His feet cross over one another, his fingers click and his head rocks from side to side as he sings and approaches me. Everybody behind him claps and whoops, cheering him on.

And I should be doing the same. Or I should be doing something, anything, but right now I am still frozen, still utterly incapable of moving as I watch Rami do a very Michael-Jackson-esque twirl that ends with a head dip and the grab of his crotch with one hand while the other tips an imaginary hat.

The show continues as Rami sings along with the chorus, inching still closer to me, although he detours and dances with Lionel's parents briefly. This goes some way to help melt my frozen state and as soon as I reclaim control over my mouth, I'm smiling. No, that's an understatement. I'm laughing. But not at him. God, no. I'm laughing with everyone else who is cheering him on, copying his moves, and shaking their bodies in the background. And they are in the background, because as the song launches into the second verse, my eyes are only on Rami who is right in front of me and...

Oh my God, is he moonwalking?

That does it. I may not have his style and I may not have his apparently endless repertoire of dance moves, but I do have good rhythm and I have been called Snake Hips more than once in my life, so I push up to stand. Miraculously, the pain in my feet has disappeared and rather than light-headed, I just feel light. Really light, as I step towards Rami and let him take my hand and pull me into something that looks like a chaotic jive. We dance together for the rest of the song, with him occasionally throwing me into a spin, only for him to then find me again and swing me the other way into a backwards arch of my back over his thigh. At other times we take turns to pull apart and dance with other people. At one point, Lionel and I are doing a ridiculous version of the Macarena routine while over my shoulder I see Luigi and Rami doing *Saturday Night Fever* finger points. A few beats later, Melanie cuts in to grab me and twist me around while I spot Bobby, Marco, Salvatore and Rami have their arms all around each other's backs doing some kicks not dissimilar to the Greek dancing I learned in Crete. As the song reaches its final stretch, Rami breaks free and rushes up to me.

"P.Y.T!" he shouts at me in time with the song.

"You idiot!" I shout back at him and when his arms come to rest on my hips, I can't stop myself leaning closer, grabbing his tuxedo lapels and pulling him against me in a big hug as we continue to dance.

"I'm going to kiss you now!" Rami shouts into my ear.

"What?" I pull back, shocked.

"It's what boyfriends do after one has serenaded the other!" He leans in closer so he doesn't have to shout so hard. "Is that okay?"

"Yes," I call back but what I suddenly and urgently mean is 'please'.

And he does. He grips my cheeks in both his hands, brings my face close to his, and places his lips firmly on mine.

Chapter Twelve

Rami

It's fake. It's forced. It's hard and dry and awkward and closed-lips and so very public. It's so far from the best kiss of my life. But it's still a kiss I know I'll always remember.

And it's a kiss I'm trying to deepen when I tilt my head to the side and lessen some of the pressure of my lips, seeing, testing if maybe he wants to do the same and open his mouth. I am far too excited when I feel that he does and our mouths lock together, his bottom lip between mine and my top one between his lips, lips that I realise taste like cherries. His stupid lip balm.

The song is seconds away from ending, but I don't move and I don't need to. I have already set up another to start immediately. It surprises me when Jake pulls away and apparently has the same thought.

"The music," he declares, his eyes dazed and his pupils changing shape as they adjust again to the disco lights. When the opening chords and cackling of Michael Jackson's *Off the Wall* sound out, I nod. "All set up."

"What the actual fuck was that?" Jake asks and it's loud because my hands are still on his face. I should probably move them. But I don't.

"The dancing? Or the kiss?" I ask, noticing behind us that the crowd have gone back to the centre of the dance floor, bodies still jumping and moving.

"All of it!" I'm not sure if Jake is trying to sound angry or shocked, but his mouth seems intent on only grinning widely between the heel of my hands.

"Just trying to shut you up," I say, and reluctantly, I drop my hands but try to cover up my disappointment with a quick wink. "I'd had enough of you moaning all day."

"Ha!" His hand swipes against the front of my tuxedo. "You just wanted to show off those obscenely good dance moves."

I swallow roughly. Is that what he actually thinks about me? All I wanted was to make him smile and dance and laugh and maybe forget all his worries for a few—

Another swipe hits my chest. "I'm joking!" Jake declares and my features relax back into a smile.

"It was brilliant," Jake says but I barely catch it because his voice has lowered, and so have his eyes, staring down at our shoes that are almost toe-to-toe below us, the shiny patent leather of my shoes catching the flaring lights. "Thank you."

"You're welcome, Forester," I say. "And you are free to go now if you want. I promise you no more public displays of affection or dancing or fake kissing. I have a dance floor to fill and—"

I'm interrupted by Jake again. This time by his body crashing against mine and his arms wrapping around the back of me. It's a hug. A real hug.

"Thank you," Jake says again, and I hear him better this time because his mouth is close to my ear. I feel his warm breath on my earlobe and a shiver runs through me. "Nobody has ever done anything that stupid or ridiculous or outrageous for me before, and I know it was all for show, but I loved it. I loved the show."

I pull out of the hug so I can focus on Jake's eyes when I say, "You're welcome."

"Now, go and make these people dance until they drop." Jake waves at the crowd behind us.

"I'll do my best," I say and I'm suddenly sad Jake won't be part of it. "And I'll do my best not to wake you up later."

"Oh, I'm not going anywhere! That performance just gave me my third, or maybe tenth wind. I'm going to get another drink and then I'm coming back to show everyone that I can match you on both dance moves and lip-synching skills."

My stomach flips with relief or excitement, or just something that I like much more than I probably should.

"I'll watch and learn then," I joke.

"Absolutely. Oh, and if you don't mind. Play me some Wham!, please?"

120

"Seriously? Are you trying to ruin my reputation?" I am only a fraction as horrified as I sound. George Michael was a genius songwriter.

"Oh, it's too late to be snobby about music or dancing. You just moonwalked at a wedding while singing Michael Jackson to your fake boyfriend!"

"True. I'll see what I can do," I say with a nod at him before I walk back to the DJ booth.

*****

The set passes in a happy, quick blur. Jake stays true to his word and does indeed dance his heart out while singing along to nearly every song I play. Each song I choose takes me back to a former version of myself and I love every single second. This is why I got into DJing in the first place; the joy on people's faces, the freedom they feel when they dance, the communal delight in sharing a dance or singing a song together. It always was as much about making people happy as it was being creative with music and I feel inexplicably grateful that I have this opportunity to enjoy this one more time.

Possibly the last time, I try not think but still the thought slices me in two.

I also like how I can play the songs that my father loved most – Motown hits, sixties soul and seventies disco – and I can mix it with my own favourite eighties synth and nineties house classics. I also honour my promise to Jake by playing Wham!'s *Wake Me Up Before You Go Go,* which Jake gets so excited. He starts an impromptu conga line halfway through the song, his hands on Melanie's waist and her husband's on Jake's hips. I laugh as they snake around the dance floor and out to the bar. When they finally return, they all have new drinks in hand. Jake, who has not one but two glasses of champagne in his hands, breaks free and darts around the dance floor with nimble ease and over the following songs I see him talking and dancing with nearly every guest. A little later he's holding a bottle of champagne as he spends many minutes dancing next to Lionel and Luigi and I have to bite back my smile when I see the two of them fold Jake into a big sandwich of a hug.

By the time the closing bars on my last song are playing, the lights come up and I can see, standing dead centre of the dance floor, Jake is still smiling and still swaying with his arm around Melanie even though the music is all but gone. I don't think it would take a genius to conclude that he's very, very drunk.

Once I've packed up and have my laptop in its case, I go to find him and hear him drawling on at Lionel's mother who doesn't look any less sober than Jake.

"... I mean that's the kind of man you raised, Melanie. A man who will drop everything, including all his clothes, when he needs to. I told him we would cancel the life drawing class, it was just a silly extra we offered that hardly any of the guests did, but he insisted on stepping in. He knew that a particular group of thirsty women in their sixties who were staying with us had all signed up to the class and he certainly gave them what they wanted to see. What a lovely man, with a lovely body..."

"Oh, you don't need to tell me. I always say to Bobby, how did Lionel get so lucky? A kind heart and an eight-pack?"

"And he barely works out!" Jake exclaims.

"I know!" Melanie agrees.

"Jake," I interrupt. "Time to get you up to bed."

"Oh, Jake, you better listen to your man. He knows what he wants." Melanie starts giggling as I step closer to get Jake to lean his weight on me.

"I'm not even tired!" Jake slurs and resists me as I try to pull his arm towards me.

"Oh, he doesn't want you in bed to sleep, honey!" Melanie explains.

"Ha! You should know something about me and Rami." Jake stretches back towards Melanie even as I manage to get my shoulder under his arm. "Rami isn't even—"

"Jake, we're going upstairs right now," I say loudly and that thankfully prompts him to shut up.

"So authoritarian!" he slurs looking at me with half-closed eyes.

"Enjoy it!" Melanie says as she stretches up to kiss us both on our cheeks. "Enjoy each other!"

I manage to lead Jake out of the ballroom, and we're almost halfway through the bar when he straightens up a little and makes a mumbled sound in his throat. We stop moving.

"Are you—" I begin.

"Gonna chuck!" he says and rushes to the double doors that lead out to the terrace. Pushing through them he disappears into the darkness outside, and I follow him. It takes a few seconds, but I finally find him sitting on a bench just to the side. It's the same bench we saw Lionel and Luigi sitting on when we first arrived earlier. Facing the pond and water feature that continues to trickle, filling the night air with a tinkling sound, Jake hangs his head between his legs but I don't see or smell any vomit and he's not retching, just sort of sitting there.

"False alarm," he says when I come to sit next to him.

"Take your time," I say with a small laugh.

"You should go upstairs. You have to get up early."

"I'm fine," I say, and I really am. I don't even feel tired.

"Don't stay out here on my behalf," Jake says, and I hear that tense, edgy tone of his again. I choose to ignore it, or rather to focus on something else. I lean back and look up at the sky. It doesn't take long to find what I'm looking for. I keep my eyes on it as I soak up the silence.

"You're still here," Jake says a minute or two later, his voice still sharp.

"Just looking at the moon," I say.

Jake lifts his head up and finds it too.

"It's a full moon. Of course, it bloody is," he grunts.

"What does that mean?"

"All the strange chaotic stuff always happens at full moons. Isn't that where the words *lunacy* and *lunatic* come from? From the moon?"

"Forester, you're surprisingly wise when you're wasted."

"You have to stop calling me that," Jake mutters, his head dropping again.

"What? Wise?"

"No, my surname. It does something to me," he says quietly.

My interest piqued, I shift forward and rest my elbows on my knees so that our heads are a little closer. "What do you mean, it does something to you?"

Jake kicks at the gravel on the ground. "Nothing. I'm just waffling because I'm drunk."

"Then let's get you upstairs and in bed," I say, readying myself to stand but I stop when Jake doesn't move.

"You go. I want to stay. The fresh air is helping me sober up, I think."

I don't move. I lean back again and watch the moon some more.

"You're still here," Jake says after a while, his voice softer now.

"Still watching the moon."

"Why?" Jake asks and I'm pretty sure he's referring to why I'm still here but I choose to interpret his question a different way.

"When I lived in California, and before that when I was travelling a lot with work, whenever I was feeling homesick, I would look for the moon. I found comfort in knowing that it was the same moon that my family could see in Birmingham. The same moon my friends could find all over the world. It was always the same moon no matter where I was."

"Ugh," Jake groans and it's not exactly the response I was expecting. "Sorry, I thought I was going to chuck up again."

I can't help but laugh. I take it all as a sign to stop trying to share more of myself, at least not with Jake Forester who is running his hands through his hair and closing his eyes, and thanks to some kind of magic, his freckles are even more noticeable in the silver moonlight. I want to touch them, maybe even kiss one or two. Stunned at these thoughts, I look away and stare at my feet.

"That was beautiful though," he says. "What you just said. It's hard being away from home for a long period of time. It's hard when you come back too. You don't really feel like you belong anywhere."

"Yeah." I nod. That's exactly how it feels, even if not for the exact reasons Jake thinks.

"I'm sorry I've been a bitch," Jake says and that prompts me to look at him. "I wasn't very welcoming to you when you joined the company. And while sharing an office has been less than ideal for both of us, I know I probably haven't made it easier for you."

"Jake—"

"No, I need to apologise. I know you go on those long walks to get away from me, to give me space. And it's very generous. But you shouldn't have to do it. I could have made it easier for you."

I risk something then. "Yeah, you could have," I say, and his eyes find mine. Sitting side by side, we're close enough that his face doesn't quite come into full focus in my eyes. The only thing I can do is narrow my gaze onto his freckles again, onto the length of his nose. Onto his lips.

"So, apology accepted?" Jake asks.

"Apology accepted." I nod.

"I can't promise I won't still be a bitch." Jake turns his head away, staring at the pond. "But I will try to be less bitchy to you, or about you."

"You've been bitchy about me? Who to?"

"Sharon, of course. What else am I supposed to do with an over-efficient personal assistant who shares my general distaste for humankind?"

"You deserve each other." I shake my head and smile to myself.

"Probably. She will be disappointed she lost her bet though," Jake says.

"What bet?"

"She assumed we'd never get away with it today. She was convinced someone would see through us. Or rather, that I would cop off with a barman or something."

"Well, you were flirting with that one fella—"

"I was not!"

"Jake, you were fluttering your eyelashes at him."

"Fine, I was doing that, but I wouldn't specifically call that flirting. My kind of flirting is much more creative than that."

"Oh, how do you like to flirt?"

"Like this." He turns his body so it's facing mine, one of his knees touching the side of my thigh. Although it's not cold, there's a slight chill in the air and I like the bolt of warmth his touch brings me. His eyes are back on mine when he speaks again. "Rami, did you know that your eyes are like pieces of the moon? Like a little bit of silver light shining in the dark? Like something I could look at forever?"

I open my mouth to speak but my tongue is too dry and heavy. Jake's almost expressionless face is still turned towards me, his eyes searching mine and all the affected, over-emphasised ways he has of looking are gone. His mouth is relaxed and level. His eyes are warm and dark in the low light. His forehead is slack, no frown, no strained smile, nothing. I suddenly find myself wondering if that wasn't him pretending to flirt. What if he's been wanting to flirt with me all night?

I lean forward ever so slightly, barely moving my body, but shifting enough that our legs touch. When Jake doesn't move back, I take that as all the invitation I need.

"Forester, I'm going to kiss you again," I say, and I give him the shortest second to tell me not to. Maybe it's not long enough because his face barely has time to look shocked as I close in on him, but I don't care. I have to take this risk.

When my lips touch his, it's not like before. It's gentle, it's fragile, it's barely there. Our lips align like they know exactly where to be and I gently, gently pull his bottom lip between mine. I feel his exhale on my upper lip and feel his bodyweight pivot to lean towards me a bit more. Bolstered by this, I nudge my mouth open a little and stroke my tongue against his lips.

It was the wrong thing to do.

Jake pulls back a few centimetres, but bizarrely, endearingly, his eyes stay closed.

"Rami," he says.

"Yes?"

"What are you doing?"

"I'm trying to kiss you."

"But—"

"Do you want me to stop?"

His eyes finally open. "Funnily enough, not really."

"Well, then shut up, Forester."

Jake hums a little and it sounds like a purr. "You know you can be very authoritative when you want to be."

"Oh, you like that?"

"Certainly better than the limp lettuce leaf you've been in the office since day one."

"Kissing you again to shut you up!" I mutter before crashing my mouth down on his. Wasting no time, I keep my mouth slightly open and let my tongue roll around and find his. Much to my delight, he responds in much the same way, his tongue stroking mine, before also finding my teeth. I groan quietly and feel sufficiently self-conscious to regret it but that only lasts a few seconds because Jake then moans into my mouth, loudly enough that it vibrates on my tongue. I bring my hands up to grip his head. I do not want this kiss to end right now. But of course, Jake being Jake, he's got his own ideas.

"Oh my God, you actually taste good," he says, pulling away again.

"You thought I would taste *bad*?"

"Not exactly but you know how people say someone tastes so good when they kiss, like in romance novels – don't judge me, I used to steal my sister's – but like you actually do. All clean and fresh and minty. How is that possible? You last cleaned your teeth over ten hours ago."

"Well, I haven't been deep throating a champagne bottle for the last hour, so there's that."

"Ha! That was nearly funny."

I tighten my grip in his hair, pulling at the roots slightly. "Less talking, more kissing, Forester, because I've had enough of this pretty mouth insulting me and my wit."

This time when our lips touch, Jake leans forward and places one of his hands on my face and the other comes down on my leg, just above my knee. As our tongues taste each other, our heads moving as we both push against the other, his hand slides up my thigh and it doesn't stop.

"Jesus, you're hard!" Jake jumps back.

"Jake." I lick my lips. I wasn't ready for that kiss to end either.

"But how?" He looks down at my crotch.

"Really? Do you need a biology lesson?"

"You're turned on?"

"Very. Although this conversation could put a stop to it."

"But I'm a man..." Jake points a finger at himself.

"Thank you for verifying."

"So, you're…"

"Pansexual," I sigh, "and more than a little exasperated with you right now."

Jake swoops back in and nips at my neck with his teeth, hard.

"Ow! What was that for?"

"You should have told me."

"I tried. Several times. But did you know you have a habit of ignoring people and talking over someone in a conversation?"

"How very dare you? I don't know what you're talking about. And stop stealing my thunder right now. It's my turn to be pissed off with you."

My eyes widen. "After everything I've done for you today? I practically put my hip out doing that dance routine back there."

"It was a bit brilliant, I suppose." Jake's words are stingy, but his smile is soft and dreamy.

"A bit? I swear you are the most annoying man on this planet. I'm going to kiss you again now, just to shut you up, and let this be your warning, I'm going to do it very, very angrily."

And I do. Our teeth clash, our tongues fight, and I suck on his soft bottom lip more times than I can count.

I don't know how long we stay like that, kissing under a full moon, but when I pull away from Jake to catch my breath, I see how his eyes stay closed and his body starts to sink to the side, so I decide for us both that it's time for us to head up to our room. Jake is reluctant at first and starts to complain, grabbing the lapels of my jacket and pulling me back towards his mouth, but I resist and stand up. Once he's upright too, I see him sway and decide that will not do.

"Stand up on the bench," I tell him as I throw my laptop bag over my shoulder.

"What?"

"Do as you're told, Forester."

"Jesus," he says on a deep exhale before obeying.

"Hop on," I say as I stand in front of him.

"What?"

"Get on my back. I'm taking you to bed."

Silently, Jake climbs on and I piggy-back him up the steps, back through the bar and eventually up the stairs and down the corridors that lead to our room. Jake is silent throughout, and his body becomes heavier and heavier with each passing second. So much so, I assume he's asleep but then he speaks as I turn the key in the door.

"Rami, I really don't want to have sex with you," he says.

"Excellent," I say. "Those are always words I want to hear."

"Not because I don't want to, but I'm suddenly very tired and suspect I'm incapable of brushing my teeth, let alone giving you a night you'll never forget."

I laugh at that. "Well, funnily enough, I don't want to have sex with you either for very similar reasons."

"How rude," he says as I lower him onto the bed.

"But I'll tell you this." I move to pull his trainers off his feet. "Nobody is sleeping in the bath or on the floor. We're going to share this bed like two sensible queer men who can keep their hands off each other."

"I can't believe you're queer. But then again, the dancing should have given it away."

"Straight people can dance," I say as I start unbuttoning his shirt while his hands go to the fly of his trousers. It takes far too much restraint to not look at what is revealed when he slides his trousers down his thighs and kicks them away.

"Not like that," he says as he shrugs off his shirt. This time there's nowhere else for me to look and I take in the generous dusting of golden-brown hair that covers his toned chest and stomach. My fingers itch to touch it.

"Get into bed," I say after swallowing. Walking into the bathroom, I quickly take off my suit and shirt, hanging it over the side of the bath. I then find my toothbrush and Jake's and load both up with toothpaste.

"Open your mouth," I say when I come back to Jake whose head is already on the pillow, his eyes closed. When his mouth falls open, I start to brush his teeth with my right hand while doing my own with my left; being ambidextrous does have its benefits.

"Please don't remind me of this at work on Monday," he says as the toothpaste starts to foam.

"I'm assuming we won't be talking about a lot of today at work," I say.

"Oh, yeah. Company policy, schmolicy," Jake says around his toothbrush. "Ridiculous really. Everyone's at it, you know. You want to know who's fucking who? I can tell you."

"Another time. Right now, you need sleep." Leaving Jake's toothbrush hanging out of his mouth, I go back to the bathroom to rinse and spit. When I return, I have the two plastic cups from the bathroom, one with water in it.

"Sit up so you can rinse," I say as I give him the water to sip and the empty cup to spit out into. Once he's done, he falls back on the pillow with a soft thump.

"I hope you don't snore, Mr DJ," he calls out through the bathroom door as I use the toilet. I roll my eyes.

"You never stop, do you?" I say as I wash my hands. But there's no reply. He must be asleep.

As quietly as I can, I go about packing my bag and setting out some clean clothes in the bathroom so I can change quickly in the morning. I also pick up Jake's suit and drape it all over a chair so he can find it easily tomorrow. I then plug my phone in to charge and turn out all the lights. As I get into bed, I finally look over at Jake who is almost certainly asleep. The room's curtains are next to useless, and they let in plenty of the moonlight, allowing me to see Jake's face at peace as he sleeps. I take in the way his eyelashes rest against the tops of his cheeks, how his nose is perfectly straight, and it makes me smile that his mouth holds a natural pout when it's not busy talking or being pushed into one of his hundreds of expressions.

And how I loved kissing that mouth.

Granted it's been years since I've kissed anyone, but I refuse to believe that is the only reason I find myself bringing my fingertips to my lips to trace where Jake's mouth was.

Do I like Jake? Do I want to be more than friends with Jake? Even though I instantly know the answers to those questions, I am just as quick to put all these thoughts to one side, because although my life is depressingly empty, a likely unrequited crush on my colleague is hardly a healthy way to fill it.

The sigh that leaves me is a lot louder than I expect.

"Hey, Rami," Jake whispers into the darkness.

"Yeah," I say, my voice dry and airy. I didn't know he was still awake.

"Wake me up before you go… go," Jake mumbles before he starts snoring.

Smiling, I roll over to face him and watch the rise and fall of his chest as he breathes deep, slow and relaxed in his sleep. And eventually, I fall asleep too.

Chapter Thirteen

Rami

One good thing about my former career is that I got quite adept at sleeping while on the move, and I benefit from this by having an almost two-hour nap on the train up to Birmingham. I'm almost as grateful for that as I am for seeing my sister, Roxie, waiting for me in her banged-up Renault Clio in the pick-up area of Birmingham New Street station. I am less grateful for the emo music blaring out of her speakers as we drive through the city and the suburbs until we are pulling up to my childhood home.

"Mom's gone all out today," Roxie says as we get out of the car. "Made all your favourites... *Bamia*, a vegan *Zereshk polo, pita, Muhammara.*"

"They're your favourites too," I point out.

"But she's not making them for me. I live here. She could make them any time but she's making them on the day her darling Rami is coming to visit. Just accept the compliment. You're her favourite. Enjoy it."

I smile but don't say anything. I shouldn't be her favourite.

Inside, the scents of all those foods flood me and I can't help but go and investigate further in the kitchen. Mom is there, busy at the stove, the same blue and white striped apron she always wears to cook worn over her clothes. Before I can call out to her, she turns to see me and her smile takes up her whole face, crinkling the corners of her grey eyes and bunching up her cheeks.

"Rami," she says.

"Mama." I bend down to give her a hug. It's a miracle I am as tall as I am as my mother is a little over five feet, and my father was only half a foot taller. Mom often says I got my sisters' height as well as my own because they are also petite.

"You look tired," she says when she pulls away, her hand cupping my face.

"I am," I admit. "It was a late night."

"A good late night?"

My smile is unstoppable. "It was, actually."

"I need to know more." She returns to the stove and starts stirring a saucepan.

"Nothing to tell," I say quickly. "Can I make a coffee?"

Mama waves her free hand at me. "You don't need to ask! This is your home!"

I don't reply how it hasn't felt like home for a while. Even when I was living here while trying to make sense of everything that happened in California, I didn't allow myself to feel fully at home here. I didn't deserve that.

"Would you like one?" I offer as I go to the machine.

"No, thank you, *habibi*," she says. We both fall silent and the sounds of sizzling food and the whirring of the coffee machine fill the room.

"So, Radia has a date today," I say, keen to talk about something, anything that isn't related to me.

"Oh, yes. She sent me a photo of her," Mom says, and she moves quickly to the other side of the kitchen and picks up her phone. "Look."

I glance at the phone and see a pretty dark-skinned woman with deep brown eyes, a heart-shaped face, and a smile just for the person taking the photo. Radia, I assume.

"Time for you to find yourself a beautiful woman," Mom says and I'm glad my back is to her when I wince.

"Mama, I've just started my new job," I say.

"Yes, tell me how that is going, *habibi*."

Inwardly, I groan. I don't know what else I can tell her that I haven't already on previous Sundays, but I suppose I'll just repeat myself so I don't give her a reason to worry.

"It's fine. Planning for the arts festival in Belfast next month is going well and I'm up in Northumberland for the next few days getting a venue ready for a food festival next weekend. And I'm getting to know people a bit better, slowly."

"And your office?"

"Yeah, I don't think I'll have that any time soon. They found some asbestos in the walls, apparently."

"That's a shame. And how is Jake?"

My eyes bolt open hearing her ask that. "He's... fine. Why?"

"Are you getting on a bit better with him? I should hope so now you did him a great favour by going to the wedding with him."

"We had fun together." I bring my cup up to my lips to hide my grin.

"Good. You deserve that."

I don't really, but I am not going to challenge her.

"While it's just you and me here, I was wondering..." Mama begins and I hold my breath. "Did you reach out to Dev yet?"

My shoulders sink and my cup suddenly feels a lot heavier than it did a second ago.

"He doesn't want to hear from me," I say.

"Says who?" Mom turns and her light eyes burn a little brighter as they fix on me. I never really understand why people say nice things about my eyes until I am staring in my mother's with their same cloudy-grey silver that seems to sparkle whenever she's agitated or excited.

"Dev knows I've been back for nearly two years and he hasn't gotten in touch," I explain with a shrug. "If he wanted to hear from me, he would have tried already."

"That's not fair. He has three kids now, Rami. Children you don't know. You're Jaden's godfather and you've not seen him since the Christening."

"He doesn't need a godfather. He must be what... ten now?"

"Exactly!"

I pull in a breath and hold it. "Mama, I don't want to argue with you. But I think you have to accept that that ship has sailed. We live very different lives. I'm in London now and he's—"

She points her spoon in the direction of our front door. "He's here. He lives three streets away. You could go right now and knock on his door and—"

"Mama," I say and I hear the edge in my voice.

I'm not sure if her timing is deliberate but Roxie appears at the door and coughs loudly, breaking some of the tension in the kitchen.

"Guys, you're not allowed to argue. Not without Radia. She hates missing out on arguments."

Mom waves her hand at us and turns back to the stove. "We weren't arguing, *habibti*. Just having a heated discussion."

My chest rises hearing those words. It's what Baba used to say if one of us walked in on him and Mom having a fight. Not that it was ever a real fight. In fact, it really was always just a heated discussion. They loved each other too much to fight.

"Ready to die, death after death after death?" Roxie raises both of her eyebrows at me, one of which is pierced. Sometimes I forget how old she really is, or maybe I do it on purpose so I don't have to remind myself how much I've missed.

"Nobody dies in Mario Kart," I say before downing the last of my coffee and pushing off the kitchen counter. I pause before I leave the room. "You don't need any help, Mama?"

Mom turns around then and I see a haze in her eyes and that makes something heavy sink lower in my stomach.

"No, thank you."

"Come on you." I nod at Roxie. "I have a championship to defend."

"You didn't win last time, Radia did."

"Well, then I will defend her crown," I say as we file into the large room at the front of the house. Unlike some homes, our living room really does live up to its name. With the dining table close to the back wall, and a large sofa filling the space in front of the bay window, it's the room where our family has always gathered over the years. Be it for family meals, family gatherings or just to watch TV together – first on a tiny black-and-white box set and then later on larger, flashier TVs – it's where we all came together when I was still living in the UK. It's also the room where I know my father's wake was held four years ago, an event I missed. While wakes are not typical in Muslim families, Radia had told me that his many friends, colleagues and neighbours had all but insisted something be held to honour his memory and that didn't surprise me in the slightest. I shudder as I sit on the sofa and imagine the room full of all my father's grieving friends and family, but not me.

"You Toad, again?"

"Like always," I say after clearing my throat.

Roxana turns the TV on and goes about connecting the console. As she does, I stare at the unit that surrounds the TV. Specifically, I'm running my eyes over the top shelf that houses a couple of my favourite masks that I wore while performing as DJ Lunar. They're positioned in between other relics from that part of my past; the framed platinum records for my first, second and third albums, three Grammy awards, two BRIT awards, and a handful of other trophies I picked up during the height of my DJ career.

Height. How funny to think of that time as a high. Most of the time, it felt like anything but.

"Here you go," Roxie says and half a second later a Joycon lands in my lap, bringing me back into the room.

"Thanks. So, how's uni?" I ask referring to Roxie being in her second year studying Maths and Economics at the University of Birmingham.

"Fine. Bit boring sometimes."

"You don't fancy trying halls next year? It's your last chance."

"Why would I do that? They stink."

"How do you know that?"

"Because I've visited them. I'm only 80% anti-social. Sometimes I even surprise myself and end up at a halls party or in the student bar. And both categorically stink."

"Maybe I didn't miss out so much not going to uni," I muse as we start to choose our vehicles for the first race.

"Pah! As if jetting around the world in private jets and schmoozing with the rich and famous can compare to 10% off fast fashion brands and BOGOF offers on sugary booze."

My jaw tightens. "It wasn't as great as it sounds. At first, it was a lot of work. I did endless gigs up and down the country for next to no money, just to get my name out there."

"Which you did," Roxie points out.

"Yes, eventually. But it didn't happen overnight. And you have to remember I also sort of broke Mom and Dad's hearts when I decided to give DJing a go."

"Really?"

"Yes, they were desperate for me to go to uni. They'd saved up for it and everything."

"Well, I can sort of imagine that."

"Absolutely." I huff out a quiet laugh. "First child of an immigrant family. I had Doctor, Lawyer, Teacher or just *Anything but DJ* stamped on my forehead."

"But they came around in the end," Roxana says, and I know it's not a question but I feel the unusual need to dwell on this more.

"They did, and I'll always be grateful for that. I'll always be thankful I got to make them proud of me in another way."

"Baba was so proud of you." Roxie nods at the shelves above the TV. "He polished those bloody awards every Saturday morning without fail."

I swear my heart cracks.

"I grew up constantly hearing stories about you and how you'd made it big in LA. I felt so much pressure." Roxana pauses and shrugs. "I still do."

"It wasn't as fantastic as Baba maybe thought it was," I say slowly, carefully. "I was... I was very lonely. And I didn't really grow up properly. I didn't have the same kind of experiences you are having or that Radia had."

"Is that why you joined a cult?" Roxie asks as simply as if she's enquiring if I want milk in my tea but I am stunned into a moment's silence.

"Yes," I say truthfully. "I think being famous had a lot to do with why I joined RemiX." I still can't say the word myself.

A silence falls between us as we set about racing around Mario Kart Stadium. We're just racing this time and Roxana's Yoshi is far ahead of me but I'm not feeling competitive, and indeed the topic of conversation has me more than a little distracted, but as more quiet minutes pass I start to feel something like relief. But it doesn't last long.

"Why don't we talk about it? Why don't *you* talk about it?" Roxie flashes me a quick look and I look at her long enough to notice her wide, curious eyes.

I swallow, audibly. "There's not much to talk about. It wasn't a happy time in my life."

"But it must have been at first. You must have thought it a good idea at one point. I mean why else would you have done it, signed up in the first place?"

"It was her," Mama says. We both turn to see her standing at the door.

"Pardon?"

"You joined it because of her. Michelle." She nods at me.

"It wasn't that simple." My shoulders sink and I try to focus on the game but even that feels wrong.

"Yes, it was. Even before you left LA, you were already cutting us off, cutting us out of your life. You hadn't been home in years."

"It wasn't just Michelle!" I raise my voice. "I have to accept responsibility for my own actions."

I may not have stuck it out at rehab, but I remember that much, and it makes sense to me. I'm not going to move past this if I just keep blaming Michelle or Gee.

"And aren't you?" Mama says, her voice louder too. "You've got a new job. You're living in a new city. You come and see your family every week. You've shrunk your life down to a small and safe space that I know doesn't always make you happy. Can't you forgive yourself like we've forgiven you, *habibi*?"

"I—" My mouth hangs open because I have no words, no explanation. At least not one I think my mother wants to hear. It's at this moment that Roxie's Yoshi completes the course in first place, and I throw down my Joycon in defeat, and not just because of the lost race.

"I don't say all this to upset you, Rami." Mom takes more steps into the room. "I say this so we can maybe talk a bit about what happened, because I think that would help. Roxie's right. We should talk about it more."

I pull in a breath and lean back in my chair. "Well, maybe we should wait for Radia to be here. As Roxie said, she'd hate to miss out." It's not like me to grab humour as a way out of a difficult conversation and it shows. Mom comes to sit beside me, and she and Roxana look at each other.

"I'm sorry for bringing it up," Roxie says with a small shrug. "Sometimes I misread a room or a moment. Blame it on my autism?"

"There's nothing to blame on anything. Your autism is never a problem," I say, and I shift forward so she can see my eyes on her, even if she doesn't want to hold eye contact. While her gaze only flickers on mine briefly, I cowardly realise that it's going to be a lot easier to look at my sister and say what I need to say rather than look at my mother, but regardless, I know she's listening. "I probably should be better at talking about what happened, and I hope one day I will be. But it still hurts. I'm still very, very embarrassed about what happened. I am still so..." The crack in my voice is tiny, but the way I stop speaking and press my lips together is much more noticeable. "I'm still so sad and angry at myself for not being here when Baba was sick and when he... died. I just find it hard to talk about."

"That makes sense." Roxie nods at me.

The warmth from Mama's hand on my arm surprises me. "We'll be here, ready whenever you are, *habibi*."

And I believe her. I don't deserve it, but I believe her. And I appreciate her, more than she may ever know.

Chapter Fourteen

Jake

Am I allowed to be pissed off Rami didn't wake me up to say goodbye?

No, I know I'm not. He did the most considerate thing when you factor how his alarm must have gone off less than four hours after we fell asleep. The great care he must have taken to not wake me up as he showered, dressed and left the room should have me smiling at his thoughtfulness, but instead I find myself questioning why he didn't want to say goodbye. Was it our kiss? Was it bad? Did he regret it? I try to replay the way he danced for me. I try to recall how long we kissed on that bench outside. I can easily remember how deliciously hard he was when my hand brushed against him... But what if that was a fluke? What if I'm not his type?

I admit it may be these spiralling thoughts that have me feeling pissed off more than Rami's actions. Perhaps that's why I spend the entire drive back to London aggressively chewing my way through a bag of Percy Pig sweets and tutting when Radio 1 plays songs I don't recognise. When I'm stuck in a traffic jam on the M25, I finally give in and call my sister on speakerphone so I can be distracted from my taunting thoughts.

"You didn't send me a photo!" she practically yells when she answers.

"Good morning to you too."

"Morning? It's nearly two o'clock in the afternoon. Must have been a good night."

My smile surprises me. "It was actually."

"So why no photo? Take one of him now and send it to me."

"Firstly, I'm driving. Secondly, Rami's not here. And finally, I didn't call you to talk about Rami. I obviously called you to talk about me. You should know this by now."

"Fine, what's up?"

"Nothing," I say in a quiet, lost voice. "Just hungover and grumpy, I guess."

"Oh, that's my favourite Jake to cheer up."

"Well, go on then. Don't keep me in suspenders…"

"Okay, well, this will make you smile. Marty and I are coming over! In three weeks actually. It's sort of for our anniversary. We found some cheap flights this morning and just booked them. Please tell me you'll be around."

"Where else would I be? Will you be staying with me?"

"If that's okay with you? It's been forever since we spent proper time together."

"We were all together at Christmas," I point out.

"But that was months ago," Jenna declares. "I used to have you all to myself all winter."

"Well, that's hardly my fault. You up and left for Dublin."

"And as soon as I did that you promptly moved to London where I'd been living for twenty years previously!"

"Let's just both say that timing is not our forte."

"Agreed. Lucky for you, we will be there when it counts. Because we'll also be over for your fortieth too. When will that be exactly?"

I groan and shove three Percy Pigs in my mouth so I don't have to reply. Jenna takes the hint but doesn't coddle me with it.

"You have to have a party, Jake. I didn't do anything big for my fortieth and I really regret it."

"What do you mean you didn't do anything big? We sat at home and watched *Mamma Mia!* while eating our bodyweight in cheese and crackers. Apart from having to pause after every song so you could have a cry over Marty, it was delightful."

"Ugh, don't remind me. That was suicidal watching a whole movie with ABBA songs while we weren't together."

"Proud of you for the suicide joke," I say wryly.

"Sorry, did that sting?"

"Not really," I say but feel the lump in my throat.

"So, what's the plan? I'm sure Derek and Harry have been on your case about it."

"And everyone else. There's practically a committee with membership badges."

"Oh, I'll have to send them a message and get myself included in the WhatsApp group."

"Please don't. They don't need any encouragement."

"Use it to your advantage. Tell me exactly what you want to do and I'll make sure they do it."

I want to do something that involves me spending no money whatsoever, because I don't have any money to spend. "I just want to keep it small and simple."

"Jake, do you have alcohol poisoning? Because you really don't sound like yourself at all."

"Parties are such a waste of money," I try again.

"Who even *are* you?"

I give up. To say any more would be to say too much. It doesn't matter anyway. I have the rest of the day free to finally do that spreadsheet I've been promising myself I'd make for months, no, wait, for years. I'll do what other people have done and I'll break down the total amount into smaller chunks and when I've paid one of them off I'll colour in a square on a grid. I'll use different colours so it all looks like a rainbow, very on-brand for me. When I've paid off a quarter of the debt, I'll celebrate with my favourite take-away and a mini bottle of champagne for one. When I've paid off half of it, it will be dinner out with one of my friends. And when I'm three-quarters of the way down, I'll go shopping and treat myself to that Mulberry man bag I've been eyeing up for the last few months. Of course, it will be dreadfully out of fashion by then, but that may mean it's discounted. And when I've paid off all my debt…

I stop the daydreaming then because it's gone from aspirational musing to outlandish fantasising. There is no way I'll ever be debt free. There's just too much. I don't earn enough. I will never earn enough or work long enough to pay it off.

"Jake?" Jenna says and I can tell from her tone it's not the first time she's said my name.

"Sorry, just driving," I say, even though I've not rolled more than fifty metres in the last ten minutes.

"Are you okay?"

"Yeah, of course." I happen to think I sound very convincing, but apparently Jenna does not.

"Did something happen with you and Rami?" Jenna asks.

"No, what... why would you think that?"

"You said he's not with you right now. And you sound kind of... distracted."

"Jesus, nothing happened," I say, and I don't know how my fingertips land on my lips but they spend far too long there tracing where Rami's mouth left all sorts of tingly feelings last night. "He just spends Sundays with his family up in Birmingham so he caught the train there early this morning."

How refreshing it feels to say a whole sentence that doesn't contain a lie. Of course, the context of me explaining it as if he's my boyfriend *is* a big fat lie.

"That's so sweet," Jenna says. "I can tell I'm going to like him a lot."

She probably would love him. What a shame they'll never meet.

"You need to make sure he's going to be there that weekend we come and stay," Jenna continues.

"Oh, shit," I say, and I realise what this means. She expects him to be there and to meet them, as my boyfriend. I quickly focus to cover up my curse at this realisation. "You know, I actually think he may be away for a work thing..."

"Are you serious? I would change the dates but I can't. It's the only weekend Marty can get off work for a good month or so."

"I'll have to check with him," I mumble now feeling all kinds of bad for all kinds of reasons.

"If he can change it tell him we'll be forever grateful and Marty will make his favourite meal for him and... actually, what is his favourite food?"

I freeze with a grimace on my face. Thank goodness this isn't a video call. I think back to what he ordered at our meal out the other week. A salad. That won't do. "I think he mostly likes whatever his mum cooks. Persian and Lebanese food."

It's an easy answer albeit possibly a tellingly vague response, but it does the trick.

"Ha, even Marty can't compete with a mother's home-cooked food."

"Indeed. Listen, I've got to go. Coming off the M25 shortly and I need to concentrate and all that jazz."

"Okay, Jakey. I'll give you a call in a few days, okay?"

"Sounds good. Big hugs to Marty O'Martin."

I hear Jenna call out this message to Marty and in the background, I hear his muffled reply.

"He says 'Love you, Sweet Cheeks.'" Jenna's smile is audible.

"Goodbye, you insufferable pair," I say, performing my role as the bitter third wheel far too well, as I have been pretty much since they got together.

After ending the call, I very briefly swipe around to see if I have any messages, any notifications, anything from Rami.

I don't. Nothing.

I sigh and focus my attention on the road ahead. I turn the radio volume back up but a second later when the song playing starts to hurt my ears, I begrudgingly switch it to Radio 2. Donna Summer is playing and I know every single word. I should be singing along. I should be smiling about how yesterday couldn't have gone better. The air was cleared with Lionel. Rami went above and beyond to convince everybody that he is mad about me. And we shared one of the sweetest, longest and weirdly most preciously innocent kisses of my life.

So why am I still so completely and utterly pissed off with him and with my life?

So pissed off I whisper "Fuck it" to myself and promise myself an hour's online shopping later plus my favourite take-away for dinner tonight, because that will make me feel a lot better than a stupid spreadsheet or budget that I'll never stick to.

Chapter Fifteen

Rami

It's Wednesday and my first day in the office this week. The last two days I was up in Northumberland meeting most of our North of England staff and getting three of our venues ready for a food festival happening this weekend that I fortunately don't need to be in attendance for.

Nerves simmer inside my stomach as I walk down the corridor to Jake's office. At her desk, Sharon looks up as I approach.

"Good morning," she says. "Good to see you, Rami."

"And you, Sharon," I say. Setting down the cardboard cup holder the café down the road gave me, I pull out her extra hot flat white and set it down on her desk. "Here you go."

"Oh, I have missed you. And not just for the free coffee. I've missed being greeted by a human who smiles."

"Oh dear. Has Jake had a hard few days?"

She nods. "I don't know what exactly has got his knickers in a twist but there's an absolute gut-tickling knot in his panties that's been making him all sorts of grumpy the last few days."

"Well, hopefully, the coffee will help," I say after clearing my throat.

"He's on his way now so let's hope it doesn't go cold." Sharon winks with me conspiratorially before I open the door to the office.

Once inside, I quickly see something that makes me feel even more on edge than I was a moment ago. The table I use as a desk is full, covered with piles of various sizes consisting of papers, magazines, unopened mail and even one stack of receipts. It's how the table looked on my first day. It's what the table would look like if I didn't work here. It's how Jake *wants* his office to look.

My shoulders sink as I take the scene in and then I set my laptop bag and the remaining two coffees on top of it on a chair. Despondency washes over me as I set about picking up piles of magazines – a mix of travel-zines and editions of *Elle Décor* and *Homes & Gardens* – and I combine them in a tall tower in one corner of the desk. Turning to then consider which stack of papers I could move on top of them, I am closer to the table than I realise and I end up knocking the tower of magazines over.

"Shit," I hiss and then drop to the ground to pick them up.

While I'm doing so, I decide to organise them a bit better, so I create stacks for each kind of magazine and then set about putting them in chronological order too. It's almost unstoppable, this urge to organise, and I spend only a passing moment considering how much more energy I have for organising someone else's belongings than I do my own. I flinch when I think of the mountain of boxes that contain my records at home. *Home.* It's not home. It's an apartment I bought so I had somewhere to sleep in London.

One day I'll make it home. One day I'll organise my records properly. One day I'll feel like I belong there. Or somewhere.

Halfway through my task I get distracted by a magazine that has a feature on Sydney, one of my favourite cities in the world. I always loved playing there and have fond memories of a New Year's Eve I DJed before I won my first Grammy and experienced a new level of fame. I played all the songs I wanted, free from any expectations or restrictions. It feels like a lifetime ago. Maybe I'll go back and visit one day.

I'm flicking through the magazine and reliving some good memories when Jake bursts in. At first, he doesn't see me and he takes a few steps into the space, meaning, when he does stop and see me, I'm on my knees, my backside resting on my heels. And Jake – or specifically Jake's crotch – is exactly at my eye level and close enough I can read the designer's name on his belt buckle.

"Morning, Jake," I say as I lift my eyes to look into his.

He blinks at me and I see a quick succession of expressions land on his face. First there's surprise, secondly, an amused, curious gaze, and finally, a cooler, sharper stare. But then that gets washed away when he promptly sneezes, loudly.

"What exactly are you doing?" he asks with a sniff.

I hold up the magazine and then point at the piles. "Organising."

"But... why?"

"I dropped them when I was trying to clear a bit of space and well, when I was picking them up I had the urge to organise. I'm a bit Type A in that respect."

"Type A?" Jake sniffs again. I wish I had a tissue to offer him.

"I guess that's a California-ism." I shrug and put the magazine on the right pile. "Type A personality. I like to be organised. Among other things."

With a quick shake of his head, Jake looks at the table. "I suppose it got a bit cluttered again."

"Yeah. It was almost like you wanted to tell me something," I say in a quiet voice.

Jake's glare snaps back onto me. "Like what?"

"Like how fed up you are of me sharing your office, which is fine, but I had thought... I had hoped we'd moved past that after Saturday."

As if to check whether we're being overheard, Jake looks quickly at the door which is all but closed. When he comes back to look at me, I see his shoulders sink. "Could you please get up... this is a bit... weird."

Jake moves to his desk as I stand. When I look across at him, he's blowing his nose while also picking up a piece of paper that apparently requires his full attention.

"I got you a coffee," I say as I bring it to him.

"Thanks," he mumbles without looking up.

"Jake, are you okay?"

He slams the letter down with a bang that makes us both jump.

"I'm fine," he says through a fixed jaw.

I pause to consider my next words. "That's a lie."

"Rami, I just have a lot of work to do and I woke up with a head full of hay fever and Sharon just told me I have a last-minute meeting with Bill and Simeon and I am neither prepared for nor delighted about any of the above."

I inhale, exhale. "How can I help?"

"By not asking me if I'm okay ten times before I've had my first sip of caffeine and popped an anti-histamine." Jake reaches for his coffee.

"It wasn't ten times," I point out gently. "And I was just wondering if you were feeling okay after Saturday. I mean, it didn't exactly end how I expected—"

"What do you mean?" he bites out, interrupting me.

It's my turn to glance at the door. "Well, I certainly didn't plan on kissing you," I say in a low voice.

Despite his hard jaw and lack of eye contact with me, Jake's cheeks turn pink. "That makes two of us."

"I don't want it to be awkward. If that was a mistake, I mean."

"If what was a mistake?"

"Me kissing you."

"I believe I kissed you just as much," Jake says with a slight shrug, as if it's not of any significance, and I suppose it isn't despite what's going on in my stomach at this moment.

"Okay, so we're okay after... that."

"We're fine," Jake says curtly. He starts rummaging in his top drawer and a moment later retrieves a box of tablets.

"And I had hoped we'd cleared the air on Saturday?" I continue, because this is important. "I thought sharing an office wouldn't be so... difficult now."

Jake swallows down two pills with his coffee before he replies, "It's still my space, you know. And I really do have a ton of work to do. And yes, I was in the middle of a bit of a long overdue clear-out yesterday that I didn't have time to finish so that's why the table was a mess which I suppose I should apologise for..." He drifts off, very noticeably not apologising.

"You know what?" I hold my hands up. "I think I'll just go work in the cafeteria or in a Starbucks somewhere."

"Well, there's no need to be so dramatic," Jake's tone is dry.

"*Me*, dramatic? You have got to be kidding me!" I move to grab my laptop and my coffee.

"Why didn't you text me?" The words rush out of Jake's mouth and fill the room.

"Pardon?" I ask, even though I heard loud and clear.

"You didn't message on Sunday, or Monday, or yesterday," he says in a much quieter voice, a voice that could possibly even be described as hurt.

"I didn't know I had to… Wait. You didn't message me either," I say, trying to keep my tone as calm as I can.

Jake considers this for a moment, his bottom lip disappearing into his mouth and being worked over by his teeth. "That's true, but I was driving home and you woke up earlier than me and… Look, it would have been nice if you had messaged. That's all. Saturday was… Saturday was fun."

I could be reaching when I say it looks like those words took something out of Jake, but then I also see how he still can't hold my gaze for more than a few flighty seconds and it has me very intrigued by what the hell is going on in his brain.

"It *was* fun," I agree. "And I'm sorry I didn't text. I didn't really have anything to say and I knew I was going to see you today and I wasn't… I wasn't sure that we were… you know, friends."

"Friends?" Jake's eyebrows arch high.

"Yes," I say and I feel like that cost me something too.

"I guess we are," he concedes. He gets up and walks towards the table. Grabbing hold of a stack of receipts and two piles of paperwork, he takes them back to his desk. "Is that enough space?"

I smile as I reply, "Yes, thank you."

We both sit and silence falls as we work on our computers. A few minutes later a new chat notification pops up on my screen.

"Looks like I'm in the same meeting as you today," I tell Jake.

"Oh God, I hope it's not bad news." Jake groans.

"Why would it be bad news?" I look up at him and he does indeed look worried, his brow furrowed and eyes wide. "It could be a new project or something good."

"Maybe," Jake says but he doesn't look reassured.

"How was everyone on Sunday?" I ask, now I have his attention. "The morning after?"

"Oh, ghastly. I mean, that was how I felt and how I looked. Everyone else still looked like Tom Ford, just this time in carefully pressed casual attire."

I laugh easily. I like how Jake can make me laugh far too much. "And your drive home?" I ask, realising I could have messaged to check this on Sunday, but surely that would have been over-stepping? Surely that would have been pointless contact Jake didn't need when he was hungover, tired and driving home after an intense day?

Was that why I didn't message him?

Or was it something else?

"Dull. Tons of traffic on the M25. I consumed two days' worth of calories in gelatine-based confectionery."

"A small price to pay for a successfully completed mission though, surely? Because it was a great success, wasn't it?"

Jake removes the plastic lid and stares into his coffee cup. "I suppose it was. Thank you again for that."

"My pleasure," I say, and I hope it's not too strange to Jake that it really was.

"And the good news is you don't need to put yourself out like that again. I'll wait a few weeks and then I'll tell Lionel and Luigi that we parted ways in a very mature, amicable fashion and that I am once again very happy to be single and ready to mingle with London's most illegible and possibly illiterate bachelors."

"Jake, it really wasn't a—"

A firm knock on the door interrupts me and we both turn to see Sharon standing there.

"Someone here to see you at Reception," she says after briefly taking in the stacks of magazines on the floor.

"Who, me?" Jake sits up straighter and reaches for the lip balm on his desk.

"No, both of you," Sharon's eyes narrow as they ping-pong between us.

"Both of us?" he asks as he applies said lip balm. It's the same as the one he was wearing on Saturday. The one that tastes of cherries.

"Says his name is Lionel and if you're free he'd like to take you both out for a coffee."

"Oh, fuck," says Jake. His eyes close as he sinks back in his chair only for them to spring open a beat later when he jumps forward in an almighty sneeze.

Chapter Sixteen

Jake

"Lionel!" I call out as I cross the marble-floored foyer. When he turns to look at me, I am struck yet again by how handsome and familiar he looks, but how I don't feel a warmth in my gut like I used to. Rather, it feels now like I'm just seeing an old friend, an old and very good-looking friend. Even if he is possibly the last person I want to see right now.

"Jake!" He walks towards me, arms open.

We embrace for a few seconds, and when I pull away, I curse out how well-rested he looks. I step back when I need to sneeze into my elbow, feeling my eyes water. I can only imagine how awful I look.

"Sorry," I say with a sniff. "Hay fever. Left my drugs at work yesterday."

"Oh, that's unfair, care bear," he says and rubs my upper arm.

"And I'm ever so sorry, Lionel, but I don't have time for a coffee right now."

"Oh, buttons, that's a shame," he says and he really does look disappointed. "Rami too?"

"Yes, he's also rather busy. We have a board meeting in an hour that we need to prepare for," I say, not adding how personally, my preparation will be all mental, in other words, lying under my desk in the foetal position while waiting for my drugs to kick in. "Besides, shouldn't you be on your honeymoon?"

"We leave on Saturday. Luigi had a launch he had to be in London for this week, and we both wanted to take a bit of time after the wedding to decompress, you know, journal about our feelings and reflect."

Had anybody else in my social circle uttered those words I would be bending in half laughing at them but because it's Lionel, I bite back my cackles.

"If I'm honest, I'm a bit restless," he continues. "Sitting at home while Luigi is out all day is getting a little boring. I probably shouldn't have taken the time off work, but then this morning I thought I'd come up and see where you work. I've been curious for so long, you know,"

I'm not surprised. Status Hotels is the kind of company Lionel and I both talked about wanting to work at for years.

"Well, I would offer you a tour but I really do have to get ready for this meeting," I say apologetically.

"Of course, of course! I shouldn't have shown up unannounced, but I was so delighted we cleared the air on Saturday, and my parents are simply in love with you and I just felt all these warm and fuzzy things about us being friends again."

My cold, stone heart beats a little faster hearing these words. And some of my frown disappears as I take in how happy Lionel looks.

"I'm happy we are friends again too," I say with a smile.

"So how about dinner? Are you and Rami free one night this week?" he asks, still beaming.

"What?" I sound as shocked as I feel at the prospect.

"Dinner, with Luigi and me? We'd love to see you both before we jet off to Bora Bora."

Bora fucking Bora. It makes complete sense that they're going to my dream honeymoon destination. I hope my scalding jealousy isn't obvious as I try my best to pull my lips out of the distasteful pout they want to jump into.

"You know, this week is a bit busy and…" I begin but then I see Lionel's face fall. A face I have made fall one too many times before. The instinct to undo his frown forces words out of my mouth, words I apparently have no control over. "But how about tomorrow?"

"Tomorrow's perfect." Lionel's broad smile is like sunshine, as it always is. "And Rami will be there?"

"Well, I'll have to check because he's also pretty busy—"

"Oh, I really hope so. We already have some of the photos from the wedding to show you. You should see some of the ones of him dancing, and DJing too, and there's also this one of him during the speeches when he's got his arm around the back of your chair and his eyes are on you and—"

"I'll go and ask him right this minute," I interject unable to hear another word about how photogenic and attractive and fucking perfect Rami is.

"And you'll text me to let me know what we can bring? Luigi should be all done by seven so we can be at your place around eight?"

"My place?"

"Oh, cherry tomatoes, is that not what you meant? I thought maybe we could come and see your place too. I bet you have it all set up beautifully. You always had the best Pinterest boards," Lionel says. "But if we're imposing..."

"My place is fine," I say through gritted teeth, and am not at all surprised when swallowing is a little cumbersome. Looks like I'll be spending this evening running around with my feather duster and hoover, which won't aggravate my allergies at all.

Fucking brilliant.

"Fabulous! I'm going to text my husband right now!" Lionel gives a little squeal that I choose to find adorable rather than letting it push me over the edge.

"I'll be in touch," I say. Giving Lionel's forearm a quick squeeze, we say goodbye and I hurriedly head to the lifts.

I'm relieved when nobody else joins me in the lift to the fifth floor so I am able to frown and tut and groan as much as I wish. Inside my brain, questions pinball at an alarming speed. Should I just not mention it to Rami? I could turn the dinner into an excuse to explain how Rami and I broke up? They would feel sorry for me and offer me lots of muscled manly hugs and encourage me to drink copious amounts of wine... and I would end the evening drunk and feeling like an even bigger piece of shit than I currently do. No, that won't work. It's possible if I do mention it to Rami that he will already have plans, so he won't be able to come. That way I'm not lying to anybody. That would certainly make me feel better, and then I could explain perhaps that Rami and I are having problems and that I don't want to talk about it. It would plant a seed that I could grow to eventually tell Lionel and Luigi that we've broken up. Yes, that seems like the safest way to proceed and get out of this mess. But what if Rami is free? What if Rami wants to come to dinner? What if Rami wants to pretend once again that we are... boyfriends?

What if Rami wants to kiss me again?

The doors of the lift pull open and I'm thankfully shaken out of this brief dream-like state where I remember how freshly sweet Rami had tasted and how perfectly innocent our kisses were. I've not kissed a man without it leading to more in years, decades possibly. I'd forgotten it was even possible. I'd certainly forgotten how lovely it could be.

But I will forget again, I decide as I march out of the lift and past banks of desks belonging to other employees, and towards my office. No, *our* office.

"Everything okay?" Sharon asks as I approach her desk. "You look like you're really thinking about something and that can't be good for your fairy brain."

"Isn't it time you made the tea?" I snap back.

Sharon tilts her head to one side. "I suppose I can do that, as long as you ignore the fact I'll be leaving work at three-thirty today. Kate got us tickets to the early evening showing of the new Marvel movie and I need to get there early to do our Venom make-up."

"You are the strangest pair of senior citizen lesbians." I narrow my eyes at her.

"And with today's outfit choice you confirm once again that you are a perpetual disappointment to the gay community," she bites back and I couldn't love her more for it.

"Ha! You can talk wearing that shirt." I lean closer after eyeing up her red and white plaid blouse. "And one sugar today, please. I need it. Stirred anti-clockwise, remember."

"Diva." She rolls her eyes at me.

"Lumberjack." I blow her a kiss as I open my office door and walk in.

Much to my agitation, Rami is back on the floor with those damn magazines, but at least he's not kneeling. I've only just recovered from having him on his knees in front of me.

"Look, I've organised your *BBC Travel* magazines. All in chronological order. Most recent on the top. Now just the *Homes & Gardens* to go..." He rises so he's up on his knees and again his face is far too level with a part of my anatomy I really don't want to be aware of right now.

"Rami, you really—" I begin but when I catch his eyes, those cursed shimmering puddles of ethereal silver, I stop and change direction completely. "What are you doing tomorrow evening?"

"Tomorrow? I... I don't have plans."

Shit.

I move to sit back at my desk so there's more distance between us. To my greater relief, Rami also stands up.

"Lionel wants us all to have dinner together. At my place."

Rami frowns. "Why aren't they on their honeymoon?"

"Oh, I don't know." I wave my hand around. "Because Luigi has to save the House of Gucci from the apocalypse or something. They leave on Saturday."

"Do you... Do *you* want us all to have dinner?" Rami leans back to sit on the table, facing me.

I try to contain my sigh but fail. "I would like to make the most of this new favour I find myself in with Lionel. I have missed his company and it would be good to get to know Luigi better now I don't want to poke his eyes out with a pair of sharpened chopsticks."

"So, you won't be making sushi, then?" Rami attempts a joke and it's hardly of quality but still I produce a courteous laugh.

"Listen, you don't have to come. I can easily make excuses for you. I'm sure you have better things to do."

"I'd love to come," Rami says and when the words land with me, I feel my stomach flip.

"You would?"

"Sure." Rami shrugs. "They're nice people. You can be nice, sometimes. And I'm very curious about your place now I know you have six months' worth of *Elle Décor* and *Homes & Gardens* magazines."

I search Rami's features for a few seconds, trying to find a slither of panic or a hint of reluctance about doing this whole fake boyfriend thing again, but I find nothing but relaxed features and a soft lift in the corners of his mouth. "But do we... We would... Do you want to do the whole pretending thing again?"

"I suppose we'd have to," he replies, still calm and composed.

"This would be a lot more intense," I say, noticing how the flip in my gut has now turned into churning but I can't discern if I'm anxious about the prospect of pretending Rami and I are together, or if it's panic at the possibility Rami will change his mind. Still, I give him one more chance to do just that. "We don't have a whole crowd of other people to disappear into. There would be questions. We would need to get some of our ducks and fucks in a row. We would have to... maybe... do stuff in front of Lionel and Luigi."

Rami pulls his head back. "Wait? What kind of stuff? Are they swingers?"

"Jesus, no. I mean, I don't know, but I assume not. Perfectly fine if they are, of course," I quickly add.

"Quite right." Rami nods. "No judgment here, just not sure I'm down for it myself. I'm a pretty monogamous kind of guy."

That really shouldn't have me feeling warm and light-headed, but it does. I flutter it away with my eyelashes.

"I just meant maybe some hand-holding, some innocent pecks on the forehead or something along those lines. And you'd have to show that you're comfortable in my place. You know? That you maybe know roughly where everything is. It's not big, so that should be easy enough."

"Jake," Rami pushes off the table and steps closer, "I am okay with it, if you are. I know your friendship with Lionel is important to you."

"It is," I admit. "But I promise, after their honeymoon, I'll tell them we're over."

Rami looks at the floor for a beat before a small smile stretches his mouth flat. "Sounds good."

"Okay, well, great. I appreciate it," I say pulling my phone out to text Lionel.

"But on one condition," Rami adds quickly pulling my eyes back to him.

"What's that?" I ask tentatively.

"You and I are going to find a home for your newly organised magazines today. And we'll also file all this other paperwork. Together. While we also get our, what did you say? Ducks and fucks in a row?"

I pout at him because I'm sure that's what he expects. "Fine, Mr Type A."

He nods and smiles at me, his mouth opening to say something but Sharon stops him by barging through the door.

"Here you go, bitches. Your tea. Made with zero love and a million scowls." Sharon puts our cups down in our respective workplaces. "Now get back to work, you lazy men-creatures."

As Sharon leaves the room, Rami and I smile at each other in a way that could be described as collusive. I try to drop my grin quickly as I turn my eyes back to my computer, but I know it sticks around for a long time.

Chapter Seventeen

Jake

I wasn't going to drink before my guests arrived. That was my intention all day. But then I made the mistake of emptying my mailbox and well, everything changed.

There's a reason I hardly ever check that bastard mailbox. It brings me nothing but bad news and today that comes in the form of three letters, all with panic-inducing red stamps and words like URGENT and NOT A CIRCULAR printed in capital letters on the front.

But I have a solution for these kinds of problems and I only have to have them feel hot and heavy in my hands for a few minutes as I carry them upstairs to my flat. Once inside, I dump my keys and bag and then take the offending envelopes with me to my bedroom. After opening up my wardrobe and pulling out the Louis Vuitton shoe box that once housed my favourite suede loafers, I think briefly about opening the letters before I stash them with their many, many friends inside. Perhaps it would do me some good to know what kind of amount I currently owe two of my credit cards and the store card I can't honestly remember opening.

A second later, I come to my senses. No, that would not help anything. That would almost certainly mean descending into a terrible mood that would make this evening even more challenging than it already has the potential to be. No, there is only one thing for it. These letters are to be tucked inside this box with the others, and one day, soon, perhaps, when I feel strong enough, I will deal with them all.

And that's how I solve that problem. That and by pouring myself a very sizeable glass of wine that gives me a boost of energy to whizz around my kitchen, joint dining-living area, bathroom and two bedrooms with a duster and a hoover in record time.

My second glass of wine which I consume while doing all the necessary meal prep is slightly less productive as I manage to cut my finger – twice – while slicing tofu and vegetables, and I also have a hot flush while searing the lamb.

My third glass of wine which I sip while getting ready – pairing my designer jeans that do wonders for my ass and ego with an ivory linen shirt I may or may not know Lionel used to like – is the most unnecessary and disastrous of all because upon swallowing the second to last mouthful I realise I shouldn't be drinking with the antihistamines that are keeping our imminent dinner from being snot flavoured.

"Bugger," I say as this particular penny drops. And then I tip my head back and swallow the remaining wine and ignore both this realisation and a sudden wave of light-headedness.

Still waiting on my guests to arrive, I spend a few minutes surveying my apartment and feeling something close to proud. It may be a rental, it may be small – one can walk from the end of the kitchen to the end of the living room in less than eight strides – and it may have a rather close-up view of the Thameslink railway line, but it's mine.

Admittedly, the rent stretches me every month and makes it very hard for me to think seriously about paying off some of my credit card debt, but at the grand old age of thirty-nine, I was determined to live alone and so my options were very limited. I could have gone for a place without a second bedroom, although the dimensions of this space truly do define "box room" but I wanted a guest room for Jenna and Marty to stay in when they visited. I also wanted friends to crash there whenever they wanted to just as I have done countless times at their places during the winters of my many years working summer seasons abroad.

In the first few months of living in London full-time, the room was often occupied. I entertained frequently and hosted many after-party gatherings once the bars or even clubs kicked out. But since the beginning of this year, it's tapered off, and more often than not I spend weekends here alone, interrupted only by gym visits and the occasional brunch or drinks with friends. But doing what I'm doing now – preparing to host a dinner, feeling proud to show off my tiny but well-decorated apartment – has become quite rare, which is a shame because it's what I love to do most.

Was it because I stopped inviting people over? Or was it because people stopped wanting to be here?

Either possibility is not one I want to dwell on, and so I am grateful when the doorbell rings. Grateful and nervous and once again feeling a little dizzy. Blasted antihistamines and Sauvignon Blanc.

Because the video monitor for the intercom is broken, I can't see who is outside as I buzz them in but I hope it's Rami. I've been trying not to, but I can't help but recall how tactile we both were at the wedding, so much so it helped convince one and all that we were an item. Furthermore, there was that kiss, the one after he danced for me, the one everybody saw.

And then there were the kisses outside in the garden. The ones nobody saw. Why have I been obsessing about these kisses ever since?

When I hear a knock on my door, I rush there. I pull in a breath before I open the door, suddenly anxious to see him. Possibly a little eager. Only because setting boundaries and getting us on the same page about how touchy-feely we can be is important to me. And not because I want to feel the warmth of his hand on mine. No, it's all about the performance we have to put on. That's *it*.

"Hello!" A chorus of voices greets me and before me stand Lionel and Luigi, the former holding a huge bunch of yellow roses, and the latter presenting me with a bottle of Château Neuf-du-Pape that I know has a triple-figure price tag. I'm suddenly very ashamed I bought wine from an eye-level shelf in Waitrose for this evening's dinner.

"Oh, hi, it's you," I stumble with my words.

"Oh, cream crackers with brie. We're too early, aren't we?" Lionel says.

"Not at all!"

"We can do a turn around the block, perhaps, if you're not ready? It's a perfectly fine evening," Luigi says and right on cue we all hear the wind howl down the corridor.

"No, no. No turn necessary." I stand to the side. "Please, come on in, I was just expecting Rami."

"Oh, he's not here yet?" Lionel says as he steps inside, Luigi following him.

I grind my molars for a second before I reply, "He's on his way."

"Oh, Jake, you have such a lovely cosy place!" Lionel declares as he walks into the kitchen. With anyone else I would absolutely interpret 'cosy' as 'tiny', but with Lionel I'm going to take it as the compliment it is.

"Thank you," I say, and I take the flowers and wine that are offered to me again. "It's small, it's a bit noisy with the trains, but it's home."

"You have two bedrooms," Luigi says leaning to look back down the corridor. "You lucky duck. We've been looking for a place with another bedroom but just can't find anything in Primrose Hill we can afford."

No shit, I think.

"You could look in other neighbourhoods?" I offer tentatively as I go about putting the flowers in a vase of water.

"That's what I said!" Lionel says as he walks over to the window at the far end of the living room.

"And be further away from Saskia and Bhavna? Never."

"Who are these people?" I ask as I retrieve some glasses and go to the fridge for the Crémant I have there.

Lionel replies while walking back to the small breakfast bar that acts like a divider between my kitchen and the living-dining area. "Saskia is his Pilates instructor, and Bhavna is the barista at his favourite coffee place who knows exactly how Luigi likes his caffe leche. Never mind that Saskia is trying to get pregnant and Bhavna is in his final year of his degree so likely to return to India in a few months..."

"He's promised me he's going to do his PhD here. Promised me," Lionel says accepting the glass I hand to him. "And you know Saskia. She'll likely be leading a reformer class on the day she gives birth..."

As I hand Lionel his glass, I take in the way his eyes are practically melting as he stares at Luigi. Surprise follows my immediate reaction of feeling suddenly very happy for my friend, that he's found someone he loves so dearly.

"To you both!" I say as I reach for my own glass, which is only half-full.

"Shouldn't we wait for Rami?" Lionel asks.

"Oh, he doesn't drink," I say, waving my hand in the air.

"Why is that?" Luigi asks, and he doesn't sound anything but genuinely curious.

I open my mouth to reply but then realise I don't have a reply. Thankfully, working in hospitality for the last twenty years has prepared me well for such moments and I smooth over my momentary panic with a broad smile.

"He's Muslim," I say, and it feels like a leap but possibly not a lie. I don't actually know why Rami doesn't drink, or if he is indeed Muslim, but I know it's an explanation that will pass well.

"He's Muslim and he's queer," Lionel says slowly as if he's not sure these words are allowed in the same sentence. "Wow."

It's my personal experience of living as a gay man in Morocco and also having very brief relationships with Muslim men over the years that has me prepared with an answer for this.

"It's much the same as being Christian and gay. Many of the ways the Quran has been interpreted to be anti-queer can easily be interpreted in a very different way with an alternative translation or just with an alternative approach. Many queer Muslims also refer to the saying that Allah made us all different, as we are, and that Allah makes no mistakes. Besides, Rami is Iranian, a country that was actually very liberal and forward-thinking until the Revolution, which is the reason his parents left."

Luigi coughs. "Goodness. We've already got to religion and politics. And we haven't even sat down to eat!"

"Yes, I'm sorry. I was being a bit nosey. But I just respect Rami a lot for having... principles."

Unsure if Lionel is referring to Rami's sobriety or to his possibly fake religious beliefs that I have bestowed on him, there's no time to clarify as the doorbell goes again.

"That will be Rami!" I say and place my glass down. After pushing the button on the intercom, I excuse myself and jog down to the front door, hoping Lionel and Luigi don't notice that I pull the kitchen door shut behind me. I'm standing at the open front door tapping my foot and chewing on my nails when I see Rami walk out of the lift and start walking towards me looking... looking annoyingly attractive.

Dressed as always in all black, this evening he's wearing jeans and a shirt that is unbuttoned at the neck, low enough for me to catch a glimpse of dark hairs lining his light brown skin. My stomach swirls in on itself and I know it has nothing to do with the alcohol or the antihistamines or the way I skipped lunch so I'd have a little extra cash to spend on food supplies for this dinner.

"Hey," he says, and I see he's carrying a box in his hands. "I'm sorry I'm a little later than I said I'd be but I went to Edgware Road after work. Really wanted to get us some some *ghorabieh*. They're Persian almond cookies. We could have them as a dessert, or maybe a nice after-dinner treat with coffee. Or you can just shove them in the bin, if you want. Whatever."

Is Rami nervous? Is that why his smile is a little wonky and his Adam's apple bobs as he swallows once, then twice?

There's no time to debate this because I only have seconds, not even minutes, so I grab Rami's arm that isn't carrying the box and I pull him inside my flat and a few steps down the corridor. Pushing open a door, I pull him in after me and then close the door. Rami takes the room in for a second – my neatly made bed, my wardrobe and the bedside tables – then turns back to me.

"You want a quickie before dinner?" he asks and I am only alarmed by his joke for a split second before my focus and resolve return.

"You don't drink because you're Muslim," I tell him.

"Pardon?"

"They just asked me why you don't drink and that's what I reached for."

"Okay, I mean it's technically true but not completely..."

"Well, tonight it's true in all senses. And Allah is completely cool about you being queer."

Rami's eyes widen and he rocks back on his heels. "Is he now? When did he call you to let you know that? Or did he send an email?"

"Rami! Don't be pedantic. This is serious!"

"Come on, Jake, it's not really serious. It's actually the opposite of serious. It's practically a Shakespearean comedy."

I narrow my eyes on him. "Do you still want to do this? Because if you don't, it's best you turn around and go right now." I don't intend to point at the door in such a dramatic fashion, but it comes far too easily.

Rami turns to set the box down on the chest of drawers behind him and then he uses his hands to hold my upper arms.

"Jake, I don't drink because I don't like drinking. I was raised Muslim but stopped practicing when I was in my teens. And yes, I'm queer and I happen to agree that *if* Allah exists, he would be very cool with that."

"Okay, so we're on the same page." I nod, feeling slightly calmer.

"We are," he says then he turns one of his wrists but keeps his hands on my arms. "Jeez, they're twenty minutes early. I thought I had plenty of time for us to do that ducks and fucks thing."

My body temperature changes and my eyes flick very quickly to the bed beside us. "Fucks thing?"

"Getting our ducks in a row. I wanted to check you'd be okay with hand-holding and stuff like that again. Like at the wedding," he explains and his hands slip down my arms, so slowly I'm aware of the glide of warmth down my skin.

I want to take a moment to think about the perfect reply. How can I tell him I'm more than okay with that? How can I tell him yes without sounding too eager? Do I say please? Do I thank him?

But there isn't time for this inner deliberating. Lionel and Luigi are waiting for us and we have already disappeared for many moments longer than it takes to walk my short corridor ten times.

"Yes, let's be like we were at the wedding," I say with a quick nod, ignoring how my mind drifts to a very specific part of the wedding – those kisses under the moonlight.

"Okay." Rami returns my nod and somehow one of his hands is now holding mine while his other arm reaches for the box again. "Let's go face the music."

"Actually, I'm relying on you to choose some music. I'm assuming you may know how to do that, Mr DJ?"

Rami holds still for a moment despite me reaching for the door handle and yanking him in that direction. I look back but see him smiling. "I can do that," he says and when I go to leave the bedroom, his hand still in mine, he follows.

Chapter Eighteen

Rami

If I'd thought about it a bit more, I shouldn't be surprised that Jake is an excellent host. While he's as sarcastic as they come and is unnecessarily scathing about anything remotely displeasing, he's also a senior director of an independent luxury hotel brand and has spent many years managing luxury resorts with all manner of clientele. I'd always known he was capable at his job – I've had to listen to enough conversations between him and his staff, suppliers, contractors and senior management – but I'd never have guessed how practical and capable he is, and how effortless he makes it look. Not to mention how much I know he's struggling with his hay fever, a fact I am reminded of when I see him subtly move the vase of roses I assume Lionel and Luigi gave him onto a side table in the living area, further away from the small round dining table we are seated at.

I also didn't know how good he would look doing it. There is something about the way he shimmies around his kitchen that is almost like dancing. There is something about the way he holds a conversation with warm eyes, all the while pouring drinks, like he couldn't be happier to have people in his home. There is something about how relaxed he looks describing the food he clearly spent a lot of time on, how he talks animatedly when he explains his wine choices, and how wide and bright his smiles become when he's talking about some of his interior décor choices. In short, a relaxed, social and proud Jake is a very, very attractive Jake.

Conversation flows nicely through dinner, dominated mostly by Luigi and Lionel talking about their wedding and upcoming honeymoon. At various moments, I steal a glance at Jake and expect to see a tense jaw, a strained smile or maybe even a frown as the happy couple effectively gush about how perfect their day was and how excited they are not only for their trip to Bora Bora but for the rest of their lives together. But I don't see it. If anything, Jake looks nothing but pleased for them, and indeed he often says as much without even a whiff of sarcasm.

"That was delicious, Jake," Luigi says as he dabs at the corner of his mouth with his napkin upon finishing his main course. "Please tell me you at least ordered in the couscous and side salad. Even they were delicious enough on their own, not even mentioning that exquisitely melt-in-my-mouth lamb."

"I would be the first to admit a cheat," Jake says after a sip of water. "But no, It was all my handiwork. And incredibly easy, I have to say. The tagine did all the hard work with the lamb, and I used a separate Dutch oven for your tofu." He nods at me. "And the couscous and salad are simple once you have the right herbs. I only know which are the right ones thanks to Samira, our head chef in one of the restaurants of the resort I worked in a few years back."

"Oh, yes, in Marrakech," Lionel says. "Where you went, after Crete."

There's a quick pause in the conversation as Jake and Lionel share a look but a beat later, a big grin fills Jake's features. "Yes, but I was only there a short summer season before I was asked to work for Status' HQ. Actually, I was already working for them – they owned the resort in Marrakech – but then they approached me for a position at headquarters and the rest is history."

"Would you have kept working abroad had they not offered you the UK Director role?" Lionel asks and I am suddenly very curious about Jake's answer.

"Possibly," his eyes turn down as if in consideration, "but I was also pretty ready to stop doing seasonal work and I'd been thinking about coming back to the UK."

"You were ready to settle down?" Luigi asks and none of us miss how his hand slides over to find Lionel's.

"God, no," Jake answers and then I see the moment when that doesn't quite add up considering he's sat next to his supposed boyfriend. I mimic Luigi's motion by reaching for Jake's hand and interlocking his fingers with mine.

"This man will never be ready to settle down completely," I say with a lightness in my voice. "Believe me, I'm trying."

Lionel looks around the room as he speaks. "For what it's worth, Jake, you seem very settled. You have a great place, a great job, and a good man."

Jake coughs and reaches for another mouthful of water. I notice then he's barely touched the red wine he poured for himself earlier. "I'm certainly very happy to not be doing seasonal work. You probably are too, Lionel?"

"Yes, indeedy-do. It was fun for a while, but it never really felt like real life, if that makes sense. It was like living in a bubble."

"Which was fun... sometimes," Jake adds, a faraway expression on his face, but his eyes firmly on Lionel.

"Yes." Lionel swallows, his gaze holding Jake's. "It was."

There's something about this exchange that makes me sit up straighter and shift my chair closer to Jake, and also, most bizarrely of all, bring our joined hands onto my thigh. Jake is just as surprised as I am as it snaps his attention my way.

"I for one am very glad that Jake is no longer doing seasonal work," I say.

"I bet you are." Luigi reaches for his glass, his lips already tinted purple from the red wine. He has not been holding back on drinking, I've noticed. "And I bet you're glad you got the job you did too, that brought you both together."

"I certainly am," I reply easily. Maybe too easily.

"And what were you doing before?" Luigi asks and I'm immediately cursing myself for not seeing that question coming. All the ease I was feeling a heartbeat ago evaporates.

"Oh, the same sort of thing. Events. But out in the US."

"In LA, no less," Jake adds.

"Oh, I love Los Angeles," Luigi says. "I'm there at least once a year for work, if not more. Where did you live?"

"A few places at first, but I eventually bought a place in Santa Monica," I say, hoping that not deliberately dishing out mistruths will help me navigate this.

"Wow. Business must have been treating you very well. Why come back here?"

"Well, I... I had a bad break-up and needed a fresh start." I turn to Jake expecting to see the same inquisitive gaze that both Lionel and Luigi are giving me but I am surprised by something else; a furrowed brow, a slightly parted mouth. He looks concerned for me, worried almost.

"I'd also been away from my family for a long time," I continue, again finding the truth easier to say even if it's not the whole truth. "I wanted to be closer to them."

"Lucky for me, eh?" Jake says. It's instinctive when I slide my hand out of his grip and hold his palm down on my leg. Again, I see Jake startle, his upper body freezing, but a beat later I feel a short squeeze and that makes it easier for me to smile and keep talking.

"I got the job with Jake in the worst way possible. I'm friends with the two owners, Bill and Simeon. But Jake has forgiven my nepotistic ways."

"Just about," Jake confirms, and I get another leg squeeze.

"And do you ever actually work together?" Lionel asks.

"Yes, we do," I answer. In fact, we just got told yesterday that we are going to be working together quite closely on a project."

"A high-profile wedding for a Premier League footballer. It's all a bit last minute and very hush-hush, of course. I'm responsible for getting the venue ready, and Rami then has to put on the show itself."

He squeezes my thigh again, a squeeze that has a slight slide to it, a slide upwards. It's my turn to freeze.

"Oh, you two... you two are just cuter than candy floss melting on my tongue." Lionel clasps his hands together and Luigi leans over to kiss the top of his husband's head.

"Well, we shouldn't be talking about work like that in front of you," Jake says removing his hand from my leg and pushing up to stand. I try to ignore how cool my leg feels now his hand is gone. "Let's clear the plates and maybe have another drink before I serve dessert?"

We all agree and together clear the table in no time at all. After stacking his dishwasher, Jake again tops up his guests' glasses without anyone noticing, and we return to the table after Luigi and Lionel take turns going to the toilet. I excuse myself to also go to the bathroom, but I stop in the doorway when I hear Lionel ask a very innocent and perfectly normal question.

"Where does Rami live, Jake? Is it far from you?"

"Err, well, not—" Jake begins but I spin on my heel and turn around, interrupting.

"I'm in Hoxton. So, a bit of a trek but not too bad," I say.

Jake's eyes widen as they meet mine but they shrink after I smile at him.

"Oh, yes, that is a bit of a distance. But no doubt you'll probably be living together soon," Lionel says and there is nothing leading or overbearing in his tone but I can tell Jake feels the same as me; completely out of my depth. Silence falls when we don't reply.

"Oh, bananas! Did I overstep? I should keep my mouth shut, shouldn't I?"

"No, no." Jake leans over the table towards his friend. "It's not that, it's more—"

"I've asked him," I say, stepping further into the room. "I'd move in with him tomorrow, but Jake wants to take it slow. He's right too. It's early days and no matter what I feel about him, we need to take it slow and enjoy dating first."

Jake's hand is still extended across the table towards Lionel but his whole body turns towards me.

"Yes, that's what I want," he says in a quiet, airy voice.

"Now, if you'll excuse me." I turn again and leave.

"Oh, Jake. He's so smitten with you." I hear Lionel say before I open the door to... another bedroom. A very small bedroom where virtually the whole space is taken up by a double bed, but still, it's not a bathroom. I open the door opposite and find what I'm looking for. After doing what I need to, I go to the sink and wash my hands. While I'm lathering the soap in my hands, I glance up at my reflection in the mirror and my smile takes me by surprise. It's not that I thought I'd look miserable – I mean, I'm having a nice evening with nice people and even Jake is on his best behaviour – but the creases around my eyes and the sheen in them indicates I'm something I haven't seen much of recently. Happy. I'm happy.

After drying my hands, I start walking back towards the kitchen-living area but stop before I walk through the doorway when I hear what Lionel is saying.

"It must have been a terrible break-up to make him leave America. Do you know much about him, his ex?"

"I know that *he* was a *she*," Jake says with emphasis on both pronouns. Suddenly I feel my smile waver.

"Really?" Lionel says with a small gasp.

"Oh, well, we've all been there," Luigi slurs.

"Speak for yourself, Jake and I are both gold-star gays over here," Lionel says with a chuckle.

"Ha! Well, many of us make this mistake, it just sounds like Rami was making his for quite some time," Luigi says with what is probably a laugh but sounds more like whooping cough.

"No, not a mistake. He's pansexual," Jake says and it's so unusual to hear him speak in such a neutral tone that I almost can't believe it's him.

Silence fills the room.

"And how do you feel about that?" Luigi asks eventually.

"Luigi!" Lionel is quick to admonish his husband and that earns him the points that his spouse just lost.

"I feel nothing about it," Jake says, his tone now almost cold. "Are you implying that I should be concerned?"

"I'm just saying that—" Luigi begins.

"I don't think you should." I hear Lionel say and it's the first time his voice has sounded anything other than soft and sweet.

"But, *mi amore—*"

"No, Luigi. We have both been far too nosey. And what you're implying sounds a little... offensive."

"It sounds very pan-phobic, or biphobic. Whatever the right terminology is," Jake says, and I can imagine his hands waving around his face like they always do. "That's my boyfriend you're talking about."

My chest shouldn't stretch out. But it does. My heart shouldn't beat a little faster. But it does. My smile shouldn't land back on my face, even bigger than before. But it does.

"I didn't mean to insult anyone. You know I like Rami, a lot. I was just curious—" I almost feel sorry for Luigi trying again.

"Curiosity killed the cat, darling," Lionel says, and I can imagine his kind, dark eyes levelling on Luigi's.

"Let me go and prepare dessert." Jake claps his hands. "And I think we need to open another bottle of wine. I'll get right onto that."

I wait until I see him in the kitchen, pulling out dishes from the fridge, before I walk in. As I approach him, I feel a nervous energy charge through my body, making me feel a strange mix of both tense and loose. It's like an electro-magnetic current and it takes me closer and closer to Jake.

"Oh, there you are! I thought you'd fallen in the loo or something." He turns to look at me and that flop of hair at the front falls down the centre of his forehead. I step towards him and lift my hand to brush it away. His bottom lip drops and I take it as an invitation to press my mouth against his in a long but chaste kiss. It's like a tempered version of the kiss I gave him after dancing to *P.Y.T.* Our mouths stay closed, we don't move our heads, but we're connected. We're joined together.

"Been wanting to do that all evening," I say in a low voice as I pull away, not that it would matter if Luigi and Lionel hear. Maybe I should have said it louder so that they can, but I didn't say it for them. I said it for Jake. And myself, because on an evening when a lot of lies are being told, it feels good to tell the truth for once.

Chapter Nineteen

Jake

Lionel is drunk. And Luigi is absolutely wasted.

There was something about the small confrontation we had about Rami's sexuality that made the latter turn to alcohol and Lionel is too polite to let his husband drink alone. They have polished off the third bottle of wine I've opened this evening and considering I've barely had a glass and a half since I opened the first, that means they've each polished off more than one each.

If Rami were drinking it would be easy to blame what happened earlier in the kitchen on him also being intoxicated, but I can't. He's as sober as ever, and thanks to slowing down my intake, I also feel clear-headed enough to be completely over-thinking not only why he kissed me, but why he said what he said.

He'd been wanting to kiss me all evening? Does that mean he's been thinking about our kiss on the bench in the same way I've been reliving it? Does he want to kiss me again? Does Rami want to do *more* with me?

I barely taste my dessert as I ponder on this while Rami and Lionel talk about music – specifically soul artists from the 1970s and 1980s that both are impressively enthusiastic about – and Luigi is in the bathroom. In fact, he's been gone quite some time. Long enough for me to excuse myself and go check on him. Lionel and Rami barely break their conversation as I get up and slip out of the room and down the corridor.

I knock on the door but hear nothing.

"Luigi," I call out. "Are you okay?"

I hear a noise that could be him mumbling words, or it could be the sink gargling. But my sink doesn't gargle.

"Luigi, can you let me in?"

More gargling comes and eventually the toilet flushes. A few thuds follow and then I hear a bang. There follow some Italian words which I would put money on being curses, and finally a loud thwack against the door.

"Too drunk to open it, sorry old boy," Luigi slurs. "Fetch my darling husband, would you?"

Wide-eyed and possibly a little delighted that this suave Italian man I once wanted to cause grievous bodily harm to has come undone in my bathroom, I rush to get Lionel.

"Sorry to interrupt, but I think Luigi has passed out in the bathroom. He's a little... drunk."

"Oh, son of a bourbon biscuit. I knew I should have made him stop three glasses ago." Lionel pushes up to stand but then he immediately plonks back down on his chair. "Oh fiddlesticks, I think I'm rather tipsy too."

Rami stands up with complete success and looks at me. "Is he locked in there?"

"I believe so," I say, still trying not to smile.

"Grab a blunt knife—" Rami begins.

"A blunt knife? In my kitchen? How very dare you!" I clutch imaginary pearls at my neck.

"I mean a knife that isn't going to sever a digit if I slip while using it to open the bathroom door," Rami explains with a roll of his eyes.

"You mean like a butter knife?"

"Yes, like that."

I retrieve one from my cutlery drawer and then follow Rami to the bathroom. He starts to knock on the door, a little too gently in my opinion.

"Luigi, can you hear me?"

Nothing.

"Luigi, it's Rami and Jake—"

"Jesus, who else is it going to be? Ronald Fucking McDonald?" I say to the ceiling, arms crossed.

"We're going to open the door and come in to check on you now," Rami says after fixing a hard stare on me. He holds out his hand for my butter knife.

I hand it over and watch him slide the end into the rivet in the outside of the lock that is currently showing red for locked. It turns to green easily and a moment later, Rami is pushing down on the handle. When he goes to push it open, it barely moves.

"He must be slumped against the door," Rami mutters

"No shit, Sherlock," I say.

"You know, you are *extra* unhelpful in a crisis."

"This isn't a crisis," I scoff. "I could write you a list of one hundred dramas bigger than this that I have navigated not only myself but also hundreds of staff through in my time."

"I'm not sure you should be so proud of that." Rami cocks an eyebrow then goes back to applying more pressure on the door, eventually sliding his arm in the crack and bending down to presumably try and find Luigi's body.

"Let me go and get Lionel to help. It may be less of a shock to have his hand groping Luigi than yours." I turn and walk back into the kitchen only to see Lionel's chair is now empty. A quick glance around the room finds him curled up on my sofa, his hands in a prayer arrangement under his sleeping head, like the beautiful Disney princess he is.

"Oh, Lionel," I say, and I unfold the blanket I have at the end of the sofa and lay it over him.

Returning to Rami, I see he has managed to now get a leg and half his body through the door.

"Lionel's passed out on the sofa," I tell him.

"That's a lot more thoughtful than where his husband decided to conk out. I can see him now and he's literally unconscious. I think it wouldn't matter if we pushed a bit harder; I can see that his head is safe."

"Very considerate of you," I say facetiously.

"I'm a considerate kind of guy," Rami replies. "Who also needs to pee."

"That makes more sense."

Rami tuts. "Jake, are you literally giving me shade right now after I've sat through another fake date with you and I'm helping you remove a six-foot chunk

181

of designer-clad Italian man from your bathroom floor so we can both empty our bladders before they burst?"

My top lip curls up in one corner. "Fine, you're being very helpful. Thank you," I say tersely.

"Now, push with me after three and I should be able to slip in. One, two, three."

In a few seconds Rami is inside and the door closes again. I hear a long string of muffled noises – thuds, bangs, grunts – and then the door opens, and somehow Rami is standing there with Luigi over one of his shoulders.

"Out the way!" he barks at me and moves forward, a strained expression on his face, which I suppose is permissible considering he's carrying more than his own body weight on his shoulder. Before I can tell him otherwise, Rami walks to the spare room opposite and dumps Luigi's body on the bed. He then sets about taking his shoes off, his chest rising and falling from exertion. I watch him for a moment, taking in the sharp lines of his nose and jawline, and I see how perfectly scattered the shards of silver-grey are in his hair and how carefully, closely cropped it is. Then I find my eyes drifting to where his fingers are at work and I notice how long and thin his hands are, like I imagine pianists' hands to be, and I suddenly have an urge to know what their pronounced knuckles would feel like, taste like, in my mouth.

Oh, shit. Watching Rami take care of Luigi is making me hard. Very hard.

I turn away to hide any possible evidence of this. "Will go find another blanket," I mumble.

"He won't know the difference," Rami calls back. "He's completely out of it."

While I wait for certain... feelings to subside I find two mixing bowls in the kitchen and place one beside Lionel's head on the floor next to the sofa, before returning to the spare bedroom and placing the second bowl on the bed close to Luigi's face which is now slack and snoring, his mouth open and his nose pointed high in the air.

"He's not a very pretty sleeper, is he?"

"Jake, you're being a bitch about someone when he's comatose. Even that is a new low for you," Rami says with a light chuckle but when I look at his face, his jaw is tense and his lips are fixed in a stern straight line as he places Luigi's shoes on the ground.

I should have asked him to say something like that a few minutes ago because it feels like a bucket of ice-cold water being thrown over me. Clearly, he no longer feels whatever it was that prompted the kiss and I was naïve to think otherwise.

"Come on," Rami says. "Let's go clean up."

He's gone before I can reply and I don't know why I do it but I stick my tongue out at his back as I follow him to the kitchen. God, I can't believe I'll be forty by the end of the year.

"You don't have to help," I say, glancing at the clock on my oven. 10:45. "It's getting late. You should go."

"I'm not leaving you with all this washing up. I'd never hear the end of it tomorrow and probably all week." Rami is already filling the sink with hot water and squeezing my bottle of washing-up liquid.

I snatch at a tea towel lying on the side. "Is that all you think I'm good for? Moaning and bitching?"

Rami's head turns to me slowly, his silver eyes sparkling a little in the kitchen's lights. "I also think you're good at making a tagine. And kissing. You're good at that."

I would have more breath in my body if somebody karate-kicked me in the chest. It takes me so long to gather myself and formulate a thought that Rami has already washed up two dishes and is about to start work on the tagine.

"Stop!" I say, a little loudly but apparently not loud enough to wake Lionel.

When Rami drops the tagine in the suds, pulls his hands out and shakes the bubbles off his hands, I take a long, luxurious look at his forearms, enjoying the way his fine black hairs caress muscular flesh and bone.

"Problem, Forester?"

Noticing his hands aren't quite dry yet, I decide to take full advantage. I step close enough so my body is pressed against the side of his, the front of my thigh against the side of his leg.

"I never know if I want to slap you or kiss you, so I'm going to do a little research," I say.

"If you slap me, HR will hear—" Rami begins but I don't let him finish. I lean in and place my lips on his, much in the same way he did to me earlier, but this kiss lasts a lot longer, and in no time at all, our mouths are open and our tongues begin to dance. At some point, Rami turns so we're chest to chest but I don't notice the warm wet patches where his hands are on my back until long seconds, maybe minutes have passed. When I do, I pull back a little, our noses still touching.

"You got me wet," I say.

"Are you complaining? Again?" He presses his forehead against mine and my grip on his shirt tightens so I can keep him close.

"I never said getting me wet was a problem," I say in a faint voice.

"So, you're not going to slap me?"

"Not yet," I say and then I dive in to take more of his mouth.

A few minutes later and it's Rami's turn to pull away.

"We should finish washing up," he says but he then leans in and pecks my lips once, twice more.

"Wow, now I don't believe you think I'm a good kisser if you'd rather put your hands in dirty dishwater than keep kissing me."

"I don't want you to wake up to it tomorrow."

"Fine," I agree because I would quite like that too, even if I would much rather see if our kissing could go a little further.

It should feel strange when we complete the rest of the dishes in near silence, but it doesn't. When we're done, I blink a few times as I watch Rami start cleaning the sink, but then I snap out of it and put a tablet in the dishwasher. As I turn back, I see Rami wiping down all the countertops before going to the table to give that a once-over. Watching him, I start to wonder if I have a new cleaning kink because there really is something about him wiping down surfaces that is doing something to me.

Or maybe it's just Rami, because suddenly I'm a balloon of fizzy, energetic air. I lean my hand on the countertop above the dishwasher as if that will ground me because I almost feel capable of floating away. My head is light and spacey, my breaths are short and sharp, and my groin is once again getting increasingly warm and heavy and full… Oh, God.

I am incredibly horny and I really need to do something about it.

"You should go," I say.

Rami looks up, his eyes soft and light, but his brows heavy.

"Yeah, I probably should. Are you going to be okay looking after these two in the morning?"

"They should be so lucky." I huff, hoping it covers up my instant disappointment that he also wants to leave, even though that is what I need in order to sort out my current... predicament. "I'll show them where the teabags and paracetamol are and that's about it."

"I'll bring you a coffee in the morning. Or would you prefer lemon and ginger tea again? For your hay fever?" he asks as he rinses out the cloth in his hand and then squeezes the water out. I swear if he hangs it up on the special hook I installed just for that purpose I may actually come in my underwear. When I see his hand move to do just that, I look away at the last second.

"The lemon and ginger would be lovely," I reply, and this reminder of something incredibly kind and considerate that he did for me this morning, on top of the last few hours of being kind and considerate, has my thoughts spinning to a fever pitch. When I then bring my fingertips to my lips and trace where his mouth was and how firm and silky soft and needy his tongue was, I think I am about to self-combust.

"Rami, what the fuck is going on?" I demand, placing my hands on my hips.

"Oh, is that not where your dish cloth goes?" Rami looks at the hanging cloth. "It seemed like the perfect hook for it."

I groan. "No, not the dish cloth, although yes, that is its rightful place. But what about us? What the fuck are we doing?"

"We were cleaning up, and I thought we were about to say goodbye," Rami says neutrally but I swear I can see the corner of his lips twitch with what could be mirth.

"But the kissing... tonight and at the wedding. The kissing when nobody else is in the room—"

"Technically, Lionel is in the same room. He's just unconscious."

"Rami," I say in two short staccato sounds. "Do you fancy me?"

"Well, if that wasn't clear from the kissing—"

"It's not clear. At all." My tone is desperate.

"Yes, I fancy you, Jake."

A rush of something threatens to sweep me away. Joy? Delight? Excitement? Anticipation? Or maybe it's panic. Because now what am I supposed to do with this information?

"You do fancy me?"

"Yes, but I don't expect anything to happen."

"You don't?"

"No," Rami says, and at first his smile seems kind and sweet but then I see, and hear, the sadness in it. "I know you don't really fancy me."

In a split second I can almost taste the regret I'll feel if I do what I'm thinking of doing, but then I push it aside and do it anyway.

"Can I touch you, Rami?" I ask my voice more serious than I've ever heard it.

"Yes, Jake," Rami says, his tone just as low.

Grabbing Rami's hand, I place it on my crotch.

"God, no, Mr Events. I don't fancy you. Not. At. All."

Rami's eyes fall to where his hand is and mine join them a second later.

"Jake, I—" His voice cracks.

I lift his hand off me and hold it.

"I'm sorry. That was inappropriate," I mumble.

"I really didn't mind," Rami says and there it is again, a little mischief in the way his mouth twitches.

"I'm just very confused about whatever is happening between us so I thought I'd at least make it clear what I was... feeling."

"You made it crystal clear. Are crystals harder than diamonds?" Rami asks with a very definite and cheeky grin.

I drop his hand. "For Christ's sake. Why would you choose this moment to suddenly find your funny bone?"

My fingers are barely at my side when Rami finds both my hands with his. He brings our joined hands together in front of us. "I'm sorry. I'm just trying to make light of the situation. As I said, I find you physically attractive, Jake. And when you behave, I quite like you too. But I know we're colleagues, and I know this whole fake boyfriends thing has an expiry date..."

I pull one of my hands free to pinch the bridge of my nose although it does nothing to relieve the headache that has just started stabbing me behind my eyes.

"And I don't want this," Rami says, and he brings his hand up to the side of my face, cupping my cheek. "I don't want you getting stressed out."

I am stressed out. I'm stressed out because I thought talking about this would be a good idea. I thought it would help clarify what's going on with us but in reality, it just made things more confusing. Now I know the physical attraction is mutual, I can't ignore it. Now that I am faced with the truth I feel even worse. And impossibly, twice as horny.

"Rami, do you want to stay over as well?" I ask tentatively.

Rami pulls his head back, tips his chin up a little as his silver eyes stare into me. "Now why would I do that? Luigi is crashed out in your spare room. I noticed earlier you don't have a bathtub. I could hardly sleep in the shower."

"That's not what I was thinking..." I say coyly.

"Oh, you're right. You do have a sofa, although that also seems to be occupied."

"I have a bed!" I blurt out. "I have a massive bed with an award-winning gel-foam mattress and the finest Egyptian cotton sheets that money can buy."

"Yes, I noticed those earlier during our fake quickie," he says and I can almost smell his obnoxiousness.

"Rami, I'm not going to beg." I detach my fingers and fold my arms across my chest.

"Beg me for what?" Rami steps closer, so close I can smell his soft spiced scent and feel the warmth of his breath on my lips.

"I'm not going to beg you to stay," I say, my gaze flitting between his eyes and his mouth.

"That's a shame," Rami says lifting his hand to push back the hair that always falls on my forehead. "I think I'd like to see you beg."

"Fuck you," I say before I pounce on him.

Chapter Twenty

Rami

You can be friends with someone and do this, right? It's totally normal to feel like you need to kiss your friend more than you need to take a breath. And yet, oxygen doesn't come easily or quickly enough after a few minutes of my tongue hungrily doing battle with Jake's. I pull away and slide my mouth to his neck, my lips brushing against the rough stubble on his jaw on their way down. As I kiss and suck and nibble on the soft skin under his chin, I take in more air waiting for the increased oxygen levels to dilute some of the desire I feel. But it doesn't happen, not when Jake has his hands on my backside and is practically purring, the noise vibrating against my teeth on his neck.

"Jake, stop me at any time," I tell him. I need him to know it's okay to stop me. In fact, part of me will be grateful. Just not a part of me that's big enough to stand up and do it alone.

"Fuck it," Jake whispers and I am not even sure if he's talking to me. "I don't know why, but I want you too much to stop this."

His words are like lighter fluid dousing the flames already in me and making them fire up tall and blisteringly hot. It makes sense that I'm feeling so turned on, because there hasn't been anyone since Michelle, and our final years were not like this. The desire was diluted and rare, tainted by everything else happening around us. For nearly two years since I left the States, all I've had to satiate myself is my hand and that got boring fast. Relieving myself was just that – scratching an itch, quickly and efficiently – but there is nothing perfunctory about the way Jake's fingers are clawing at my back as if his nails want to cut through the black cotton of my shirt. There is nothing boring about the way he just nipped at my earlobe before sucking it into his mouth. Wanting Jake and discovering his body for the first time – his narrow waist, his tight butt cheeks and the firm thigh that is now between my legs – it's not surprising that the desire is so fiery hot. It's new and exciting and such a long, long time coming.

That's why I'm so incredibly turned on. That's why I'm going to ignore the warning signs telling me this could be a bad idea. That's why I'll deal with the consequences another time.

But right now, I'm going to take Jake's hand and...

"Ugh, traffic bollards, the room is spinning!" Lionel's voice calls out.

"Shit," Jake hisses as he rests his head on my shoulder.

"Indeed," I agree as I take a half step back and use a hand to quickly rearrange my trousers.

"It's okay, Lionel," Jake says as he rushes to his friend. "I'm here. Put your foot on the floor. There you go. That should help ground you."

"Did I fall asleep? Where's Lulu?"

"Lulu, I mean, Luigi is asleep in the guest room," I say, coming to stand behind Jake who is kneeling beside the sofa. "Would you like to join him?"

"I don't think I can move." Lionel flops his forearm over his eyes. "I think I drank too much."

"It's a fine hypothesis." Jake nods as he and I share a smile.

"I'll get you a glass of water," I say and move to the kitchen to do that. When I bring it back, Jake is holding Lionel's hand and stroking his forehead. I'm gripped with momentary panic. No, more than that, it's fear. Fear that Jake still has some of those feelings for his friend that he almost certainly had only a few weeks ago.

"I think he's gone back to sleep," Jake says when I'm behind him again.

"I'll put this here by the bowl," I say, placing the glass on the floor.

Jake tucks the blanket up a bit higher on Lionel's body and then pushes up to stand. He turns so we're facing one another, and I'm about to say something, make an excuse and suggest I leave, but I see his eyes rake down my body and up again. So I wait.

"Where were we?" Jake asks with a smirk.

I cough. "I was about to take you to your bedroom, undress you and do unspeakable things to you."

He cocks one of his over-used eyebrows. "Unspeakable, hey? That's a shame. I quite like a bit of dirty talk."

I echo his brow pop back at him as I hold out my hand. "Duly noted. So, shall we?"

As he takes my hand, Jake's confident expression breaks and he puffs out a couple of sigh-filled giggles. "I can't believe we're doing this. You know it's a terrible idea."

"It's like you said, I want you too much to stop it. I want you, Forester. Get in your bedroom, right now," I say in my sternest voice and his reaction is the greatest reward.

Jake steps closer so our chests touch and his chin tilts up a little. "Oh, fuck, yes. I love it when you call me by my surname."

With his neck more exposed to me, I step in and run my tongue up its arch. His body shifts as if he just lost his balance but then a second later he places his hands on my hips and pushes me away. As I follow him down the corridor I watch him slide his shirt off his body, revealing a map of lithe back muscles that ripple a little as he walks. And is he shaking his hips more than usual? Is he strutting like that for me? I put a little more effort into my last strides and just as he walks through his bedroom door, flicking the light switch on, I grab his waist and lift him up. Twisting him as I throw him on the bed, he lands looking up at me with wide, astonished eyes.

"What the—" He stops when he sees me go to pick up his foot and I start taking his sock off. I do the same with the other, resting his foot on my groin, close enough that his toes can feel how hard I am for him.

"Jesus," he says and his shoulders relax. I take in the plains and angles of his torso and smile at the dusting of light brown hairs curling on his pecs and in a strip down the middle of his abs. His body is toned and sculpted in a different way to mine. His muscle tone clearly comes from hard work, hours upon hours in the gym, while mine is naturally lean and defined, more like the runner I am now, and the yogi I used to be. I've never liked the gym – too busy, too competitive – but I have always liked the peace that comes from running. It's the closest thing to meditation after meditation itself.

I'm grateful for meditation now as I feel completely present in this moment when I lean forward and bring my hand to the fly on Jake's jeans. After lightly caressing the bulge that presses up against the material, I pop open the top button. Pausing before I move to the zip, I look up and see Jake watching me intently. I kiss him roughly because that's what his open mouth and glazed eyes demand, but our heady, hungry kiss leads me to fumble as I try to pull the zip down and fail. Without taking his mouth off mine, Jake moves his hand to help me out, relieving me of the duty. He then lifts his hips up and slides his jeans down his legs before kicking them onto the floor.

"You have such a good body, Jake," I say. "You're beautiful."

He promptly shuts both his mouth and his eyes, turning his head away from me. Had I known complimenting him would make him fall silent so easily I would have done it a lot more over the last few weeks, but still I savour watching him blush and squirm under the praise.

"I mean it, Forester. You are fucking sexy."

"You just swore." He blinks up at me, one of his hands scratching through the scruff on my cheeks and chin. "You never swear."

"I swear when it matters. When I really want to make a point. Or when I need to tell someone to fuck off."

"Understood." Jake nods and then his eyes fall down my body. "You have too many clothes on."

He's right so I start removing them and Jake's eyes darken as he watches. First, I get rid of my socks, then I loosen my watch and place it on the chest of drawers behind me. After pulling my shirt off, I look down and see Jake's gaze dance over my torso. He sits up straighter and reaches out his hand to graze his fingers over my chest and down one side of my abs. I feel and watch my muscles tense in response.

"You don't look so bad yourself, Mr Events," Jake says in a low voice and he leans forward to place a kiss on the line where my ribs end.

Suddenly a little nervous to reveal more of my body to someone else – it has been years, after all – I bring my fingers slowly to the waistband of my trousers as

Jake continues leaving the softest kisses all over my chest and stomach. I'm surprised therefore when I feel his hands find mine.

"No, let me," he says and looking up at me, holding my eyes the whole time, he undoes my fly and slides my trousers down. I kick them off my feet and then look down to see Jake staring at my boxers.

"Baby pink? And silk? That is a big surprise."

I try to contain my embrarrased giggle, but fail. "I like the way they feel."

"It's not the silk part that I'm amused by." Jake's hands come to rest on the side of my hips. "It's the pink part. You literally dress like a long-lost member of the Addams Family but underneath you're a Care Bear, apparently."

I point a finger down at him. "Firstly, Gomez Addams is a fashion icon. And secondly, nothing wrong with the Care Bears. That's my childhood right there."

Jake shrugs. "Same here. No wonder our families weren't surprised we turned out queer."

Inwardly I baulk at this comment, but it's easy to move past it when I feel a wet warm pressure on my cock. I look down and see Jake tonguing me through the silk of my boxers, leaving obscene but erotic wet marks up and down the outline of my penis. If I wasn't already too far gone to stop this, I would be now. The heat. The slickness. The hunger in his eager movements and closed eyes.

I bring one hand up to stroke his cheek and that makes him hum and lean into my palm. He pulls his mouth off and looks up at me. "Can I take them off?"

Unable to speak, I nod and keep my hand on his face. He watches his fingers as they tuck into the waistband of my boxers and he pulls them down slowly, freeing me.

"Oh," he says on an exhale as my cock bobs in front of him.

The panic at such an ambiguous noise is quick to rise in me, but then Jake wraps a hand around my penis and I'm more focused on not letting my knees buckle.

"What does 'oh' mean?" I ask, breathless.

"I think this may be the most beautiful cock I've ever seen in my life." Jake moves his head in various angles, studying me.

I laugh a little. "I bet you say that to all the guys."

"Trust me, I don't," Jake says, still inspecting, but now his hand is moving almost unbearably slowly up and down my length. "It really is perfect."

"Jake," I say wanting to advise him that he doesn't need to say things like that but he seems oblivious.

"It's the perfect length. And that girth. Not too much, but more than enough. And this curve. Wow. That's a promise and a dream. So beautiful," he muses, still looking at my penis. "And believe me, I've seen hundreds, if not thousands of cocks."

"That's great to hear," I say dryly although some of the tension in my voice is because of what Jake is doing, his pressure and speed increasing, his grip firm on the bottom half of my dick, then suddenly featherlight and teasing around my head.

"I can't believe you had this hiding in your pants the whole time we've been getting on each other's nerves. That actually makes you even more annoying."

"Speaking of which," I say, my jaw tense and breaths hurried. "Are you going to show me how much you like my dick? Or are you just going to keep staring at it?"

When Jake's eyes flash up to mine I watch his pupils dilate, claiming more of the chestnut brown they are framed with, I see he wasn't lying. He does like dirty talk.

"Can I taste you?" Jake says, shuffling forward on the bed so his feet are on the ground and I'm standing between his open legs.

"Taste me," I demand, my chest rising and falling. "Lick me. Suck me. Fuck me with your mouth, Forester."

Chapter Twenty-One

Jake

It's like a switch I didn't even know existed in me has just been flicked. I've wanted a lot of men in the past. I've felt so turned on I can't see straight before. And it really doesn't take much to make me horny if someone shows me even half a minute's interest. But this. This is something else.

The way Rami talks to me. The way he uses curse words when he never normally does. The way his eyes turn an almost effervescent silver when he stares down at me telling me what he wants me to do. I am so turned on and so hungry for his beautiful cock, I doubt I'll ever get enough of it.

Starting with long, lazy licks up and down his length, I keep my hold on the base of him tight. When I notice his stomach rise and fall a little quicker, I take him in my mouth for the first time. Pulling in only the head, I swirl my tongue around it and place my hands on his hip to keep him close. After doing this for a while, I push down a little more, bringing more of him into my mouth. When Rami then brings his hands to hold my head, his fingers combing through my hair, I smile around his cock. I suck and pull on his dick, wrapping it in the warmth of my mouth and I get the best reward, a long, rough groan that only makes me take more of him, forcing the head to the back of my throat.

"Fuck, yes, Jake, yes," Rami starts to thrust and I hum in response. I bring a hand up to caress his balls which are tight and firm in my hand.

"Jake, I'm going to— Fuck, Forester. Your mouth..."

I mumble something that wasn't even words to begin with.

"Shit, it's been so long..." Rami mumbles, barely audible. "I'm going to come. If you don't want me, pull off now." Rami's grip on my head loosens, as if to give me more space.

If you don't want me?

Do I want Rami? Yes, physically, so much. But do I want an intimate moment like this, him coming inside my mouth? Him practically choking me with his perfect dick? Do I want his cum sliding down my throat? I know it would be perfectly fine, hot even, to lift my lips off him and finish him off with my fist and have him come on my chest.

But I don't want to do that. I want Rami. I want him to come undone inside my mouth. I want to taste him.

My answer is to grip his hips and push him further inside my mouth, as far down my throat as I can stand. I breathe through my nose and let my barely controlled gag reflex do the work. With my nose pressed to the firm flesh of his lower abdomen, the hairs there fine, wiry and soft, he grunts and moans in a deep voice. A second later, I feel him thrust once, twice, and then his warm cum spills down my throat.

"Fuck," he says as he continues to rock into me.

Eventually, I pull off and wipe my mouth with the back of my forearm. "Good?" I ask, because of course I still need validation despite how quickly he came.

His hand slides down to cup my chin. "I could write a song about your mouth," he says with bright eyes. It seems a peculiar thing to say, but it's beautiful regardless. When his hand moves down and grips the sides of my neck, applying the gentlest squeeze, it forces me to stand up. When our eyes meet – lined up perfectly because we are close enough to the same height, a fact that has somehow escaped me until this moment – I admire their colour openly. The same colour as the full moon on a clear night.

"Tell me what you want," Rami says, one hand still on my neck, and the other coming to stroke me through my boxers. "Tell me what feels good for you."

I make an incomprehensible noise, but then quickly clear my throat. "I... I don't know."

He pulls back slightly. "You don't know?"

I look away from his intense stare. "I've never been asked that before," I admit and turn back to him waiting to find surprise or confusion or worst of all, pity. Instead, I just get a slow smile and a slight push of his hands on my shoulders, forcing me back on the bed.

"Sit back," he nods at the pillows. "Relax."

Perplexed by where this is leading, I follow his instructions. When I'm sitting there, unsure what to do with my hands, I watch as Rami puts his boxers back on, something that makes me feel irrationally sad. He kneels at my feet, feet he pushes open so he can move into the space between my legs.

"Touch yourself," he says.

"What?"

"Pretend I'm not here," Rami says. "And touch yourself."

"You're a very handsome man wearing pink silk boxer shorts. It's a little difficult to ignore you."

"I don't want you to ignore me. I just want you to imagine you're alone, so you can touch yourself however, wherever you like to be touched."

"Does that... would that turn you on?"

"Yes," Rami says and he almost looks shy but a second later shakes it off, that deep stern voice returning. "But more than that, I want to know exactly what you like. How you like to be touched. What turns you on. What makes your eyes roll back. What makes your toes curl. What makes you come. I want to watch it all so I can then do it to you myself."

If it was possible for the human body to melt from arousal, I'm fairly sure that's what would be happening right now. As my hands fist the duvet I'm lying on top of, I level my eyes on Rami and watch how his gaze rolls around my body, searching, waiting. I really do think he's serious, which means he wants to do this, with me. He doesn't want to just get an orgasm and run. He wants to please me too.

"Forester, did you hear me?"

"I heard you," I say in a whisper.

"And yet, you're not doing as I ask," he says and I know now that he is well aware how much being spoken to like this turns me on. I don't even care that he knows this about me, I am enjoying it too much.

"Kiss me," I say and I am half-certain he's going to refuse, because that's not how this usually works. Some men who have dominated me before only kiss when they want to, others not at all. But I need this too sometimes. I crave the stern words, the demands and instructions, and I also long for the kissing, the caressing, the terms of affection sprinkled here and there amongst the harsher, dirtier words.

So yes, I'm surprised when Rami leans forward, balances his hands on either side of my body and kisses me, hard. As he pushes my head back onto the headboard, I bring my hands up to grip his face, ready to deepen the kiss but then he stops and lifts his lips off mine.

"Are you going to give me what I want?"

"Yes," I say, a word made of nothing but air. His crooked smile is like a reward as he sits back on his knees. His hands slide down my body and rest on my shins.

As I already said, it's impossible to pretend he's not there, but I do set about showing him what he wants to see; what turns me on. First, I start stroking myself through the material of my boxers. I do this until I can't take it anymore and I need more of a squeeze, more friction, and I rush through taking them off. I surprise myself by holding Rami's gaze as I grip the base of my dick and hold it outright for him to see. When he licks his lips, my desire kicks up another notch. As I then start to slowly fist my cock with one hand, I bring the other up to play with my nipple, flicking my finger over it, pinching it. After doing the same to my other nipple, I lazily slide that hand down to play with my balls. When I give them a gentle pull, a moan escapes my lips and my eyes dart to Rami, feeling embarrassed but he just smiles. I drag my eyes down his body as I speed up my strokes and I delight at the sight of another erection filling the silk of his pink silk boxers.

"So good, Jake," Rami says, urging me on.

"Jesus, I think I like you watching me," I say bumpily.

"I like watching you." Rami strokes my shin almost in the same rhythm I'm using to stroke myself. "You're being such a good boy for me, Jake."

I groan at that and close my eyes, leaning my head back and chin up. With this new darkness, taking away the intensity of his stare, my hand dives down lower still and plays with the outside of my hole.

"Yes, Jake." I hear Rami hiss and I feel his hands ride up my thighs and push them further apart. Still, I can't look at him.

"Fuck," I whisper as I feel myself get closer.

A few seconds later my hand is pulled away from my ass and that prompts me to open my eyes, which I really shouldn't have done because that's when I see Rami hold my hand out in front of him and he bends his mouth close to my fingers, and spits. He then moves my hand back to where it was.

Oh, God. That was hot.

My breath is coming so irregularly now, there are long moments when I don't inhale, don't exhale, just stay in this heightened state of wonder, where all I'm aware of are my hands working myself to a perfect peak, and Rami's eyes on it all.

"Such a good boy, Jake," Rami says again. "Are you going to come for me?"

"Yes, fuck, yes," I reply. And yet becoming so aware of how much his words affect me stalls my fast-approaching orgasm a little and I struggle to find the place where I was, the tingling in my spine and the tightness in my balls dissipating.

"Shit," I gasp and maybe Rami can't hear the frustration there. Maybe it just sounds like I'm cursing in the early throes of my climax. I don't know what he thinks and I definitely don't know what makes him lean forward and start to press light, lingering kisses up the length of my inner thigh.

"Please don't stop doing that," I say when I feel how it relaxes me, and gets me back on the path I was on, the path that is leading me into the white-hot tunnel that will be my orgasm.

"I'm not going anywhere." I hear Rami say. Wondering why he chose those words and wondering why they land so heavily inside me are the last conscious thoughts I have before I come.

"Fuck!" I yell out as I feel the warm spill land on my stomach before it coats my hand.

"Fuck," I say as my breaths bump into one another.

"Fuck," I whisper as I lean my head back and wait for the shame to waltz in, like it always does.

"That was—" Rami begins as he comes back into the same position he was moments ago, on all fours straddling my body. "Fucking brilliant."

I don't have any words. Instead, I just laugh, looking up at him.

"So fucking good," Rami speaks again as if to set the sentiment in stone.

"You are so not what I expected," I say eventually, and his smile becomes one of confusion.

"What do you mean?"

"Nothing," I say and I feel my stomach flip with that all familiar lull that follows an ill-advised sexual encounter. Looking down at myself, at my softening dick and at the splashes of white on my body does little to make me feel better.

I'm about to move, got up and go and clean up, but I feel a warm weight come crashing down on top of me.

"Rami, what the fuck—"

"Kiss me, Forester," he says, trying to line his mouth up with mine, but I'm not having any of it.

"Rami, you're going to get messy," I say.

"Does it look like I care?" he asks, still trying to find my lips.

"Seriously. I should shower or—"

"We'll shower together, in a minute. But first I need your mouth, and now," he demands before finally winning his fight and rolling me over in his arms so I'm lying on top of him.

I don't kiss him back at first, still convinced he'll push me away in a few seconds, and I keep my body braced, tense for the onslaught of shitty feelings that I detected just a moment ago.

But they don't come. And instead, slowly, tentatively, but eventually wholeheartedly, I relax into kissing Rami back.

PART THREE – FULL MOON

"So imagine that the lovely moon is playing just for you - everything makes music if you really want it to."

Giles Andreae

Chapter Twenty-Two

Rami

I'm not saying I've missed Jake, but I'm also not *not* saying that.

It's only been four days since I slept at his place after the dinner with Lionel and Luigi but it feels like much longer. I would like to say that the time has disappeared without me realising it but in reality, I've felt it drag.

On Friday I was out all day at a site visit with Bill and Simeon, a fact that helped us avoid what Jake described as "life-threatening embarrassment" of walking into the office together that morning. It wasn't clear who he implied should feel embarrassed, him or myself. I thought about texting him on Saturday to see if he wanted to meet up, have a coffee or some lunch together, but each time I had the words typed out, I would stop myself. It wasn't really that I was afraid of getting rejected, it was *how* I would get rejected. I didn't want to hear that Jake was busy with other friends. I didn't want to know if he'd already made plans with a buddy or two. And I definitely didn't want to know if he had a date.

In short, I didn't want to be reminded that Jake had a whole city of friends and possibly lovers, and me… I have him. And that's pretty much it.

Instead, I went on a twenty-kilometre run, treated myself to lunch in a sushi restaurant and then after meditating for twenty minutes, collapsed on the sofa playing Mario Kart virtually with Roxie and told myself my aching legs were the reason I stayed in on a Saturday evening. On Sunday I headed up to my mom's, as grateful for an activity that would fill my day as I was happy to see her. It also helped a lot that Radia caught the train with me this time and so the one-and-a-half-hour train journey was filled with her recounting her latest dates with Barista Babe. It helped because it diluted my many, many thoughts about Jake.

So, is it now Monday morning and am I all excited to see him? Yes, and yes. Am I twenty minutes early waiting for him at the entrance of a Georgian manor house a couple of streets away from Clapham Common? Yes, I am. Am I holding his coffee order in one hand and craning my neck to see if he's walking down the street towards me? Yes, I am doing that too.

The appropriately named Clapham Manor House Hotel is one of the company's signature properties and it's where one of the country's most famous footballers wants to marry his equally famous supermodel fiancée in August. Considering their budget and the fact it's all being organised very last minute, I'm not surprised Bill and Simeon asked both Jake and me to be at this meeting with the happy couple and the hotel's manager, and because I am so keen to talk to Jake, I'm not mad about it either.

Reaching to check my phone to see if Jake has texted – not that there's a reason he would – I see a new email notification. Once in the app, my stomach sinks when I read who the email is from.

It's not Michelle. It's not Gee. It's the one other person whose name stops me in my tracks. It's Cassie, my former manager and I suppose, former friend too. My instinct is to jump out of the email app and pocket my phone, but a quick glance at the time shows me I still have another ten minutes before Jake is likely to show up and I really don't want to spend that time wondering why she's got in touch. There's also the subject title of the email, the crafty witch of a woman that she is.

Don't Open This Unless You Want Your Life to Change... For the Better.

I sigh, take a quick sip of my coffee, then open the email.

Rami,
Long time, blah, blah, blah.
I hear you're back in the UK. Is the weather still as abysmal as it was when I last visited in 2002? Never again.

Anyway. I've waited long enough to send this email and I won't put it off anymore.

I've been fielding calls and demands for you since you decided to go AWOL and they've officially started to slow down in number and offer size.

What does this mean? Well, it means your time is officially running out. The longer you leave it now to come back, the harder it will be.

I'm telling you this as the best manager you ever had and as an average friend.

Get in touch if you want to talk about it. My number is still the same (but my rates have gone up!).

Nix sends their love, by the way. They miss you a lot more than I do, just FYI.

Cassie x

I can't help but smile. Even if what she's telling me is not what I want to read or think about, I have missed Cassie and her partner Nixon. They were good people to work and socialise with, and we had countless fun nights in LA together. Her, them, me and... Michelle. It feels so strange to think about her as my partner. I can't imagine sitting down to dinner with her and another couple, like we used to, like I did so naturally, so easily last week with...

Jake.

I see him approaching me over the top of my phone. He's in a navy suit with a pastel blue shirt that captures something in his colouring that makes me think about what he would look like with a suntan, smiling against a deep blue sky on holiday. Thinking about this has me grinning to myself.

"Who's got you smiling like that?" Jake asks as he comes to stand opposite me.

"Nobody, nothing," I say in a rush.

Jake blinks at me. "I was just implying you may have had a text from someone you're enamoured with. No need to bite my head off." He holds his hands up but then spots the coffee. "Ooh, is that for me?"

"It is," I say, and I know now that I can't bring up last week. That little comment, delivered so easily, without hesitation, tells me that whatever happened last week, Jake has clearly moved on from it and so must I. Telling myself this only adds more weight to that sinking feeling in my stomach. How am I going to be able to even salvage a friendship with Jake from whatever it is we had going on between us after he's sucked my cock and I watched him get himself off so intently I can recall many minutes of it in my mind's eye. And I have – multiple times.

"Shall we go in?" Jake asks interrupting my thoughts.

"Sure," I say.

Walking up the steps, a smartly dressed butler in a top hat opens one of the double doors for us and we step into the vast, high-ceilinged lobby of the hotel. On the floor are alternating black-and-white square tiles and the space is furnished with warm coloured leather sofas and chairs. A row of reception desks line the wall to our left and that's the direction we move in when we are intercepted.

"Looney Tunes!" A voice from my past bellows.

I freeze.

"Is it really you?" I hear all the hard edges and piqued vowels of the cockney accent, all the depth of the baritone it belongs to. "No fucking way!"

"Jamison." I turn around to face the music, which on this occasion is my old friend and one-time colleague Lyle Jamison, a one-time member of an early Nineties boy band turned songwriter for other pop stars. In other words, he fell from a great height into obscurity but probably earns a lot more money and has a lot more sanity for it.

"What the fuck are you doing here?" the stocky man asks me as he approaches us both, arms open wide. I step into them, but don't get very far because of his sizeable stomach, but he truly looks all the happier and healthier for the weight gain.

"I thought you was out in the middle of nowhere in California, you know doing that—"

"I'm here now," I quickly cut in as I step back from him. I spare a quick glance at Jake who is looking at Jamison like he's speaking a foreign language. "Working in London. Doing events for the company that runs this hotel."

"Events? Serious?" Jamison claps me on the side of my upper arm. "Fucking 'ell you look good. Seems that whatever happened out there in the desert didn't do you any harm."

I daren't look at Jake now, daren't draw his attention to the inevitable pink in my cheeks and the way I'm gritting my teeth so hard I can feel every millimetre of my cheeks and jawbones.

"What are you doing here?" I ask quickly.

"Oh, also work. I'm recording down the road with Minx, you heard of them?"

"Can't say I have." I shake my head.

"Don't look them up neither. Not worth it. Only one of them can hold a tune and of course she's the one on the cusp of having a drug and drink problem so she's nearly always five hours late to recordings. It's been a massive waste of my time but I'm not complaining because I get paid by the hour, don't I?" Jamison laughs and I try to laugh with him, I really try, but frankly I'm not finding anything about this situation very funny.

"How's Louise? The kids?" I'm grateful I pull his wife's name out of nowhere.

"Oh, a massive pain in the arse, all of them. They bust my balls dawn to dusk, but I fucking love 'em. Couldn't live without 'em. You know how it is." Jamison puts his hands on his hips. "How's 'Chelle doing? Where are you guys living now if you're over here?"

"Oh, we broke up. She's still in the States," I say and it's now that I become painfully aware again of Jake standing there witnessing this whole bizarre exchange with a chunk of my past I rather like him not knowing about.

"Fuck, sorry to hear that." Jamison whistles through his teeth. "That's a shame, I thought you two was the real deal."

I'm not sure if it's deliberate but that's the moment Jake decides to make his presence known by clearing his throat, loudly.

"Oh, sorry, this is my colleague, Jake. Jake, this is Lyle Jamison. Jake is head of UK properties for the company I work for."

"Pleasure to meet you, Lyle," Jake says politely.

"Call me Jamison. Unless you're my mother, which you probably aren't because she's been dead the last fifteen years."

It's almost worth the awkwardness to see Jake lost for words and it does give me a second or two to get my thoughts in order.

"Listen, Jamison, so good to see you." I hold out my hand for him again. "But Jake and I've got a meeting and the client will be there and we don't want to hold them up."

"Will you be around all day? I dare say I'll be back here by five as that's when they all start getting the munchies. We could go get a drink. Catch up a bit."

I do my best to feign disappointment when all I feel is relief. "I'd love to, mate, but I really can't. I'll be back in the office by then which is in the West End and tonight Jake and I are going for dinner." The words tumble out of my mouth.

"We are?" Jake asks, sounding almost horrified.

I turn to him with a glare. "Yes, don't you remember? You owe me from last week." I know instantly from the way he slams his lips closed, he's got the message.

"Oh, yes, that. Yes, I do owe Rami dinner tonight. Or actually, I think he owes me dinner." He turns to me. "I seem to recall I went above and beyond for you last week so it's really your turn to treat me." He gives me an almost sickly-sweet smile. "To dinner that is."

My smile is a lot less innocent. "You're right, I do owe you. Last week was so good, I've been thinking a lot about the things I could do to make it up to you."

For the second time in as many minutes, Jake falls silent. I turn back to my old friend.

"Jamison, good to see you again. Are you still on the same number? I'll call you should I ever be in New York."

"Make sure you do, Looney. It's been too fucking long." I get pulled in for another hug. "Pleasure to meet you, Jake."

"Pleasure was all mine but tell me, how do you know—"

"Love to Louise and the kids!" I say and then place a hand on the small of Jake's back and push slightly so we head further towards a reception desk.

"Who the hell was that?"

"I introduced you, Lyle Jamison," I reply, possibly a little snappily.

"Yes, I got that, but who is he to you? And what did he call you? Looney Tunes? What is that all about?"

"Oh, just a silly nickname." I wave my hand and look around the open space desperate to see someone who may be the hotel manager that we're supposed to meet.

"And he seemed surprised you were working in events? And what was all that about the desert?"

"There are lots of deserts in Southern California. We would go out there with friends for holidays now and then. Jamison came on a few trips." The lies I tell Jake taste bitter and sour.

"But what about—" Jake begins but I pull away and walk to a newly available receptionist before I can hear the rest.

"Excuse me," I ask the woman standing behind the desk. "We're here to meet Elliot Marcham, the manager, at ten o'clock."

I give her our names and then follow her instructions to take a seat on the leather couches behind us. As Jake comes to sit next to me, I avoid his eye contact and find myself staring through the glass doors that open onto a courtyard in the middle of the property, the very courtyard where the footballer and his future wife will make their vows, and then later, where they'll eat dinner, dance and start the rest of their happy lives together.

"You don't need to worry," Jake says, and I look at him, alarmed and curious what he means. Has he figured it all out? "About owing me. I didn't really mean it." He leans against my body in a quick nudge.

I couldn't stop the smile that takes over my mouth if I tried.

"Oh, I do," I say in a voice that takes me back to that night. "And I meant what I said. I have been thinking about exactly what I can do to make it up to you too."

And what do you know, that completes a hat trick of moments when Jake is completely lost for words.

Chapter Twenty-Three

Jake

Elliot Marcham is very close to getting on my last nerve. And it has nothing to do with his chiselled good looks or his striking dark hair and ice-blue eyes combo. Fine, it has a bit to do with that. But there's more to it than *just* that. First, he interrupted Rami and I at a critical moment – namely when I was searching for a suitably flirty rejoinder to what seemed to be a thinly veiled proposition of us doing sex stuff again – and secondly, he has decided my name is Jack despite Rami introducing me and using my name many times in a way I strongly suspect are attempts to correct Elliot.

Finally, the salt in my wound is the way he is flirting with Rami as he gives us a tour of the building. He's complimented Rami's eyes no fewer than three times. He's casually asked if Rami and his 'significant other' have sampled many of Status' hotels and he commented on Rami's explanation that there was no significant other with an almost villain-esque "Hmm, interesting." And now, as we near completion of the tour and circle back to the lobby to meet Wayne Bell and his fiancée Alison Wentworth, he's telling Rami all about how his ex-*boyfriend* loved the company discount and how he's practically convinced this ex-*boyfriend* was more upset about losing that than losing a *boyfriend*.

"So, you're gay and single, are you?" I say glibly as we approach the same leather couch Rami and I had our rudely interrupted moment on.

It's not that I'm jealous of Elliot or feeling possessive of Rami. I have no right to be either of those things. I just find it a little unprofessional to flirt with a colleague – a senior colleague – in such a blatant way. Once I've stated this case in my mind, I have to do considerable mental gymnastics to ignore the fact that Rami and I are colleagues and we have actually done more than just flirting.

"Takes one to know one, I see," Elliot says with a fake smile I would almost be jealous of if it didn't also come with a dagger-like stare that has me shrinking into the leather as I take a seat. Much to my further dismay, neither Rami nor Elliot sit and so that leaves them standing opposite each other talking about how the next hour's meeting will go, and I'm completely excluded looking like a child sitting at the kids' table.

I'm about to stand again when both front doors burst open and a wave of noise from outside rushes in. We all turn and look to see an impossibly tall, slim and well-put-together couple march through the entrance as the clicks of cameras and shouts of names fill the lobby. On their heels is a short man wearing a very tight-fitting suit and boasting far too much gel in his hair.

As they approach us, I stand and decide to stop sulking for the sake of this meeting seeing as the paparazzi uproar outside clearly indicates they are something of a big deal despite me personally always skipping their stories in the Mail Online. I won't mention that to them.

"Alison, Wayne, welcome to Clapham Manor," Elliot says extending his hand.

"Nice to meet you," Wayne says in a voice that is surprisingly soft and almost high in pitch.

"Sorry about the carnage outside," Alison says. She is much louder and her Home Counties accent clashes considerably with Wayne's gentle Lancashire tone. "They followed me from doing Lorraine this morning."

I resist the urge to make a joke about her 'doing' Lorraine, and instead shake their hands when I am introduced by Elliot, once again as Jack.

"It's Jake, actually," I say, tightly.

Finally, the mouse-like man with an entire pot of gel in his hair is introduced to us as Sergio, their wedding planner and he shakes all our hands with a limp, lacking grip and a very noticeable head-to-toe eye-fucking of Rami. Just as well he and I are only fake dating. Going out with someone that striking in real life would make me even more paranoid than I already am.

"Thank you for the last-minute meeting, and well, last-minute everything," Sergio says, and I notice then that he has a tablet in his hands, which he is swiping away at furiously. "Wayne and Ali only have an hour now so we really need to make sure they see everything as quickly as possible."

"Right." Elliot claps his hands together in a way that makes me jump. "Let's show you the courtyard."

The only part of the property we didn't see in our whistle-stop tour earlier, Elliot proudly opens the glass doors to the courtyard as if he's revealing a new kingdom to a lost nation. But I almost can't blame him.

It's stunning.

A rectangular space surrounded by red-brick walls and glass windows, the courtyard is easily big enough to host a wedding party of a few hundred guests. Filled with pot plants of various shapes, sizes and styles, it has a jungle-feel to it, making it a veritable oasis from the hustle and bustle of the city outside. With all the greenery and flowers, I feel like I'm back in the gardens of the stately home where Lionel and Luigi got married. The gardens where Rami and I kissed for the longest, sweetest time.

"Wow, Wayney, look at this." Alison yanks her fiancé by the hand into the centre of the space. She does what can only be described as a twirl – long copper-red hair blooming out around her – and beams a very bright and very white smile. "It's amazing. Just think how good the photos will be."

Wayne turns around taking it in. "Is it big enough? We've got two hundred and fifty people coming for the ceremony. Plus, photographers and the documentary crew."

Elliot steps in, literally, as if we're a circle of dancers and it's his turn to jive or something. "Absolutely. Half of the plants and shrubs you see here now will be removed and the whole space will be cleared to seat 132 chairs on either side. That's eleven rows of twelve in case you couldn't do the maths."

Oh, God, is he implying that our clients are dumb because one's a model and the other's a footballer. I resist the urge to slap my palm to my face.

"We don't want all the plants to go though. They'd make such a lovely backdrop for photos, don't you think Wayney?"

"I'd rather have enough space for all our friends and family, to be honest," Wayne mutters in a way that suggests he is a little fearful mentioning this and I soon see why when I spot a slightly red tinge push its way through Alison's flawless make-up.

"You know what we could do," I say, seeing an opportunity. "We could turn the rear wall into a living wall."

Alison blinks at me before her heavy lashed lids narrow on me.

"A live wall?"

"I mean, a wall of plants. It's called a living wall. That would work to keep the aesthetic the same but also mean we can remove more of the potted plants and shrubs so Wayne doesn't need to worry about space as much. And you will have the perfect backdrop for photos. We could even get one of those rotating platforms with a smartphone holder."

"Now you're talking! Such a great idea!" Ali shimmies her hip into mine, or rather, into my waist because she's a good half a foot taller than me, in her ankle-breaking heels.

"Great idea, Jake," Rami says and I practically purr internally at the praise in his voice.

"A rotating platform? How do you even know about these things, Jack?" Elliot asks with a sardonic tone.

"Oh, my sister's sister-in-law is an influencer. I spent Christmas with her and she had one and we all had far too much fun with it. I also discovered that while my right side is nothing to be proud of, my left profile is a work of art," I say with everyone's eyes on me.

"Oh, is she famous?" Alison asks.

"Do you know Mae O'Martin?"

"Mae! Yes! We follow each other. She's amazing. Gorgeous too. I love her content and she's so brave, what with all the stuff she's been doing recently about her—" Alison chooses to lower her voice at this moment and it also seems one side of her mouth has stopped working. "Her sexuality."

I fight the urge to fold my face into a cringe because I don't want to have a conversation like this about someone I consider a little sister and dear friend, especially as one of the key facets of Maeve's recent content on this topic relates to her curiosity about her sexuality, rather than putting a fixed label on it, but Alison is our client, and arguably one of the most important – or rather, high paying – ones our company will work for this year so I manage to turn it into a smile.

"Maeve is a really special human," I agree, and I risk tapping Alison on the forearm. "One day when we have more time, I'll tell you a funny story about how she single-handedly saved my pert backside from getting fired in my first hotel manager job seven years ago."

"Oh, I'd like to hear that story. What did you say your name is again? I'm going to message Mae to let her know I met you."

"Jake," I say with more than a fleeting glance at Elliot. "Jake Forester."

My next thought is wiped away when a chemical scent fills my nostrils. Sergio and his hair gel have taken their turn to step into the centre of our group.

"Do you really have time to install a living wall? We don't want false promises at this late stage in the game." What Elliot's tone has in slime, as he replies with overly enthusiastic reassurance, Sergio's has in exhaustion. He reminds me of Tasha, our old Head of Events. Always a bit too busy to care that her tone was blunt and brusque. Thinking on this makes me realise how different Rami is. Rami doesn't have that hospitality shine that is in reality anything but shiny, rather an over-buffed or over-waxed effect of always putting customers' and clients' needs before our own. Rami is much more relaxed, almost detached from the work. From the way he's barely said more than twenty words in the last hour to how he is standing back, letting Elliot and Sergio argue over which plants should stay or go, Rami really is something of an anomaly in our industry.

"It's pretty cool, huh?" Rami's low, steady voice lands in my ear from behind me. I'd like to say I stop the shiver it pulls from my body but I'm not sure I do.

"Well, it's no orangery," I say a little slyly but it gives me the reaction I want, a quick but real laugh from Rami. "But it should do. For the happy couple, I mean."

"You are much more relaxed about this wedding than the last one we were at."

"This one is going to help pay our salaries." I lean a little closer so only he can hear that. Yes, that's why I lean in closer.

"It's a really cool venue. You'd never know this was all here."

I nod in agreement. "These are my favourite kind of places in London. It's why I wanted to work for Status in the first place. You really feel like you're looking after important pieces of history. I know it's trivial to a lot of people but I think it really matters, having places like this that people can enjoy just for a night or two. And if they can do so for the happiest day of their life, or heck, even just a party, then it's a very special honour. It's pretty much why I got into hospitality."

When Rami doesn't respond for a short while, I turn to check he's still there, and he is, still standing behind me, slightly to the side, both of us now gazing straight up at the blue sky.

"I think Elliot was trying to come on to you earlier," Rami says out of nowhere.

"Me?" I squeak. "That wasn't for me. That was all for you."

"Ha! I doubt it. I think you've caught Sergio's eye too."

"Rami, don't do this," I say in a part-hiss, part-whisper. "You should know better than to just assume when queer men are in a room together we all automatically fancy each other."

It's Rami's turn to lean in a little closer. "But I do fancy one of the gay men in this room."

After another shiver has worked its way down my spine, I turn to look at him and try to elongate this conversation, but he's no longer behind me, instead he's walking over to Elliot who is standing with his hands on his hips watching Sergio, Wayne and Alison stand at the other end of the courtyard.

"Elliot, can you remind me again what the staff discount is that your ex-boyfriend used to love so much?" Rami says.

"You don't know? Blimey. That's the first thing I asked at my job interview." He laughs loudly. "It's fifty per cent. You need to start taking advantage of that."

Rami hums before asking, "And would that still apply if a staff member was to hold a function here, like a fortieth birthday party for example?"

"Rami," I warn through gritted teeth.

"It still applies. My ex-boyfriend and I looked into possibly having an engagement party here. It was like a sick game of Call My Bluff waiting for him to propose, and I guess he called mine when he broke up with me via text message."

"Do you have your calendar on your phone?" Rami asks as he pulls out his own device.

"I do indeed, are you asking me out on a date?" Elliot does that slimy laugh again. I cough loudly enough so that I get Rami's attention and when I do, I give him my best I-told-you-so look.

"Do you have availability on or around the third of September?" Rami asks.

Why the hell does he have my birthday in his calendar?

"That's a Saturday, right? Oh, yes, I remember now. We had a cancellation just last week and so we have the courtyard and adjoining function room all available. But the ballroom is taken for a retirement party."

"We'll take the courtyard, or rather, Jake over here will." When Rami emphasises my name to Elliot once again, it almost makes up for the chaos he is causing everywhere else in my body and brain.

"Oh, what's the occasion, Jack?" Elliot asks.

"Nothing big," I say, considering whether to allow myself a moment of imagining all my friends in this space. It would be amazing to have Jenna and Marty here too, maybe Maeve could also come for the occasion. Could I even invite my father and Carol? Would they come? I reverse a little and even let myself have the thought that I think has been trying to burrow its way to the surface for a long time; I'm never going to get married, so why not make this something special? Can I maybe just relax and say "Fuck it" to this proposition? I'll find a way to pay for it somehow, or rather, I'll find another credit card to do so.

"It's his birthday and it's going to be the party of the year," Rami says with confidence, coming to stand next to me, his arm touching mine.

"That's exactly what we want!" Ali interrupts. "The party of the year!"

I don't mind her interjecting and making all my vivid daydreams disappear. I don't even mind her assuming the only thing the four members of her queer wedding organising army have on their minds is making her day the best of her life. And a part of me doesn't even mind that it now seems I have to go through with this birthday party and its hefty price tag, even with the healthy discount. Because Rami's body heat is still radiating through our suits from his to mine and that, honestly, is all that seems to matter.

Chapter Twenty-Four

Rami

The meeting has been a great success. Wayne and Alison walk away happy. Jake has a venue for his fortieth birthday party, and his pout upon arranging that was more begrudged amusement rather than outright rage.

I've got quite good at judging his pouts. But none of this is the reason I'm smiling. That has more to do with the fact that for me the meeting was a great success because he and I managed to squeeze in some flirting and possibly completely meaningless, but also just as possibly very meaningful touches in passing.

And we're doing more of it now, our shoulders brushing against one another as we sit side by side on the Tube together, replying to the emails that have filled our inboxes during the meeting.

At least, I'm sure that's what Jake is doing, but for some reason I can't concentrate.

"Jake," I begin.

He doesn't look up for a few seconds but then lowers his phone and presses a single finger to his chest. "Oh, sorry. Are you talking to me? Or Jack?"

I sigh. "I did try to correct him multiple times."

"I noticed. Thank you for trying."

"He was a bit..." I begin but don't have the right word.

"A bit of a slimeball?" Jake finishes for me, because of course he has the right word.

"Something like that." I chuckle.

"He really did like you, you know," Jake says and briefly his gaze and busy fingers return to his phone. "You could have got his number, if you wanted."

"I did not want," I say easily.

Jake's mouth twitches and I half expect a smile to land there but it doesn't.

"So what do you want?" Jake says and his question stuns me a little.

"Sorry?"

"You said my name," he says, his curious eyes searching my face.

"Oh, yeah," I say, abruptly feeling stupid. I suck in a deep breath.

"Would you like to have dinner with me on Friday night?" I venture feeling waves of nerves rise and fall in my gut.

Jake doesn't speak for a few seconds. He doesn't even look at me and his expression remains almost neutral, which for him is nothing short of alarming.

"Are you asking me out on a date?" he finally asks with only the slightest head turn towards me.

I decide to answer this question as truthfully as I can. "I'd like to spend some more time with you away from work, and away from fake dating scenarios."

"So, it's not a date?" Jake says, still frustratingly empty in the expression department.

"Not if you don't want it to be," I say. And I realise this much is true. If Jake isn't interested in me like this, then I would still like to be friends. I want that so much I'm prepared to try and find a way to nuke the other feelings that have been bubbling up in the last week.

"I'd love to have dinner with you, Rami, but I'm afraid I can't," Jake says, and my stomach wastes no time in plummeting to the ground. "At least not on Friday. I have literally just agreed to have dinner with Derek and Harry, having just informed them I was bullied into agreeing to have my 40th birthday party in the most sumptuous venue. I would try and rearrange but Harry is jetting off to Lisbon early on Saturday and I am honestly quite looking forward to gloating about how impressive it is my party will be at Clapham Manor House. Thank you for that, by the way."

"Pleasure." I nod. While I'm relieved I'm not getting rejected because Jake doesn't want to have dinner with me, I don't enjoy the reminder that he has such a busy social life. I let myself wince a little before I ask my next question, feeling like I'm revealing a lot about myself, about how dull and lacking my own social life is. "How about Saturday night?"

If Jake is confused or put off, he doesn't let it show.

"Let me check," he says raising his phone and swiping and tapping. "Shit, no can do. My friend Dana is in town. She's only here for the weekend then flying back to Barcelona on Sunday so I really can't move it around. Sorry."

It should be a comfort that he does sound sorry, but I don't feel comforted at all.

"How about Sunday? I could do brunch or lunch instead of dinner?" Jake's suggestion helps me feel a little better, but my answer quickly mitigates that reassurance.

"I can't," I say. "Sundays I spend with my family."

"You can't miss one?" Jake doesn't sound pushy or condescending, more curious.

"No, I'm sorry, I can't."

Jake takes a moment to consider his response and that blank look returns to his face.

"I understand," he says. "And I think that's very admirable."

I lean back against the window of the Tube carriage behind us and look at Jake. "Maybe we can try another time? I would really like to have dinner with you, somewhere nice."

Life returns to Jake's features. His cheekiest pout and eyebrow raise materialise as he also leans his head back and looks at me.

"Oh, you really did want to have dinner? Here I was thinking that was a euphemism for sex stuff."

I don't have words for that, only wide eyes and difficulty swallowing.

Jake briefly glances around the carriage which is still mostly empty before continuing, "You're such a different man in and out of the bedroom."

"Am I?"

"You practically blushed when I said 'sex stuff' and yet when we were doing the aforementioned 'sex stuff' your mouth was filthy."

It's not the first time I've heard this, but it is the first time I have an explanation for someone.

"That was all you, Forester." I let my eyes drop to his lips. "You brought that out of me."

Jake does the same thing, his gaze falling on my mouth. "I liked it. I liked it a lot."

"Shit," I say in a whisper, aware of every drop of blood in my body rushing to my groin.

Jake straightens up in his seat. "Uh oh, he's swearing again."

Also lifting my head, I stare at my feet. "So no dinner or sex stuff this weekend?"

"Apparently not. But if you decide to change your mind about Sunday, let me know," he says tucking his phone in his pocket.

"I really won't," I say and I hate how snarkily it comes out. I know it's because I'm annoyed at my own stubborn rules.

"Fine," Jake says abruptly, and I don't like how his tone has changed. Did he think I was annoyed at him for suggesting I wouldn't change my mind? I open my mouth to reassure him but he's quicker. "You know, maybe it's a good thing. I mean, us doing dinner and or sex stuff is probably the worst of bad ideas. We are colleagues after all, and when Lionel and Luigi are back from their honeymoon next week I'll be telling them we've broken up. So, actually starting to have some sort of physical relationship would only make that more complicated and chaotic, and frankly, I'm trying to reduce the amount of chaos and complications in my life."

I study his face to find maybe a crack of doubt, but I don't see it. He looks calm, almost. This is what Jake wants. He wants us to be colleagues, not lovers. He wants us to be colleagues, not friends.

And I have to respect that.

Chapter Twenty-Five

Jake

"It's just a crush," I say, wine glass aloft in my hand.

"Jake, I've not seen you go this gooey-eyed about a man in years, possibly a decade," Dana says with undeniable sincerity.

"Well, there's no need to draw attention to the drought of decent men that's been my love life."

"I mean, because I've been living abroad for five years," Dana slurs and playfully taps my forearm, and her touch lingers as she starts stroking my shirt. If she keeps drinking at this pace, I'll have her leaning on my shoulder in an hour and possibly shortly after that she'll be offering me a feel of her breasts.

"But it's actually true," I say nodding to myself. "Rami is one of the more decent specimens I've had a crush on in a long time."

Apart from Lionel, I think to myself, but I'm not going to bring that up with Dana because I never told her about him. I didn't tell anyone. Maybe that should have been a sign that Lionel and I were never meant to be.

"So, what are you going to do about it?" Dana gulps back another mouthful of prosecco.

"Absolutely nothing," I state the obvious.

"What? Why?"

"Oh, you want a list. Here we go. One, we work together. Two, he's way out of my league. Once he's been in London for more than five minutes he'll be fighting off people left, right and centre so he'll soon get bored of me. Three, based on this and well, *me*, my relationships never last more than five minutes and having to work with him after we've ended a short-lived situationship will be even more painful than it already is. Despite how easy on the eye he is, and how he occasionally gives me butterflies, I still don't really enjoy sharing an office with him."

Dana squints at me. "Do you really think that?"

"That it will be awkward and uncomfortable? It already is, Dana. After I told him that we should put the brakes on a few days ago, the tension in the office has been unbearable. He's gone from taking three-hour walks to make his calls to being out for nearly six hours every day. I actually can't believe he walks so many miles in Louboutin loafers, but I guess that's what you get when you spend more than a week's rent on shoes."

Dana tuts me. "Trust you to know exactly how expensive his shoes are." She reaches to grab the bottle of wine and top our glasses up, but I intercept and take over because I am a gentleman with hospitality training… and I also think there's a decent chance of her spilling half of it.

"The point is, I feel like I've probably dodged a bullet. I'm turning forty this year. It's time to be a bit more sensible and not just jump into bed with the first inappropriate man who shows me a little bit of interest."

"You know that forty rhymes with naughty?" Dana says with an evil wink.

"Can we talk about you now? How are you? How's Barcelona? How's married life? Please lie and say all the above are terrible."

"All the above are terrible," she says dutifully. "Which of course is not true. They're all wonderful. But I'm not going to let you change the subject, Jake. I want to see you happy."

"I am happy!" I say, possibly louder than necessary.

"Well, you could be happier," Dana suggests and I'm starting to think her glass is now glued to her hand as it hasn't touched the table since I topped it up. "What does Jenna think about Rami?"

That shuts me up. Because Jenna knows a different version of this story, the one where we're supposedly dating, which I didn't tell Dana because then I'd have to tell her about Lionel. *Goodness, lies get messy very quickly.*

"Jenna wants to meet him," I say, which is true. "I guess to check him out or something."

"I do too," Dana says after another swig. "Oh, wait. Can we call him? Get him on a video chat? Or better yet, get him to come down and meet us. Where does he live?"

"Hoxton, I believe."

"That's literally just around the corner!"

"It's around several corners."

"But he could be here in minutes, not hours. That's lightning fast in London!"

"I'm not calling him," I say but I don't miss how a part of me wakes up with this suggestion.

"Oh, but you said he wanted to take you out, so I bet he's free. I bet he's sat at home waiting for you to call."

I glance at my watch which requires an elaborate flick of my wrist that comes far too easily. "It's gone ten o'clock. He's probably getting ready for bed. He's going up to Birmingham tomorrow to spend the day with his family."

"Ah, what a sweetheart," Dana slurs.

"He does it every week." I smile.

"Stop, you're killing me. A family man and a dirty talker, this is an elite pairing, Jake. I think you should definitely call him."

"I'm. Not. Going. To. Call. Him," I say but out of sight my fingers tap my jeans pocket where my phone is.

After briefly narrowing her eyes at me again, Dana flicks out her long black hair and then changes the direction of the conversation.

"Have you seen Dove recently?" she asks referring to our other best friend from college. I used to call them my Double Ds.

"Not for a few weeks. But no doubt she and Keeley are very happy," I say with a genuine smile. See, I can still be happy for people who are luckier in love than me.

"I miss them." Dana pouts. "And how is Jenna? Still in Dublin? Still ridiculously in love?"

"Sickeningly so," I say.

"Don't you want that?" Dana asks and it stuns me a little.

"What?"

"Someone to fall in love with." Her eyes are all misty again.

I groan. "It's not like I've been out here dating men with the intention of doing jigsaw puzzles with them, Dana."

Much to my surprise, Dana bursts out laughing, her small frame shaking in her oversized blazer.

"What's so funny?" I put my glass down.

"You actually believe you've been trying to fall in love? Ha!" She continues to laugh.

"What do you mean?"

"Jake, you meet men, yes, all the time. You have a lot of sex with them too, but you never let them get close enough to have anything more than that."

"That is absolutely not—" I can't finish the sentence. I need to think on it.

"Sorry, I don't mean to be harsh. Perhaps we shouldn't have ordered the second bottle." She nods at the wine cooler. "You know bubbles make me a bitch. But regardless, you can't honestly say that you've given a real relationship much of a chance can you?"

My mind drifts briefly to Lionel. Does Dana have a point?

"You know it takes two to tango. It's not just me who has a say in whether a relationship works or not," I protest.

"Oh, so you mean when you told Rami that it was good that things weren't going to happen that was a discussion?"

I clamp my mouth shut and suck my cheeks in between my teeth.

"What time is your flight again?" I say deliberately contrite.

"Oh, Jakey." Dana slides her chair a little closer to me and then right on cue, her head comes down on my shoulder. "It will happen one day. Maybe not Rami, but someone will make you so happy you don't want to be without him and you will risk it all for that."

Finally, I have something to say to fight my corner. "But I don't want to *risk it all*. I don't want to risk anything. I want to know it's a sure thing. Why else would I bother unless I know that for certain?"

Dana lifts her head slightly so we can make eye contact. "Oh, you're such an idiot. It doesn't work like that. If there's no risk, then it's not love."

226

"Then thank you, but no thank you," I say. "Not everyone needs that, you know."

"I know," Dana says and her head slumps back down after she polishes off the prosecco in her glass. "And if that's really what you think, Jake, then tell me to shut up."

"Shut up," I say but it sounds weak.

"Fine," she says then pushes up to sit a little straighter, her hands coming to either side of her ribcage. "Hey, I've been meaning to ask. Do you think my tits are saggier than when you last saw me?"

*****

After I wave Dana off in her Uber, I open the same app on my phone and start to find a taxi home, but before I take the final necessary step, I pause.

It's 11:15. It's late, but not super late. It's an inconvenient time to call someone, but probably not a horrifically anti-social time. At least, not one that couldn't be apologised for.

I tell myself I'll do it just to hear his voice and clear the air. I want both things more than I can describe and it suddenly feels very urgent that I do it now. I know that's the prosecco talking, but I also know I'm not drunk. At least not horrifically anti-socially drunk or drunk in a way that couldn't be apologised for.

I think again about the way Rami's face fell on the Tube when I told him I thought we were a bad idea, and how his eyes roamed my face for a few seconds before he agreed. It had taken more energy than I care to quantify to stick to my guns in that moment but the stubborn Virgo in me persisted.

It's not that I'm calling him to undo that conversation. I'm calling him to make sure that we are indeed on the same page, and that we can be civil with each other. Friends, maybe.

With the win-win of this situation clear in my mind, I tap out of the Uber app and go to my Contacts. The phone rings four times before he answers.

"Jake? Are you okay?"

I am not prepared. Prepared for hearing my name, yes, but not for the way he says it in his sleepy voice. Despite sharing a bed twice, I've not heard this low, deep, purr of a voice before and it throws a bucket of cold water all over the resolve and intentions I had firmly in place a moment ago. No, not cold water. Fiery hot water.

"Shit," I say. "I'm sorry. It's late. You were asleep and—"

"No, no. It's okay," he says, still gruff and sexy and probably wearing another pair of pastel-coloured silk boxers. *Fuck, this was a terrible idea. Damn you, Dana!*

"What's going on? Where are you?"

"Just off Brick Lane having just put a very drunk Dana in an Uber."

"That's just around the corner," Rami says.

I chuckle to myself. "It's really not."

"Do you need some help? Money for a taxi?"

"Jesus, no," I say and I'm about to berate him for thinking me incapable enough to get myself in a pickle like that, but I stop myself just in time. It would certainly be harsh to be angry with him after I've woken him. "I just... fuck."

I hear some muffled rustling and imagine him sitting up in bed, the sheets falling down to reveal his dark, hairy torso. *Focus, Jake!*

"Do you need me to come meet you?" Rami asks.

"You'd do that? For me?"

"If you're in trouble or stuck somewhere, of course."

I sigh into the phone. "I don't need help. I'm not stuck. I was calling – stupidly and perhaps a little under the influence – to try and clear the air between us. I'm aware things have been... tense."

"That's one word for it," Rami says with a gentle laugh.

"I don't like it when things are tense," I say and it feels freeing to say something so deeply true.

"Neither do I, Forester." It's hearing my surname in that gruff sleepy tone that makes me reach for my magic phrase.

Fuck it.

"Rami, I—" I begin, but he is just as quick.

"Jake, do you want to come over?"

Chapter Twenty-Six

Rami

Jake doesn't look out of place in my apartment. He looks like he could live here, despite what he's saying and how he's behaving.

"What the fuck are you doing living in a place like this?" he demands standing at the floor-to-ceiling window and staring at the sparkling lights of London's night sky.

I walk over to stand beside him. "What do you mean?"

"It's a fucking penthouse apartment with a view that alone would have cost a million pounds."

"Well, then that would have made the apartment very cheap," I mutter, attempting humour.

"Seriously, what the hell were you doing in LA? Drug smuggling?" Jake puts his hands on his hips as he turns to me.

I look him up and down again, deciding this is possibly my favourite look on Jake. The slightly undone version of his once most done up appearance; his shirt a little creased and untucked on one side, his cheeks pink with warmth from good conversation and wine, and his hair suffering from his hands running through it all night, that front tuft threatening to fall down the centre of his forehead.

"I can assure you I was not drug smuggling," I say, choosing to deny falsehoods rather than create my own.

Honestly, when I bought this apartment, I didn't realise how flashy it would look, or how out of other peoples' price brackets it would be. I could blame that on over a decade of acclimatising to the LA-lifestyle where money has a very different value and your status depends on where you live as much as how you live, but it wasn't quite that simple. I bought this apartment without seeing it on a whim because I needed the kick up the backside to leave my mom's house. I needed to have somewhere else to go, a new life to start living, and I promised myself I'd make it a home, eventually. I'm still working on that part.

"It's incredible." Jake's breathless tone suggests he means it.

"Thank you," I say. "Do you want a tour? Or a cup of tea? Or something else?"

I didn't mean to say that in such a leading way and I regret doing so as soon as I hear the hidden connotation, but Jake doesn't seem shocked, in fact, it seems to make him smile.

"I'll take a cup of tea, and something else," he says, nothing mistaken about the emphasis he adds. But then he clarifies, "By which I mean, a chat. I really did call to talk."

After I have made us both tea — all the while Jake stands at the window and studies the view — I bring it to the large L-shaped couch that dominates the living area, and he meets me there.

"So, what did you want to talk about?" I ask after we are both sitting down.

"Well, this wasn't on the agenda, but can we talk about how aggravating it is that you look this good in joggers," he says and pokes the side of my thigh.

"I wasn't going to greet you in my boxers."

"Shame. I wouldn't have minded," Jake mutters before taking a tentative sip from his mug. "I blame your narrow hips, by the way."

"You blame what on my hips?"

He rolls his eyes. "Everything."

I laugh at that and I'm somewhat relieved that this quick wittedness suggests that Jake isn't as drunk as I previously thought when he called. To be honest, I'm just grateful to see Jake in a different environment from the office as it had become increasingly stuffy as the week had gone on.

"What did you want to talk about, Forester?" I ask and get the reaction I was aiming for when his eyelids lower a little and he gives me a quick side glance.

"What are we going to do about the tension in the office?" he blurts out.

So he's felt it too.

"I am trying," I begin. "I'm taking all my calls outside and—"

Jake puts his hand on my arm and that stops me. "You shouldn't have to do that. Sharon told me on Friday that your office is still weeks away from being ready, maybe even a month or two, so we need to figure this out."

I run a hand through my stubble and move it to rest on the back of my neck. "I don't know, Jake. Maybe we'll just get over it and move on."

"Get over what?"

"The tension," I say.

"Forgive my direct use of words but do you mean the sexual tension? Or the tension because we're not being sexual?"

"Aren't they one and the same?"

"I suppose they are." Jake nods at his cup.

"Maybe I should start working from home," I say. "I'm sure Bill and Simeon wouldn't mind."

"Because you're their favourite," Jake adds in a low voice.

"Jake, comments like that don't help," I say.

"Help what?"

"The tension?"

"Oh, are my snide remarks a turn on?"

"I wasn't—" I begin but then notice him giggling into his cup of tea.

"It's nice to see you laugh," I admit.

"It's nice to be in the same room as you and not feel like you hate me." Jake rests his head against the back of the sofa.

"I don't hate you, Jake," I say softly copying his movement, putting us in much the same position as we were on the Tube a few days ago.

"I know, but whatever it is that's going on with us, or not going on with us, it's getting to me." Jake's eyes are steady on mine.

"Yeah, me too," I say, aware of how talking about this is making me feel better. Not that it's making the tension go away, but rather it's shaping it into a different form, a lighter, headier thing.

"So, what now?"

I don't have a suggestion, but I do have the sudden strong urge to hold his hand, so I do.

His eyes drop to our fingers and I wait. I wait for him to take his hand away. I wait for him to say something. I wait for him to tell me this isn't helping. But he doesn't do any of that. Instead, he wriggles his fingers in between mine.

"You know, we could try something," Jake says staring at our hands.

"What's that?"

"We could try… we could just have sex. Get it out of our systems. Scratch the itch. Kill the tension."

Holding my breath, I study Jake's side profile. I suddenly want to kiss the pointed tip of his nose, want to run my tongue along the pronounced edge of his jawline, want to taste his rough stubble and his soft lips.

"Jake, I—"

"Don't overthink it. You either want to or you don't, and I really don't mind either way."

"You don't mind?"

"I mean, obviously I want to, because of all the aforementioned tension, but I understand if you don't want to go there with me."

"Jake, I want to go there," I say quickly and speaking the truth loosens one of the knots inside me. "But I just don't know if it's a good idea."

"I'm very good at sex," Jake says then and I have to put my tea down on the coffee table in front of us because I'm laughing so hard.

"I'm sure you are," I finally manage to say.

"And I bet you're at least average." Jake puts his tea down too before twisting his body towards mine.

"Thanks for the vote of confidence."

"Actually, it doesn't even matter if you're bad. I'll just enjoy looking at you." Jake scans my body. "You are that hot."

"Jake, I'm not going to have sex with you thinking I'll be bad at it," I say levelly. "I'd want you to enjoy it. I'd pretty much do everything I could to make sure you did."

Jake clears his throat before he replies in a hoarse voice, "Rami, when you say stuff like that to me… I can't…"

"What?"

"Nobody has said stuff like that to me before."

"Nobody?"

He shakes his head. My reaction is visceral. I want to hold him. I want to show him. I want to please him. I want to make him see how worthy of pleasure he is.

It almost hurts to pull my stare away from Jake with his features so small and his body turning in on itself but I need a moment where he doesn't fill my gaze or my mind. I lean forward and rest my elbows on my knees. "I don't know what's the right thing to do."

The silence that follows feels like it could go on forever, which would be impractical considering I have to get on a train in nine hours, but I still don't know what to say. I want Jake. I want Jake as a lover and as my friend, and it feels like I can't have both. That it's asking for too much.

Eventually Jake is the one brave enough to end the silence and make a decision.

"I should go," he says, and I feel the dip in the sofa that comes as he stands to leave. When I look up and see him run his fingers through his hair, but not catching that bit at the front, I know exactly what I want to do.

"Don't go," I say, and I grab his hand. "Don't you fucking dare go anywhere."

Chapter Twenty-Seven

Jake

I told myself if he stopped me going, if he said something to make me stay, then I would stay. But if he let me go, then I'd go. I'd walk away and find some peace with it all. Eventually. What I didn't expect is how I would feel if he spoke to me in that way again, that heavy, loaded voice, the rare curse words and the gravel in it all. Now I know I couldn't leave even if I wanted to.

I look down at him then, wanting to see if his face matches his words, and I see they do. There's his stern jaw, low brows and a shimmering quality to his silver eyes, a soft glow that reminds me of the moon on a clear night.

"Jake," he says, another growl of a word.

I don't speak, but I step back towards him and slide my body on top of his, straddling him. I exhale deeply when his hands land on my legs and glide up my thighs. When they come to rest on my butt, I roll my hips once, twice, and find his eyes, locking in his gaze.

"Say it again," I say, possibly over-indulging myself but I don't care. I want to hear him say it, feel that voice roll through me. "Tell me not to leave."

"Don't go, Jake," he says, pushing up to press his body against mine. "Stay with me. Stay here with me tonight."

They're softer words, and I wait to feel disappointed because I was craving more of the swearing and the rough demands, but they have just as much impact on me as I grind down against him. If anything, they reach more parts of me, parts of me that are melting and bringing heat to every inch of my body.

"We'll just fuck this out of our systems, right?" I say, wanting to make it very clear what I want, what I am almost starting to think I need.

Rami lifts a hand and places it on the back of my neck, readying me for a kiss.

"You can tell yourself that, Forester, but I don't think it's true. I don't think one night is going to be enough."

Swallowing is clumsy and laboured as my chest rises and falls with anticipation. I didn't even notice how much I was rolling against his body, his length hardening underneath me and mine against his stomach.

"Kiss me," I say. "Kiss me before you say more stupid, annoying, ridiculous things."

I feel a tug on the short hair at the nape of my neck.

"Tell me I'm not speaking the truth," he says pulling my head back so my neck is open to him. He grazes his teeth down one side. "Tell me it's a fucking lie."

I shudder as another fresh bud of desire blooms inside me. "I just want you, Rami. I want you so much it drives me up the wall."

"Good boy," Rami says into the skin of my neck. "I like it when you tell me how you really feel."

I only see the smile that opens his mouth for a split second before his lips come crashing down on mine. Our first kisses on that bench in front of a stately home were playful, curious, exploratory. Our second night of kissing at my flat had more hunger and less patience. But these kisses. These are the kind of kisses that almost feel like they could kill. There's no space to breathe, no room for air to find us, but we don't seem to need it. Because all that I need in this moment is in his kiss.

As Rami pushes me against him with the hand on the back of my head, I feel like he wants to sear this kiss into my memory. Even if I've got that wrong, I know that's exactly where this kiss will always live. I'll never forget it, and that both aggravates me as much as it thrills me.

Finally needing air, I push against his chest to create a little space and take in a lungful of oxygen. Rami takes my pause as an invitation to run his teeth, his tongue, his lips up along my jawline.

"You promised me a tour," I gasp out.

He pauses and lifts his head. "You want a tour? Now?" he asks incredulously. Part of me wonders if he would actually give me one if I demanded it.

"I want a tour of your bedroom, Mr Events," I clarify with a smile as I stand up.

Rami stands and grabs me around my neck, pulling me closer to him. A flash of a thought crosses my mind, in which I consider how much I would like it if he was taller than me so I could look up into his eyes, feel the full force of his power and dominance over me. But a beat later, I find myself liking how we line up perfectly, eye-to-eye, mouth-to-mouth, cock-to-cock, our bodies meeting in all the right places.

God, I want this man.

"Get your perfect backside down my hall and in my bedroom. Right now. Don't make me wait longer than you already have."

Partly-skipping, partly-stumbling, I obey his orders and find his bedroom through the second door on the right out of the corridor. A space that's almost as big as my entire flat, his bedroom has the same view as the living room and I find my attention briefly drift there, marvelling at how small this impossibly big city looks out of more floor-to-ceiling windows. But then I hear a click and a whir, and my eyes lift to see a blind coming down, taking the twinkling lights and the grey silhouettes of buildings away.

"Wait!" I say, holding my hand up. "Can you leave it up?"

"You want to do this with it open?"

"Can people see in?"

Rami considers this for a moment. "Not unless we leave the lights on."

I turn back to the window and look up at the sky briefly, searching for the moon. It's not difficult to find, hanging low and in its crescent form, it smiles in the sky above the cityscape. So I guess I can't even blame a full moon for feeling so utterly on edge with desire tonight.

"Lights off, blinds up," I say, still staring at the moon. It's not providing much light but the city's illuminations will give us enough to see what we're doing.

There's another click and more whirring, turning the light off and lifting the blinds out of sight. Still a little mesmerised by the view, I don't turn back to Rami immediately and I'm only thinking about doing so when I feel his arms snake around my waist and the warm solid heat of him press against my back.

I lean back into his touch for a few seconds, still admiring the irregular pattern of lights on in other buildings, but then I shake my head and pull away. This is not part of my "fuck it" – or rather "fuck him" – plan. Cuddles and admiring the view – no matter how impressive the latter may be, or how grounding Rami's embrace is – is not what I came here for. Because yes, I've long since stopped trying to convince myself that I didn't come here for sex. In fact, as soon as I suggested we try obliterating this tension by simply fucking it out of us, it made perfect sense. Of course, this will work. Rami and I will have a night of passion, and we will burn up all this lust that has been disrupting our professional relationship, and maybe even a friendship.

If it sounds like I have some authority on how this will play out, it's because I do. This is how it always goes for me. I meet a guy. I fancy him. I chase him a bit. I let him chase me back. And then we fuck. And after that, well, invariably nothing happens. Aside from a few outlier relationships of a few months, things between me and men just don't last. Twenty odd years of this behaviour on repeat is as good as ironclad evidence of how tonight will go. Rami and I really will get this out of our way and working together in the same office will get considerably easier.

Furthermore, we get to share a fun night together, because there's no doubt in my mind that it will be fun. It's written in Rami's darkening pupils that look me up and down as I turn to face him. It's clear to see in the way he licks his lips before placing them on mine. It's evident in how our bodies bend towards one another on instinct as our mouths lock together.

As our kiss deepens, Rami starts to push me towards the bed. When the back of my legs hit the side, I stop kissing him and pull back.

"Do you... What do you... How do you want to do this?"

"What do you want?" he asks me, breaking his commanding presence, but I'm actually grateful for it.

"I want to top you," I say in a hurry before I can change my mind.

"You do?" He's as surprised as I expect, as men often are when I say I want to top them. So surprised that normally I take it back.

As Rami stays quiet, I feel the need to explain. I swallow before I speak. "I want to see your cock while I fuck you. I've not been able to stop thinking about how perfect it is."

Rami looks away, down at the floor, and I know if the lights were on, I'd see a dark blush rise in his cheeks.

"Unless you don't want that," I quickly add. "Or you're not ready for that now."

"No, I'm ready. I had a shower just before you came here," he says and his hands slide up my back.

"Did you now? That was... presumptuous."

"You booty called me!" he protests.

"Booty call? Really, Rami, nobody has used that phrase since the mid-2000s and even then I think it was only permissible if you were in an American R&B group."

"You're talking too much again," he grumbles, but delivers it with a winning smile.

"What are you smiling at?"

"I was just thinking how good we are together."

Those are the last words I was expecting to come out of his mouth and for that reason, when they land, I don't know what to do with them. Luckily for me, Rami hasn't finished talking.

"You're full of surprises," he says and he lowers his mouth to kiss the base of my neck. "Really, really good surprises."

"You thought just because I'm a bitchy diva with good taste in interior décor that I'd be a bottom?"

"If I say yes, is that going to put the brakes on things?" he mumbles into my skin.

"Well, I thought you were a straight man with no sense of humour, so it looks like we're both learning not to judge a book by its cover," I say and I'm impressed I manage to get a whole sentence out fully formed considering how the sensation of his teeth nipping at my ear lobe is making my mind go fuzzy around the edges.

"Stop. Talking. So. Much." His mouth travels up over the ridge of my chin.

"Who me? Not possible. I am—" My words are swallowed by Rami's mouth and his tongue silences me for good as it finds my own. Floored by the hunger in his kiss, I grip hold of his body as I fall backwards onto the bed, bringing Rami with me.

Supporting his weight with one hand, Rami holds up his body so he has space to find my shirt buttons with the fingers on his other hand, and he begins fumbling with them, completely incompetently.

"An excellent fake wedding date you may be, and a pro at lip-synching Michael Jackson while also doubling up as a last-minute DJ, yes. But a magician who can undo buttons with one hand? I don't think so," I say and I swot his hands away so I can undo my own shirt.

"Talking too much again." Rami grunts but his eyes stay fixed on the skin that I'm exposing as I wriggle out of my shirt. Before I've even got it off fully, his mouth is on me. His tongue snakes a path up my stomach and to my chest, pausing to flick and play with one nipple before crossing to the other and doing the same thing. I'm no longer rocking against him but instead my body shudders in helpless, almost pathetic little jolts of need.

Rami has considerably more success unfastening things when his hand finds the fly of my jeans and somehow, he single-handedly pops the button open before lowering the zip. Waiting for his next move, I curl my head up so I can see what he's doing, but I'm surprised when he looks up and his eyes find mine. We stay locked in eye contact as his fingers slip inside the open fly of my jeans and he rests his hand on my achingly hard cock.

I huff out a breath as he shifts his hand so he can grip me. My stomach muscles start to shake from the position I'm in, or maybe it's the way his fingers start to stroke me.

The truth is, I've been touched by many men. I'm not proud of it, but my past is full of different men who have gripped me, grabbed me, stroked me, played with me, manhandled me. But none of them have touched me the way Rami is touching me right now. With barely-there glides of his fingertips and the occasional grasping and squeezing, he's exploring, he's curious, he's intentional, he's tender.

This only continues when he pushes up to lean on his side and brings his other hand over to pull my jeans and boxers down.

Once completely naked, I'm briefly aware that he is still fully dressed and my instinctive reaction is to do something about that, but I don't reach for him, because my second thought is how sexy I find it. How much I like his attention on me and considering this is a one-night only thing, I'm going to soak it all up.

"So beautiful," he says to me as his eyes roll up and down my body, and the way the shimmer of his silver eyes pops in the dim light of the room, I almost feel like believing him.

"Kiss me," I say, wanting to bury how his words make me feel in another hungry kiss. Wanting to replace the ache they arouse in me with the burn of his stubble against my lips.

"I will," he replies but he doesn't bring his head up to mine, instead he lowers it to my dick and leaves a lingering kiss at the tip where I already know I'm leaking.

A moan rushes out of me, and I close my eyes, tilting my chin up to the ceiling. Part of me expects that kiss to turn into licking, sucking, tasting, but it doesn't. Instead, he comes up to sit on his knees by my side.

"Lie back and relax," he says and he proceeds to start touching me. First, he glides the flat of his palm over my erection, slow and prolonged. Then he grabs the base of me and squeezes, hard. With his grip staying tight, he brings his other hand up to one of my nipples and plays with it, flicking and twisting. After doing the same to the other, he starts to move his fist, up and down. The speed slowly, steadily increases as the hand exploring me comes down to play with my balls, and when he pulls lightly on them, I moan, long and loud.

The fuzz in my brain only multiplies when I realise what he's doing; touching me in the very same way I touched myself, complete with one hand now stroking around my hole, just like I did to myself when he watched.

But then Rami lowers his head again and while still gripping me and fisting me, he opens his mouth and sucks the head of my dick into the wet warmth there.

"Rami," I whimper. I hope he thinks it's because I'm turned on, which I really, really am, but in reality, the shake in my voice has much more to do with how overwhelming I'm finding this moment, this attention, this intimacy as he continues to suck on me, lick me, kiss me, taste me.

"You taste so good, Forester. I could do this for hours," Rami says into the crevice of my groin in between kisses that lead lower down.

"No, you couldn't, or rather you wouldn't. Because I'd not last more than a few minutes," I explain.

After licking around my balls, and coasting his tongue down my perineum, Rami's voice practically drops an octave. "Maybe I should insist on you waiting to come until I said so. And I'd only let you come when you were a really good boy."

Oh, Jesus. He really is speaking my language. I am so beyond fucked if this continues.

"Okay! Enough!" I say gripping the bedsheets, which I can't help but notice are possibly softer than my own. "I need to get you ready."

Rami's reaction is not unexpected as he stops moving his hand and lifts his mouth off me. I didn't mean for that to sound like an outburst, but I'm not wholly surprised. I just need to take control of this situation. I can't let him and his deep voice and his kinky words have such an effect on me.

"Are you okay?" Rami's voice is back to normal.

"I'm fine," I say quickly while pushing up to rest on my elbows. "I just want to stop wasting time. Let's fuck already."

Chapter Twenty-Eight

Rami

I don't believe him. He's not okay.

I also want to argue that what I was doing was not wasting time. It was anything but. It was giving me all kinds of pleasure watching him squirm and wriggle beneath me while his cock got harder and harder under my tongue.

Besides, I wasn't finished with Jake yet. I was just getting started driving him wild, but something about his strained voice and the way he's avoiding eye contact with me now makes me realise he is indeed losing his cool but not in the way I wanted.

"Jake, you seem a bit stressed," I begin.

"I'm horny, okay," he snaps at me. "I get grouchy when I'm horny."

I'm not convinced that's true, but I know his tone well enough not to challenge it. That said, I'm not about to drop my trousers and carry on where we left off because that won't get rid of whatever it is he's feeling.

"I'm nervous too," I say simply. Somehow, mercifully, it works. Because as Jake finds my eyes again, I see his shoulders lower and the tension in his jaw ease.

"I'll be gentle with you," he tells me, and I understand then what he thinks I'm referring to – the bottoming. While I appreciate the sentiment, that's not what I'm the most nervous about. I'm anxious about giving myself to him in a way that I haven't with anyone in over two years. Even before Michelle, I didn't do random hook-ups. I've always preferred being in a relationship to one-night stands or failing that having a friends with benefits type arrangement that has some sort of connection or longevity in it. That said, I'm only too aware that whatever is happening between Jake and myself doesn't fit in any of these categories. I have no clue what we are or what we're doing.

But as I take in the sight of Jake splayed across my bed, the shadowy light in the room highlighting where his muscles rise and fall, and his cock so straight and proud, I know I want this. I want this so much that labels don't matter. I feel close to him even if he maybe doesn't feel the same.

"Do you want *me* to be gentle with *you*?" I ask and it's both a tease and a test.

"Don't you fucking dare," he says his brown eyes firing up again as they fix on mine.

"Then kiss me," I say as I come to straddle his body keeping up on my knees. "Kiss me and tear off my clothes and grab me and hold me, Forester," I sit on his stomach and wrap my hand around his throat. He nods at me just like I want him to. "And then fuck me. Fuck me so good."

It's like watching the last shred of whatever resistance he was feeling melt away instantly as he moves his hand to grab the back of my head and pull me down. To say we're kissing doesn't feel quite right, more fighting with our tongues, our teeth, our lips. I groan when he bites my bottom lip. A few seconds later, he moans when I suck his tongue into my mouth.

Obeying the first of the orders I just gave him, he brings his hands down to the hem of my T-shirt and pulls it up and over my head. His hands then explore my chest, my stomach, and my arms, before finding their way to the waistband of my joggers. I bring a hand down to help him slide them down my hips. Kicking them off the bed, I feel Jake's hand on my dick, squeezing it through my silk boxers.

He breaks our kiss to look down. "Powder blue today. Very cute."

I should say something back, something equally as sarcastic, but I don't want to, nor do I think I'm able. The way he plays with me, his fingers curling around the head of my dick, their pressure varying in a way that kicks up my desire many notches, I don't want to talk at all anymore, at least not unless it's to get a reaction from Jake.

"Let me grab what we need," I say and I stretch to rummage in the drawer of the bedside table. I find what I'm looking for and throw the lube and the box of condoms over my shoulder onto the bed.

"Ow!" Jake calls out.

Turning my head, I see his hands clutching his eye and the bottle of lube lying on the bed close to his head.

"Shit," I say, moving back so I'm directly on top of him again. "Sorry."

"I better not have a black eye tomorrow," he says still wincing in pain. "For fuck's sake. It's been years since I've had a sex-related injury."

I chuckle at that. "Let me see," I say trying to move his hands.

"I'm fine," he says, again in that tense voice.

But I'm not having any of that. He's not going to slip back into being grumpy, so I push my body further down the bed, and line my mouth up with his groin.

"Rami, what are you—" Jake says but his words descend into a deep groan as I hold his cock in my hand and run my tongue up the underside. "Oh, Jesus Christ, yes."

I keep lapping at him until I see my saliva glisten all over his skin, and then I move to the head, letting my tongue explore its smooth texture and lick at the pre-cum that emerges at the tip.

"Fuck me, your mouth." Jake grunts and his hand comes down to grip the back of my head. I moan at his touch when his fingers start digging into my skull. Then he shifts and sits up a little. "Rami, I should be—"

Holding his cock in one hand, I use my other to press on his stomach and push him back down. "Lie down and shut up."

"Yes, Daddy," he says and falls back on the bed. I stop moving my mouth, observing how new flames of longing burn bright at the base of my spine. When I don't resume he lifts his head again. "Too much?" he asks.

"No, not too much," I say in my normal voice before turning my more serious, lower tone back on. "You're such a good boy, Jake."

He hums at that, a noise that only gets louder when I suck his dick into my mouth. I quickly get lost in lapping at him and sucking him into my throat as deep as I can stand. It's only when I hear the click of the lube bottle being opened that I pull away.

"Please, Rami, let me fuck you now," Jake mumbles.

I come off him and climb up his body. After lifting up my legs one at a time and sliding my boxers off, I sit on his thighs and hold out one hand to him. With my other I grip our dicks together and squeeze.

"I want to—" Jake begins but then his eyes flutter shut when I start rubbing my hand up and down our lengths, pressing them together.

When his eyes open again, I shake my head. "I'll do it," I say. "And you have to watch."

He pulls his mouth into a quick scowl, but he sees sense a second later when he then props himself up on his elbows and casts his eyes on my hand. A beat later he squeezes a generous amount of lube on my palm. Regretfully taking my other hand off our cocks, I place it beside Jake's head to hold myself up as I lean forward. I then bend it at the elbow and come down to kiss him. With my other hand I get to work applying lube all around my hole, and starting to push two fingers inside.

"I can't watch you if you're kissing me," Jake mumbles into my mouth.

"Fine," I say with a grunt as I move to sit back down and grab his cock and mine again. Jake groans as I then find the lube and squirt a generous amount on both of us. I start to stroke us both again, up and down, twisting my hand over our heads each time I reach the top. Behind me, I push another finger inside.

"God, I wish you weren't so good at this," Jake says, his narrow eyes and slight sneer suggesting what he says really is true.

"You haven't seen anything yet," I say as I speed up my strokes. It's not that I think I'm good in bed. I haven't given it much thought over the years, if I'm honest, but one thing I am confident of is that I'm going to make this good for Jake. Just in case it never happens again, I know I'm going to make this something he remembers.

Jake's stomach muscles tense as he curls up further and watches my hand work. When I feel his dick swell a little more under my grip, I drop my hand to squeeze the base of us both.

"Fuck," he hisses.

"Not yet," I say and after a few seconds, I return to slowly stroking us both, something like a smirk curling my lips.

"You're going to make me beg for it, aren't you?" Jake asks.

"You would sound so pretty," I say. "I often imagine what you sound like when you beg."

"Rami, stop saying things like that," he grits out as he squirms a little on the bed as if he doesn't know what to do with his hands.

"Like what? Like how I've thought about doing this with you every night since we kissed at the wedding? How when I fuck my hand, only the thought of you lying on my bed, helpless and needy, is what gets me off?"

"Please, don't…" he says but his hips start to thrust up.

"Tell me what you want, Jake. Beg me."

"I want to fuck you," he says in such a rush I can barely hear the words. "Please can I fuck you?"

"I told you to beg," I say and lean down to bite his nipple.

"Please, Rami, please. I'm fucking begging you. Please can I fuck you?"

After flicking my tongue over his other nipple, I look up. Taking in the rapid rise and fall of his chest, and the way his mouth is open, panting, I smile.

"Put a condom on," I say reaching for the box. "And fuck me."

Jake scrambles to open the box and I do my best to avoid thinking what impression that gives of me – to have a brand-new unopened box of condoms in my drawer – and luckily for me I have the perfect, cutest distraction as I watch him bite on his bottom lip concentrating as he rolls a condom down.

God, he's a good-looking man. A good-looking man who has no idea how much more beautiful he is when he becomes unravelled like he is now, his hair flopping over his forehead, heat in his cheeks, and his hands shaking a little.

I reach to stroke the side of his face. He flinches at the touch and his eyes dart up to look at me.

"Relax," I say, returning to my normal voice once more.

He nods at me and I watch him pull in a breath.

Content that he's calmer now, and the way he continues to rock his hips slightly and breathing heavily suggests he's still very turned on, I grab the bottle of lube and squeeze a dollop out on top of his condom-covered dick. I slick some of it around the full length of his shaft and then I keep hold of the base, positioning him where I want him as I rise up high on my knees.

"I'm going to ride you first, get used to it a bit, and I want you to be a really good boy for me and take it," I say holding eye contact. "But don't come."

He licks his lips. "Yes. Yes, okay."

A burst of inspiration puffs out my chest.

"Yes, what?"

"Yes, Daddy," he replies on a ragged, shallow exhale.

"Good boy," I say and I cup his face again and keep my hand there while I shift so I can press the head of his dick against me.

I am expecting it to hurt, I'm expecting to feel the hot ache that I know will pass, and I have to be honest and say half of the role I'm playing is so that I can focus on something else other than the trepidation about that which has been running through my veins since Jake told me what he wanted to do. By being stern and demanding for Jake, and seeing the instant, heady effect this has on him, it has eased a lot of the nervous excitement I feel about being with a man in this way again after a long, long time.

But what I don't expect, what I am not prepared for is how *good* it feels as Jake's dick slides inside me and I slowly, tentatively come to sit down on him. It's not just the fullness and the pressure in exactly the right spot, it's the connection, the intimacy, the way Jake is inside me, and my body is welcoming him, squeezing him, holding him. It's the way we are connected.

"Fuck, yes," I say in a whisper as I rock a little on my knees.

Jake makes no noise but looks just as blissed out as I feel, his head tilted back and slightly to the side. I watch his throat work through a deep swallow.

"You feel—" he begins.

"So good," I finish for him.

After a few more moments adjusting, where I just look down into Jake's eyes and smile, I start to move. His eyelids fall and he pulls his lips into his mouth.

"Watch me," I say suddenly desperate to not have him drift away from me again.

Like the good boy he is, he obeys me, first holding my gaze, but eventually lowering his eyes so they watch how my hands are placed on his chest, and how I push myself up and down on top of him. Finally, his stare is on my cock, and he licks his lips again.

"Why do you have to have the most perfect penis in the whole goddamn world?" he asks but he looks anything but angry about it.

"Touch me," I say and I mean my dick but it's not a disappointment at all when he rests his hands on my thighs, sliding them up and down in the same rhythm I use to ride his cock.

"Yes," I gasp out, feeling tingles from the way his dick presses against my prostate, feeling sparkles from the way his hands flicker over my legs.

"This is better than I thought it would be," Jake says and the way he pulls in a deep breath at the end of that sentence makes me wonder if he even meant to say it. This is somewhat confirmed when his tone of voice changes. "Your cock, I mean. It's so pretty. I love watching it bounce."

There's something about this censoring of himself and his showmanship in paying me a compliment that irritates me and I know it's time.

I pull off Jake and lie down on the bed next to him, for a moment we're side by side, both a little breathless, and his confused eyes staring at me.

"What are you—"

"It's time for you to fuck me, Jake. Are you going to give me what I want?"

"Yes," he says.

"Yes, what?"

"Yes, Daddy."

"Good boy." I lean over and take his mouth.

We keep kissing as he turns and climbs on top of me. I lift my legs up at the same time he reaches down and plays with my dick, stroking it with a firm grip, then his hand drops and he slides a finger over my hole. I grunt into his mouth. He circles it again and again, before he then cups my balls, applying the faintest pressure when I hiss again. The need to have him filling me up again is too great to ignore for a second longer.

"Fuck me," I say with his bottom lip between my teeth. "Now."

He pulls up on his knees and looks down. "Rami, I—"

But he doesn't finish, and I am too desperate to feel him again that I don't even ask what he was about to say. Instead, I prop my head up with pillows, lift my knees up higher and use a hand to fist my dick.

Jake takes his time sliding in, and his eyes dance around my body as he does, as if he's not sure where he should look.

"You fill me up so good," I say deliberately, wanting to encourage him again to stay with me, to stay in the room.

"I want to fuck you good, just like you want me to," he says, and I delight when I hear how eager he is to please, and a note of needy desperation in his voice.

"Yes, Jake, fuck me. Fuck me like the good boy you are."

The words are barely out of my mouth when he starts to move, thrusting in earnest inside me. His hands come down to my hips and he pulls me back onto him.

"Tell me if it's too much," he grunts out and it's all I can do to nod, mesmerised by the concentration on his face, and how good he's making me feel.

"More. Harder," I say finally and I keep stroking myself as Jake ruts into me.

A couple of times I feel him speed up only to slow down again and I wait until it happens a third time before I speak.

"You want Daddy to tell you when to come?" I offer.

Jake moans. "Jesus, fuck. Yes."

"Good boy asking my permission." I bring one of my hands to his hip, digging my fingertips into the supple flesh there.

His thrusts slow down again, and he hangs his head. "Your fucking words. They're too much," he says, sounding defeated.

"Did I tell you that you could stop fucking me?" I demand, hoping this is the right way to keep him with me.

He responds by looking up, gritting his teeth and thrusting into me again, our bodies slapping against one another.

A few seconds later his angle changes and I feel a new rush of pleasure as he hits my prostate again and again and again, every single time. I don't want to come yet, I want to drag this out all night, but it feels too good. When my eyes roll back and I curl my toes, despite taking my hand off my dick, I know I'm done for.

"Grab my dick, Jake," I say. "Make me come."

Jake fumbles at first, his hand clumsy and heavy but it doesn't take long for his strokes to even out and for him to match them with the thrusts he pounds me with.

"Are you going to come with me?" I ask, knowing he hears the breathlessness in my voice just as clearly as I do.

"I don't... I don't know."

"I want you to come with me, Forester. Are you going to do that for me?"

"Yes," he says and I don't even have a chance to pull him up. "Yes, Daddy, yes," he adds in a rush.

"Good boy."

Jake's eyes close and his thrusts and strokes speed up even more. I watch a trickle of sweat glide down his neck and I am thirstier than I have ever been to reach up and lick it off his skin, but I don't move. I fix my eyes on his face, on his eyes. As if feeling the intensity of my stare, they snap shut.

"Open your eyes," I tell him as I feel a delicious prickling pressure at the base of my spine. "Watch what you do to me."

"Oh, God," he says when his lids lift and his gaze drifts down to where his hand is working me. A deep grunt comes from his throat and I lock the sound away inside me, knowing I'll think about it again and again in the days to come.

"Yes, Jake," I say as I feel my balls tighten and my dick harden in his grip.

"Fuck," I say as the first surge of my orgasm rushes up and out of me.

"Such a good boy," I gasp as Jake continues to pump me and I spill more of myself on his fingers.

As the pleasure sucks me under, my vision clouds but still I watch him as he thrusts into me, his movements hard and sharp. He's staring at my dick in his hand, looking at all the places on my stomach where my cum now lies, and I moan with sweet satisfaction as the hits of my own pleasure fade into gentle waves.

"Oh, God," he says again and he stills after thrusting up into me. I feel his dick twitch once, twice and I fix my eyes on his face, finally discovering what he looks like when he comes. Eyes closed, mouth slack, brow completely wrinkle free, he looks blissed out. He looks relaxed. He looks beautiful.

I can't stop the hand that lifts to stroke his face, and there's no restraining myself from using my other arm to pull his body down on top of me and the mess we've made there. And there's definitely nothing in the world that could stop me from kissing the top of his head and squeezing him close to my body as I say, "My beautiful boy," over and over and over again.

Chapter Twenty-Nine

Jake

I wake in a bed that's not my own, and my first thought is pancakes, because that's what I can smell. A sweet, warm and airy fragrance, my nose is full of it before I even open my eyes. When I do, I realise where I am, and then it doesn't matter how good the scent is, I panic. I panic because in just a few quick seconds I relive the whole of last night.

The way he spoke to me. The way he bossed me around. The way he let me call him Daddy. The way he studied my face as I came. The way he held me afterwards, whispering the most unbearable of sweet words until I must have fallen asleep.

I close my eyes and take a moment to replay those final moments in his arms. I remember so clearly wanting to cry. I remember wanting to sob my tired heart out so I could carry on without it. I remember fighting so hard to not let a single tear fall, but I don't know if I succeeded. God, I hope I didn't cry in front of Rami.

"Good morning," a voice says from beside the bed and I jolt my eyes open as I let out a squeak of shock.

"Sorry," Rami says, standing next to me wearing just the jogging bottoms from last night. *God, he looks good. The bastard.* "I thought you were awake."

"I was, just didn't realise you have a stealth mode." I push to sit up but keep the covers around my waist.

"I brought you coffee and pancakes. American style of course. Didn't get much from living in LA for ten years, but I did learn how to make good pancakes."

A little hint of that helpless urge to cry reveals itself inside me once more as I take the plate and mug he's offering me.

"And I'm allowed to eat in your bed?" I ask, placing the mug on the bedside table.

"I brought them here, didn't I?"

"I just have a strict no-eating rule in my bed," I say but then embrace the opportunity to cock my eyebrow. "Unless…"

"I don't think you need to finish that sentence," he says, but he's smiling at me indulgently.

It should be jarring, seeing him switch back to his slightly prudish self. I should be feeling paranoid or self-conscious that our dynamic last night was so different to what it is normally, but of all the things I'm feeling, that is not one of them. It's actually nice he's being normal with me. It possibly suggests he doesn't think differently about me. Possibly.

After Rami sits on the bed next to me, and I've taken a few delicious bites of the food, I watch him sip his coffee. Maybe he's acting *too* normally. Maybe the pancakes and being nice is all an act. I blame it on my self-sabotaging tendencies that I feel the need to test this theory.

"So now you know I have Daddy Issues," I say and Rami promptly spits a mouthful of coffee back into his mug.

"Pardon?" He coughs.

"Last night. The whole calling you Daddy thing." I close my eyes and wave my hands around.

When I open my eyes again, I see Rami looking at me with a furrowed brow, his eyes darting around my face. "I don't think that means you have Daddy Issues."

"Well, I do," I say as I take another bite.

"Jake, are you okay?"

Chewing gives me far too much time to formulate my reply. "Am I okay? Well, I just shagged my co-worker and the only way I was able to climax was from him calling me a good boy and giving me permission to come, all while I was calling him Daddy like the pathetic man with abandonment issues that I am."

"Jake, I—" Rami tries to speak.

"It's fine. I'm not shaming myself. Not really. I'm nearly forty fucking years old. I'm well aware of what pushes my buttons and what doesn't, I just don't always share those things with someone else and rarely is it so—" I stop speaking.

"So, what, Jake?" Rami asks and his voice has the edge I love in it again. The one that slows my senses and melts my insides.

"Nothing," I say quietly and fill my mouth with hot coffee. Damn it. It's an extra strong coconut milk latte, just how I like it.

Rami sighs. "Would it make you feel better if I told you how much I enjoyed it?"

"You did?" I turn to look at him.

"Yes, Jake. I loved it. I haven't... I haven't had a night like that in a long time."

"Oh," I say.

I don't miss the sharp inhale that follows Rami's next words, words he says without looking at me but instead staring down at the plate I'm holding. "I liked you calling me Daddy. I liked it a lot. It made me feel powerful, strong, important."

"Did it?" I ask, suddenly aware I've never thought about it from this angle before.

"Yes." Rami's eyes are on mine now and we stay connected like that as silence falls. And it's the worst possible thing that could happen, because it allows me space to feel something I was really dreading feeling. I still want him. I still desire him. Last night did not scratch the itch. In fact, it only made things... itchier.

Clueless if Rami feels the same, I drop eye contact and reach for my coffee again.

"Can you lift the blind?" I ask, realising he must have closed it last night, after...

"Sure," he says, hopping off the bed and flicking the switch.

"A bazillion-pound penthouse apartment but no remote for the blind, you're roughing it," I say in my snarkiest voice.

"Oh, I have a remote, but it's in the drawer next to you," he says coming back to sit on the bed.

"Then why didn't you just ask me to get it?"

Rami shrugs. "Because I like doing things for you," he says and he's lucky the view outside grabs my attention so I am distracted from pulling him up on saying silly, soppy, untrue things like that.

"Wow," I say. "I'd never get bored of this view."

"Me neither," Rami agrees but when I glance at him a second later, I don't see him looking out of the window. I see him looking at me.

*****

"I should go," I say when I finish the food and coffee. "I need a shower and you've got a train to catch."

"You can shower here," Rami says. "And I still have an hour before I need to leave."

"You don't mind?" I ask. I am already imagining how incredible his bathroom is. I'm too nosey for my own good sometimes.

"Not at all," he says getting off the bed. "Do you want to use my ensuite or the guest bathroom? I should also have a shower."

My jaw drops. "You have two bathrooms?"

"Possibly," he says tellingly, coming to collect my plate and mug.

"Hmm. I bet they both have bathtubs too."

Rami's mouth pulls up on one side.

"They do? Jesus, Rami. Are you a secret millionaire or something!"

"Possibly," he says again but it sounds less leading.

"I'll take the guest bathroom. Should I go first or wait for you to finish?"

"We can shower at the same time… In separate showers, I mean," he adds carefully.

My mouth falls open. "It won't affect the temperature or water pressure? What kind of utopia is this?!"

"I'll get you a towel," Rami says and leaves the room.

After making sure I know where my underwear is before I get out of the bed, I grab them and pull them on in record time. However, I'm not quick enough to find my jeans or shirt, so I'm standing in just my underwear when Rami returns to the room carrying a folded towel. A folded towel that looks annoyingly fluffy. For fuck's sake, I bet it smells good too.

"Can't find my clothes," I say as if to explain my partial nudity. Every square inch of my skin rises with goosebumps as Rami's eyes rake down me from head to toe.

"I should have hidden them," he says before nodding at a pile at the end of the bed. "Bathroom is just down the hall."

And then he goes through the door to his ensuite bathroom. I spend far too long waiting to hear the click of a lock, and then even longer wondering why it doesn't come. Eventually, I hear the running water of his shower and I shake away all the possible reasons he leaves the door unlocked as I take my clothes and his ridiculously fluffy towel and walk out of the room.

There are three other doors in the short hallway and they're all closed. With no real sense of my bearings, I open the one nearest me on the opposite side, and I know immediately it's not the bathroom. I know this because when I walk in, I see a bed without sheets, and surrounding it, are stacks of boxes. No furniture, no soft furnishings, just rows and rows, and columns and columns of moving boxes, and they all look like they're packed full.

On the side of the boxes are handwritten letters and this tells me that whatever is inside is organised alphabetically. Curiosity gets the better of me and I go to the nearest box and try to look through the hole that provides a handle. Unable to see the contents clearly, I open the top flap and peer in. Records. The box is full of vinyl records. If every single box is full, this is quite an impressive collection and I wonder why Rami doesn't have it all on display. It also suggests maybe his love of music and those amateur DJ skills have more roots than he claims.

Closing the box, I leave the room and find the bathroom in the room next door. I spend more than a few seconds admiring the finishings – black marble floor and walls, gold taps and details, and fuck me, a heated towel rail three times bigger than the radiator in my pokey bathroom – and then I switch the shower on. I groan when the pressure is instantly perfect and the water becomes warm before I've even dropped my boxers.

"Fuck him and his perfect apartment."

It is the best shower of my life. Of course, it's a waterfall shower with water pressure and I stay under the spray for far too long, using copious amounts of Rami's designer lemongrass shower gel.

After I dry off and dress, I steal a bit of toothpaste from a tube I find in the sink drawer and run it around my mouth on my finger.

Leaving the bathroom, I feel sheepish and a little out of place, and I hate it. This is exactly the feeling I've deliberately tried to avoid by purposely not partaking in any one-night stands or dating app action for the last six months. I feel ashamed and embarrassed and awkward, and I hate that I feel all those things in relation to Rami.

It's not because it's him. I don't feel judged or disliked by him, and it's not even because we work together, although I know this is only going to make the awkwardness bleed into my working week. It's the worst possible reason; it's because I know I like him. I like him in a way that always gets me hurt.

I have to leave. Now.

Hearing movement in the large living area, I stand in the doorway of Rami's kitchen to tell him goodbye. "Thanks for the shower. I left the towel hanging up."

"You want another coffee?"

If this man gives me one more perfectly prepared coffee, I'm going to implode.

"I have to…" I start. *Go feel sorry for myself until my alarm goes off for work tomorrow.* "I have things to do."

"Like what?"

"Like…. Okay, I have no plans. But I just don't think being here is a good idea."

"Because it didn't work," Rami says putting down the spoon and coffee he was putting into a press.

"What didn't work?"

"Us scratching the itch? Getting this out of our systems," Rami says and his eyes are determined in holding mine.

"I guess not," I admit and saying it out loud helps relieve a little of the weight on my shoulders.

"So, what next?"

I pull in a breath. "I guess we go back to being weird with each other and ignoring the elephant in the room."

"Now, Jake, that's a terrible way to describe Sharon," Rami says and the curl in his lips lets me know he was trying to make a joke. It's more his attempt than the actual words that have my insides melting a little and a dry chuckle leaving my lips.

"Your sense of humour is getting worse again," I say. "And to think we'd made such good progress at the wedding."

"I think I need to spend more time with you then."

"Oh, that will create more problems than it solves. And will make my life a living hell."

Rami looks taken aback. "Because you don't enjoy my company?"

"No, because I will want last night to happen again," I say and while being honest again relieves more weight, it also makes me feel like I'm free-falling a bit, especially when Rami drops his eyes from mine.

I watch as he pulls his lips into his mouth and sets about finishing making his coffee. When the water is in the pot and the coffee is swirling around, he finally speaks.

"Maybe we need to spend time together without having sex?" Rami offers. "And not at work."

"Oh, you want to go for a country walk? Play Scrabble? Go rock-climbing?" I offer, the sarcasm thick and heavy in my voice. It has a depressingly familiar bitter taste too.

"No, I mean, let's put ourselves in a situation where we physically can't... succumb to temptation."

"Isn't that exactly what work is? And that tension is what we're trying to nuke."

"The tension at work is different. We're forced to spend time together there, but what if we just hung out for a while? Maybe we'd find a better way to communicate and just be in each other's company without it being weird."

"Or without it involving nudity," I add.

"Well, what I have in mind definitely would be better if we avoided nudity," Rami says with a wary smile.

"What do you have in mind, Mr Events?"

"Come with me to visit my mom and sisters today," he says it so casually it's like he's asking me to put the kettle on but my reaction is anything but calm.

"What?! Your family?"

"Yes, why not?"

"I don't know them, and they don't know me."

"That's kind of the whole point of you coming to meet them," he says as he slowly pushes down the percolator.

"I don't know, Rami, it's a bit—"

"Look, you'd be doing me a favour. It's a long story, but my mom worries about me living here in London and not really knowing anyone yet. If I brought a pal over, it would put her mind at rest."

"But we're not teenagers, Rami. Isn't it a bit odd that you feel the need to bring a friend home?"

"I know it sounds strange, but it's true. If you don't want to, I understand."

"No, it's not that I don't want to. I just don't want to impose. It's your family day."

And nobody has ever asked me to meet their family. Nobody. Not one man in my life has ever invited me into their life in that way.

"Jake, you'd be the star of the show. And you'll love my sisters. They rip into me way harder than you ever could. You'll pick up some tips."

"That does sound tempting," I admit. But I don't think that's the main reason I want to say yes. I am also intrigued at the idea of meeting his family, at the prospect of finding out more about this man who continues to surprise, and frankly, impress me.

"Then you'll come?" he asks and I see the lift in his body at the possibility. Before I have time to confirm or deny, he's moving to grab his phone.

"I'll just go call Mama to tell her to cook enough food for you," he says halfway out of the door.

"She doesn't need to—" I call after him, but he's gone. Uncertain why he had to leave the room to call his mother, it does nothing to calm the new nerves I have that now mix with the agitation I was already feeling at realising how much I like Rami. But I can't deny how both things are also making me smile.

Chapter Thirty

Rami

"Just put them in a cupboard somewhere. I don't care where, just get them out of sight."

"Rami, it's like you think I don't have better things to do," Roxie grumbles.

"Well, do you?"

"I'm on my twenty-fifth row of a candy floss baby blanket even though I know nobody about to have a baby."

"Then why are you making a baby blanket?"

"My OT suggested I try screen-free hobbies that keep my mind and hands busy when I need more sensory input but I'm tired. So, knitting it is."

"That sounds... nice."

"It's awful. I suck at it. But again, I've got to try and be bad at things. Another challenge. Is your therapy this nightmarish?"

"I don't go to therapy," I say before thinking it through.

"Seriously? Why not? You're way more fucked up than me!"

I laugh lightly while my heart also breaks. "Thanks, Roxie."

"But it's true! You joined a cult, for crying out loud. I was just born with a weird brain."

"Your brain is not weird," I say quickly, sternly. "It's a beautiful brain, you just need some extra help figuring out how it works."

"You really don't think you need therapy? I thought you told Mom you'd be starting again when you moved to London."

I did say that. I also said two years ago I'd go back to LA and do the residential therapy I never finished. Since when did I become a man of so many broken promises?

Unsure why he darts into my mind, I feel something shift when I remember Jake is sitting in my kitchen.

"Maybe I'll start soon," I say more to myself than my sister.

"Ugh. Why can't I earn enough money to move out and live my life exactly how I want to. You rich, old, neurotypical folk have it so easy." Roxie moans.

"I'm not sure that's a compliment, but thanks. Listen, Roxie, can you pass me to Mama while you go hide all the discs and awards? And can you also fill Radia in on everything when you pick her up? How she can't mention DJing or RemiX or Michelle or—"

"Anything else? Need me to cut your fingernails?"

"That won't be necessary," I say. "Just do the awards and—"

"Shit! Yes, that's why I stood up."

"And pass me over to Mama," I add.

"Oh, no, *that's* why I got up. Jesus Christ."

"Thank you, Roxie. I love you."

There's no more talking for a few seconds, only rustling until I hear my mother's voice.

"Rami?"

"Mama," I say. "How are you?"

"Good, good. Looking forward to seeing you. Unless you're calling to say you can't come, which is completely fine and you should go have a nice day off in London…"

"No, I'm calling to say I am bringing a friend with me today. I hope that's okay?"

"A friend?"

"Yes, someone from work. His name's Jake."

There's a quick pause. "Of course, that's okay. I look forward to meeting him."

"The thing is, Mom, he doesn't know… about my past."

"About the cult?"

"Or even the DJing," I add in a low voice. There's a twist of something sharp in my chest and I don't know if it's at the thought of Jake overhearing me or just because I'm still lying to him about this huge part of myself.

"Why haven't you told him about that?" Mom's question sounds innocent enough but it lands with me loaded in guilt.

"Because it just hasn't come up in conversation. I will fill him in eventually but just for today we want to be with you and Radia and Roxie and enjoy all your good food," I say forcing a smile in my voice.

After another pause, my mother says something that kicks me in the gut. "I don't like lying to people, Rami. It never ends well."

"I'm sorry, Mama. But it really will be just today."

A silence stretches on and on. It lasts so long I pull the phone away from my ear to check the screen. We're still connected.

"Okay, *habibi*. I trust you," she says eventually and although I am relieved, it feels like a lot more than I deserve.

*****

Despite the usual extra shot in his second latte, Jake falls asleep within minutes of us leaving Euston station. I try to rest my head back against the seat and fall asleep myself, but it doesn't come. Although my eyes stay closed for a few minutes, invariably I find them opening to roll up and down Jake's sleeping body, pausing on his face and the way his mouth hangs slightly open and how his eyelids flicker in a dream. His head is resting against the window and I envy the sheet of glass, wishing it was my shoulder he was leaning on.

When I finally admit that sleep isn't coming for me, I pull out my headphones and stick them in my ears. I scroll through my playlists waiting to feel inspired but nothing grabs me. That is until I see the same playlist I put on for Jake when he was getting ready in the ensuite bathroom of our hotel room at Lionel's wedding. I smile to myself, then shake my head, clueless at how I can feel nostalgic already even though that day was only a few weeks ago. It's then that I realise just how little time has passed since I met Jake, and yet how well I feel I know him. No, that's not quite right. How much I *like* him.

Because I do like him and not just in the way where I want him to be my friend. It feels greedy to admit it but having him only as my friend would feel inadequate now. I don't want to be friends with Jake. I want more, but I'm pretty sure that's wanting the impossible because that would require Jake to know things I haven't told him yet. Things that I'm not sure I want him to ever know, as selfish and impossible as that may be. As I chew on this conundrum and find it curdles my stomach and creases my brow, I am relieved at the interruption that is my vibrating phone. I pull it out of my pocket and see a message from Radia.

<Roxie just filled me in on your 'friend' coming to visit today. Is it fake boyfriend Jake?>

I grit my teeth, <It might be. Did she also tell you that we're not to mention DJing or the other thing.>

<The cult. Call it what it was.>

<Tomato, tomato.>

<That doesn't work in a text message.> She sends back with the face palm emoji.

<Has Roxie taken down all the awards and discs?>

<Yes. They're stashed in my old room so unless your fake boyfriend goes snooping upstairs, you're safe.>

<No fake boyfriends. Just friends.> I clarify.

<Whatever.>

<How's BB?> I ask, desperate to move on to something else.

<Changing the subject like the avoidant you are.>

<Actually, avoidants would never ask that. Avoidant behaviour would never start a conversation about close emotional connection, even between other people.>

<Wow, you did learn something in those few days of therapy.>

How can I tell her that I didn't learn that in therapy but in... the cult? The cult that started off like something resembling therapy, a wellness movement, no less. Founded by two people who I do believe at some point thought they were improving others' lives, Gee and Michelle weren't uninformed – they were both sponges for information, reading books and studying several Eastern philosophies that centred the body and our natural energies – but they weren't professionals either. They were self-taught at best, and reckless rookie amateurs at worst. And somewhere along the way, they got lost. Or at the very least their priorities did. Because nobody who wants to charge their so-called friends thousands upon thousands of dollars to "remix" your life, to "weed out the bad and nurture the good in your soul", is actually doing that when they're wiping away people's life savings, retirement plans and investments.

I'm only lucky a constant flow of royalties kept me more than comfortable. I also had a decent chunk of money tied up in the house that Michelle and I owned together, a property that I didn't agree to sell to put the equity into RemiX. That had been the first of many red flags.

Not that it was all about money. The real pain came when I realised how comprehensively I'd been manipulated, and it was a double-edged sword because like one therapist told me in the week of rehab I did do, there is no brainwashing in cults, not really. People do not join cults blindly. They want to believe whatever the message is. And I know I did. I wanted to believe life could be simpler, calmer, more fulfilling than the treadmill I was on when my DJ career was at its peak. That part of the equation I have no problem understanding. I was burnt-out, overwhelmed and on the cusp of a physical and mental breakdown. What I struggle to understand is why I turned to Michelle and Gee, and eventually the retreat, no, the commune, we established in the Mojave Desert. Why didn't I come home to the UK? Why didn't I turn to my family? Why did I cut off Dev and all my other friends? Why didn't I seek out real professional help?

Was I really that proud? Was I really that susceptible to the wrong kind of influence? If not brainwashed, was I really that blinkered to what was good for me? And if the answers to these questions are yes, then what kind of man does that make me? Is that the kind of man who is worthy of someone like Jake?

Desperately not wanting to answer those questions, I switch my focus back to Radia's text conversation. **<I also learnt to be grateful for my sisters who help me out when I need them to.>**

<Save your gratitude for Mom. She's tutting approximately twice a minute over this whole Don't Mention the DJing/Cult Thing.>

<It's for the best. For everyone.> I text back.

When I see Radia go offline, I put my phone away and close my eyes, listening to the music and mentally travelling back to an English country garden bathed in moonlight. And I stay there lost in that memory, as well as recollections of last night until we're in my home city.

Jake stirs as we approach Birmingham New Street, and I know I only have a few minutes before we meet Roxana who has confirmed she's waiting in the car park outside. I need to talk, and quickly.

"Jake," I say but then pause to take in how adorably cute he is just waking up, all scrunched up eyes and pouting lips.

"Yeah," he croaks.

"Bit of a random request, but don't mention my whole being pansexual thing in front of my mom."

Jake blinks and with that single movement instantly wakes up. "You're not out to your family?"

"My mom, no. My sisters, yes."

He doesn't reply as I see the station's platform begin.

"So, you won't mention it?" I prompt.

"Is your mum a homophobe?" Jake asks in a rush. "Because in case you aren't aware, I reek of gay. And I refuse to go back in the closet for anyone."

"No, of course not!" I say, horrified he would even think that. "She knows my sister's gay. She will be absolutely fine with you being gay too."

Jake blinks again. "Then why aren't you out to her?"

I sigh and it is such a long, heavy breath that it almost hurts my chest. "It's a long story, but my mother and I had a very distant relationship for a while. We didn't talk much and we weren't very close."

"When you were living in the States?"

"Yes, and I am trying to repair it, and I just don't want to do anything to rock that boat."

Jake lowers his voice to a whisper. A loud whisper admittedly, but I appreciate the gesture. "Rami, have you been with men before? Was I your first?"

I chuckle a little. "Yes, I've been with men before."

"But no relationships?"

"None that I told my parents about."

As the train comes to a halt, I grab my bag and stand. I am relieved when Jake does the same as I move out into the walkway. Just before we approach the doors that are still closed, I turn back to Jake. "Look, I know it's nothing to be ashamed of, and I do plan on addressing it in the future, but please could we just not mention it in front of my mother."

I hear the beep and start walking towards the doors. Over my shoulder, I hear Jake's response. "It wasn't like I was planning on mounting you at the dinner table. But yes, you can count on me."

I can't help myself turning my head back towards him. "That's a shame. What about in the kitchen? Any chance of some dry humping there?"

"Not in front of your mother!" He pushes my back lightly. "And did you forget already? We're supposed to be spending a day together without heavy petting."

"What about *light* petting?" I ask after I'm off the train and turned around to watch Jake step down. He comes to stand right in front of me and I lean towards him.

"Rami," he warns, and I can smell his breath – coffee and mint – and feel its warmth on my lips. "Let's at least try, shall we?"

"Okay, I'll try," I say but drop my gaze to his mouth.

Maybe I do it because I want him to know that while I'm not out to my mother, I'm not ashamed of who I am or who he is. Maybe I do it because I want to thank him for his promise of confidence. Maybe I do it because I just can't stop myself and I know this is my last chance to touch him like this today. Whatever the reason is, I close the gap between us and rest my lips against his, closing my eyes to the people walking down the platform around us. While neither of us open our lips to deepen the kiss, our mouths stay locked together for many long seconds before I release Jake and step back.

"Starting now," I add and when I look at him, I see the same mischievous glint that I know is dancing in my eyes.

Chapter Thirty-One

Jake

While I didn't have long to imagine what Rami's family home would look like, as we pull up to the semi-detached Tudor-style 1930s house, I realise it's exactly what I expected. It's also exactly what I wish I had as an adult – a childhood home I can return to where older versions of my parents wait eagerly on the doorstep – but that dream shattered a long, long time ago.

Of course, it's not all dream-like for Rami either. I'm sure he desperately wishes his father was standing next to his mother on the driveway, but he isn't. She does, however, seem to do her best to make up for any missing hugs as she embraces her son at length, a hug that he returns just as willingly. After Rami hugs his other sister – Radia, I assume – he introduces me to them both. They all greet me with warm enthusiasm and I do my best to return it. When his mother, Raina, shakes my hand she doesn't let go and uses her hold to lead me into the house ahead of everyone else, something that warms parts of me that have possibly been lying dormant since my own mother passed.

Inside, the house is cosy and tastefully decorated and the walls are covered in artwork and photos. A bittersweet feeling settles inside my stomach when I realise all the framed pictures are of the three children, or alternatively, they are treasured artwork created by them. Part of me wants to stand in the hallway and study each photo, each messy, colourful painting, but Raina still has my hand in hers and she's taking me through to the kitchen where she insists I sit at a small round table in one corner.

"Would you like a coffee, Jake? Or a tea?"

"A tea would be lovely," I say and I notice Rami lean against the kitchen counter opposite me. He's smiling and looking a lot more relaxed than I feel.

"Rami, see to that will you," Raina waves her hand at her son and after only a quick beat, he jumps into action.

"I'll have one too," says Radia as she comes to sit next to me.

"And me," Roxana takes the chair on the other side of me.

"Don't get used to this," Rami says, pointing a teaspoon at us all.

"So, what's he really like at work?" Roxie leans closer. "Rami's never really had an office job before. I bet Radi he wouldn't last six months. Do you think I'll get a tenner out of it?"

"Why, what was he doing before this job?" I ask.

"Oh, you know, travelling the world, and—" Roxie stops abruptly. Her eyes snap to Radia who is looking cautiously at her brother.

"Travelling the world and pretending it was work," Radia finishes.

"Yeah, there was a lot of travel," Rami says but he has his back to us as he retrieves mugs from a cupboard. "But it *was* work, I can assure you."

His mother's cough is a sharp, curt sound.

"We're going to have a beef bazella, which is like a pea stew, with tabbouleh and rice for lunch, Jake. Or there will be a vegetarian version for Rami and Radia, if you prefer that. I hope that sounds okay." She comes to stand by my chair.

"The beef sounds delicious." I hope the smile I'm offering Rami's mother is as warm as the one she's giving me.

The kitchen quickly descends into a rumbling cacophony of conversation and cooking noises. Rami busies himself chopping vegetables by his mother's side, while Radia tells me more about her work, and Roxana asks me questions about my job. Both of his sisters are incredibly easy to talk to and they have sharp, lively senses of humour that occasionally reveal a dark side. I like them both immediately.

Just as I'm telling them a bit about this one time in Crete when I saved the resort from a suds tsunami after a guest put bubble bath in a jacuzzi, Roxana jumps up and leaves the room without saying anything. When she returns, she's carrying a stack of photo albums. Over the course of the next hour, I learn that Rami was right to say spending time with his sisters would provide me with instant ammunition for our future conversations. While he and his mother cook behind us, Radia and Roxie take me through countless photos of Rami's formative years, including the most adorable pictures of Rami in dresses, Rami in make-up, Rami in criminally short shorts, and cutest of all, Rami completely naked watering plants in the garden that is just outside the window.

How his mother doesn't know her son is queer is beyond me.

My face sore from near-constant grinning and chuckling with Rami's sisters, we are called to the dining room where lunch will be served.

The meal lives up to the promises the scent of Raina's cooking gave me and I happily take a fully loaded plate from Rami.

It's not long after I've practically licked my plate clean that Raina asks me if I have a boyfriend. Before I reply, I shoot Rami a quick look that I hope conveys how foolish he is to think she would ever have a problem with his sexuality.

"No, I don't," I say, and I reach for one of a handful of my default responses to this question. "I like to keep my options open."

"That's exactly what you should do while you're still young," she says with a kind smile.

Her comment is polite if a little misplaced, but regardless I think I am in love with this woman. Briefly, I wonder if this is what my mother would have been like if she was still here, if she had had a different life. Would she have been so welcoming? Would she have been so visibly delighted to have her grown-up children sitting around her table?

"And Rami hasn't caught anyone's eye at work?" Her question is followed by silence as all three of her children stop moving their knives and forks and ping-pong looks at each other. If they think they're being subtle, they're very mistaken and I'm in half a mind to think that their mother knows it too.

"Rami? Oh, I'm sure he's caught many peoples' eye but he probably doesn't know it. He's too busy working hard and trying to get on my nerves."

"I do not..." Rami tries.

"Work hard? I should hope you do. You're lucky to have that job!" his mother says and she is rewarded by her daughters' laughter.

"I meant, I don't try to get on your nerves," Rami says to me while waving a hand at his giggling sisters. "It just... happens."

"And yet you're so very successful at it." I purse my lips at him and watch as Rami's face flickers from annoyed to amused.

"Well, Jake likes to annoy his assistant." Rami turns to his mother and sisters, sounding like a scorned child.

"I do indeed," I say proudly. "Sharon is a wonderful butch lesbian who keeps my life from descending into utter chaos. The least I can do is communicate my gratitude for her in her love languages which are derision and degradation. And she does exactly the same to me, because they are also my love languages." I deliberately avoid Rami's gaze when I say this.

Rami's mother chuckles, her whole body moving slightly. "It sounds like you both have a lot of fun at work." She looks at Rami. "I'm very happy to hear this, *habibi*."

"And for the record, Rami does work hard," I add. "And he has been very accommodating to my need for space sometimes. Sharing an office has been a bit challenging at times, but I take most of the blame for that."

Rami blinks at me before his smile grows. "It's been a learning curve for us both, Jake."

"Well, you do bring me coffee every morning. That does make it somewhat less sufferable having you around."

Rami arches an eyebrow, and is he trying to impersonate one of my typical pouts back at me? I squint as if to scrutinise it but we both end up laughing at our expressions and I then pull my glare away, only to see Rami's mum watching us, closely.

"Who's ready for dessert?" Radia pushes up to stand in such a hurried way it makes me wonder what she knows about Rami and myself. "Roxie, help me clear the plates."

Roxie groans. "Do I have to?"

"It's fine, I'll do it." Rami stands up too.

Raina has the final say as she stands and reaches for two dishes on the table. "No, you helped cook. You sit and talk with your guest. The girls are happy to help me." She walks out of the room.

"I wouldn't say that," grumbles Roxie, not moving.

"Happy is a stretch," Radia says with a wink at me as she reaches for my plate. She quickly glances to check her mother has left the room already. "Come on, Rox. Let's leave Rami and his boyfriend alone for a minute."

"Radia, Jake is not my—" Rami begins.

"Ssshhh, Mom might hear!" Radia sticks out her tongue before walking away.

"Are you really boyfriends?" Roxie asks looking from me to Rami and back again. I can't quite read her open-mouthed expression but I'm going to choose it's excited rather than horrified. I'm also choosing to ignore the way my stomach flips every time the word 'boyfriend' is said.

"We are not boyfriends," Rami says, not exactly holding his sister's eye contact but still leaning towards her. "We are friends, and we work together."

"Do you not want to be Jake's boyfriend?" Roxie asks and heat climbs up my neck and cheeks. If Rami is having anything close to the same reaction, he doesn't show it.

"Jake would be a brilliant boyfriend," his voice stays calm and he still doesn't look away from his sister. "But it's up to Jake who his boyfriend is, isn't it?"

I pray silently that Roxie doesn't direct the same question at me and for once my prayers are answered. With a quick shrug, she stands and collects a handful of remaining plates and then leaves the room.

"Roxana sometimes doesn't have a filter," Rami says finally looking at me again. "And Radia too, it seems. Sorry if that made you feel uncomfortable."

Hot? Flustered? Intrigued? Restless? That's what the boyfriend comments made me feel. I wouldn't say any of it was uncomfortable though.

I wave away his apology. "No big deal. You have a lovely family, Rami."

He looks down, smiling. "I know. I'm very lucky."

Because of the angle of his head, I can't see if that smile reaches his eyes or if it's as sad as his voice sounds.

"You know you're not so bad yourself, right? I know I tease you and stuff, but you're a good guy, Rami."

The way Rami's head snaps up, his eyes blown wide and his mouth slightly open is a shock to me. Surely, he knows he's one of the good guys. A good guy who travels hours every Sunday to see their family. A good guy who goes out of his way to make my life easier whether it's taking his calls out of the office or traipsing across half of Southwest England to go to a wedding as my fake boyfriend. A good guy who buys me and Sharon coffee every single morning. A good guy who didn't humiliate me for my weird sexual preferences. A good guy who maybe, possibly even enjoyed them himself as he indulged them.

"Thanks, Jake," Rami finally replies, the words small and swallowed away quickly as he reaches for his drink.

*****

I eat more than my fair share of dessert – five different kinds of delectably sweet halva – and then I am treated to a cup of possibly the world's sweetest tea. During the latter, Rami's mother humours me while I test out what little Arabic I learnt in Morocco. She compliments my accent, which makes me blush, and then teaches me a few words of Farsi, which I enjoy far too much. Maybe I should look into getting some lessons. I always have enjoyed learning other languages.

But no, lessons cost money. And money is not something I have, a fact I was reminded of earlier when I felt far too much relief when Rami insisted on buying our train tickets. I shouldn't be approaching forty and experiencing such gratitude when I don't have to pay for things. The tension from this kind of shame straightens my spine and makes me drift away from the room as Rami's mum goes about correcting her children's pronunciation of words and they all laugh together at jokes I don't understand.

I try not to dwell on what life would be like if my mother were still alive, or if my father lived closer. I haven't really let myself feel the full weight of loss I feel at Jenna living in another country. But as I already feel low thinking about all my debt, it seems to open the door for more negative thoughts and feelings.

As I often do, out of the blue, I feel the sadness of my mother's death, and all the same questions it brings to my mind. Was there more I could have done? Why did she want to leave me? Why wasn't I enough?

I've worked through these questions countless times with Anita and in the past I have been able to find peace with never knowing the answers, but today I feel like I can't ignore how much I will never understand her decision to end her life, to miss out on seeing the people Jenna and I grew up to be.

"You okay?" I feel a hand on my arm. I look up and see Rami's silver eyes on me and above them a concerned frown. From nowhere, a daring thought crosses my mind. Could I talk to Rami about my mother? Would he listen and offer words of reassurance? Would he hold me as I shared the pain I still feel at losing her when I was so young?

"Yeah, yeah," I say quickly then reach for my tea, only a little surprised it's gone cold. "Just a bit tired."

Rami scans the room before he replies, "Me too. Let's go soon."

"No, we can stay as long as you want. Don't leave on my account. I really am having a lovely time."

Perhaps too lovely, in fact.

"It's okay, Radia is sleeping over tonight so we can go anytime, and I normally would go around now anyway. I have a busy day at work tomorrow."

"Do you?" I realise I haven't even thought about work tomorrow or the week ahead. I've not even thought about what I'm going to do with the rest of my day.

Rami leans a bit closer when he talks next. "Jake, will you come home with me? I've liked being with you today and I sort of don't want it to stop. Will you come home and have dinner with me?"

I also check my surroundings before speaking, but Rami's mother and his sisters are all crowding around Radia's phone on the other side of the table, laughing at something.

"Rami, if I do that, I feel like something… else could happen."

"Would that be so bad?" Rami replies with a gleam in his moonlight eyes.

Yes, it would, because I like you. Yes, it would because I don't want to get into this deeper. Yes, it would because the deeper I get into it the harder it's going to be to climb back out when it inevitably ends.

"I don't know," I decide to say.

"We don't have to. If you don't want to," Rami says and it sounds like a peace offering, permission to walk away, and yet I can't ignore how disappointed it makes me feel.

"Okay," I say, noticing movement among his mum and sisters. "I'll come back to your place."

"Good boy," Rami says in a hoarse whisper, and I have no time to react because his mother is offering me more tea and his sisters want to show me another photo album and Rami is explaining to them all how we have to go soon.

But I do react. Inside. I react with every fibre of my being. I react by feeling more alert, anxious and excited than I have in years. I react by feeling more alive, and despite myself more hopeful than I have in the longest time.

Chapter Thirty-Two

Rami

The train home is a lot more comfortable than our journey up to Birmingham, which has everything to do with how Jake's sleeping head is resting on my shoulder. It may or may not have been tactical, my claiming of the window seat when we got on, but I have no regrets, not now I feel the weight of his body against mine as I watch the blurred greens of the English countryside rush past me.

I'm almost ready to fall asleep myself, my cheek resting on top of Jake's hair when my phone buzzes. It's a message from Radia.

<We all agree Jake is amazing.>

<I co-sign.> I reply.

<Good then you need to tell him about California. The whole story.>

I drop my phone to my lap. I've not even begun to formulate a suitable response when a buzz tells me another message has arrived.

<And pleeeeeeease come out to Mom already. Today was super fun but the lying in too many directions was not a good time. Poor Roxie has gone for a lie-down she feels so pooped.>

A burst of guilt stabs inside me and I can only imagine how hard Roxana found it, not least because she probably doesn't fully understand why I feel the need to lie to my mom, or why I don't want Jake knowing certain things about my past. Truth be told, I don't even understand it fully.

<I'm sorry.> I message back to my sister.

<I know. We just want you to be happy.>

<Didn't I look happy today?>

<You did with Jake, yes. But something tells me that's not as happy as you could be.>

<Don't want to be greedy.> I joke.

<Be greedy.> Radia messages back instantly and I can almost hear her saying the words. <You're allowed to be greedy.>

No, I'm not, I want to roar back at her. *I have to pay my dues. I have to amend for what I did. I have to keep life as calm and normal as possible for myself and everyone else I love.*

<When are you going to bring BB up to visit on a Sunday?> I change the subject rather than respond.

<Ha! That proves my point. Jake not your boyfriend? MY ASS!>

<He's not.>

<Do us all a favour and ask Jake out on a proper date. And on that date tell him all about DJing, California, Michelle, Gee and RemiX. Then send a photo of you and him on said date to Mom with the caption 'Jake is now my boyfriend'. Job done.>

The noise that leaves my mouth is half-groan, half-laughter.

<I love you, Radia.> I type back, because I really do. I then open my latest chat with Roxie and text her the same thing, while also apologising for making today more difficult for her.

<Ew. Emotions.> She texts back immediately.

I shake my head and pocket my phone, but as I do it vibrates in my hand.

<Love you, too.> My sister messages and the smile it puts on my face stays there as I rest my head on Jake's and fall asleep.

*****

There's a moment when we're walking to the Tube when I think Jake is going to change his mind and head in the opposite direction back to his flat, but he doesn't. He just walks by my side as I lead us into the station. Maybe I do it in celebration, but once we're through the ticket barriers, I take his hand and hold it in mine. And when we stand on the escalator, descending to the platform, Jake turns to face me from his lower step and wraps his hands around my waist. The escalator's end comes far too soon.

Back at home, I am quick to instruct Jake to sit on the couch while I go about making him a ginger tea as I noticed he started sniffling again this afternoon. Once he's settled drinking his tea and looking at a coffee table book of Annie Leibovitz portraits – handily not the one that features a photo of me – I go to the fridge to decipher what we can have for dinner.

"Marinaded tempeh with new potatoes and asparagus sound okay?"

"Sounds very elaborate for a quick and easy dinner."

"Who said anything about being quick and easy?"

Jake lifts his head from the book. "Are we still talking about food?"

I snort loudly and then start moving around the kitchen preparing the vegetables and the tempeh.

"Can I watch you cook?" Jake's voice is louder and I look up and see him standing at the island. Again, I find myself thinking how perfectly at home he looks.

"Sure," I say and as he sits, I let my eyes wander over his body, especially as I believe he's opened a few buttons on his shirt, or rather my shirt that he borrowed so he'd have something clean to wear to my mom's.

"You look good in my clothes," I say as I take a few steps towards him around the island.

"Rami, something's about to boil over." Jake points behind me.

"Shit!" I say and rush back to the hob. When the heat is turned down and I've cleaned up the mess I turn back to Jake. "Looks like you were saved by the boil."

"Oh, God." Jake groans and drops his head to land on his forearm. "That was your worst joke yet. Has spending all this time with me done nothing for you?"

I turn half my body back towards him and wait for his head to lift. "Spending time with you, Jake, has been everything to me."

Jake doesn't respond but instead gives me another silent and unusually empty expression, so I turn back to the hob a little unsettled at the possibility I said too much. But I don't regret it. It was completely true. A few seconds later, he's by my side, the length of his body pressed up against the side of mine. I turn to face him and he leans forward and grazes his teeth down the side of my neck, which I elongate for him.

"Jake," I say and it's full of heat and air. I don't know if it's a warning or an invitation, but Jake takes it as the latter as I feel his hands on my fly while his tongue laps at the places his teeth scratched down my skin.

"Don't say anything," he says into my jawbone. "Just cook."

When my trousers are hanging open, he drops to his knees and pulls them down, my boxers too. Not yet fully erect, I feel heavy heat rush to my cock immediately when Jake takes it in his hand and then licks the tip.

"Jake," I repeat. Another indecipherable instruction or admonition.

And again, Jake silences me with more pleasure by lapping at the head of my penis as it swells in his grip. His tongue then slides down to lap at the full length, on all sides, and I quickly turn down the heat on the hob, knowing I don't want to have my eyes looking anywhere but at him on his knees in front of me. I lift my shirt so I can see him better and then I lean back a little, thrusting my now rock-hard dick closer to his wickedly talented mouth.

"Forester," I say and this time the meaning is clear. *Keep going. Don't stop. Fuck yes.* "You look so good on your knees for me."

He moans and then takes me in his mouth. As his teeth graze over the edges of my cock I feel my pleasure intensify and not in a way that gets me closer to my climax but rather a bolt of heat that revels in how dirty this is. In an ideal world I would have had a shower, and we certainly wouldn't be doing this in my kitchen, but the spontaneity and the unexpectedness of Jake wanting my cock only makes it more thrilling.

"You're so fucking good at this," I say as Jake continues to suck all of me into his mouth, moaning again at my words.

Pulling my hips back when he takes a break from taking me down his throat, I move my cock away from his mouth and reach down with my hand to cup his chin.

"Look at me," I say, and he does, beautifully obedient.

"Open your mouth," I say, and after a second-long display of confusion creases his brow, he does.

Slowly, carefully, and with a tenderness I know may get lost in the moment, but it's there, so very there for me, I spit into Jake's mouth. "Suck me, Forester."

I watch as his eyelids flutter shut but he keeps his mouth open, my spit on his tongue as he pulls my cock back into the slick wet warmth there.

I have a suspicion that Jake is trying to make this last, because every time his sucking and deep throating gets me closer, has me thrusting into his mouth and my eyelids lowering although never fully closing, he pulls off and goes back to using his tongue to tease me. Zigzagging licks up my length, gentle laps of my balls, and careful flicks across the leaking tip of my sensitive head. It's only when I start to swear and dig my fingernails so firmly into his hair that I suspect it hurts, he finally takes me back into his mouth and lets me fuck him there in earnest.

"I'm going to—" I can't finish the sentence.

"Please." Jake lifts his mouth only to rush the words out. "Please, Daddy, please."

When I come only a few seconds later – a white-hot sensation that almost forces me off my feet – and I'm spilling down his throat, I'm glad he took his time. His mouth made me so desperate for my orgasm, but now I'm almost sad it's over. Or maybe it doesn't have to be.

"Get up," I say once my breath is back in my body.

Licking his lips, Jake stands. I remove any distance between us and grab his face with both my hands.

"Kiss me," I say and he does. Eyes closed, head tilted, his mouth on mine. Jake kisses me like it's the only thing he wants to do and I use my tongue to search for traces of my cum in his mouth.

It surprises me when Jake pulls back at exactly the moment our kiss deepens and I have moved my hands down to his waist.

"Was that good for you?" he asks and he looks concerned, worried almost.

"So fucking good," I say into his mouth because I don't want to take my lips away from his yet.

Jake's half-smile nudges at my own. "You swore, so I believe you."

This comment has a sobering effect on me. "Why wouldn't you believe me?"

Jake pulls back a little more. "I don't know. People say sex is good all the time. It's like the standard parting ritual. *Great sex, thanks so much, see you never.*"

"Except, I'm not going anywhere," I say, running my nose against his.

"Well, you do live here," Jake says in his joking voice.

"I want to kiss you again." I'm not in the mood for banter.

"We're ruining dinner."

He has a point albeit one I am willing to ignore. I run my hands to the front of his trousers and find what I'm looking for.

"I want to make you feel good," I say.

Jake pulls his hips back. "Maybe later."

I stare into his chestnut eyes and find them a little duller than I would like. There's something there I sense but can't name. Whatever it is, it makes me back off.

"Okay." I make a mental note to not let Jake dodge me later. I quickly go back to making dinner while Jake and I make small talk. It doesn't take long for us to be seated at one corner of the island with full plates in front of us. From his first mouthful, I can tell Jake is both impressed and surprised by what he tastes.

"You can cook," he says with an arched eyebrow.

"I try."

"Did you cook a lot in LA? I've always imagined it's a place where people eat out a lot. Especially working in hospitality."

"Yeah, you're right. I rarely cooked at home. I think that's why I enjoy it so much now." Not to mention how we were only 'permitted' to eat raw vegan food in the desert. Any other permeation of nutrition was deemed sub-standard and capable of tainting the "pure vessels" our bodies needed to be. I shudder not because of the ridiculous notion, but because I can still tap into the part of me that was happy to believe it. I'm not yet comfortable even thinking about eating animal products again, let alone trying to do so.

As we eat in silence, and possibly to distract myself from more memories of RemiX, I find myself looking at Jake more than I'd care to admit, watching his jaw work and his eyes close as he savours the flavours. I shouldn't find it erotic, but it only adds to the returning desire I feel thinking about all the things I'm going to do to him later.

"So, I don't want you to think I was snooping…" Jake says out of nowhere and my line of thought quickly halts. "But I found your guest room by accident earlier and I saw all your boxes. Your boxes of records."

"Oh," I say. I know this is as incriminating a response as any, but my brain is simply not working fast enough to come up with something better.

"What's the story there?" Jake asks, an intrigued tilt to his head.

I think about telling him everything, really I do. It's the perfect opportunity, I see that clearly, but then I also see the way he's looking at me – curious, caring, hopeful – and I just know telling him everything will wipe all of that away. I'm not ready for Jake to not think of me as somebody other than the confident, assured man who has the power to make him come undone in his arms.

I suck in a breath.

"Well, I just haven't really gotten around to getting them out and I was also thinking of getting rid of some," I reply and this is partly true.

"Why? You must have collected them for a reason."

"Some of them belonged to my father," I say, another truth. "That's actually how my collection first started. He gave me some of his duplicate vinyl, a long time ago."

"Then you mustn't get rid of those."

"No, I won't, but some of the others…" And I drift off because how can I tell him I need to get rid of these records because I'm never going to be that person again. Lunar. Award-winning DJ. One of the best-selling music artists of the 2000s. And the man who threw it all away, and so much more, to join a cult.

"You have plenty of space in this apartment, Rami. Maybe you don't need to get rid of as much as you think. I'm guessing those shelves were installed just for those records…" He nods behind us to the empty purpose-built unit lining the wall behind the sofa.

"Yeah, they were."

"So, just get them on display. And maybe start playing some of them too. You clearly love music."

You have no idea, I want to say but I don't.

"It's complicated," I say with great effort.

Jake puts his cutlery down with what could be described as a flourish. "Well, I have ears and my heart doesn't feel quite as stony today as usual. You could talk it through with me?"

"It's a long story," I reply, my voice sounding shaky.

"I have time." Jake leans a little closer. He looks up at me and I see his freckles, the curl of his eyelashes and his beautiful mouth waiting for me to tell him my story. I know what he's doing; acting coquettishly to lure an explanation out of me. And I am about to do that, I really think I am, but then he opens his mouth and adds two words that instantly make me stop. "Please, Daddy."

Because that's how Jake sees me. He sees me as strong. He sees me as capable, and all put-together. He sees me as predictable and reliable and in control. And I need Jake to see me that way. I really do. It's what has made today feel so brilliant, so affirming. I don't want to ruin that. I don't want to ruin this perfect day.

"I will tell you, just not now." I stand and collect our plates, dumping them quickly in the sink before turning back to Jake. "Because now is not about me. It's all about you."

Chapter Thirty-Three

Jake

I am torn. Part of me wants to push Rami away, because I want to know this long story he is hesitant to tell. But another part of me wants to fold myself into his arms, and as much as I want him to fill in some of the blanks that still exist in my mind, I can't stop my body from melting at the dark, hungry look in his eyes.

I didn't drop down on my knees for him to do this as payback. I knelt in front of him because I was suddenly desperate for a taste of him. I was desperate to thank him for including me in his family day. I was so very desperate to give him pleasure.

Could it really be true that Rami is now just as desperate as I was?

In a weak last-minute attempt to try and go back to talking, I stand and open my mouth to speak, lifting my hands to keep some space between us, but nothing holds any ground with Rami. He crushes my hands between our bodies as he presses his mouth against mine, taking my open lips as an invitation to have his tongue ravage me.

I moan as he spins me and pushes me up against the island we were just sitting at and he kicks away my chair so we have more space.

"I want you so much," he says, now all stern and commanding. "I don't like being made to wait for what I want."

"But dinner—" I say weakly.

"Was for your benefit. I want you well fed and watered before I do what I'm about to do."

"Oh, God, Rami. What are you doing to me?" I whimper although it was supposed to be a thought not something I say out loud.

"Call me Daddy," he says as he bites my chin, tipping my head back.

"Jesus, Daddy, yes, whatever, Daddy, please," I mumble, and I stop trying to even find some sense in my head let alone in the words that are tumbling out of my mouth, words that Rami sucks into his body when he comes to kiss me again.

"On the rug," he says into my mouth after several long minutes of kissing as our erections press against each other through our clothes. Holding me so tightly around my waist and upper back, Rami's grip is so strong and firm I can barely move to seek out more rhythm and friction.

Rami is in complete control. And I love it.

I look briefly at the sheepskin rug over Rami's shoulder before I move. "Is it real?"

Rami takes his lips off my neck to also follow my gaze.

"Honestly, I don't know," his voice is back to normal, "I paid someone to decorate this apartment for me and I never asked."

I roll my eyes but I don't think he sees because of what he says next.

"If you don't want to lie on it, I understand. We can go to the bedroom."

There is something almost heart-shatteringly charming about how he breaks character to address my possible concerns.

I smile at him and rock my hips against his. "I'm pretty sure I ate close to a quarter of a cow at your mother's house. My animal welfare ethics are already pretty sketchy today."

It snaps him back into the persona I instantly crave. "Then lie down, Forester."

"Yes, Daddy," I whisper, then walk, no, *skip* to the rug.

I have mere seconds to panic about whether I'm supposed to adopt some semi-erotic pose or not before he is also on the rug, on his hands and knees, stalking his way up my body.

"Tell me what you want, and I'll do it," Rami says.

"I don't want anything special," I say looking up into his cloudy eyes.

"Not what I want to hear. Be a good boy, Jake, and tell me what you want."

Feeling myself get pulled back into the trance-like state that comes with us playing these roles, I briefly take a moment to consider my answer. All the while I look into his eyes and watch how his pupils dilate and the silver-grey swirl around them is like watching an oncoming storm.

He really does want to know.

"Undress me," I say finally. "Then kiss me, everywhere. All over my body. And bite me. Bite me wherever you want. Touch me, get me so hard and close I'm begging you not to stop. But then do stop. Stop and wait. Then take me close again. And again and again."

"Edge you?"

"Yes," I say feeling my quick, ragged breaths shake my stomach.

"And then what? How do you want to come? Inside me again?"

"No," I say again. "I want to feel you this time. I want to come with you inside me."

Rami dips his head and growls, literally growls, into my ear.

"Fuck, yes," he says and then he sits down straddling my body and his hands come to pull up my shirt, or rather his shirt that I've been wearing all day.

Rami follows my instructions to the letter. He strips me of all my clothes apart from my underwear and quickly gets to work running his tongue up and down my body, lapping at the sides of my torso, flicking the tip over my nipples, kissing a line from my neck to my belly button and nipping at the flesh he grazes along the way. Then he slides down further and kisses my thighs and groin, his lips and tongue getting lost in the hair there, and his touches are so light and soft and unnervingly tender, that I find myself squirming under his touch.

"Keep still," he says gripping my hips and pushing me down. "Be a good boy and keep still."

I am not a good boy because I cannot keep still, not completely. I writhe under his kisses and nibbles. I tremble when he pulls my boxers down and his mouth comes down on my dick. I shiver when his hands come up to pinch my nipples as he sucks me down his throat. And I rut into empty air when he takes his lips off me when I'm frighteningly close to climaxing, just like I asked.

But still he calls me a good boy. He calls me *his* good boy.

After he has edged me three, four times, he lifts his mouth and kisses me just below my belly button.

"Don't move," he says and he gets up and leaves the room.

The panic I feel when he leaves me is utterly irrational but a very real thing to feel. When I see Rami returning with a condom and bottle of lube in his hand, I relax… until I don't.

I sit up. "Rami, I should probably go and… you know."

He nods at me, understanding. "Do you feel ready?"

I mentally trace back how the day has played out. I nod.

"I trust you, Jake," he says as he drops to his knees beside me and his mouth dives in to kiss my neck.

It still feels like a risk, and I'm not sure I'm only talking about bottoming, but when Rami's hand comes down to stroke my perineum and lower still, tracing circles around my hole, I know it's a risk I want to take. Even if the worst happens, I feel like I will survive it with Rami, which is an absolutely wild thing to think, but believe it I do.

When his head comes up, I reach for it and hold the back of his neck.

"I trust you too, Rami," I say. The wave of tender emotion I experience as he holds my gaze is terrifying but also like something divine, holy, almost. As time teeters on the edge of becoming everlasting, I stare into his eyes and also sense he is experiencing a very similar sensation. It's bittersweet when he looks away.

"Have to have you," he says on an exhale and then lies down between my legs.

We kiss as he removes his clothes and I moan each time I feel his skin on a new part of my body: his chest on mine, his legs on mine, his dick on mine. When he's completely naked, he shifts back and reaches for the lube. I watch him as he pours some onto his hand and I can't help but smile at the sight of him. His lean torso covered in soft dark hairs. His brown nipples alert. His stomach muscles flexing as he moves and positions himself lower between my legs.

When his hand comes to press up against my hole, I suck air in through my teeth, and instinctively pull my legs up a little, giving Rami more room.

"Yes, just like that," he says and his fingers start to tease me open.

"Is it… Are we okay?" I ask, the panic threatening to return.

Rami's smile is wide and confident. "It's all good, Jake. You're all good. Always."

Relief mixes with something else, something like validation.

"Rami, please fuck me," I say, suddenly desperate to have him inside me.

"I will, but don't take this away from me." His voice has an edge, but it's not the stern tone he normally yields over me so captivatingly. It's softer, brighter. Still, I'm confused.

"Take what away from you?"

"Seeing you come undone. Seeing you give yourself to me and the moment. Seeing you at your most beautiful." He slides two fingers inside me.

I groan and close my eyes. How dare he speak to me like that? How dare he affect my heartrate so uncompromisingly? How dare he make me feel like he could, maybe one day, love me?

"Please just fuck me, Rami." I rock against him, taking it back to a place that feels safe.

"Let me do this, Jake. Let me take care of you." He comes down to graze his lips and teeth across my chest.

No! I want to scream, but for some reason, I don't.

"Yes." I sigh instead and the relief I feel just admitting that that is what I want is all-encompassing. It's like breathing the freshest air.

"Good boy," he rewards me and adds another finger.

And Rami does take care of me. He gets me so ready I am sure I will come as soon as his cock enters me, and he does it all while lavishing sweet kisses all over my body, while running his other hand up and down my torso, while claiming my mouth with his and moaning into it more times than I can count.

When Rami finally, finally puts a condom on and slides his dick slowly inside me, we are staring into each other's eyes and his hand finds mine just above my head and our fingers lock.

"Oh, God," I say when he glides over my prostate for the first time.

"Yes," he hisses as he pushes up on his forearms and starts to fuck me.

At times Rami's thrusts are slow and considered, but at other times they become erratic, and it feels like he's trying to claw his way into my body. I love both. I savour every move he makes. And not just because it feels good, but because it's Rami.

Rami, Rami, Rami.

"Jake, you feel... you feel like..." Rami's breathing is laboured.

"Rami," I say as I wrap my legs around his body.

"I don't want to stop but..." Rami tries again. "I don't know if I can hold on."

"Don't hold on," I say. "Give into it."

Because I think I want to, I want to say. *I really think I could give into this.*

Rami shifts to kneel back with his bent legs under mine. His hands come to grip my thighs.

"Come first," he says nodding at my dick. "I want to watch you come."

I reach for myself and start to stroke, obeying him willingly. As he watches me fist myself, he rocks into me slowly. As my hand increases speed, so do his thrusts. When I feel the tell-tale tingle in the base of my spine, I look up at Rami's eyes and see him already looking at me.

"You going to come for me like the good boy you are?" he asks and his voice sounds uncharacteristically strained. There's something almost heart-breaking in hearing him still try to be this persona I need while also being so close to the edge himself.

"For you, Daddy, yes," I say as my stomach muscles clench and my breathing stops as the first delicious surge of my orgasm rolls over my body. The pleasure thunders through me and a beat later I feel my cum land on my stomach.

When I open my eyes many long, heady seconds later, Rami's eyes are still on me as he keeps thrusting into me. His silver stare is so intense, I look away and down at where he ruts into me.

It was the wrong thing to do. His hand jolts up to grip my chin and he tilts my head up so my eyes find his again.

"Stay with me," he says and it's an order. An order I obey. I hold his eye contact as he crashes into me over and over again. I bring my hands up to hold the back of his head until his mouth falls open and with a deep, guttural groan, Rami comes.

Just like last time, Rami thinks nothing of the mess between us as he collapses on top of me. His body convulses a few times, almost of its own accord, and then he starts to kiss along my collarbone.

"Jake, I—" He begins.

But I don't want any more words. His words have already devastated me.

"Rami, please don't talk," I say and it's a miracle my voice doesn't break.

He lifts up to look at me then.

"Are you... Are you okay?"

I nod quickly, convinced if I open my mouth to speak again I'll cry.

"Jake," Rami tries again.

This time I shake my head and close my eyes. It seems to get my message delivered because a second later, Rami lowers his head and just holds me.

And even though part of me wants to push him away and run from this room, from this scene where I felt more than I have for anyone ever, I let him. I stay and I let him hold me. I may not be ready for his words, but I'm ready to let him do that.

Many minutes later, Rami slides carefully out of me and kisses my cheek before getting up, slipping the condom off as he walks away.

"Stay where you are," he says and I don't have the energy not to conform.

When Rami returns, still gloriously naked with a light sheen of sweat and cum covering his torso, he has a warm wet cloth in one hand and a couple of blankets in the other. He sets about cleaning up our stomachs and then throws the cloth towards the kitchen. I have no idea where it lands, nor do I care, because Rami is covering me with blankets and finding one of the couch's cushions to place under my head. Eventually, he comes to lie down next to me and I roll over so I can tangle my legs in his.

"So, you're not one for pillow talk?" Rami shifts so his arm is behind my shoulders and I come to rest my head on his chest.

I give him a short, rough laugh. "Your words have a lot of power," I say honestly. "Sometimes they catch me unaware."

"Are you saying I render you speechless sometimes, Forester? Wonders will never cease."

I know he expects me to banter with him but I don't want to. "I'm saying..." I pause. I feel I owe it to Rami to be as transparent as I possibly can in this moment. "I'm saying I'm scared."

"Scared? Of... this?" He squeezes my hand.

"Terrified," I reply, my voice small and raw but still undeniably brave.

Rami takes so long to reply I'm not sure he even will but just as my thoughts drift elsewhere, he speaks.

"Me too," he simply says. "But maybe, maybe we can be scared together?"

"Maybe we can," I agree.

And we lie there, scared together, until night falls and a waning moon appears high in the sky.

Chapter Thirty-Four

Rami

On Monday, I woke up with Jake in my bed and in my arms.

On Tuesday, I got to work an hour early and so did he and we brought each other to orgasm with our hands while leaning and moaning against the closed door of our office.

On Wednesday, I was out of the office all day and missed Jake so much I showed up at his flat at seven o'clock armed with a bottle of wine, take-away sushi and a hard-on for him.

On Thursday, I went to work wearing his clothes. While everyone I passed in the building did a double take because my shirt was white, not black, and Sharon gave me more than a few knowing looks, it was easy to ignore because I was too busy lifting the material to my nose and inhaling his sweet citrus smell.

And on Friday, today, I am taking him on that date my sister rightly told me I should take him on. And I am going to tell him everything about my past – the DJing, the cult and the way I estranged my friends and family.

At least that is the plan, but as I step out of the bathroom, a towel wrapped around my waist, I hear my phone ringing on top of the chest of drawers. I answer and bring it to my ear.

"Arse cracks, shit, fuck, balls and cunts!"

"Hi, Jake," I say. "Everything okay?"

"Can you not hear my voice is an octave higher than usual? Clearly, everything is far from okay!"

I'm glad he can't see my smile. "Would you like to tell me why?"

"My sister and her life-partner-boyfriend-toy-boy-whatever-the-fuck-he-is are on their way!"

"Yeah, you said they're coming to visit tomorrow..."

"No, Rami, I mean they're about to arrive at my apartment any minute now!"

"Ah, so you can't do dinner?" I say, keenly aware of the lull of disappointment that sinks my stomach.

"No, I can't fucking do dinner tonight! I swear to God, she told me they'd be arriving tomorrow not today."

"It's not a big deal," I say. "You love your sister. You'll have a great time catching up."

The silence that falls surprises me after all Jake's previous commotion.

"But I wanted to go to dinner with you," he says in a small voice.

"We can do that next weekend," I suggest.

"That's forever away!"

"No, it's seven days away."

"Semantics, Rami!"

"I don't actually think that applies—"

"The other part of the drama is I haven't told her we're not fake dating anymore."

"Oh, I didn't know you'd told them we *were* fake dating." I shouldn't be feeling all puffed up with this new slice of information, but I am.

"It's a long stupid story but when I was going to Lionel's wedding, it served me to also tell Jenna I had a date and that he was also my boyfriend. Since getting coupled up with Marty she's been rather keen for me to meet someone so I figured it would buy me a little relief from that. But then I just neglected to tell her we'd fake split up…"

"Okay," I say. "Are you going to tell her tonight?"

Jake pauses. "I suppose I should."

"You don't have to," I say quickly.

"I don't?"

"Well, we're obviously not too far from dating anyway right now so maybe it's just easier for you to not create a break-up. In fact, have you told Lionel and Luigi yet that we fake broke up?"

"No, I've not had a chance since they got back from their honeymoon. Or rather, I've actively been avoiding them until Luigi's tan fades."

"Then maybe don't tell anyone anything about us breaking up, okay?"

There's a beat of silence.

"Rami, do you… *Are* we dating?" Jake asks tentatively.

"Would you like to be dating?"

"Would *you* like to be dating?"

"Are you going to keep answering questions with questions?"

"Are *you*?"

"If I stop, will you stop?"

"That was a question, wasn't it?"

I groan. "You're ridiculous!"

"So are you!" he says and we laugh together.

"Rami," Jake says in that small voice again. "Seeing as your dinner plans have so very rudely been cancelled, would you like to come over and have dinner with my sister and Marty?"

I'm so grateful he can't see how brightly my smile beams down the phone. "I'd love to. I'll be there as soon as I can."

*****

Marty and Jenna give me my first pansexual panic in years. First, there's the way they look – his lean height, angular features and dazzling dark eyes, and her swaying curves, full lips and freckled nose – but also just the way they are with each other. They're practically always touching, regularly finish each other's sentences and their faces light up as they watch the other speak. And finally, it's how they are with me, and in a very different way, how they are with Jake too.

With me, they're attentive but not creepy, inquisitive but not nosey, and are quick to laugh at any weak attempt at humour I make. With Jake, they are kind and loving. Jenna literally has a different laugh that she uses when Jake makes her giggle and I count Marty winking at his partner's brother more times than maybe some people would find comfortable. I'm not even sure what I think about him calling Jake 'Sweet Cheeks' but it makes Jake smile and that's fast becoming all that matters.

I'm enjoying myself thanks to such good company, and also thanks to the fact I get to watch Jake move around his kitchen cooking and preparing food that already smells incredible. When Marty insists on helping Jake and begins chopping an onion with a finesse that surprises me, Jenna notices my shocked expression.

"He's a professional chef." She leans over the table towards me.

"That will explain it," I say, just as the music gets louder and promptly changes to ABBA's *Gimme Gimme Gimme*.

Wine glass in hand, Jenna grunts softly. "And that's just his terrible taste in music."

"ABBA is one of the greats," I say in response.

"You like music, Rami?"

"Love music." I remind myself that that's an innocuous thing to say. Lots of people love music.

"Jake told me all about you DJing at Lionel's wedding. What an awesome thing to do! Where did you learn to DJ?"

I suppose people can know how to DJ too without it meaning they were once a multi-million selling artist and producer. "My father, a little bit. And then mostly self-taught."

"Oh, yes. And I think Jake mentioned your dad has passed. Sorry to hear that," she says with real concern in her eyes that I notice are the exact same shade of chestnut brown as Jake's.

"Thanks," I mumble and take a quick sip of my tonic water, the one Jake grumbled about pouring for 'the bingo-hall going Grandma' I apparently am even though he added a slice of lemon and ice cubes unprompted.

"Does Jake..." Jenna pauses and shuffles a little closer to me. "Does Jake ever talk much about our father?"

Her question is unexpected, and I have to quickly mentally search through our conversations to answer. I choose not to mention our Daddy Issues conversation. "Not really. Just that he lives in Scotland, and they don't see each other much."

Jenna chews on her bottom lip. "Hmmm, yeah. That's pretty much it. I had hoped it would change as we spent a few Christmases up there recently but then Jake came to Dublin last year and I don't think he has plans to go back this year, unless Marty and I do."

I stay silent and watch as the furrow in Jenna's brow deepens. "Do you think Jake would invite our dad to his fortieth birthday party?"

Considering Jake barely wants to attend his own party, I'm not confident in answering that question. "I think that's up to Jake."

"You're right." Jenna nods and moves to pick up her wine glass, but she pauses before taking a sip. "What about our mother? Has Jake told you much about her?"

"Only that she died," I say. "When Jake was younger. I'm sorry for your loss too."

Jenna's smile is composed and genuine, reaching up to her eyes, but I don't miss that they also mist over. "Jake was thirteen when she died. Did he tell you that it was by suicide?"

Stunned but not sure why exactly, I fall silent and feel my neck muscles work when I swallow.

Jenna continues, "It was complicated further because our father was already in a relationship with the woman he's now married to. We don't know the full details but basically our father lived a double life with Carol, and he re-married very quickly after Mum died."

Part of me is perplexed why Jake never told me this, but a bigger part of me has this strange sense of confidence that he would have, eventually, so I try not to let my surprise show.

"That must have been very hard on you both," I say.

"It was harder on Jake," Jenna says, and I understand now why she wanted to bring this up. "He was closer to Mum. I know this is probably over-stepping, but I often think it would do him good to talk about Mum with someone. He and I… we do talk about her sometimes, but never as often as we should. I know he has a therapist, but it's not the same. I was only really able to talk about her properly when I met Marty. It would make me very happy to know he was talking to you about her."

The weight of her loaded comments is noticeable immediately and I half expect myself to attempt to shrug it off, to change the subject, but I don't. If anything, I feel more full, more ready and more eager to help Jake with this. I don't know how I'll do that yet, but I know I want to.

"I'll see what I can do," I tell Jenna and I'm about to ask her more questions about her work and life in Dublin, but I turn to see Jake and Marty approach us carrying plates and big smiles.

I always want to make Jake smile. I don't know how I'll do that yet, or even if he'll want me to, but I know I want to.

Chapter Thirty-Five

Jake

I am fighting the urge to be annoyed. Annoyed with Rami. Because he is too good. He is too good at all of this, and by this, I mean charming the pants, socks and any other possible undergarments off my sister and Marty. And I'm annoyed because it feels good. It feels so wondrously good to have two people I care deeply about laugh, smile and joke with the man I am starting to care about in a way that is far from shallow.

But it's still annoying, because the sooner we admit our feelings for one another, the sooner those feelings will fade on one or both of our parts. And I'm not ready for that. I don't want to lose him, which means it will likely be his feelings that fade and not mine. Therefore, if I go any further into this, I am just taking more steps closer to my heart possibly breaking into little shards that will be so small and so lost who knows if I can ever piece them all back together again.

It's remarkable that I can have such devastating thoughts while pouring us all cups of after-dinner coffee.

"Sugar, anyone?" I point at the sugar bowl as I place the cafetiere back on the table.

"I'm sweet enough," says Marty, picking up his cup. "Besides, I have another important job to do."

"Oh, God, please don't tell me he brought a board game." I glare at Jenna. "I still haven't recovered from Risk at Christmas."

Jenna chuckles, shaking her head. "Ryanair's meagre luggage allowance barely allowed us to bring enough pants let alone entertainment."

"I'm talking about the washing up." Marty stands.

"Oh, sit down! You don't have to do that! Rami and I will do it in the morning," I say, only feeling the clumsiness of the words after they're gone. I look at Rami. "You are staying, aren't you?"

"Good to know you only want me here for my washing-up skills the morning after," Rami jokes and I'm about to defend myself but he continues, "Yes, I'm staying over. I packed my toothbrush."

"Don't you have one here?" Jenna asks and it's an innocent enough question and yet it feels like a bit of a bullet wound, because it only goes to highlight how fake this thing between us has been. Until now... Maybe.

A little at a loss of what to say, I keep my eyes on pouring milk into my coffee.

"I've been trying to leave one here since the first time I stayed over, but my red toothbrush didn't match Jake's bathroom aesthetic," Rami says.

"Pah! I was just surprised your toothbrush and toothpaste weren't black like the rest of *your* aesthetic!"

"I'm still going to make a start on the washing up," Marty says and heads to the kitchen sink. "Least I can do to thank you, for that incredible meal, Sweet Cheeks."

"Don't stop him." Jenna lifts her hand to me.

"But this is his weekend off," I say.

"He's a head chef now, don't you know? He barely does any menial labour these days."

"I'm going to go help him." Rami stands then, and before I can tell him to sit down, he's gone.

"Good! Just us!" Jenna declares as she slides over to sit in Rami's vacated seat.

"God, you're so happy, aren't you? Like violently happy?" I say, studying her.

"I really am." Her eyes flicker over to Marty who has changed my music again, this time to the BeeGees. *Give me strength*. I spare a quick glance at Rami to see how he and his ultra-cool taste in music is coping and I find he's smiling with Marty who is shaking his hips like he shouldn't be that cheerful washing up.

"Aren't you happy too? I mean, you *look* happy with Rami," my sister asks.

"Rami is a great guy," I say honestly.

"And..."

"And what?"

"And are you happy with him?"

"Yes." The word flies out of my mouth easily. Because I am. I really am.

"And he's besotted with you." Jenna leans a little closer.

"Besotted is a strong word." I tsk it away.

Jenna pulls back and blinks at me. "Jake, why are you resisting this?"

"Resisting what?"

"Your relationship with Rami. I can tell you're not giving yourself fully to it."

As I put my coffee cup back on its saucer with a light chime, I'm flooded with the urge to tell Jenna the truth because it would explain everything. It would explain how Rami and I aren't really months into a relationship but in fact we're standing on the precipice of starting one. It would explain how chaotic the last few weeks have been and why I've been terrible at replying to her messages and vague about what I say regarding Rami. It would explain why I'm not comfortable sitting here and declaring unequivocally how much I like Rami and how good he makes me feel.

My desperation to avoid this line of discussion gets the better of me in the worst way possible.

"So, you're not pregnant yet?" I ask.

Jenna's face doesn't fall, more morphs into a question. "Oh, Jake, that was an awful way to change the conversation. Even for you," she says with a dry laugh.

I close my eyes as my shoulders sink. "I'm sorry. I know it's much too personal. I was just feeling the heat of your... attention."

"Or maybe it was the heat of your feelings for Rami?" Jenna challenges me back and I take it. It's what I deserve. "But no, I'm not pregnant. Not yet. Although, I can assure you we're doing anything and everything we can to change that. In fact, you're lucky I'm not ovulating right now or we'd have had several quickies in between courses."

"Delightful," I mumble.

"My turn to change the subject and make you feel awkward," Jenna says re-crossing her legs.

"Oh, goodie."

"Have you heard from Dad recently?"

"Oh, yeah. He calls me up weekly to check how I'm doing. Texts every day and regularly emails me articles he enjoys from The Times."

"Jakey…" Jenna's eyes narrow on me.

"Well, has he been in touch with you?" I dart back at her.

"No, but that doesn't bother me like it bothers you."

"It doesn't bother—" I stop when I hear how loud my voice has become. It's almost louder than *Stayin' Alive* which Rami and Marty are now shuffling their hips to side by side at the sink. "It doesn't bother me as much as you think," I say in a quieter voice and I taste the surprising truth in the statement, because it's true that in recent weeks, thoughts of my father haven't plagued me as much as they usually do.

"Are you going to invite him to your fortieth?"

"Ugh," I say, annoyed at the reminder of a party I am yet to organise even though I don't really want it to happen.

"I think he would come." Jenna reaches for my hand, cups it between both her palms.

"It will be a room full of shrieking queens, queers, and beards. He and Carol will need to take sedatives to survive it."

"He's not a dinosaur. And he's never had a problem with your sexuality."

It's true my father never gave me grief about being gay. In some ways, I used to wish he would. It would at least show in some sick, dark way that he cared.

"It's one thing to put up with *my* gay flapping, but quite another to celebrate it."

Jenna waits a moment before speaking again. "Jake, nobody puts up with you. We love you."

Looking away is the only way I can stave off the threat of tears. My sister squeezes my hand a little tighter.

"Can I give you some advice, what with me being a little knowledgeable about matters of the heart?" Jenna leans closer still.

"Jenna, you wrote a best-selling book about falling in love. You have more knowledge about love in your little fingernail than I do in my whole brain and body."

"That's not true – you know a lot more about love than you think – but because it strokes my ego a little, let's pretend I am an expert. I want you to listen to me very carefully. That man right there." Her eyes glance quickly at Rami. "He wants to love you. And I think you should let him. Because I think you want to love him too."

I let out a huff. "Even if that were true, it wouldn't last."

"Says who?"

"Me, and I have twenty years of evidence to support this."

"Did you actually read my book? There are literal chapters on how relationships ending are not a bad thing."

"So it's a good thing that hurts like hell?" I spit back.

"Yes, it could be. Because that's life, and that's love."

"Love is overrated—"

"Love is everything, Jake," Jenna interjects, her voice now has an edge to it. "But it's ultimately what we make it. Love can be as boundless and hopeful as you want it to be. Or it can be as devastating and hopeless as you believe it is. It's up to you, Jake. What do you want love to be for you? Because love is what you deserve. You always have, you always will. So, do it. Let him love you."

PART FOUR – LAST QUARTER

"I want to be in love with you the same way I am in love with the moon with the light shining out of its soul."

Sanober Khan

Chapter Thirty-Six

Rami

Before I open my eyes, I reach for Jake, but he's not there.

After our post-dinner conversations with Marty and Jenna went on past midnight, we fell asleep tangled together in our underwear, promising we would make up for the lack of sex in the morning, and yet, he's not here for me to do that.

Maybe I should have pushed him harder to make love last night, but I actually found it just as satisfying and intimate falling asleep together, dazed and exhausted from an enjoyable evening with good company. There was something meaningful in us choosing sleep over sex in that moment.

But now, I'm hungry for him.

After quickly checking the time – 8:40 – I get out of bed and reach for my trousers. I'm about to pull them on when I see a red tartan dressing gown hanging on the back of Jake's door. Feeling a little bold, I slide it on and tie it around my waist. I bring the material up to my nose to inhale Jake's scent before I walk out.

As I make my way to the end of the corridor, to Jake's kitchen and living area, I walk past the guest room and hear a noise that at first sounds strange and almost worrying, but half a second later it's very clear what it is and I am not at all worried. Smiling a little to myself, I move away from the creaking bed and muffled moans.

I find Jake busy at the hob, also wrapped up in a robe, but this one is light blue cotton, and I quickly smell the French toast he's making.

"You're unstoppable," I say.

"Unstoppable, maybe, but not unflappable. Shit! Pass me that spatula, this one's got a burnt bottom already!"

I hand over the utensil and Jake quickly gets to work flipping the bread.

"That will teach me to try being a good little hostess with breakfast ready on the table before everyone wakes up."

I yawn and stretch, before coming closer to Jake at the hob and nuzzling my lips in the crook of his neck.

"What are you doing wearing my robe?"

"Making it look good," I quip.

Jake tuts but pushes back against where my mouth kisses his neck.

"I don't know why you're doing this. I would have made everyone breakfast." I keep my chin on his shoulder and come to stand behind him.

"I... I couldn't sleep," he says and I feel his shoulders fall.

"Any particular reason?"

"Yes and no," he says. "But we'll talk later, okay? Maybe after Jenna and Marty have gone out. That is... if you don't have plans."

"Those are my plans," I say, although my stomach falls when I now realise what conversation is imminent. Will I feel more ready to have it in a few hours? Only time will tell.

"Good." Jake rests his cheek momentarily against mine. "Now make yourself useful and make some coffee. Oh, and can you put on some music, preferably nothing recorded by men with mullets and women in flares."

"I can do that," I say but let my hands slide further around Jake's front and into the opening of his robe. "But I'd rather do this first."

I move one hand to find a nipple and I play with it, tweaking and pulling. My other hand heads south to cup Jake over his boxer shorts. When he reacts instantly, with warmth and stiffness, I smile into his neck as I start kissing him there.

"Rami," Jake says, breathless. "I don't want any more burnt bottoms."

"Turn the hob off," I say as I start to stroke in earnest, feeling more of Jake come to life.

"You don't have to do this," he says. "Just because I went down on you last weekend while you were cooking..."

"That's what you think I'm doing?" I peck at his shoulder. "Tit for tat?"

Jake huffs out a very quick laugh. "I know I've been slacking at the gym recently, but last time I checked neither of us have tits."

"Jake..." I say warningly.

"My sister could walk in at any moment," he says after a little moan.

"I'll be quick," I say, my voice low. "But also, that makes it hotter."

Jake sighs. "You know you are nothing like what I expected when you first walked into the office that day."

"You thought I worked in the post room." I nip at his neck with my teeth. Jake rocks his butt back into me and I know he feels how much this is turning me on too.

"I got a lot of things wrong that day," Jake says softly.

I lift my head and stare at him. "You're lucky I'm too turned on to throw a party and send out a company-wide email because I do believe that's the first time you've ever admitted you were wrong." I tuck my hand under the waistband of his boxers and finally, rejoicingly feel his hot smooth skin in my hand.

"Rami, I am so far from perfect," Jake says, his head leaning back now.

"You're perfect for me," I say as I feel goosebumps break out on his chest as I move my fingers to his left nipple.

"Don't say stuff you don't mean," Jake says and he lifts his head off my shoulder.

Taking my hand out of his boxers, I use it to grab his waist and turn his body to mine. I don't stop my fingers as they come up and wrap around his neck, forcing him to look me dead in the eye.

"I never say things I don't mean. Never doubt anything I say to you, Jake, especially when it's telling you how I feel about you."

"But how can you… It doesn't… How can you feel…" He stops and starts in a spluttering staccato.

It's far too easy to step into the confident, dominant man he needs me to be, especially when I also get the opportunity to tell Jake how I really feel. "You can doubt yourself, Jake, and I know you do, even though you shouldn't, mustn't, because you're a brilliant, brilliant human being. But never doubt me. When I say you're perfect for me, I mean it. I've not felt like this in the longest time. I never thought I would feel like this again, if I'm honest, and I want you to know that it's all you. All you with your host-with-the-most skills, your snarky comebacks for anything and everything, and your one hundred different, adorable pouts."

Jake says my name again but this time there is less resistance in it, possibly even a new hint of compliance, or perhaps, surrender. As if to test how pliant he really is, my hand drops around the back of his body to find all the parts of him I go on to talk about.

"It's all you with your tight backside, this sexy arch in your back, and your delectable dick."

This time when I grab hold of him, he groans and closes his eyes. Stroking him with one hand, I lift on my toes a little so I can place my lips on more parts of him. "It's all you with your honey-coloured eyes, those ridiculous freckles on your nose, and these soft pink lips that always, always open for mine."

Right on cue, as my mouth touches his, his lips fall open and I'm able to slide my tongue inside, searching for and taking as much of him as I can. When he moans again, I feel the vibration travel up his throat and into my mouth. This man and the way he reacts to my touch unlocks parts of me I didn't know I had but now I've found them, I want to keep hold of them forever. I think I want to keep hold of Jake forever.

After kissing him hard and fast for a minute or two, my hand still stroking him slowly, but not too tight, I pull away with reluctance but a lot of anticipation for what's going to happen next.

"Is the heat off?" I nod at the hob behind him.

"Yes," he says, his pupils blown so big they dominate his eyes.

The corner of my mouth kicks up. "Yes, what?"

"Yes, Daddy," Jake replies without hesitation.

"I'm going to go down on my knees now, and I'm going to take you in mouth and you're going to fuck my throat until you come," I say slowly and deliberately.

"But Rami," Jake says and he finishes the sentence by flashing his eyes quickly to the door.

I think about the noises I heard. "They won't come in. Do you trust me?"

Jake nods but doesn't look convinced so I know I'm going to have to take his mind off the possibility the only way I know how. Dropping to my knees, I make quick work of pulling his boxers down and licking my way up and down his length.

With my hand firmly gripping his base, I look up at him again. "Promise me you're going to be a good boy and fuck my mouth until you come?"

"Jesus, Rami. The way you talk to me..." Jake's hand comes down to stroke the side of my face. Something changes in his eyes when he speaks again. "Nobody has cared about my pleasure as much as you."

"Maybe that's true," I say before kissing the head of his cock.

"What do you mean?" Jake looks confused.

"Maybe it's true that nobody has cared about you the way I do. And if that's the case then lucky, lucky me." I flick my tongue across the tip of him.

"Rami, I—"

I don't know what he wants to say but I silence him by guiding his dick into my mouth. I suddenly want nothing more than having him inside me this way, hot and hard and heavy, and completely at my mercy.

It takes him a while, but like the good little boy I know he is, Jake finally starts to thrust inside my mouth. I focus on keeping my lips wrapped around my teeth and I bring my hands up to grip his backside, urging him to keep going. His strokes are shallow but fast and I roll my tongue around the head of his cock. When that gets me a deep, rough moan, I do it again, and again, and again until Jake is gasping out a warning that he's going to come. I'm unable to reply because I don't want to take my mouth off him, but I palm and pull at his buttocks in encouragement. Then it's only a matter of seconds before he's spilling down my throat and a long string of curses are sailing out of his mouth.

"Oh, God, Rami," he says as I pull his boxers up, then stand up, wiping my mouth on the back of my arm.

"Good?"

Jake shakes his head at me, his eyes dazed. "I have no words."

"I like speechless Jake," I say and I kiss his neck again.

"Do you... Don't you want to..." Jake's words drift away as he stares down at my erection that is visible even through his robe.

"Later. When Marty and Jenna have gone out."

He brings his hand down to squeeze me and I close my eyes at his touch. "You'll stay for the day?"

"Try and get rid of me."

"I'll do my best," he whispers into my cheek and I hear his smile.

Reluctantly I place my hands on his hips and push him away. "Finish the breakfast. I'm going to have a shower and then we'll eat together. I think your sister should be finished with Marty by then."

Jake goes to open his mouth but instead opts for a swift eye roll.

"You can help yourself to my clothes. In the wardrobe," he says then seems to gather himself. "I may have a black T-shirt somewhere that I forgot to give to a charity shop."

I ignore his dig and instead bite the corner of his jaw before I walk away.

In his bedroom, I open his wardrobe and find a lilac short-sleeved shirt I know I will surprise him by wearing and I'm grinning to myself thinking about this when something catches my eye.

I'd been thinking about buying Jake a very specific gift for a while now and kept stopping myself because it felt too much, too intimate for where we were but after this last week, after today, I feel more confident and reassured.

So I bend down and pull out one of the shoe boxes from the bottom of his wardrobe. Holding it in my hands, I turn it around to find a label that will tell me his shoe size, but it's a designer box – Louis Vuitton – and there's no markings. That's why I then open the lid to check the shoes themselves, but there aren't any shoes inside the shoe box. In fact, what I do find, is the very last thing I expect to discover.

Chapter Thirty-Seven

Jake

I love my sister and Marty more than is possibly healthy, but it feels like they are never going to leave when breakfast rolls into a two-hour meal and then they both insist on doing the washing up. But finally, finally, just after midday, they leave to spend the rest of the day with Jenna's friends.

When the door closes behind them, I move quickly to press Rami up against it. Flashbacks of him on his knees in front of me have been running through my mind all morning and I want to do the same to him, or maybe fuck him again or have him fuck me. I don't care what it looks like, I just want to be close to him. I just want to make him feel as good as he makes me feel.

But as Rami's hands come up and press on my chest, I learn he has other plans.

"Jake, we should talk," he says.

"Oh, yes, that," I say to him while internally I curse the version of me who suggested it. But I know it needs to happen. My insomnia last night was ultimately me giving myself a pep talk to admit my own feelings for Rami. My feelings, and my desires. My desire to try and be with him.

Shit. Is this really going to happen?

"Okay, let's talk," I say and I give him a quick peck on the nose before leading him back into the living area. "Shall I make us some tea?"

"I'll do it," he says and gestures for me to sit. I watch him in silence as he fills the kettle.

"I don't really know where to start," he says as he leans back against the counter and faces me. The kettle rumbles towards its boil beside him.

"Well, I could start," I say and slap my thighs as if summoning some energy. "But how do you know what I want to talk about?"

"Don't you want to talk about… us?"

Rami's face falls for the briefest moment. "Yes, yes, I do, but I also want to… Oh, fuck." He rubs a hand down his face and he suddenly looks tired.

"You just swore," I say, my stomach lurching. "Now I know this is bad."

"No," Rami practically shouts over the kettle's deepening roar. "It's not bad. But I just… I have to confess something."

"Okay," I say and wait, breathing apparently now something I will do once I know what Rami wants to say.

"When I was getting this shirt, earlier, from your wardrobe, I also found something."

Any air that was there rushes out of my lungs.

"I was trying to find out your shoe size because I wanted to buy you some shoes, like the ones I wore at the wedding because you said you really liked them and…"

I am frozen in my chair and I'm losing the ability to see clearly.

"You found them," I say. My shoe box full of red-stamped envelopes and letters from creditors I owe tens of thousands of pounds to.

"I wasn't prying," Rami defends himself. When I don't speak, he adds, "Okay, I suppose I was a bit, but not to find… that."

"My debt," I say and as if it was timing it perfectly, the kettle clicks off as it starts to boil.

"Yes," Rami says.

As the shock keeps rushing through me, wave after wave of possible implications freezing me on the spot, there is a small enough part of me that is conscious enough to be grateful that Rami goes about making the tea in silence so I can try and find some clarity in the mental mess. When he brings the mugs over to my coffee table, I am surprised that he comes and sits next to me on the couch rather than have a bit more distance.

"It's not a big deal," he says.

I make a strangled noise. I'm still not breathing quite right. "Then why are we having a big sit-down chat about it?" I ask, sounding as flustered as I feel.

"Because I wanted to be honest about stumbling upon the shoebox."

"Well, you've done that now so I guess you can go." That is exactly what needs to happen. Rami needs to go so I can hopefully stop feeling the hot flames of shame lick their way up my body. Or at least feel them without an audience.

Rami leans forward as if to put himself in my line of sight because I'm very deliberately not looking at him.

"Jake, I'm not going anywhere," he says, and I flinch at how it sounds, the potential figurative meaning in his words. But I can't fall into that romantic notion. To think I was minutes away from telling him I wanted us to be in a relationship together. I should at least be grateful he came clean about what he found before I made an even bigger idiot of myself.

"I don't know what you expect me to say," I say sounding undeniably angry. "I can't deny it, clearly. And I can't even say it's under control although I am paying it back, slowly, but it's still not pretty."

"You don't need to explain yourself. I just want to know if I can help?"

"Help?" I spit out.

"Yes, like if talking about it would help…"

"It wouldn't," I say quickly and shoot him a quick look which I instantly regret because he's sitting there all calm and collected, and my lilac linen mix shirt has never looked better.

"What does your therapist say about it?" Rami asks, reaching for his tea.

"Oh, God, I haven't told my therapist!" I say, appalled.

"You haven't?"

"Lord, no, she's far too busy dealing with my real problems, she doesn't have time and I, ironically, don't have enough money to pay her to help me with this almighty and ultimately inexplicable fuck-up."

"It's not a fuck-up…" he says and his delicate tone snaps the last thread of patience I have for myself, for him, and for this conversation.

"Rami, I'm nearly forty years old. I have earned good money for the last ten or so years and I have nothing to show for it. In fact, all I have to show for my years lived is a mountain of debt. Not to mention how my mother left me a decent-sized inheritance that I burned through in less than a year. I am one massive fuck-up when it comes to money."

"Jake, you're not listening to me." He puts his hand on my arm, and why does it have to be soft and warm and just the perfect amount of pressure? "Your relationship with money is not about debt and spending and whatever. It's about much more than that. If you get to the bottom of why your relationship with money is hard work, then maybe it will all get a bit easier to pay the debt back."

I laugh at that. "I have no reason to have a shit relationship with money. That's what I'm telling you. I have never wanted for money. My mother came from money. My father's job was well paid. I have never been poor, and yet I haven't been out of debt since…." I freeze. I've never told anybody this before. I'm not sure I can.

Rami squeezes my arm. "You can be honest with me. I'm not going to judge you."

Maybe that's why this is happening, this untangling of my deepest darkest secret. Maybe it's exactly why I'm telling him more than I've told anyone else. Because I can see just how little judgement there is. In fact, there's something else there rippling his features and pulling at the corners of his mouth. Concern? Care? Worry? Surely not.

"I've never not had some kind of debt," I say on an exhale. "From my first pay cheque until right now, I have always overspent. First, it was owing my friends a few quid here and there when I wanted to go out at the end of the month and I'd run out of cash. Then it was my overdraft. And then in Sydney, I spent my inheritance upfront on a year's rent, but then still went over what I budgeted for expenses. My wage barely touched the sides so I borrowed money from my dad to get home, and he's never asked for it back, but I promised myself I would re-pay him, I just never did. Maybe that's why he's so disappointed in me." I suck in a breath, feeling more words ready to tumble out. "Then in my mid-twenties I started using credit cards and store cards, and I just rolled it over from one new card to another. From one bank to the next. Each season I was working abroad I was able to pay off some of it because my living expenses were covered and there was no time to shop or spend, but each winter I would pretty much undo all that good work." I swallow. "Now it's all I can do to pay off the very minimum."

Rami pulls in a breath but keeps his eyes on me. "How much debt do you have now?" He puts his mug back on the coffee table.

Now is when I should shut up. Now is when his cool and calm facade will crack. Now is when he will be so shocked, he'll be unable to hide his disdain.

Good, I think. Because the steady warmth in his light eyes is starting to make my skin feel clammy.

"Just over fifty-five thousand pounds," I say with a half-hearted shrug as if I'm almost considering laughing it off. "But that's not the total I've accrued over the years."

"Oh, Jake," Rami simply says and he squeezes my arm again. I realise I'm still not breathing, not properly. I'm waiting for his features to fall, for the whites around his pupils to widen. But his expression hasn't changed.

He's still looking at me like he wants to hug me.

"Oh, God, please don't hug me." I lift up my hands which knocks his grip off my forearm.

"What?" Now his eyes do indeed widen.

"Please don't be nice to me about this!" I don't mean to shout but I can't keep my voice low either. "Don't be kind to me when I'm telling you how I'm a shitty person who spends way too much money on awful materialistic things."

"Jake. I wasn't—"

"Seriously. Just have a normal reaction to it, please. Be shocked. Swear about it. Tell me I'm an idiot. Ask me if it was all worth it."

"I don't—"

"Because it wasn't, okay?" I shout out. "None of my clothes, none of my designer bags, none of my shoes, no matter how stylish and shiny, were worth this. This noose around my neck, this tightness that is forever entwined around my body, this constant pressure on my chest..." I rush the words out because there's a ball of tears climbing up my throat.

"Jake, just shut the fuck up, will you?" Rami grips my wrists and brings my flapping hands down to rest on my thighs. "For fuck's sake."

"Better. That's a much better reaction." I nod, trying to feel self-satisfied but it doesn't materialise.

"I'm swearing because of *your* reaction. As for your debt, I have no strong feelings about it. Money is just money. Numbers—"

"Spoken like a man who has never been in debt in his life," I interject grumpily.

"You don't know what my relationship with money is like," he says and his brows pull together.

I take a leap. "But am I right? Have you ever been in debt?"

I watch his neck move as he swallows. "No, but that's not the point I was trying to make. Your debt is a symptom of a bigger issue, a bigger blockage—"

"Blockage? I'm not a sodding toilet!"

"Jake, don't try and joke your way out of this. This is serious."

I wave a hand at him. "You just said money is only money!"

"And it is. But that's not what I'm talking about." His forehead crumples and his jaw tightens with effort. "Your debt, does it cause you stress?"

I sigh. "Like you wouldn't believe."

"And by the sounds of it, not many people know about it?"

"Nobody knows. Apart from you."

Rami pauses. "Not even Jenna?"

"Especially not Jenna," I say with emphasis.

"And why's that?"

My shoulders sink when I realise what he's done. "Because I don't want her to think less of me. I… I couldn't stand it."

"You're ashamed." Rami's hands slide over mine, covering them. Seeing and feeling his fingers on mine makes me feel protected, safe almost. It's a moment of calm in the chaos.

Maybe that's why I start crying. Because I finally feel I can.

When I make a wrenching whelp of a noise in the back of my throat as my tears quickly turn into sobs, Rami's hands come off mine.

"Jesus," I say, rubbing at the skin beneath my eyes. "I'm sorry. I'll get my shit together and—"

I run out of words and am painfully aware of how Rami isn't saying anything. Eventually, he stands and I look up at him, ready to watch him leave.

"It's okay. You go," I say. "I'm just sorry I—"

"Shut up and get up, Jake," Rami says in a low voice. That low sexy demanding voice of his.

"Okay," I say, my own tone faltering and weak.

I'm barely standing all the way up when I feel Rami's arms wrap around me and his body step closer to mine. He holds me against him like he needs *me* to stand up. He grips me so tightly my breath is now irregular for a very different reason.

"You are not your debt," he says. "You are so much bigger and brighter and better than that or any one thing."

I don't have words in response. Only tears, which keep on coming and coming. But Rami continues to hold me, and he doesn't let go, not until my tears stop.

Chapter Thirty-Eight

Rami

Our train is stuck in the middle of nowhere and Radia is not okay about it.

"I should be lying in Barista Babe's bed not here stuck in a metal box in the arse end of Staffordshire with you," she grumbles as she stares out of the window.

"I'm not sure who should be more offended by that. Staffordshire, me or your *girlfriend* who has a name."

This changes Radia's expression, melting her frown into a giddy smile. "My girlfriend, my girlfriend, my girlfriend!" She taps out every syllable of each word on the table that fills the space between our seats which face each other.

"It's a shame Chloe had to work later today so she couldn't come," I say.

"Next week," Radia confirms and she looks a lot less grumpy than she did a few minutes ago. "Maybe you can bring Jake with you too?"

It's my turn to feel my mouth melt into a silly grin and I don't even try to hide it.

"Oh, Rami. You've got it bad, bab."

"You can talk!"

"Yes, but I *know* I've got it bad. I talk about how bad I've got it all the time. You're still trying to deny it."

"I'm not denying anything."

"Apart from your sexuality and your new boyfriend to your mother," Radia says under her breath, but I don't miss a single word.

"That's different."

"How?"

I look away. "We've talked about this before."

"Correct, and I failed to understand the logic in your argument then and I will probably fail again now."

"Not you failing at something when you've always been such an over-achiever," I tease and also hope it provides a change of conversation topic.

"Me? Don't you mean *you*? You're the one who was a multi-millionaire by the time you were twenty-five."

"Which I hate," I add quickly.

"You didn't hate it at the time," Radia says.

"I didn't love it as much as you think. And it cost me in the long run, didn't it?"

Radia's shoulders fall with a sigh, but then rise again on a deep inhale. "Rami, you need to move on from that chapter of your life. Bad things happened. There was pain, and loss, and suffering, but you're out of it now. You're making amends and you've moved on. You've got a good job, and you've got Jake."

I listen to what she's saying but for some reason the words don't offer much reassurance. They don't calm the simmering unsettled feeling in the pit of my stomach that has been lingering since yesterday became another missed opportunity to share my truth with Jake. But that's how it had to be. Yesterday was all about Jake and his struggles. It would have been so wrong to open up about mine at the same time.

"I don't think I can ever forgive myself," I say still looking out the window. I feel the weight of every word because it's the first time I've said it out loud.

"For Baba?" Radia asks gently.

"Yeah."

Radia holds my eye contact and leans forward, her chin extended. "Well, that's not good enough."

I snap my head to look at her. "Pardon?"

She flicks her wrist at me and the black-and-white pattern of her houndstooth suit jacket flashes before my eyes. "You're going to have to try and find a way to forgive yourself, Rami. Because we all have already."

"But how can I? I abandoned you all when you needed me most."

"Rami, we had each other. We weren't on our own. Yes, we wanted you here and of course Baba wanted to see you before he died. But that's not the way it played out, and as I've said before, I understand why you did what you did."

I lean forward so only she can hear my response. "But… but how can you? What I did… it was madness."

"Yep, it's pretty out-there. Nobody is denying that. But guess what? So is being world famous by your mid-twenties. That is not a normal thing to happen to someone and you didn't exactly have many people helping you out with that. Apart from Gee. And then you met Michelle…"

I bite my lip and look out of the window. I don't want to hear this but I know I have to.

"As much as I despise the woman now, I recognise that Michelle gave you things you needed, and things we couldn't give you because we were on the other side of the Atlantic. She gave you support, love, care… And Gee was the friend you needed too. He knew what it was like being famous, and I do believe he cared about you. They both did, at a time, but they also had other motives."

"They weren't all bad," I say but I can't ignore the unease I feel defending them both.

"Maybe not. But they are still there, aren't they? They're still taking money from people and promising them things they aren't qualified to deliver on."

I shake my head. "They're not wholly to blame. I have to take responsibility for my own actions, and the consequences."

"That's true, but it's also valid that you were impressionable and vulnerable, and they took advantage of that."

I shake my head as I watch rain droplets slip down the window. "They have their own problems. Michelle grew up with so much pressure to achieve, and Gee, he barely had a family," I say before changing my tone purposefully. "Unlike me who had a loving family I just ignored and abandoned."

"Because that's what they told you to do!" Radia slaps a hand on the table.

It's hard to say what's more difficult for me to admit; that I abandoned my family of my own will, or that I was persuaded to do so by others who claimed to have my best interests at heart. Both possibilities make my head and heart hurt.

"I don't want to fight about this," I say.

"Me neither." Radia sits back, briefly adjusting her gold hijab around her hairline. "What does Jake think about it all?"

My silence is very loud and telling.

"Please tell me you've told him by now." Radia's brows pull together in disbelief.

I force a brittle smile. "I could tell you that, but I'd be lying."

"Oh, Rami." Radia sighs with audible disappointment.

"Jake has his own stuff going on right now," I say, thinking back to the way we spent the whole of yesterday talking about his debt, discussing ways we could come up with a repayment plan, and after that when he was so drained and exhausted from it all, I just held him and stroked his hair as he fell asleep.

"So what? We all have stuff going on. The whole point of a relationship is that you share your loads with each other." Radia lifts a pointed finger and wags it at me. "And don't you dare try and make that into a filthy joke. My sensitive lesbian guts would not be able to stand it."

I don't even laugh at the innuendo. It suddenly feels like there isn't much to smile or laugh about.

"I will tell Jake," I say.

Radia makes sure I'm looking at her again before she replies, "You better do it soon. Before it's too late."

As if to punctuate the doom in Radia's words, the train jolts once, twice, and then slowly starts to move off. As the fields start rolling by again, a soft buzzing pulls my attention to my phone on the table, but it's not lit up. Radia instead is bringing hers to her ear.

"BARISTA BABE!" Radia says and has that giddy grin back on her face.

While I smile back at her and feel a little flip of excitement for my sister and her new relationship, I can't deny that most of my body is feeling almost nauseated with what my sister and I just discussed, and it's not because these are new topics of consideration for me. More that they've been haunting my sub-conscious for weeks, and more recently my very conscious thoughts.

There's the issue of coming out to my mother and then there's also the fact I haven't told Jake about my past. I so desperately want to tell myself that they're separate issues, but my gut knows they're not. Both of these problems – problems that involve various levels of deception and lying – relate to one key issue; my fear of disappointing people, especially those I love.

Because, yes, I think I love Jake.

The thing is, my fear of disappointing those I love isn't irrational. Because I *have* disappointed people I love in the past. I disappointed my parents and sisters when I cut them off to join RemiX. Even before that I'd intentionally created distance between us by moving to LA. And with Jake, I am terrified of him seeing a version of me – the real me – and it not being who he thinks I am. I'm frightened of not being the man he wants. Whether it's in the bedroom, or now with his battle with debt, Jake needs me to be strong for him. Jake needs me to support him, not the other way around. Jake needs to know I won't let him down. And yet, by keeping a huge part of myself from him, aren't I already letting him down? How can I applaud and support him in being honest about his own struggles, when I have been keeping my own challenges locked away in a bunker of my deep, dark shame? Jake is not a man who suffers fools lightly, and I don't blame him. It's one of the many things that I like, no, love about him.

It's for that very reason I feel trapped. Because if I tell him, I risk losing him. But if I don't tell him, the risk is just as real if not greater. There is no way out of this, not without risking losing Jake. And I can't make sense of it. I can't figure out the right thing to do.

It's like my thoughts are not my own and my true feelings, wants and desires are slipping further and further out of reach. It's like when I was in RemiX.

The panic I feel at this realisation is interrupted by another vibrating noise. This time a short and sharp one that indicates a new email. Somewhat relieved to have a distraction from the hopeless direction of my inner thoughts, I check my phone. I keep staring and blinking at the front screen and the small extract of a new email that appears in the notification there.

Subject: LUNAR ECLIPSE: THE COMEBACK WORLD TOUR (This is not a drill!)

Rami, don't be a dick and delete this before you even…

I read these two lines four, maybe five times before I swallow the lump in my throat and with my heart beating loudly throughout my body, I open the email and read.

Chapter Thirty-Nine

Jake

A week is a really long time when you're waiting to ask someone to be your boyfriend. Even the minor PR crisis of a group of prankster influencers setting fire to our farmhouse hotel in Gloucestershire didn't help pass the time, nor did the way I demanded Sharon hide my phone from me all Thursday and Friday because I'd gotten to the point where I was only taking my next breath for a possible message from Rami. Not that she knew that. At least I don't think she knew it.

It's not like Rami and I haven't been in touch, but while he was in Belfast for the week-long arts festival that was being held in our three properties there, he was busier than I would like so I'd sometimes have to wait an hour or two for a message from him. And they were long, long hours. I'm not usually this needy for attention and contact, but when I've spent this whole week effectively getting my life in order and doing so because I want to make Rami proud, I've felt a little desperate for some, or any kind of reassurance. And Rami has been offering me reassurance. His messages are always kind and are signed off with multiple Xs. He's annoyingly lacking in the humour department still, but this week I'd rather have had one hundred 'I'm thinking of you' or 'How's my boy today?' messages than witty but pointless banter.

But now it's Saturday and I am waiting for Rami in a restaurant that has more white linen than a hotel's store cupboard. I only got here twenty minutes early which I think is respectable considering I've been ready for the date since over two hours ago.

Our date. *Our first real date.*

It feels so strange to be having such a thing now after all we've done together, but I wouldn't have it any other way. It feels almost poetic that it will be on our first date that I ask him to be my boyfriend.

Because how can I not?

I can't deny how different I've been feeling all week since I finally opened up about my debt to someone, to Rami. It's like someone has turned on a long forgotten and broken light in my brain and I am now able to see things more easily than before. Of course, what I see still looks like an almighty mess; my debt is still there, everywhere. But now I have a new clarity of mind to deal with it. And most surprisingly of all, I am dealing with it.

On Sunday morning after Rami left to spend the day with his family and while Jenna and Marty were still asleep, I created a spreadsheet and entered in all the various debts I owed. I went through every single statement and got all the debt out of my head and out of my shoebox of shame and into that spreadsheet. It wasn't pretty, and the final total was actually more than I expected, but it felt freeing to at least know it now. To know the dark truth and to still be breathing after the shock and shame had faded.

On Monday, during my lunch break, I called a debt consolidation service and scheduled a phone call with an advisor for the following day.

On Tuesday, after the call with the advisor, who was perfunctory and efficient in a way I appreciated, I went to my therapist appointment. I told Anita about my debt and I cried a thousand more tears, but she didn't look at me any differently. It seems she can be impressively immoveable about all my issues equally which is as comforting as it is ridiculous.

On Wednesday, after work, I created a new spreadsheet and mapped out a budget that would help me make those monthly repayments, while also putting a little bit of money aside for savings, something the financial advisor told me was still important.

By Thursday, I finally felt ready to take the next step and so after dinner, I got my wallet out and chopped up all of my credit and store cards. I took a photo of their colourful fragments and sent it to Rami and his reply had been worth all my hard work that week to get to that point.

<So proud of you. Good boy.Xxx>

On Friday, yesterday, I celebrated a week of homemade lunches by treating myself to my first take-away coffee in seven days and I swear it tasted richer because of the wait.

It's not all been plain sailing. I've had many moments where the panic has crawled up my body and almost claimed me. When I think of having to explain to friends why I can't go out for dinner as often as I'd like, my breath stalls. When I think about telling Jenna about my debt, my throat tightens. When I think about not being able to cheer myself up with a little designer treat here and there, my skin feels taut across my chest. But all these fears and all those threats of panic are minor inconveniences compared to the heavy weight I now know I was carrying around by keeping my debt a secret.

Facing my debt has made me feel brave. Making plans to deal with it and release its hold on me has made me feel like I can do scary and impossible things. Sharing my truth with Rami has made me realise how beautiful and hopeful life can be when you share it with someone, even the hardest parts.

So that's what I'm going to try and do. I'm going to try and share my life, with Rami.

"You look a million miles away," a wonderfully familiar voice pulls me back from staring out at the rising and fall of the Thames out the window.

"Hi," I say and I just know from the stretch across my face that I'm beaming up at him as if he's the first day of sunshine after a long dark winter.

Jesus, Jake. It's been a week.

I stand then and step to the side of the table, but before I get closer I feel frozen by uncertainty. Do we kiss? Do we hug? Do we shake hands? Or do we just sit down?

Rami decides for me by stepping in close and bringing one hand around my waist and the other to cup my jawline. He leans in close and nudges the tip of his nose against mine.

"I missed you," he says, his breath dancing on my lips.

I close my eyes and don't even try to hide the tremble that now runs up my spine.

"I missed you too," I say when he pulls back.

God, I really, really hope he wants to give this a go too.

After sitting back down we make small talk about his trip and as he talks, explaining how the event went well but not without a few last-minute glitches, I see tiredness in small shadows under his eyes and the way his smile doesn't quite claim his whole face like it usually does.

"And how was your week?" he asks after we place our orders with one of the restaurant staff.

"Oh, you know, same old, same old. Sorted out my life. Spoke to a financial advisor. Consolidated my debts and made a payment plan that may see me debt free by the time I'm seventy. Nothing special."

Rami stretches his hand across the table and takes mine. "Have I told you how proud I am of you, Jake?"

"Only a few times, but I could always hear it more. You know how shy and unassuming my ego is." I flutter my eyelashes at him and that gets me an eye-crinkling grin.

"So, I was hoping we could talk," Rami says after that smile fades a little quicker than I'd like.

Trying not to read too much into that, I open my mouth ready to say everything I want to say before I talk myself out of it. But then a waiter appears with our drinks and that pulls us away from the moment, not least because he brings over two glasses of wine when we only ordered one. Rami starts to insist that I should keep it as my second glass but I protest that I don't want to drink more than one – although he doesn't yet know it's because I want to stay sober for what feels like the most important conversation of my life – and then the waiter suggests he leaves it for Rami in case he changes his mind, which Rami scoffs at and bluntly asks for the glass of wine to be taken away.

"Sometimes I think the universe is trying to make me drink," he says after the waiter leaves, and I have never heard Rami sound so tense or uptight.

"Are you okay?" I ask leaning over the table.

"Yeah, sorry. I just… It's been a long week."

It's not that his mood has changed. He's still looking at me with kind eyes, and his hand is back on mine, stroking my knuckles, but I sense something else about Rami that I haven't noticed before. He's on edge, distracted, and possibly also a little nervous.

Maybe it's because he finally wants to tell me more about what happened in California.

"You said you wanted to talk," I prompt him.

"I do, yes."

"I do too."

"You do?" He seems surprised.

"Yes, I wanted to tell you… I wanted to tell you how happy I am when I'm with you." My intention in saying this, in getting this ball rolling is two-fold. Firstly, I hope it helps soothe a little of whatever tension he is feeling and get his mind away from whatever it is that is making him frown so deeply. And secondly, it's a test. A test to see if he is receptive to me saying these kinds of things.

"Jake, you know I feel the same." His hand squeezes mine. "At least I hope you know that."

"I think I do." I feel so buoyed by this comment, I press on, "Rami, I know this is like our first date and that's not the typical time to be saying such things, but I suppose nothing about how we met and how we got to this point is typical, and I for one kind of like that. But still, I wanted to make sure you knew how… how much I care about you."

He blinks at me, his expression unreadable. It's not like he's surprised, more like he's listening so intently he has no other energy for any kind of decipherable reaction.

Despite the panic that rises in me at his immediate silence, I still feel brave. Rami makes me feel brave. Even if he is struggling with whatever it is he wants to talk about with me, that doesn't matter because I can be brave for him. I can be brave for both of us.

"Because I do care about you, a lot," I continue. "And I'm aware that maybe I haven't shown it. I haven't gotten up and danced in front of you and a large crowd of drunk wedding guests. I haven't brought you coffee once since we started working together. I know I drive you up the wall sometimes and occasionally you return the favour, but Rami... I didn't know it was possible for someone to know all of me and still like me."

"Jake—" He tries to interrupt but I hold up my free hand.

"Please let me finish. When you stayed last weekend and talked through everything with me, you made me feel accepted in a way that I have possibly never felt because my debt has been hanging over me for most of my adult years. To have you know about it, and not just want to stick around but also help me overcome it. That means more to me than I can really say, and as you know I am rarely lost for words."

"Jake, I didn't do anything special. You were the courageous one last weekend."

Palpable relief pulses through me at knowing he still doesn't judge me, still thinks highly of me after having a week to have the full horror story of my debt sink in.

"But you are special, Rami," I quickly interject. "You're kind, you're generous, you're charming, you're reliable and loyal, and you're even funny, sometimes." I lean over the table so only he can hear. "Also did I mention you have the world's most perfect penis?"

Rami closes his eyes when he smiles at that so I can't see if it reaches them, but I tell myself it does. I mean, who wouldn't smile at being told they have a perfect penis?

"I don't know if I've ever told you this before, but I don't have the best track record with relationships. In some ways, I've never had a real relationship before. And whatever I've had in the past... It hasn't felt like this. *I* haven't felt like this."

"Please, Jake, I—" Rami leans towards me but again I stop him talking by continuing. I need to say this now or I may never get the words out.

"And I haven't exactly figured out the details in my own mind, because of course, it is a problem that we work together but I'd like to think we could make it work somehow. I mean, if I had to, I'd look for another job. I'd be more than happy to do that. I just want to..." I stop because my increasing rate of talking is starting to alarm even me. I take in a deep breath and level my gaze on Rami's moonlight eyes. "I know I'm far too old to be asking such a question, but I want to ask it for the first time in my life. I want to ask you," I bring my other hand to sandwich his palm between both of mine, "Rami, will you be my boyfriend?"

Another untenable expression lingers on Rami's face and his silence makes my stomach sink at a frightening rate. Maddeningly, he takes a sip of water before he puts his eyes back on mine and speaks.

"Jake, I feel the same. I also haven't felt like this before, and I *have* had previous relationships. That should go a long way to tell you how much I care about you. You are special too. You're hilarious, full of life, and sometimes utterly ludicrous, and I love that. I also love your ginormous heart that does so much for others even when you're determined to act the grump. The way you host people in your home. The way you banter with Sharon. The way you came to Birmingham with me and spent a day with my family. The way you love your sister and Marty. Even the way you wanted a fake date to Lionel's wedding so he wouldn't worry about you still having feelings for him. The way you stick up for people you care about. The way you want to make your friends happy, so you agreed to a party you don't really want to have." He leans over the table, closer to me. "And then there's what you do to me. The way you make me feel when your whole body responds to my touch. The noises you make when you come. The way you look lying naked on my bed in the moonlight. You are beyond special. You are everything."

I grin at him like a madman, soaking up every one of his words. I almost want to look down to see if my chest is puffing out the way I feel it is, like a huge balloon inflating in my chest. I can't believe what I'm hearing. And I can't believe what is about to happen. Rami squeezes my hand and unblinking I wait for his next words.

"Which is why it destroys me to say, I'm sorry, Jake. But no, I cannot be your boyfriend."

And just like that, the balloon in my chest and my stupid, stupid heart both burst into smithereens.

Chapter Forty

Rami

"Well, I'm not sure how I'm going to eat my beef tartare now," Jake deadpans as he pulls his hands away from mine. I want to be relieved he's making a joke when his chin is trembling, but I'm not.

Nothing could erase or even dilute the ache I feel for him and what I just said. Nothing can ease the pain I feel at having said what I said. But it needed to be said.

I can't be Jake's boyfriend, not like this.

"Jake, I want to explain—"

"I'm not sure I want you to." He won't look at me, his eyes darting around looking out over the view of the Thames. What an incredible view for such a devastating moment.

"It's really complicated," I begin.

"I'm sure it is," he snaps.

I open my mouth to try again but the waiter brings our starters and I find myself grinding my molars as he takes a painfully long time to explain the ingredients and flavours of our respective dishes.

When he's gone, I ignore my food and focus on Jake who is now chewing on his bottom lip and staring at his plate like looking anywhere else would cost him too much.

"Jake, there are a lot of things I haven't told you."

Jake nods then and glances up at me. I want to feel relieved he's looking at me again, but I'm not because I can see the sheen in his eyes, and all the hurt. "Yes, I've always been aware of that. Like the boxes of records in your room. The way you never told me exactly what it was you were doing in LA. The way you're not out to your mother. The way you don't seem to mention any friends from that time, or even many people back here in the UK."

"Yeah, it's not right I haven't explained… things."

"But I don't care. I actually don't care about any of that, Rami," Jake says and he sounds unusually quiet, like he's suddenly feeling tired, or defeated. "I kept things from you too, remember? But you know sharing that made me realise it didn't matter. I believed you'd tell me eventually. I just sort of had this crazy idea that if we tried to make this work, there would be time for us to share more of ourselves, as and when we're ready. So, I don't really care you have stuff you haven't told me."

"Well, you should care," I say with emphasis.

"You *want* me to be angry with you?" His expression can only be described as a scowl.

"No." I shake my head. "I definitely don't want that. But you have every right to be."

Jake pushes back in his chair and folds his arms. "Well, I am angry, because, honestly, none of this makes sense. The way you've been messaging me all week. The way we were when we were last together. The way we've been for a while now…"

"This isn't about how I feel. I'm not doing this because I don't care. I'm doing this because *I do*. I'm doing this because I need a bit more time to sort some things out. I can't give myself to you fully until I do."

"And yet, you haven't told me what those things are?"

"I could," I say and then it's my turn to shrink in my chair, because I know telling him now won't help. I can't help but believe it would make things even worse. "But I'm scared you'll not want to see me again if I do."

"Rami, are you a serial killer?"

"No."

"Have you committed any other major crimes?"

"No, it's nothing like that."

"Do you put cats in wheelie bins?"

"What?" I stare at Jake until I realise it's a serious question. "God, no."

"Well, then I don't even care what it is. I know what it's like when you have a dark secret you don't want anyone to find out, and irony of ironies, it was you who made me see how people not knowing my truth was more toxic than the actual problem itself. Why can't you see that?"

"People do know. My family know. Bill and Simeon too," I say but his reaction instantly tells me I was stupid to share this with him.

"But I don't," he says and his chin trembles again.

What can I say to him? I can't even give him a fragment of the truth because it all interconnects. One piece of the puzzle ultimately reveals the full picture and that's terrifying.

"Jesus Christ, this is the worst first date of my life and considering some bloke once threw up on the brand-new Patrick Cox shoes I bought with my first pay cheque, that is saying something," Jake says with a bitter laugh and picks up his cutlery.

I suck in a sour breath. "Jake, we should try and enjoy the meal. I am leaving for the US on Monday and I don't know when exactly I'll be back but I—"

"You're leaving?" His knife and fork crash onto the plate.

"Yes, I've resigned from Status and I'm going back to LA for a while."

"Resigned?"

"Yes," I say heavily. I knew this would be a difficult conversation, but I didn't fully appreciate how much it would pain me to hurt Jake over and over again. It's not even like telling him the whole truth would make him feel better. No, that would only make everything much, much worse. Now is a time for damage control. Now is a time to do what I can to try and make Jake feel better.

"I need to go back to the States for a few weeks, maybe a month or so. And then I'll be back. I'll be coming back for you, Jake. If you'll have me."

Jake tilts his head to the side and his eyes narrow. "And what do I do while you're gone? Sit and wait and file my nails? Put myself in the freezer next to the frozen peas and a tray of fucking ice cubes? Spend the whole time gluing glitter onto a sign for your return at Heathrow?"

"No, Jake, I don't expect you to wait for me. I'm just telling you when I come back, I won't be coming back for my job, and not only for my family. I'll be coming back for you."

"Or you won't." He shrugs. "Maybe whatever it is in America that has you running back there will be too enticing to stay away from. Maybe you will get there and realise that's what you want – perpetual summer, pissing macadamia nut milk lattes, and Botox on tap. Maybe once you're back living your millionaire lifestyle with actual millionaires you won't want to slum it with the likes of me."

I risk lowering my voice and fix him with one of my looks, the ones that have affected him so resonantly in the past. "Stop talking about yourself like that, Forester."

He points a finger at me and his words come out in a hiss. "No, Rami. No. You don't get to talk to me like that anymore. Not if you're not my man."

It's a perfectly aimed kick to my gut, because God, I want to be his man. I want nothing more than to be his man.

"You're right." I swallow down my pain.

We stare at each other, a million things being said with his sad, confused and enraged eyes. I have no idea what mine tell him, but I hope somewhere in there he gets just a hint of how much I... how much I love him. How much I want to love him. How much I hope I one day get to love him.

Much to my horror, a tear rolls out of his left eye and slides down the faint dusting of freckles on his cheeks, the ones that took my breath away that day we went to a wedding together.

"Jake." I am ready to move, to stand and come to him and hold him in my arms like I did a week ago.

"No," he says and he folds his napkin and places it on the table next to his untouched food. In the next beat, he stands up and looks down at me. "I can't do this. I can't sit here any longer. But what I can do is walk away with my head held high. I gave you a piece of me today, and although it hurts like hell that you don't want it, I don't regret offering it up. I was brave and vulnerable and hopeful. Fuck, no. I *am* brave and vulnerable and hopeful. I will not let you take that away from me."

"I would never—"

"Goodbye, Rami. I hope you find what you're looking for. But I'm not going to wait around to find out if you do."

And that's it. I've run out of words. I've run out of everything. It's all I can do to watch Jake walk away from me, and he doesn't look back once.

Chapter Forty-One

Rami

I don't know how I make it through the loneliest and saddest Saturday of my life, but somehow I do. I also don't know how on Sunday I get on the train to Birmingham, nor do I know how I walk off it and find my sister's car, but somehow I do. I say next to nothing to her as we drive to my mother's house, and when she asks me what's wrong it's all I can do to reach my hand over and squeeze her shoulder, and I hope she can forgive me the impromptu physical touch.

As I go through these out of body motions, I swim in thoughts of Jake. Specifically, how hurt he was, how lost he looked and how beautifully brave he sounded with his final words to me. The only comfort I have now is knowing that I have a few hours alone with Roxie and my mother before Radia and Chloe arrive on a later train. Because I need to talk to my mom, and truth be told, I need one of her biggest, warmest hugs.

It's as if Mama knows as soon as she sees me when I walk into the living room. She looks up from the recipe book she's holding on the couch and lowers her reading glasses.

"Rami?" she says, her tone filled with questions; *Are you okay? What's wrong?*

"Mama," I say and I am flooded with gratitude when she comes to stand as I approach her. Her arms open a moment before I step into them and she lifts up on her toes to embrace me as wholly as she can. I squeeze her body back in return, bending my head to hide it on her shoulder, her floral perfume filling my nostrils.

The urge to sob is strong. I fight it and with some success, although a few rebellious tears break through and land in my mother's hair. When I finally pull back, Mama is quick to swipe her thumb under my eyes, taking others away.

"Tell me about it," she says simply as she takes my hand and gestures for us to sit together.

"Shall I make tea?" a quiet voice says from the other corner of the room.

"You never make tea," I say weakly to Roxie.

"And you never cry like a baby on Mama," she points out.

"Tea would be great," I concede with a small laugh, a chuckle I don't feel I deserve but still it helps.

After Roxie leaves the room, I exhale and find my mother's eyes. They haven't left my face.

"It's such a mess, Mama."

"What is?" she asks gently.

"Everything," I huff out.

"Then just start somewhere, *habibi*." She pulls on me to move next to her on the couch. Her silver eyes have never looked kinder or more full of love. I think about what Jake said about being brave and vulnerable and hopeful. I know that's exactly what I need to be now.

"Mama, I'm not straight. Did you know that?"

A flash of shock shakes her calm expression and she blinks hard once, twice.

"You're gay?"

"No," I say with a small smile. "Pansexual. It means gender isn't important to me. Attraction is about the person, not what gender they identify as."

It's Mom's turn to half-laugh. "I am aware of what pansexuality is. I've read a few articles and watched the odd TV show, you know."

I feel heat rise in my neck and cheeks. "Well, that's what I am," I say looking down at my knees.

Mom's hand squeezes mine, harder and harder until I look at her. When I do, I see her smile is back on her kind, concerned face. "Jake?"

My whole body caves as I breathe out. "Yeah."

"He's such a lovely man. Rami, I'm so happy for you."

I shake my head quickly. "No, we're not together... we're.... This is where it gets messy. And there's more I have to tell you."

"Well, you've already started talking, so just keep going, *habibi*. Tell me whatever you want to next."

"I'm going back to the US."

This gets me the exact reaction I dread, her body tensing and her shoulders lifting. "Why?" She gasps.

"I'm going to go back to finish the rehab," I explain.

"In California?"

"Yes, I've emailed them and they'll let me check-in again on Monday morning, as they should considering how much they're charging me," I add dryly.

"And how long will you do that for?"

"It's a minimum of five weeks to complete what I should have done two years ago."

Mama shakes her head. "But you're already doing so well. Why do you have to go back there? Why can't you do something similar here?"

"This place is specifically for people recovering from cults and cult-like institutions. What I started doing there did work. It set me up to recover, but some of the things I've done since and the way I've been acting recently has highlighted that I've still got some work to do."

"What do you mean?"

"The way I've kept my sexuality from you. The way I can't talk about my past, with anyone, even you all. The way I've kept it all a secret from Jake. I'm still not at peace with certain parts of my story, and it's taking its toll on me. It's stopping me from being with Jake and I don't want anything to get in the way of that."

"Oh, Rami, you really care for him." Mama reaches a hand up to cup my face.

"I do, but I also... I care about myself enough to know that I need to do this." I pull in another deep breath. "I'm also going to have a meeting with Cassie, my manager. You remember her?"

"The one I got in touch with to try and find out where you were, when you were in RemiX?"

I swallow down a jagged-edged lump. "Yes, she's talking about me maybe going back to DJing. I've honestly not considered it until the last week or so but I can't stop thinking about it. I think it would make me... happy."

Mama considers this for a moment. "Yes, Rami, you deserve that. But what would that mean for you and Jake?"

"I don't know, but I know I would only do it in a way that meant I could be with Jake. That's why I'm going to meet with Cassie."

Mama stares off into the distance for a few moments and I let her. She has a lot of information to digest.

"Whatever you do, Rami, chase your happiness. Life is too short to do anything but that," she says, and I know exactly where the roots of her words lie.

"That's why I'm going back to rehab. Because I need to believe that more than some of the other things that my brain tells me. I need to learn to trust myself again."

She sandwiches my hands between hers and for a long time just stares into my eyes.

"Well, I trust you're doing the right thing," she says eventually. "When do you go?"

"Tomorrow."

There's another flash of shock but this one dissipates quicker. "What about your job?"

"I resigned. I don't think it was the right role for me anyway and that's what I'm going to be meeting Cassie about. She's been working on me possibly doing a comeback tour."

Much to my surprise, my mother laughs, loud and heartily.

"What's got into her?" Roxana says as she brings a tray into the room and places it on the coffee table near us. I spare a quick thought to how it is almost a perfect copy of the tea trays Mama makes for guests and I smile at my sister.

"I'm just dropping a few bombshells. Want me to catch you up?"

Roxie shrugs as she kneels and pours the tea. "Sure."

"Well, I'm in love with Jake, that guy you all met a few weeks back. I've also left my job and tomorrow I'm flying back to the States to do rehab and to discuss a possible work thing, a DJ work thing."

Roxie nods while her brows pull together. "Okay. But like, none of those things make sense together. If you're in love with Jake, why are you going to

America? And why would you go back to DJing when you were working with him every day?"

I nearly laugh with how absurd it all sounds when spelt out in Roxana's natural black-and-white logic. "You're right, none of it makes much sense, but I am hoping while I'm in the US I can do some things that help it make complete sense. And then I'll come home."

"For Jake?" Roxie asks.

"Yes," I say in a faltering voice because his damning parting words echo in my mind. "And to see you all. I'll always come home and see you again."

Roxie shrugs at this. "It's okay if you don't. If you want to move back to California, I mean. I'm still annoyed I didn't get to visit you there."

"I'll take you to California one day," I promise, and I mean it.

"I just don't want to join that cult. That sounded awful. I like playing Nintendo and eating meat too much."

I laugh despite myself then, and I smile when I see Mom chuckling too.

"I promise nobody in this family is going to be joining a cult ever again."

"Thank goodness," Mama says. It's as close as she may ever get to joining in a joke about that whole episode, and I treasure it. "And you must come back, *habibi*," she adds. "For us, yes, but also, for Jake."

"I want to," I say but I can't stop the sigh that escapes me. "But when I told him yesterday I was leaving, he sort of made it clear that he wouldn't wait for me, and part of me doesn't want him to. Part of me wants him to go live his life and forget all about me."

"Rami," Mom says and it sounds like a soft warning.

"Why would you want that?" Roxie blurts out. "If you're in love with him, like, really in love with him, then you shouldn't want that."

"Well, sometimes when you love someone, that's what you do. You let them go," I explain in a careful tone. "I think Mariah Carey or someone wrote a song about it actually."

"Bullshit," Roxie says then looks apologetically at our mother. "Sorry, Mama."

Mom shrugs and finds my hand again, pulling it onto her lap. "Roxie's right. Sometimes when you love someone you do let them go, because you have no choice." Her eyes glaze over. "But other times when you love someone, and you do have a chance to get them, you have to do everything you can to get them back and keep them close. And trust me, *habibi*, when you have them close again, it's worth it. So very, very worth it."

Chapter Forty-Two

One Month Later

Jake

When Rami said he was leaving, he really meant it. He disappeared completely and it was almost like he was never here. There was nothing left in my office to remind me of him apart from an empty space at my table, and it hurt in the most twisted way that he didn't even have a toothbrush in my bathroom for me to stare at while cleaning my teeth and fighting back the tears like I did most mornings and evenings.

The second week was when I started looking for him. Despite his overbearing absence, a pathetic and idiotic part of me kept looking for him. Down every corridor in our building, on the Tube to and from work, on the busy streets of London, my eyes kept betraying me by seeking out his silver eyes, dark skin, and relaxed gait. That was also when I began handing over my personal phone to Sharon the moment I arrived at work. It was as much to not have the reminder that Rami wasn't texting me or calling me, as it was to not have the temptation of doing some spontaneous online shopping I couldn't afford. Sharon never asked any questions, and she was dictator-like about hiding the phone from me although her smiles when she handed it over each evening were kind and warmly received.

By the third week I was almost too busy to stay lost in thoughts of Rami. In what was the biggest irony of ironies, Rami's leaving meant that I was given the responsibility of Wayne and Alison's wedding at Clapham Manor House, which is to be held this coming Saturday, tomorrow. I'm dreading donning the same tux I'd worn when Rami and I had kissed in the moonlight for what felt like hours, but I'm trying to approach it like an exorcism. If I can expose myself to these bittersweet memories and survive them, maybe it will help it all move further behind me. Maybe it will help me forget Rami.

By the time this last week rolled around, the wedding had me working all hours of the day and many evenings, which I was grateful for because it also gave me an excuse to turn down offers of dinner or drinks with friends, something I wanted to avoid not only because of my reluctance to pretend everything was fine, but also because I didn't want to spend any of the money I was still dutifully putting aside to pay off my debt.

At least Rami's departure finally prompted me to tell Lionel and Luigi we were over. I had thought it would bring relief, but Lionel's text response only brought more pain.

<If it's meant to be, Jake, he'll come back for you. And something tells me, he will.>

The possibility of Rami coming back for me is the hardest thought of all. It twists my insides and makes my head spin. I don't want to want it. I want to forget how he had made me feel seen, valued, *loved* in a way no other man ever had. I want to forget it all.

Except I also don't want to forget. Because forgetting would mean losing something I thought I'd never have. Even if I never do have it again, even if reliving it hurts like hell, I don't want to lose the memory. I don't want to lose the feeling of being loved like that, even if it really is over.

Sometimes I try to sedate the sadness with anger. I try to focus on the way he hurt me. I recall how he'd kept things from me, things I still don't know. I tell myself that it must be unthinkably bad. I tell myself that it meant I never really knew Rami at all, and that whatever we had together, whatever we'd been together, it was a lie.

But again, this doesn't stick.

Rami may have told me lies, but what we had together, that didn't feel like a lie. Not at all.

The moment I realised this came last Sunday evening. I had been sorting out my wardrobe collecting clothes and shoes to sell online to make a little extra cash to pay back my debts, and I'd had the radio on. When I'd heard the opening guitar riffs of Michael Jackson's *P.Y.T* I'd dropped the Gucci loafers I'd had in my hands, scuffing them and drastically reducing their resale value. My first reaction was to reach for the radio and shut it off. But I didn't.

Instead, I lay down on my bed and listened to every beat, every note, and I replayed how Rami had danced and sang for me. It was the strangest sensation to have tears pouring out of my eyes but a real, solid smile on my mouth, but that sort of perfectly summarises how I feel about Rami now. I reminisce with a smile on my face and a hole in my aching heart.

I still find myself thinking of Rami in ways I really shouldn't, and it's completely spontaneous and unstoppable. Like earlier this week when I made my first payment towards my debt, a respectable £1250, the first person I wanted to call was Rami. I even got his number up on my phone's screen and hovered my thumb over the call button. But a beat later I swiped away.

Instead, I told Anita at our next appointment and while her acknowledgement had been lacklustre – a quick nod of the head and a curt 'Congratulations' before asking me how I felt about it – it had reaffirmed many of the things Rami had told me when I confessed to him over a month ago. That I was not my debt. That I could overcome the shame.

Today, with the wedding and venue all but ready to go tomorrow, and an otherwise quiet day ahead of me in the office, I have set myself the task of clearing out the last magazines that Rami organised for me. They're a tenuous reminder of him and I'm coming to realise now how I've cancelled all my subscriptions in another money-saving step, it feels right to get rid of them.

Sharon is supposed to be helping but she's currently sitting with her feet propped up on the tabletop reading a Lonely Planet magazine article about Lesbos and bemoaning how little is mentioned about Sappho and the lesbian travellers who put this Greek island on the map.

"You don't understand. For decades, it was the only place we could travel safely and be ourselves."

"Oh, you're right, as a gay man who has lived and worked all over the world, I really don't understand that at all." My sarcasm comes easily.

"Everything always comes back to you, doesn't it?" Sharon says snidely over the top of the magazine.

I tut at her. "I'm trying to assure you that I do understand. I believe that's called empathising."

"Then why do it in such a sarcastic way? You don't always have to be such a little man-bitch." Sharon throws the magazine on the table.

"And you don't always have to be a big fat man-hater," I snap back and then can't help the laughter that tumbles out of me as I drop the final stack of magazines in the bin liner and sit down.

"God, I needed that laugh," I say.

"I can tell," Sharon says and she takes her feet off the table and leans towards me. "You've had a face like a slapped arse for weeks now."

"You mean I don't usually have a face like a slapped arse? That's practically a compliment. Thanks, Shaz."

"The last one you'll get this year." She shrugs and slides the magazine across the table to me so I can throw it out with the others. "Come on, I'll take that outside to get collected, and then I'll make you a cup of tea for all your hard, back-breaking work."

"You say that, but I actually did break a fingernail and got three papercuts."

"Such a brave little soldier," she says getting up. Much to my surprise as she comes to collect the bin liner, she places her hand on my shoulder. "I know you miss him."

"I don't know what you're talking about," I manage to say before my chin wobbles.

"Well, *I* miss him. He's so much prettier than you," Sharon says and then she's gone, leaving me alone with a wistful smile and Rami's sparkling-eyes in my mind.

A minute or so later when I'm back at my desk replying to an email, I hear a knock at the door. I sigh and get up.

"Come on you useless wench, you can open the door with two cups of tea," I say as I come to push down the door handle.

But when I open the door, it's not Sharon with two cups of tea. It's my bosses, Bill and Simeon.

"Afternoon, Jake. Do you always speak to your assistant like that?" Bill asks peering at me over his glasses.

"Why do I feel like we may have a tribunal in our future, if you do?" Simeon puts his hands on his hips.

"Bill, Simeon, errr..."

"Oh, God, not two more overpaid white men I have to make tea for." Sharon's voice breaks up the awkward silence.

"Sharon, long time, no see! Milk and two sugars for me." Simeon steps aside.

"No milk, no sugar for me." Bill taps his stomach. "Missus has me on a bloody awful dairy-free diet but it does appear to be working. Do you think I've lost weight? Jake?"

"You're looking very... svelte," I say and then quickly usher Sharon out of my office and invite them to sit.

Considering how hands-on these two are with their company, they spend surprisingly little time in the head office. Partly this is because Bill recently relocated to Yorkshire with his wife and five children, and Simeon lives half the month in Paris with his French husband and their two teenage sons, but it's also because they like to spend time at all our venues and keep a close eye on how they are all doing. And when they are in the London office, they have never once shown up in my office spontaneously, so to say I'm a little surprised at having them sitting around my meeting table is an understatement.

"I didn't know that you were both in town," I say stumbling over my words.

"Oh, yes, we're going to the wedding tomorrow," Bill explains.

Of course, they are.

"We're really looking forward to it," Simeon says as he adjusts the cuffs of his shirt under his corduroy blazer. They are almost comically opposite in their stature and appearance. Bill is a ruddy-cheeked, portly man that you would never describe as tall, while Simeon is long and lean and boasts wiry features. "We have heard nothing but good things about your planning and organising of it."

"Well, proof will be in the pudding. And I'm not talking about the chocolate fondant we're serving."

Bill and Simeon laugh harder than I expect, but it does ease my nerves.

"That's actually why we're here. We wanted to come and thank you for your hard work on the wedding. You stepped up when we really needed you and we appreciate that."

"Just doing my job," I say a little meekly.

"Well, you're doing two jobs, actually. Don't think we don't know that. You'll be getting a bonus for your efforts, that's for sure."

"A bonus?" I say and for the first time ever I envision putting that money towards my debt rather than a collection of shiny shopping bags from various designer labels.

"Absolutely. When Rami left so suddenly we were really up shit creek without a puddle-"

"I think you mean up shit creek without a paddle," Simeon corrects Bill.

"You know what, that does make more sense." Bill nods to himself. "Anyway, the point is. Rami let us down and you have not."

The most bizarre need to defend Rami rises in me. "I think Rami had his reasons."

"Did he tell you he was going to do it?" Simeon leans forward. "Did he tell you when he got the offer?"

"The offer?" I ask, confused.

"To go back and do a world tour," Bill replies.

A world tour? Has Bill finally lost the marbles that were frankly barely there in the first place?

"I told Sim we can't blame him. He always loved DJing and after all that cult nonsense it's good that he finally wants to go back to it," Bill continues.

Cult nonsense. My head spins. *Did Sharon spike my tea?*

"And it's not like he wasn't good at it. How many Grammys does he have?" Simeon asks Bill.

"Oh, three or four, at least."

"Rami has Grammy awards?" I ask, breathless.

Bill's laughter is more of a bellow. "Ha! Rami has a Grammy! Why have I never noticed that before? Hilarious!"

"I'm sorry... Rami's a... DJ?"

Bill blinks at me like I am growing another head. "Not just any DJ. He's DJ Lunar, but you knew that, didn't you? Oh, God, do you gays not listen to dance music anymore?" He throws that last question at Simeon who waves his hand dismissively at his business partner.

"Oh, I never did listen to dance music. Barbara Streisand show tunes is about as disco as it gets in our household."

Sharon returns then with their tea and they talk with her briefly, allowing me some time to gather the thoughts that crash into each other in my brain.

DJ. Cult. Rami. World Tour.

My mind does cartwheels trying to place the name DJ Lunar and I surprise myself by recalling a handful of songs that were very popular about ten or fifteen years ago. I have danced to them many times over the years, and certainly quite frequently in my younger adult years. Is Rami DJ Lunar? Why on Earth would Rami not tell me that? How on Earth did I not figure it out? Then a loud penny drops.

DJ Lunar always wore a mask.

But why did DJ Lunar stop making music? The word cult pulses in my temple and I bring a hand to my forehead to ease its hard, heavy beat.

"So, you haven't heard from him, Jake?" Bill asks me and I lift my gaze to look at him and Simeon, one by one.

"No, I've not heard from him since he left," I say and my voice barely sounds like my own.

"Oh, well, I did get an email a week or so ago apologising again for leaving us hanging. He has a conscience at least."

It's Bill's turn to wave a hand at Simeon as he sips his tea. "We're hardly allowed to be angry with him. He was working for us for practically nothing."

"Pardon?" I bark out.

"Oh, he didn't tell you? Yes, we paid him a pittance. He insisted on it," Simeon clarifies.

"Said he had enough money," Bill scoffs. "Must be nice."

"Well, if you just stopped having children," Simeon banters.

"I can't help it if I'm so virile," Bill says and they lose me again, because all I can do is sit there and try and put a very complex jigsaw puzzle together when I know I don't yet have all the pieces.

Chapter Forty-Three

Jake

I promised myself an early night. I need to at least try and look a little less haggard for tomorrow's wedding despite the exhaustion I feel after four weeks of missing Rami and working far too many hours, but that is not going to happen.

I'm two hours into reading articles about DJ Lunar from a wide range of different sources ranging from long-abandoned gossip blogs from the 2000s through to a 2017 *New York Times* article about the cult that DJ Lunar joined. The cult Rami joined.

Almost unanimously, the articles agree that DJ Lunar joined the so-called RemiX cult because he followed his girlfriend, Michelle Saunders, and close friend, Gavin Lough, into it, the latter reportedly being the creator and leader of RemiX.

There isn't much detailed information about Gavin Lough other than he was also a DJ around the same time that DJ Lunar was climbing in the charts and together they headlined multiple festivals and gigs all over the world. Although nowhere near as successful, Gavin Lough, or DJG as he was known then, had a couple of top 20 hits and released a few semi-successful albums. The most recent interview I find with him is many years later and it's for Men's Health magazine. In it he's discussing at great length the benefits of a raw vegan diet, and talking about how our bodies have the innate ability to heal themselves if we remove all toxins from our diet and immediate environment. The next time he is mentioned in the media is when reports of DJ Lunar's disappearance start to circulate and that's when I first see RemiX, a one-time wellness movement, described as a cult.

After searching her name, I find Michelle Saunders referred to as anything from a D-list actress and influencer to wellness guru and it feels impossible to gauge exactly what kind of a person she is from the articles I've read, nor can I discern what kind of relationship she and Rami had. Even the photos don't give away much because there are only a handful of them photographed together and the quality of the photos are terrible. These long-zoom images blur the edges of their bodies that are never captured mid-embrace but rather walking down various LA streets together wearing sunglasses and late-2000s fashion that comprises mostly of low-rise flared trousers and crop tops for her, and skinny jeans and vintage T-shirts for him, the latter mostly in black, of course. The paparazzi photos of her alone don't reveal much more, are often just as pixelated and she nearly always has oversized glasses on. But even those obstructions can't deny that she is beautiful to look at. Fair colouring, dainty features, pointed chin, and a fashion model's physique.

But I don't feel jealous. Far from it. I feel curious. I want to know what really happened. I want to know how it was for Rami when he was in the cult. How did it all begin? And more importantly perhaps, how did it all end?

There is no official DJ Lunar website or social channels other than one on Spotify that has all his albums and songs, all of which are still available although the profile lacks a bio or any other photos other than one of him, masked up and facing the camera head on. I can't bring myself to listen to a single song while I'm on his channel; the thumping bassline and upbeat rhythm would just mess with my head too much.

Because I'm not yet ready to admit that Rami is this whole other person I didn't even know existed.

I'm also not yet ready to consider the possibility that he returned to LA for Michelle, or for RemiX, or indeed to do this comeback tour that only one music industry webzine has referred to in its rumour section from a few weeks ago.

Because all of those possibilities will mean one thing; that Rami is not coming back for me.

How am I still even wondering if he will return to me like he said he would? How is a traitorous, stubborn part of me still hoping for it, yearning almost? That is not the strong, independent man I want to be. That's not the whole person I am fighting to become now I have finally, finally tackled my biggest darkest secret head on.

Except I haven't, have I?

Groaning I close my laptop and slide it to the side on my bed. I then reach for my phone and do what I have been putting off doing for nearly a month, the longest time I have ever gone without speaking to my sister.

But I need her now. I need her to help make sense of these new revelations about Rami. And I need her to hear my truth and hopefully, hopefully, love me despite it.

Jenna answers on the second ring.

"Jake Malcolm Forester, you better have spent the last month trapped in a bed with Rami or have another equally excusable reason for not calling me back in far too long."

I suck in a breath as I grimace. "How about, Rami and I broke up?"

The silence is loud. "Oh, Jakey, no."

"Oh, Jenna, yes."

"I'm so sorry," she says and I realise how much I needed her voice and her comfort. I will always need my big sister. "That really sucks."

"Yeah, it does."

"Do you want to tell me about it?"

"I sort of do, yes, but I also want to tell you something else. In fact, I have a lot of things to tell you, but first I want to apologise for not being in touch much recently. It's been hard since Rami left and I didn't want to talk about it and work's also been really busy and—"

"Jake, you don't need to apologise to me. I only want to speak to you because I care about you."

"Well, I hope that will still be the case after I explain some of the chaos that is my life to you."

I pull in a deep breath and then I tell her. I tell her all about my debt. I tell her the numbers. I tell her how it started, and how I let it get as bad as I did. And I tell her how now things are different and how the beginning of this hopeful end began with a long conversation with Rami where he held me until I stopped crying.

"But I don't understand," Jenna says eventually. "If Rami was there supporting you through that, where is he now?"

"In California."

"He moved back? Is that why you broke up?"

"Yes, no, I don't really know."

I hear Jenna's slow exhale down the phone. "Jake, I'm so sorry you felt like you couldn't tell me about your debt. If I ever gave you the impression I would judge you or think less of you, I'm truly sorry."

I shake my head as I squeeze the phone against my ear. "It's not that at all. It's more I judged myself for getting in this mess and I couldn't bear anyone else to have similar harsh, horrid thoughts about me. Especially you."

Jenna's voice quivers when she speaks next. "Oh, Jakey, I can't bear the thought of you struggling with this on your own for all this time. And I hate that you're alone now. Let me look up flights. I could come tomorrow and spend the week with you."

My sigh comes out more like a groan. "I'm touched, really but there's no point. I have to work tomorrow. We have a wedding at one of our venues. In fact, it's the venue where I'm going to have my fortieth."

"Speaking of, and before I forget. That's sort of why I've been trying to get in touch with you. Well, on top of the fact I love you and I need to hear your voice at least once a week or I start going a bit senile."

"I think I'm the same. It may explain my current state of mind," I say realising I still haven't told her the most outlandish part of this whole saga but I wait for her to tell me what she wants to first.

"So, firstly, Maeve has confirmed she'll come with us. A bit reluctantly, I have to admit – she's worried she'll be out of place—"

"As if! I'll text her myself to tell her she better be there. She'll be guest of honour!"

"That's what I said!"

"I'm so glad she's coming," I say, and I really am. It melts a little of the tension in my shoulders and the ache in my gut. There are good people in my life. People who love and care about me. Maybe a part of me will always wish Rami was one of them but I have others. I have people. I have love.

"And she won't be the only other extra guest," Jenna says in a weird voice.

"Oh, who else are you dragging over here? Are Cynthia and James coming? I hope they know they're very welcome," I say referring to Marty's parents who have also come to feel like family.

"No," Jenna says slowly. "I'll be bringing the extra person… not that they're a person… yet."

Realisation crashes into me and it almost knocks me sideways as I grip the phone even tighter and feel my mouth fall open. A second later, I burst into tears. Maybe they're tears that I've had stored up for Rami and now I finally have a reason to shed them, or maybe they're tears that are just deserving of this occasion.

"You're pregnant?" I gasp out.

"Yes," Jenna confirms and the delight in her voice is beautifully audible. "It's still very early but I've taken several tests and had it confirmed at the doctors too."

"Oh, Jenna," I say. "That's wonderful news. I'm so very happy for you."

And I am. The happiness is bubbling up inside me in a way that feels miraculous. The last few weeks have left me wondering if I was even capable of feeling such joy and it is instantly healing to know I am.

"I wanted you to be the first person I told," she says with a sniff. "If only you had answered your fucking phone two weeks ago."

Here is where the blade of guilt strikes. "Oh, shit, I'm so sorry, Jen. I wasn't thinking. I was—"

"Shh. I'm not really angry. I'm just sorry you weren't the first person I told. Cynthia guessed it from the moment I ordered a decaf coffee after yoga together."

"She's quite the detective," I say, imagining her and James' excitement.

"You have no idea. She's already quite the amateur midwife. I think she'll be very offended when I explain I'd prefer her son, the baby's father, in the room when I give birth rather than her."

"Oh, gosh, Marty. He must be in heaven?"

I swear I hear Jenna swallow before she answers. "I've never seen him happier."

"God, I can't wait to see you at the party now," I say, wiping more tears from my eyes.

"Me too," Jenna says. "How are you feeling about the party now?"

"Oh, like it is costing me three months' worth of debt repayments," I say with a groan. "Honestly, it's strange how much of a shift has happened with money for me. A month ago, I would be seeing it as costing me a new Tom Ford suit or a holiday in the Caribbean but now I only think in terms of paying off my debt. It's good. It feels... healthy."

Jenna sniffs again. "It's because you're working through the shame of it. Shame is such a cockblocker."

"I sincerely hope that's not a quote from your next book," I say and smile when Jenna laughs.

"It's not, I promise. Hey, did you give any more thought to inviting Dad and Carol?"

"Honestly, Jenna, there's been so much else going on, I really haven't."

"Right, yes, of course. You've been grieving Rami."

I roll my eyes. "God, he didn't die. He just... he just has his own shit to sort out. And he decided to go and do that somewhere with a better climate and more attractive people."

"Am I allowed to ask what he has to sort out?"

A groan leaves my mouth. "Jenna, it's possible you wouldn't believe me if I told you."

"Try me," she says.

And I do. I tell her all about what I've just discovered. I tell her all about him not telling me about any of it. I tell her about him possibly going on a world tour. And I tell her my theories – or rather, my fears – of him going back there for Michelle or for the cult.

What I don't tell her is what he said when we broke up, about how he said he'd come back for me. And how I told him I didn't want him to. What's the point in telling her that when both statements are now untrue?

"My God, Jake. How do you even start processing all this?"

"I was hoping you would help me with that," I say, only half-joking.

"Well, it will take time. And you must give yourself time. I'm so sorry Rami felt he couldn't tell you himself. It must have been awful for him to feel like he couldn't. That's shame, again."

Her words and their similarity to what we just discussed about my debt ring in my ears like an alarm.

"But I would never have judged him," I say and I wonder who I'm telling, myself or my sister. "I would have wanted to help him."

Jenna sighs. "Sometimes people feel they're not worthy of help, especially when shame has a hold on them. I think we can all relate to that in one way or another, but I think especially for Rami, considering how he must have caused his loved ones a lot of pain when he cut them off, he may well believe that so thoroughly that it's unthinkable to lean on someone else or to ask for more than he thinks he deserves."

"But his family aren't angry. Not at all. I've met them. They love him."

"And you? Do you love him?" Her question hits me like an arrow.

I sigh. "Jenna, it doesn't matter. He's gone."

"It matters, Jake. It matters more than you realise. It's okay to still love him. Honestly, you just need to admit it to yourself if you've got any hope of moving forward and getting over this."

Another alarm rings out as I hear these words and the most foolish, stubborn part of my brain issues a single clear and precise thought. *I don't want to get over him.*

I close my eyes and shake my head at myself. *Wow, my self-sabotaging tendencies know no limit.*

"I think I could have fallen head over heels for him," I admit.

"Whatever you do, Jake, don't build those defences up again. Don't waste the energy. It's okay to feel raw and vulnerable. It won't feel scary and awkward forever, I promise."

"Jenna, I barely have the energy to tie my shoelaces at the moment, let alone re-build thirty-odd years of impenetrable walls."

"Hmm," my sister mumbles. "So, you have to work tomorrow, but what about Sunday? I could fly in and work from your place for a while. Marty is working all week so he'll barely notice I'm gone."

"That's bollocks and we both know it."

"Fine, I'll tell the truth and say after the last few years trying to get pregnant we're actually rather shagged out and he'll probably be grateful for a few days off from sex."

"Also probably untrue, rather depressingly."

"Jake, please. Will you let me do this for you? I want to come and look after you."

Sensing my instinctive resistance to her offer, it's almost like I feel the foundation of those walls being dug and I purposefully stop myself from digging deeper.

Jenna's right.

I shouldn't build up my defences again, and I should do the one thing that I wish Rami trusted me enough to do. I should accept Jenna's love, and help.

"As long as you don't mind, I'd love that, Jenna. Thank you."

I feel noticeably better after hanging up, and it's not just because I know I'll see my sister in two days. It's also because I see glimmers of the man I never thought I could be still shining through this hazy mess. I see how brave I was telling my sister all about my debt. I see how bravely I told her mine and Rami's story. I see how brave I was in accepting her offer of help. I see my courage, and I feel it too.

Maybe that's why I pick up the phone again, scroll until I find a number I have been thinking about dialling far too much recently and I press call.

As the ringing starts, I quickly glance at the clock. It's nearly ten o'clock. Hopefully, that doesn't mean it's a bad time to call him.

"Hello?" His deep voice makes me feel far too many things, but I push on anyway.

"Dad, it's Jake."

"Jake." A pause. "Are you okay?"

"Yes, I'm sorry to call so late. But I wanted to ask you something."

Another pause. "Okay."

"What are you and Carol doing the first weekend of September? Because I'm having a party for my fortieth birthday, and I would really like you to be there."

Chapter Forty-Four

Another Month Later

Rami

"Well, it wouldn't be a comeback tour if you weren't fresh out of rehab." Carrie's tone is as harsh as ever, but it doesn't cut me like it used to. Who knows if that's my age or the work I did in rehab, a huge chunk of which was focused on building resilience, but Cassie's brusqueness doesn't even phase me. I let it wash over me.

However, it would seem I need time for that to happen because when I don't reply, she shifts in her seat and starts to look uncomfortable.

"Sorry, was that too soon?" she asks.

"I left over a week ago, so not really," I say and bring my coffee cup to my lips. The sun is shining bright above us and while the LA heat is a balm, I can't help but wonder what the weather's like in London these days. Has the sun been shining on Jake? Has he enjoyed his summer? Has he thought about me at all?

As always, my thoughts end up back with him. Most of them start with him too.

"How was it?" Cassie asks and I am taken aback by the genuine concern that has softened her voice.

I think about my answer for a moment. It feels too extreme to say that it saved my life and it's possibly inaccurate, but there is some truth in how essential it was, and how with hindsight, I can see how without it, I wouldn't be where I am now, feeling what I feel. Because I feel proud. Proud of myself and proud of the decision I made to go to rehab, even though at times it felt impossible, like I was putting myself through hell with all the distance from Jake and the excavating of deep-rooted problems relating not only to my rise to fame and joining RemiX, but also my relationship with myself and my family. Turns out Jake isn't the only one with so-called Daddy Issues. I swallow the small smile this thought prompts before I respond to Cassie.

"It was fine. Good, in fact. Did the full six weeks in the end. Should have done it two years ago," I say and again my mind drifts to Jake. I can't help but think how much upset I could have saved him, saved us both, had I just completed the therapy when I was supposed to.

"Yeah, but you had your reasons for not doing it back then. And to be honest, not everyone would do it at all."

"Not everyone would follow their girlfriend and a middle-aged man who wears far too much linen into a cult either," I say although my weak attempt at humour makes me cringe a little.

She waves her hand in the air in front of her. "Pah, RemiX isn't even a real cult. Just sounds like a crappy techno dance event no act would ever want to headline. You said there were no orgies or body maiming so…"

I know she's joking too but suddenly I don't feel like laughing anymore.

I speak slowly and deliberately so she can hear every word, and so can I. "It was a cult, trust me."

"That's the first time you've actually called it what it is," she says bluntly and I see from the self-satisfied look on her face she's achieved what she set out to with these jokes. "I'd say rehab worked."

I think about how the words were always too heavy to leave my throat whenever it came to telling Jake and I know she's right. And I also can't deny how much the urge to tell Jake is fast becoming an obsession. It's all I think about. It's why I've written countless draft emails and text messages, but didn't send any of them. I have to tell him to his face. If he ever lets me get in front of his face again.

"So, can we talk business now? I've enquired about your welfare, so I can tick that item off the to-do list." She says this with no sarcasm and I wouldn't be surprised if it was indeed on her list for the day.

"Go ahead," I say putting my coffee down.

"You've read through everything I sent, right? What did you think about the proposed venues? The dates? We have some wriggle room on those as long we make decisions before the end of September. A January start date would also give you plenty of time to get back in the studio—"

I hold my hand up. "Wait a minute, you want me to do an album before the tour starts?"

"Come on, Rami, get your head back in the game and out of the watercolour painting and flower arranging you were doing in rehab. You know you need an album for this tour to really make us the money we all want it to—"

I shake my head. "Money is the last thing I want from this tour."

"Well, that makes only one of us. Nix and I have got our eyes on a lovely ranch in Montana."

"What would you do with a ranch?"

Cassie shrugs. "Stay on it a few weeks a year. Buy chaps to wear while we look at the horses. We already have the fedoras and cowboy boots."

I'd forgotten how she has an answer for everything. "Cassie, I'm not sure I want to do another album. Playing is a different story. I'm keen to do that again, but I don't want to play my own music. I want to go back to my roots. I want to do a really varied, vibrant set. Switch up night by night too."

"Rami, that sounds charming… for a prom. But you're not going to be playing proms. You're going to be playing the biggest stadiums in the biggest cities of the world. Your old school fans will want to relive their misspent youth with all your hits from back in the day, and then we want to get a whole new generation of butts on seats with some new material. Don't tell me you don't have it in you. Nobody pulls a good tune out of their ass like you do."

I almost don't care if she sees me flinch as I fidget in my seat. It's not the way she's talking to me, or even what she's saying, it's more this over-arching assumption that I'm just going to give her what she wants. But what about what *I* want?

I want to DJ again, yes, but on my own terms. Do I want to tour the world and reconnect with fans who I abandoned just as abruptly as I did my own family? Yes, part of me would love to do that. Am I ready to bear the media scrutiny that will certainly come with that? Yes, sort of. I finally feel able to do it in a way that will serve me rather than feed the machines that get rich off me. And I'm currently staring at one of the hungriest, greediest machines. A machine who does care about me on one level or another, but not as much as she cares about her bank balance, or a ranch in Montana, apparently.

"Cassie," I lean forward, "I am going to need a bit more time to think about this. The recording part, I mean."

She starts to scroll around again, this time on her iPad. "How much time? Shall we schedule a meeting for next week?"

"No," I say. "I'll be gone by next week."

"Gone where?"

"Back to the UK."

"Oh, not that dump." She curls up her top lip.

"That dump is my home," I say, and my thoughts of Jake have never been clearer, or more colourful.

Cassie points her finger at me. "I am not letting you leave without your signature on a very lucrative contract."

I have to hide my smile because I've got her where I want her.

"If you can forego the album requirement, and the exact tour length and venues can be TBC, you can have all my signatures."

"Rami, Rami, Rami, you're throwing away hundreds of thousands of dollars. Millions potentially if the album takes off."

"I don't want any more money," I say. *I want Jake*, I finish in my mind. I want Jake and I want to see my mother and my sisters again. I want Jake and I want to tell him everything. I want Jake and I want to spend the rest of my life making up for some of the hurt I've caused him.

Cassie narrows her eyes at me. "Sounds to me like you're still brainwashed, but I will see what I can do."

"Thank you, I appreciate that," I say and I stand up to leave.

"Where the fuck do you think you're going?" She looks at me appalled. "We still haven't gone through the list of tour managers I think will be almost as good as me."

"You really don't want to do it?" I ask, sitting back down.

"Fuck, no. My luggage stays in storage unless it's Mexico or the Maldives." She flips her iPad over. "So, here's my shortlist."

"Wait," I say without looking at it. "I don't need that list."

"Yes, you do. You're not managing a fucking world tour all on your lonesome, not when you're already going to try and dodge every single media interview I set up for you. You managing this tour will mean half-filled stadiums and us all in the red by the time you're back in LA."

"That's the thing," I say.

"What's the thing?"

"I'm not moving back here."

Her eyes and mouth pop open. "You're not?"

"No, I still want to live in the UK, even if I'm touring. That's where I'll be going home."

"Because of your family?" she says with a hint of disdain.

"Yes, and… other people."

Cassie's eyes narrow on me. "Rami, do you have someone else you're going home for? Because if you do, that could really fuck up this world tour and my summer house in Cabo purchase plans."

"It was a ranch in Montana a minute ago!"

"Oh, God, you're in love, aren't you? Jesus fucking Christ."

"Why is that so shocking?"

"Well considering the last time you fell in love you ended up lost in the Mojave Desert eating nothing but raw vegetables and fermented leaves."

I swallow roughly. "And you think this is the same?"

"Tell me it's not. Whoever they are they want you to be in the UK! For all we know the UK could just be one big cult. It would make an awful lot of sense, to be honest."

"The UK is not a cult," I say, feeling a flash of pride at saying that word out loud for the second time.

"You all drink tea with milk in it!"

"At least we have gun control!"

Cassie slams her fists down on the sides of her chair. "Goddamn the guns. They silence me every fucking time. I hate not being able to win an argument. Anyway, are you going to tell me more about them?"

"No, I'm not," I say with a smile on my face but it quickly fades when I speak again. "Besides, it may not… work out."

"Why not?"

"Because I walked away when he needed me most."

Cassie shrugs. "Needing someone is not a safe place to start a relationship from. If you're lucky they won't need you anymore."

"Great, thanks." My stomach sinks.

"No, I mean it. If you're lucky they'll have moved on, they'll be in a place where they don't need anyone at all and so when you do show up again and start grovelling – and grovel you must, by the sounds of it – then if they do take you back, you know it's because they *want* you and not because they *need* you."

I blink at Cassie. "That almost sounds like good advice."

Her smile concentrates in one corner of her mouth. "I'm a ruthless bitch when it comes to business and the UK's unsavoury refreshment habits, but when it comes to true love, you'll not find a bigger fan."

I smile again, but this time more to myself. What she's just said feels like permission to do something I spent most of my time in rehab envisioning. "Then maybe you can help me with something."

Cassie leans forward. "I'm all ears."

"I need to get in touch with a semi-famous influencer," I say pulling out my phone. "Mae's her name on social media , but she's Maeve in real life. She's Irish. I can show you her profiles but I really need her private number."

Cassie rolls her eyes as I show her my phone screen. "Too easy. You could at least have made it a challenge for me."

Chapter Forty-Five

Two Weeks Later

Jake

I'd be lying if I said I hadn't allowed myself a daydream or two about tonight.

In those daydreams, I'm wearing couture and the glossiest polished shoes, the music is exactly to everyone's taste and the champagne flows without end. In those daydreams, the people I love most in the world all mingle together and share laughter and smiles, I dance with my sister, Marty and Maeve, and I am hugged by Dana and Dove, and their spouses. In those daydreams, I have my photo taken with Lionel and Luigi, and with no shadow of a doubt, I am the one who looks the most handsome in the resulting photograph. In those daydreams I give a speech that everybody laughs and cries at in all the appropriate places. In those daydreams, my father seeks me out of the crowd to tell me how proud he is of me.

And sometimes in those daydreams, if I let them get this far, Rami is by my side. Rami, looking sharp in his tux with his velvet bow tie. Rami, holding my hand like he did at Lionel and Luigi's wedding. Rami, slow dancing with me to Stevie Wonder or maybe to some of the George Michael I have insisted the DJ play later. Rami, staying close as we circulate and make small talk with the guests, and then later, Rami, piggy-backing me up to one of the suites upstairs after the party is over. Rami, laying me on the bed and peeling off my clothes and calling me his beautiful boy.

But Rami is not here. Rami is still in LA, I assume. Rami has not been in touch. Rami has not come back for me like he said he would.

And I am trying to be okay with that. I'm trying because the alternative is too bleak to entertain. Furthermore, a quick glance around my current surroundings confirms I have more than enough entertaining duties in this present moment.

It's shortly after eight o'clock and everybody is here at my birthday party, apart from my father. I didn't expect him to be prompt, but I also didn't expect him to be the most fashionably late. But this is another thing I'm trying not to think about.

I've said brief hellos to almost everyone, excusing myself from protracted conversations on account of new guests arriving, and now I am standing at the bar taking my much-needed first stationary sip of champagne as I look around the room.

And I'm not alone. Maeve is standing next to me, having accompanied me to the bar, but she's now focused on her phone and I'm grateful for the moment of peace that gives me. It also means I can finally take in the scene in front of me.

I watch as Jenna and Marty chat with Luigi and Lionel, and in barely a minute I count at least four occasions when Marty's hand comes up to caress Jenna's stomach which is only slightly showing her pregnancy. Close to them, Dove and Dana are holding hands and are deep in conversation while Keeley, Dove's tattoo-covered wife, and Javier, Dana's bespectacled accountant husband, make what is clearly awkward small talk beside them. At a table to the side, I see Sharon and her wife Kate with full plates of the canapes the hotel arranged. I watch them for long enough to see Sharon pop something in Kate's mouth and they both share a smile and eye contact as Kate kisses the tip of Sharon's finger before it leaves her lips. Although the DJ has yet to start playing any of my long list of requested song choices, Harry, Derek and a handful of my other friends are on the dance floor trying far too hard to outdo one another with their moves.

The whole scene is perfect. My friends are all here. They are people who love me, care about me, and they're all here for me. I just wish I didn't feel like one very important part was missing.

"Oh, God," I groan loudly enough for Maeve to hear.

"What's up?" She lifts her head.

"Nothing, just London's most depressingly loved-up newlyweds on their way to make me feel worse about turning forty as a single man."

"Ugh, I hate loved-up people," Maeve says with what sounds like genuine distaste. "Need me to come up with something to save you?"

I sigh. "No, I should probably face this car crash head on."

"Okay, I'll leave you to it," she says. "Good luck!" And Maeve shimmies away, her long blonde hair swaying behind her.

I swallow a large mouthful of champagne and plaster a firm smile on my face. "Lionel! Luigi! So good to see you."

I'm pulled into a hug with both of them that I should hate but in truth, their closeness warms me.

"What an incredible party, Jake!" Lionel enthuses.

"Fantastic location," Luigi adds. "You know we tried to host a catwalk show here last year but couldn't get a look-in. You were lucky to secure it."

"Perks of the job." I shrug.

"We were just talking with Jenna," Lionel says, his eyes sparkling. "She mentioned your father's coming. That's wonderful."

I'd forgotten Lionel knows a little about my complex relationship with my father.

"Yes, he said he's coming but still plenty of time for him to not show," I say feeling the need to pre-empt that out loud, just in case.

"Oh, no, I'm sure he'll be here." Lionel taps my arm in reassurance.

There's something about the depths of Lionel's kind eyes, or maybe it's the progress I've been making with my debt, and in therapy recently, that has me pulling in a deep breath and launching into a conversation that months ago I never would have dared to start with Lionel and Luigi.

"Actually, there's something I've been meaning to talk to you both about. If you have a minute."

"We are here in our finest attire just for you, old boy," Luigi says with one of his guffaws.

"Well, you know at your wedding. How Rami was my date... my boyfriend."

Lionel and Luigi share a quick look that I can't decipher so I just push on.

"The thing is, we weren't exactly together, then. Or really maybe ever. I don't really know what we were." I pause and need another deep breath before I can continue. "But we weren't together at your wedding. Rami was my fake date, my fake boyfriend. He came with me so I wouldn't be alone at your wedding."

"He was your *fake* date?" Lionel's face creases in confusion.

"You weren't really together?" Luigi asks, also with a heavy frown. "But that's impossible. What about the dancing…"

Lionel takes over. "At our wedding. When he did that dance in front of everyone and he… he kissed you."

"That was all part of the pretence," I say glumly.

"What about that other night?" Luigi's eyebrow lifts into a very impressive arch. Of course, he has overachieving facial features as well as everything else. "You know, when we made drunken fools of ourselves at your place, I believe there was a lot more than kissing happening then…"

"Oh, God." I groan and cover my face with my hand. "Did you hear us?"

Luigi gets as close to blushing as is maybe possible. "I was in no fit state to make sense of anything that night, but hindsight did make me question if I heard… something."

"Well, yes, there was something going on then, and after that. For a while…" My voice and my mind drifts away from Lionel and Luigi. It goes back in time to a place where Rami laid me out on his sheepskin rug and covered my body in kisses

"But not anymore?" Lionel asks and he sounds like he's genuinely intrigued.

I swallow the lump in my throat. "When I texted you we broke up, that was when whatever we were ended. That was when he went back to LA and I've not heard from him since."

"Nothing at all?" Luigi has the same curiosity.

"Nope," I say and I do try to smile even though I'm almost certain it doesn't convert. "I'm sorry I lied to you about him being my boyfriend."

Lionel chuckles then and the sound helps ease some of my own discomfort. "Well, tickle me under the arms with a feather duster, I can't believe you weren't really dating! You seemed so good together."

We were, I want to call out for him and anyone else to hear but I feel I have no right.

"You know, it could all still work out," Luigi says but doesn't continue after Lionel gives him a pointed look.

"I really do think that ship has sailed," I say to Luigi before turning to Lionel. "Not everybody gets the happy ending you both did. And I'm okay with that."

That's the thing. I really am. In the last few weeks I've seen glimmers of something that could be called peace. In the way my debt is reducing. In the way therapy actually feels like it's making a concrete difference rather than giving me soundbites to cling to when I need to ride out the latest chaos in my life. Chaos that invariably used to involve me doing online shopping in the middle of the night or treating myself to a big night out my bank balance or my liver could ill afford, all things that I have now stopped doing.

"Oh, biscuits. I want to hug you again," Lionel says and this time when he leans in, it's just me and him. As his arms envelop me, I think about how much our relationship has changed. Four months ago, I was actively avoiding Lionel's calls and dreading his wedding and now I am closing my eyes and relaxing in his embrace like it's a little extra oxygen.

Part of me wants to thank Rami for this evolution, for being by my side as I cleared the air with Lionel, but a bigger, stronger part of me just feels proud because *I* did that. I may have done it with Rami somewhere in the background, and certainly Lionel's big, kind heart helped us both get to where we are today, but still, I was part of it too. Albeit long overdue, I was humble enough to own up to my mistakes and apologise for them. I was strong enough to keep Lionel in my life when pushing him away felt like the easiest thing. I am still brave enough to keep these hopelessly in love idiots close to me when a former version of myself would have banished them forever.

I've been feeling brave a lot recently, which is just as well because when I open my eyes and lift my head off Lionel's shoulder, I see my father and Carol entering the courtyard.

I quickly excuse myself and make my way to them.

"Dad, Carol, you're here," I say as I come to stand in front of them.

"Looks like it," Dad says with an awkward shrug. The cumbersome lift in his shoulders and the slightly humourless tone of his voice threatens to make me turn on my heel and walk away from them. How could I be so stupid to think my father would actually *want* to be here? But then I recall how it's not like he's lived his life with a strong sense of duty to his children so there must be something that brought him here and I'm curious about that. Curious in the way Anita advises me to be about my feelings.

"Come over to the bar and get a drink," I say and I lead them there.

Once they've placed their orders, they both turn and take in the courtyard.

"Very impressive," Dad says.

"It's beautiful," Carol says and her dangling silver earrings catch some of the glow of the fairy lights that criss-cross overhead. She looks very elegant in a long plum coloured shift dress and I like her new cropped hairstyle. When I tell her so, she blushes and smiles. I see then how much more comfortable in this setting she is than my father, which suggests she provided no resistance to being here, something that is also a relief.

"Jenna and Marty are here," I say. "And Marty's sister, Maeve. I'll introduce you later."

"That would be nice," Carol says.

"It's a very... colourful party," Dad says and I can translate perfectly. Colourful, meaning queer. For some reason I don't want to speak his language today.

"Yes, we are a veritable kaleidoscope of the LGBTQIA+ spectrum." I wave my hands around at the crowd and briefly see Jenna turn to cast her gaze on us. Feeling her eyes on me I look at our father to see how much I've shocked him, but I am the one left surprised when I see half a grin curling his lips.

"And then there's us," he adds, and I can't help but laugh with him.

"And yes, there's you," I say nodding at my sister who is smiling back at us, no doubt encouraged by our shared laughter. "And also Jenna. She rather lets the side down too."

"Oh, yes. I see Jenna now. I'll go say hello," Carol says and she picks up her drink and heads in that direction.

More surprise washes over me when my father doesn't follow her but instead stays with me at the bar.

"You know, I was surprised you called," he says as he plays around with the cufflinks on one sleeve of his shirt. He's wearing a blazer over a crisp white shirt, but no tie, and I realise he is simply not used to dressing up like this, which makes me feel a strange mix of grateful and uncomfortable that he did it for me.

"You were?"

"Yes." He clears his throat.

"Well, I am your son," I say bitterly.

"Yes, you are." I search his reply for a hint of hidden meaning; regret, pride, love, disappointment. But I hear nothing. I turn then to face my father.

"You know you could have called me," I say. "You are my father."

"Yes, I am," he says and I hear it then. Resistance.

"Dad—" I begin and I'm astonished when he cuts me off.

"I know I should have called you. To find out how you are."

"Yes, you should have," I say and both of our bodies move at the boldness of these words. My father turns towards me a little more, while I stand a bit straighter, suddenly a little lighter after speaking that truth.

"Well, we agree on that at least," he says in a way that suggests he's slightly put-out by my honesty, but he knows he doesn't have a leg to stand on in terms of contesting it. In many ways, this spurs me on.

"Dad, I think we agree on a lot of things. Like how we've both been shit with contact in the past. Like how we could both make a bit more effort going forward. And maybe we could see each other more often too."

Dad takes a sip of his drink and looks out at the crowd. "You know, it was lovely those years when you and Jenna came up for Christmas. It was a shame you didn't come by yourself last year."

I feel my jaw tighten. "You didn't invite me."

Dad thinks on this for a moment. "I suppose you're right about that too."

"I've not been perfect either," I admit. "I've thought about calling you many times, but I never did."

"Why didn't you?"

I quickly glance around the room again, noticing how everyone is getting a little louder and more bodies are starting to move to the music. I know I shouldn't be getting into this at my birthday party, but I also don't know when I'll get the chance again. And Lord knows I've waited long enough for it to happen.

"Because you hurt me, Dad. I've wanted to have a better relationship with you for years, decades. Indeed, I wanted to be closer to you when I was younger, but it's never felt possible. You've always kept us at arm's length…" I brave a look at him.

His colouring has faded a little and his eyes are fixed on his glass, I can't read what he's thinking. So I keep going.

"And it hurt me, Dad. Jenna will never say it because, frankly, she doesn't need you in the same way—"

"What exactly are you trying to say, Jake?" He interrupts in a rough voice. His eyes are on me now looking angry or confused, or both. I've said too much. I've pushed him too far. The clutches of panic wrap around my throat, threatening to silence me, but I refuse to let them do so before I say what I really need to say.

"Part of me still needs my dad," I push the words out even though they are heavy leaving my mouth. "I still need to know that you love me, and that you're proud of me."

The silence between us stretches into a deafening nothingness, even despite the music and chatter that fills the courtyard. It's a fertile ground for doubt and fear and more panic. But my dad's voice is like sunshine warming the stubborn seed of hope that was still there regardless.

"I love you, Jake," he says just loud enough for me to hear. He coughs again and then his voice is louder. "And I couldn't be prouder of you."

"Really?" I face him, unable to stop my smile.

"Yes, and I'm sorry—" My father's voice cracks. "I'm sorry I haven't told you that enough. Probably ever, in fact."

"You're saying it now," I say as if to confirm he really is, but Dad doesn't seem to listen.

"I know I've been selfish. What happened with your mother and with Carol…"

"We don't have to talk about it. At least not now," I say quickly. In all honesty, I don't want to rehash the past. I'd rather focus on a better future.

"Well, I won't lie and pretend that's a relief because I find it hard. I find it very, very hard to think about what happened to Cathy and how she died and how you and Jenna had to grow up so quickly and…" He trails off.

"So, you don't think about it," I finish for him.

"No, I don't. Which I know is very cowardly."

"Yes, it is," I agree, but I can't honestly say I'm much better. Too often I avoid talking about my mother, even with Jenna.

My father releases such a heavy sigh I almost expect him to say something else or walk away or do something to end the conversation, but instead I get the opposite.

"God, it's such a relief to say these dreadful things out loud."

"It is?"

"When I read Jenna's book—" he begins.

"You read Jenna's book?" The shock pushes my shoulders back.

"Of course. Carol and I read it together, a chapter a night, when it first came out."

"Have you told Jenna this?" I look up to see my sister chatting with Carol, Marty's arm around her back.

"No, I don't suppose I have."

"Jesus, Dad. She would love to know this!"

"Jenna? No, I'm not so sure. You said yourself, Jenna doesn't need any kind of praise from me. She knows she's a fine writer and an excellent researcher, just in the same way you know how remarkable it is that you have lived and worked in countless countries across the world. Learning the languages, the customs, and climbing the ranks in hospitality."

"No, Dad. I *don't* know this. And I definitely don't know that that's what you think about me."

Dad's face falls. "Oh... Well, that's... That's a shame."

I pull in a breath. "The good news is that it can change," I say. "I've learnt recently that you can change almost anything about yourself as long as you put your mind to it. So, tell me what you were going to say about Jenna's book?"

"Yes, that. Well, when I read the chapter about communication, I realised I'd made many mistakes with you kids. There was so much I didn't tell you, and what I did tell you was done in the wrong way. Especially after you lost your mother."

My head feels a little fuller as I listen to my father effectively give me the apology I have always wanted to have from him. I keep expecting some new feeling of peace or calm to waltz in, but it doesn't come. It's not that I feel agitated or on edge, rather I am realising I didn't need this as much as I thought I did. I had already made some peace with it. It's great to hear my father apologise and sound vulnerable for the first time in my life, but it's not the missing jigsaw puzzle piece I thought it was. As mystifying as that is, it's also reassuring too.

"So, perhaps, if you would like to, you could come up to us for Christmas again this year?" My father finishes by asking. I open my mouth to tell him how I'd like that, but I'm distracted by the instantly identifiable first notes of a song I specifically told the DJ not to play.

When I hear Michael Jackson's voice talking over a lilting guitar melody, I feel goosebumps prickle my skin from my head to my toes. I try to peer through the crowd towards the DJ to see what the hell he's doing, but that's exactly the moment everybody starts to move to the sides of the courtyard and a single figure is standing in the centre of the dance floor, looking at me.

Chapter Forty-Six

Rami

The moment Jake sees me he looks exactly how I have been fearing the last two months: horrified. But it's too late to back out now. Not when *P.Y.T*'s tempo kicks in and it's time for me to dance.

And dance I do. I dance like my life depends on it, and in some very real ways, I think it does. I lip-sync too, just like I did three months ago. I sing every word of the first verse to Jake as his mouth falls open and he looks pinned to his spot by the bar. As the song winds into the first chorus, I do the routine that I came up with in a hotel room in LA just over a week ago, which involves a series of side steps, a spin and a little shuffle with my shoulders. When I look up, I am given the greatest reward on this Earth, Jake's smile. It looks cautious and careful, like he daren't let it fully bloom, but it's there. He's smiling.

As the chorus repeats, I turn my back to Jake and quickly scan the room looking for familiar faces. When I see them scattered around the crowd, all standing to the side, dancing on the spot and grinning knowingly at me, I turn back and proceed to lip-sync the second verse as I dance a little closer to Jake. When he gives me a few long moments of eye contact, it feels like a gift and I treasure it until he looks away, laughing to himself.

The closer I get the more my body itches to reach out and touch him, to pull him against me and dance the rest of the night, and maybe our lives, away together, but I don't. Not yet. And maybe not ever. I tell myself I have to be satisfied with this if this is all I get with Jake again. The opportunity to dance in front of him and make him smile while singing him a song that will always make me think of him.

Just as the second verse ends, I stand still and look over my shoulder, clicking my fingers. Right on cue I see a few people step away from the crowd and come forward. Because they're all behind me, I can't see if they do what I asked them all to do – copy my dance moves, based on the video I sent out a week ago – but I hope they're all giving it their best shot as the chorus kicks in again and I dance through the same sequence.

When Jake's grin widens and his eyes dart around the room, I know they're doing it and I allow myself to imagine how good it looks. When his smile cracks into a laugh that bends his body, I feel pure peace wash over me.

We repeat the sequence as the chorus replays and that's when I become aware of how much noise is in the room. There's cheering, clapping, and whoops of encouragement. I can't contain my smile as I look to the side and see my sisters dancing the routine next to me, wearing matching sky blue three-piece suits Radia made. While she is wearing a bright pink hijab that makes the blue pop even more, Roxie's long black hair tumbles down her back and she proudly boasts the new septum piercing she got a few weeks ago while I was away.

When I look back at Jake, his hand is over his mouth and his eyes look shiny. He glances quickly to his side at the older man next to him and I realise then that it's his father. A slither of panic throws me off the beat for a second but when I see that man bouncing his knees and clapping slightly off rhythm, I'm able to fall back into the dance.

As the song goes to the bridge, I turn around and watch everyone freestyling like I told them to do. I see Marty using both hands to spin Jenna and Maeve around on either side. I make a mental note to seek Maeve out later and thank her for all her help making this happen. Then my attention is captured by Lionel and Luigi doing some rather odd robotic dance together but they're grinning at each other in the same way they did all day at their wedding and their love feels almost contagious. Next to them is Sharon and who I assume is her wife, both of them singing the "Na-na-na-na-nah!" loudly at each other as they dance. And behind them are a small group of others who I don't know but assume to include some of Jake's London friends as well as Dana and Dove, Jake's friends from college, all people Jenna was able to put me in touch with a week ago. I laugh as I watch them dance in a row together, all linked with their arms behind their backs and doing high kicks like a can-can.

Smiling wildly, I look back to the bar, to find Jake and see his reaction to this beautiful love-filled celebration of him.

But he's not there.

Panic ripples through me and I spin around again trying to place him. The song is on its last bars and I just want to see him smile one last time before it ends. I want to know that even if we aren't going to work this out, I still made him smile and feel good on his birthday. And maybe, maybe, part of me just wants to have the opportunity to talk to him, even if that is only to say goodbye.

When I can't see him, I turn to look for Jenna and see her already walking towards me.

"I'll go find him," she says in my ear as the music changes and the moment is so clearly and definably over. Jenna rushes past me and as the room starts to whirl around me, I search for my sisters, suddenly needing them close.

As I do, people start to fill the space around me and I'm promptly pulled into a big hug with Lionel and Luigi. Over their shoulders I see Sharon wave at me, while Marty and his sister also approach. I want to talk to them all, really I do, but more than anything I want to find Jake.

I just want to know Jake's okay.

Finally, I see my sisters standing to the side and I politely make excuses to everyone else saying I need to check on them.

"That was amazing!" Roxie says, grabbing my forearm. "Can we do it again?"

"You did great, Roxie," I say but can't stop myself looking above her head, searching.

"Where did he go?" Radia asks me, understanding.

"I don't know. One second he was there, and then he wasn't. Maybe it was too little, too late," I say and the self-doubt settles far too easily inside my stomach.

Radia shakes her head. "No, he was smiling. He was laughing."

"I've been gone two months," I say, raising my voice over the dance track that now plays. "And there's so much I need to tell him."

"And you will. That's why you're here, isn't it?" Radia grips my other arm. My sisters' hold on me is exactly what I need to find a little focus again.

"I need some fresh air," I say, thinking if I can just go outside and meditate for a few minutes I'll feel so much calmer to think about what needs to happen next.

Radia nods at me and I'm about to go but Roxie jolts forward and throws her arms around me.

"Seriously, that was like the most fun, ever!" she says and she kisses my cheek.

Roxie's embrace and her beatific smile are great comfort in the chaos. They're a reminder that although Jake was at the forefront of my mind when I returned to the UK, my sisters and my mother are as close a second as you could get. And I will always come home to them.

When I leave the courtyard, the comparative quiet of the lobby is sobering but my mind is still busy as I search for Jake on the couches and in the corners. He's not here. When I walk outside, I stop at the top step, standing slightly to the side and close my eyes. I do three long and deep Ayurvedic breaths and feel the tight grip on my nervous system ease a little. When I open my eyes, I expect to see the traffic I hear and people coming and going from the hotel, but all I see is Jake and Jenna sitting on the bottom step, their backs to me and her arm around his shoulder.

Immediately, I take a step down, eager to speak to him, to check he's okay, but then I stop myself. He has his sister. If he needed me, he would have sought me out. I should go back and wait in the lobby and leave it up to him whether he wants to talk to me tonight. I repeat what I've been telling myself ever since I boarded the plane for LA two months ago; I will fight for Jake, but I will also wait if that's what's required. I'll do whatever it takes, for as long as it takes.

I turn around to walk back inside but a voice stops me.

"Got another plane to catch?"

I smile at his tone – the same stinging sarcasm that caught my attention the first day I met him – and I take another deep breath before I turn around. Jenna and Jake are still sitting but they are turned towards me. While Jenna has a sympathetic smile on her face, Jake's mouth can't seem to decide whether to frown or pout.

"Hi, Jake," I say and I sound as pathetic as I feel. There are so many more things I want to say to him but now he's finally engaged in a conversation with me, I have no clue where to start.

Jenna stands up. "I'll go back inside," she says, brushing her hands against her hips. As she passes me, she squeezes my arm and I hope one day I can tell her how much that means to me. It's the thinnest slice of hope but it's one I desperately need.

When I look back at Jake, I see he's standing up too, adjusting his suit with what is now a definite and furious pout. And yet he still looks so, so good.

"Happy birthday," I say tentatively. "I'm sorry I didn't get you anything but..."

"I think you've done enough," Jake bites out and while the words are sour, his face doesn't hold onto the same fury anymore. He looks more lost than anything.

"Can we talk?" I ask him, suddenly frozen on the spot even though my whole body wants to rush down the steps to him.

"You don't want to communicate with me through the medium of dance like you just did? Or considering how many people you roped in to join you, should we call it a flash mob? I'm not sure what the rules are on flash mobs. How many bodies does one need for such a thing?"

"Jake, I... Could we go inside? Sit down?"

"I'm fine here," he says and at that moment we both smile awkwardly at a couple walking up the steps.

"Okay," I say after they've gone. In all the ways I imagined our reunion would go, it never went like this, with us outside in the dark on some stone steps, illuminated by the streetlights and passing cars. I glance up at the night sky and find the moon high in the sky. It's a full moon just like there was on the night we first kissed. It gives me another sliver of hope to cling on to.

I watch Jake as I take two steps down to get closer but stop when he speaks.

"So, a cult, huh?"

"Yeah," I say and I am not shocked he knows. I am only sorry I didn't tell him myself, that I wasn't ready when I should have been. "I should have told you."

"Yes, you fucking should have," he says and while his words have a bite, I can't say for certain it's pure anger.

I swallow and hold his gaze. "There are a lot of reasons why I didn't, but none of them can excuse what I did. I went to rehab to try and address some of these reasons. And I've been working on it, on myself."

Jake's lips press together so tightly it looks painful. "Rehab? How very LA of you."

My body lifts in a light laugh. This man and his humour. "So, I guess you also know about the DJ thing?"

Jake rolls his eyes. "'DJ thing', Rami you've won Grammy awards. Why the hell wouldn't you tell me about that?"

"If you knew about that then you'd have ended up knowing about everything else. I know it's wrong, but I just wasn't ready."

"And I wasn't ready for feeling quite as foolish as I have since I found out. Honestly, when I think about you doing the whole 'DJ thing' at Lionel's wedding… What an idiot I was. You had me thinking you were some amateur who was honoured to do a last-minute wedding set."

"I *was* honoured to do that wedding set," I say truthfully.

"Rami, according to Hello! Magazine you DJed at the wedding of a Swedish princess in 2007. *That's* an honour! Lionel and Luigi's wedding was hardly the same!" Jake's voice threatens to become a shrill squawk.

"No, it wasn't the same. Their wedding was much better," I raise my voice, "because I was there with you."

This silences Jake and I'm not pleased because he looks a little off kilter, but rather I'm glad his silence gives me an opportunity to take another two steps closer to him.

"I know it's more than I should even think of asking for but could I just say a few things? They're things I should have said months ago, I know that, and it won't take long – it is your party after all – but you deserve an apology from me and I'd like to give it to you."

"Rami, it's really not—"

"Please, Jake."

Jake looks skyward and I briefly wonder if he also notices the full globe of the moon and how brightly it shines in London's starless night sky. I wonder if he finds comfort in that too.

"Okay," he says on an exhale.

"I'm sorry," I begin. "I'm sorry I left you like I did. I'm sorry I didn't tell you about my past. I'm sorry I couldn't be your boyfriend two months ago. I'm sorry I disappeared completely. I'm sorry I showed up at your party and caused what now feels like a bit of a scene..."

Jake's eyebrows peak. "It was... a lot."

"Too much?"

Jake inhales sharply through his nose and tilts his chin up. "Speaking as somebody who is often too much for most people, I can confirm that it wasn't even close to being too much."

Something clamps around my heart at his words, but I know I'm not in a place to reach for him or offer him a soothing response.

Please, let me one day have that honour again.

"Well, I'm sorry if it upset you. The way you left at the end—"

"I left because I needed air. I needed some space... to think." His voice drops and so do his eyes. "I never expected to see you tonight."

"I told you I'd come back for you." I square my shoulders.

"And is that what you're doing? Coming back for me?" Jake asks with widening eyes. It feels like a gift to see their chestnut colour swirl in the moonlight again.

"Yes," I say resolutely.

"But... why?" Jake says with a sigh. He sounds exhausted, empty.

"Jake... everything you said that night we were supposed to have dinner—"

"Our first and last date," Jake sneers and I take the hit. I deserve to feel pain right now and I know I can deal with it, especially if Jake keeps talking to me.

"Well, everything you said is still true for me. It's never not been true. But I knew I couldn't be with you properly, fully, until I finished the therapy I had to do. You see, after I left RemiX, the cult, I did go to rehab but I left after a week because

I found out about my dad dying and I just had to get back home and see my mom and sisters."

The softness in Jake's expression disappears as quickly as it comes.

"But why couldn't you tell me all this? Why couldn't you be honest with me? And after I told you everything about my debt. Don't you see how unfair that was?" Jake's hands move almost as quickly as his mouth and his neck strains as his voice gets louder again.

"Yes, it was very unfair. And it was wrong. It's wrong I still haven't told you everything, in my own words, but I want to, I want to tell you everything, and I want to keep telling you everything."

Jake's shoulders rise and fall as he takes a deep breath.

"You still haven't answered my question." He crosses his arms. "Why have you come back? *Why* are you coming back for me?"

I look up to the dark grey sky for inspiration, and I find it.

"Because I am your moon."

Jake blinks. "Pardon?"

"You are the world, *my* world, and I am your moon."

I watch Jake's neck work as he swallows, his mouth firmly closed.

"Do you know how the moon came to be?" I ask him.

Jake shakes his head.

"There are a few different theories but the one that most modern physicists agree on is that over four billion years ago, Earth was in its early stages of being formed and it collided with another huge mass, one believed to be roughly around the size of Mars. This implosion caused pieces of both masses to break off and over time all those broken bits of rock, dust and particles found each other and formed a new mass, the moon. And you know how gravity works, right?"

Jake purses his lips at me and it's perfect, so very perfect. "I'm not just a pretty face," he deadpans.

"No, you are not. You are so much more. But back to the moon. Well, gravity caused that new mass, the moon, to stay close to the Earth because you know gravity pulls us to bigger things."

"I believe it's more about density," Jake cuts in. "So, what you're actually saying is I'm very dense."

I rock back on my heels and laugh. "Not going to make this easy for me, are you?"

"Did you expect me to?" Jake almost, almost smiles with me. This makes me feel brave and I take the final step to stand just one above him. I can finally smell him – soft citrus tones with a floral twist and the faintest hint of his godforsaken cherry lip balm – and it takes all my inner strength not to pull in the deepest inhale.

"I think I told you before that for the longest time the moon has kept me company when other people or things haven't. When I was DJing and touring all over the world, I always looked for the moon because it was the same presence wherever I was. And also, yes, it reminded me of my dad because of his DJ name, and the one I also chose for myself—"

"Which I assume you did in your dad's honour?" Jake sounds interested and it makes me feel so close to ecstatic.

"Yes, but also Lunar is a very, very cool name," I say, smiling at him as he groans, another reaction that buoys me.

"When I was living in LA and feeling a million miles from home, I always looked for the moon on the nights I couldn't sleep or whenever I missed my family and friends. Then when I lived in the desert, after I pretty much gave up everything and everyone I loved, I still had the moon. Even when I was here, in London, when I knew barely anyone and I was working at Status and invading your office and constantly getting on your nerves, the moon was still with me. So when I went back to LA and to rehab, I also looked for the moon when I felt lonely, which was a lot, Jake. I missed you so much. I felt sick with how much I missed you. And at some point, when I was looking at it, I would find myself thinking about how much I would love you to be my moon, to always be somewhere for me. But now I realise that's not the right way round."

"Why not?" he asks with his brown eyes locked on me.

"Because you are bigger. You are more alive. You are full of life. You are the person that gives people light and life. You are the world. You are *my* world. And

I always want to be close to you. I feel that pull, constantly. So that must make me your moon..." I pause, my breath now feeling thinner. "And I want to orbit you for the rest of my days, Jake. If you'll let me."

Jake opens his mouth to speak, his chin tilted up towards me and I wait feeling like my whole life hangs on the next words he speaks. The rumble of cars continues, a few other people walk down the street we're standing on, and in the far distance I hear sirens, a plane flying above, and other muffled noises of the busy city. But it all fades away as I stand in front of the man I love and wait.

Chapter Forty-Seven

Jake

I'm not angry. I didn't leave the courtyard because I was mad at him showing up out of the blue. Even though I know I am acting that way, even though I know it's exactly what I sound like, I'm not annoyed or irritated or displeased.

I'm in shock.

First my father says words I've been waiting to hear all my life, and then the only man I think I've ever been in love with shows up and serenades me. And not only that, he does so with my family and friends all dancing in sync together. It's like a dream. No, it's better than any dream I could have conjured up.

But that's the thing with scenarios that I have never imagined happening before; I don't know how to deal with them. This is ironic considering solving unforeseen problems is a huge part of my professional life, but when it comes to my personal life, the unexpected is a huge curve ball. Because things like this just don't happen to me. Men just don't show up like this for me.

At least they didn't before Rami.

I didn't know what to do when Rami did this the first time, playing *P.Y.T.* at Lionel's wedding and dancing for me. I didn't know what to do when Rami ran me that bath before the ceremony, or when he kissed me for what felt like hours on that bench in the gardens afterwards, or when he piggy-backed me to bed. I didn't know what to do when Rami showed up again for that dinner with Lionel and Luigi, and I certainly felt nothing but astounded when he became everything I craved and desired when we slept together. I was clueless and helpless when Rami discovered my debt and got me to open up about it in a way I had previously thought unthinkable. I didn't know what to do with myself, with him, or the love I felt when Rami stayed with me that whole day and tucked me up in bed when the crying and the talking got too much.

Rami has constantly exceeded whatever expectations I had, and tonight, this moment is no different.

Maybe that's why now the shock is fading, I realise I believe him. I believe he left two months ago because he really had to. I believe there was something stopping him from telling me his story before. I believe he had to do rehab to feel able to be with me fully. I believe he wouldn't have left me if he felt there was another way. I believe him. I believe *in* him.

Rami may have disappointed me by not telling me about his past, and by leaving at the very moment I was ready to give myself completely to him. But he said he would come back for me, and he has. He's here, right here. And by the sounds of it, he's not going anywhere.

Because Rami loves me.

He may not have said it yet, but I see it. I see it in the way his moonlight eyes search my face for answers as he waits for my response. I saw it in the way he danced his socks off and presumably somehow reached out to my sister and many of my friends to join him in doing so. And I heard it in everything he just said to me. And I am reeling from it all. Seeing and feeling someone's love for you is almost more powerful than hearing them declare it.

Rami coughs when I still don't reply. He rocks back as he speaks. "Jake, I know I'm not allowed to rush you, I barely have the right to stand in front of you and tell you all these things, but I'm sort of dying to know what's going on inside that beautiful head of yours," he rushes on before I can even open my mouth, "and it doesn't matter if you don't feel the same. It doesn't matter if you need more time. I'll happily wait the longest time until whenever you're ready."

Well, that makes it easier.

"No, I don't want that," I say firmly.

"You don't..." Shock pulls Rami's eyes wide.

"I don't want you to wait." I'm amazed my voice is as level as it is.

Rami shakes his head and looks like he believes the ground under his feet is about to give way.

Finally, I lift my hand to touch him, something I've been dying to do since I saw him standing in front of me in the courtyard. I cup his face with my hand and treasure the way he leans into it. "I want you to start today, little moon. I want you to start your orbit, today."

There are more things I want to say, more ways I want to acknowledge what he just told me, but I don't get the chance. Rami's hands grab me and pull me close to his body and because he's one step higher, I'm forced to crane my neck as his mouth presses down on mine.

And I swear the Earth tilts a little more on its axis and spins a little faster. Because everything else disappears. The noise around us. The traffic behind me. The buzzing busy thoughts in my head. They all vanish as Rami deepens his grip and his kiss.

This man loves me. I believe it in my bones.

And I love him.

Suddenly, I have to tell him. I pull away from the kiss.

"Rami, I—"

"I fucking love you." He beats me to it.

I smile against his lips. "You swore."

"Yes, because it fucking matters," he says and kisses the tip of my nose. "I fucking love you, Jake Forester."

"I fucking love you, Rami Kazimi."

"You do?" He leans back further, assessing me as disbelief keeps his expression open.

"You literally just stole all my thunder at my fortieth birthday party and I'm still letting you shove your tongue in my mouth." I push my forehead against his lips, claiming another kiss there. "Yes, I love you."

Feeling his hands grip either side of my face, I'm pushed back again as he takes my mouth once more. My arms slide under his tux jacket and up his back as our tongues clash and I love how familiar his warm body feels. I've missed it so much. I hope I never have to miss it again.

"I have so much to tell you," Rami says after sucking my bottom lip into his mouth. "I want to be completely honest with you about everything, totally transparent. I mean, you probably have some questions."

He's right, of course. We have so much to talk about. Because I want to know it all. I want him to fill in this frustrating void that has admittedly haunted us, but I also know now it hasn't consumed us. Because just as he told me, Rami is so much more than his past. He is the man standing before me offering me his heart and his future. And that is more important than anything.

Besides, we hopefully have long years of filling in blanks ahead of us. I'm only forty, after all. I'm still young.

"I only have one that I need you to answer right now," I say. "Are you going to come in and celebrate the rest of my party with me?"

"Yes," he says and moisture lights up his eyes. "I'd love to. And after that, I'm going to carry you upstairs to the suite I booked."

"That was… confident of you." I'm trying to bite back my smile. *So, daydreams really can come true, huh?*

"I would have used it for crying in had you not been ready or willing to join me."

"Rami, it looks like you're crying now." I lift a finger to wipe away a tear that is sliding down his cheek.

"It's possible," he says and sniffs lightly.

"You're so beautiful." And then I push up on my tiptoes so I can find his ear. "Daddy."

He nuzzles his stubble against my cheek and I love how rough and raw it feels. "Can I still be that for you?" He sounds genuinely worried I'm going to refuse him.

"You already are," I say. I suck on his ear lobe and rock my body against his.

"Jake, keep doing that and you'll spend the rest of your party tied up to a bed upstairs."

God, yes, please.

"No." I sigh. "We have to go face the music inside."

"We do," Rami says and his hands come down to find mine. Our fingers locking together. "But guess what?"

"What?"

Rami kisses my lips one more time. "The music sounds better with you."

Epilogue

New Year's Eve
Sydney, Australia

Rami

"Jake, you can stay in the hotel room tonight if you want?" I say to my boyfriend's back. It's been many long minutes since he looked away from the floor-to-ceiling windows that give him a full view of Sydney Harbour Bridge, Sydney Opera House, the North Shore and the vast harbour itself.

"I think I can see my old apartment building," he says, pressing a finger to the glass. I move to stand next to him.

"Look, that one. The lighter-coloured building with the rectangular windows."

"Wow, nice location."

"Yeah, it was. And it should have been. It cost enough."

"How long did you live there?"

"Just over a year. I would have stayed longer but I hated my job and I missed Jenna. I also ran out of money," he adds in a quieter voice.

"Where were you working?"

"At Harbour North Hotel. Look, you can see that too. There," he points to another tower block, "I was assistant manager of the restaurant."

"I don't think I've heard of it," I say.

"I bet all the hotels you've stayed in over the years just blend into one another."

"Depressingly it is a bit like that. When were you working there?"

Jake looks up, thinking. "Sixteen, seventeen years ago. In fact it was exactly sixteen years ago today I saw in the new year there with this awful guy. He was married to a woman, had terrible style, and opened beer bottles with his teeth."

"Sounds like a real catch. You think you've moved up since him?" I come to stand behind Jake and I wrap my arms around his waist. He leans back on me.

"Well, on paper you're hardly an upgrade. Ex-cult member. Closeted until your forties. Turned down a multi-million two-album deal."

"So I could spend more time with you!" I tighten my hold, on him.

"As I said, on paper, you're a dubious prospect. But in reality, you're a sure thing." He grips my arms. "You're my sure thing."

"Always," I say before I kiss his neck. When Jake pushes his arse back against my groin I curse how we don't have more time before I need to be at Blues Point for my set. "You know you really don't have to come tonight."

Jake spins in my arms. "It's New Year's Eve in Sydney and you're playing a Harbour-front set. You really think I'd rather be stuck inside a hotel room, even if it is *very* luxurious and has possibly the best view of the Harbour Bridge fireworks?"

"You have been the supportive partner many times before. We're both jetlagged. You don't need to come, if you don't want to."

"Sod being your partner. What kind of tour manager would I be if I wasn't there to keep an eye on you?"

I smile at this. It had taken quite a few weeks of persuading Jake to become my tour manager, but I was glad he had taken his time. Leaving his job with Status wasn't an easy decision, although they assured him he would always be welcome back once the tour was finished. It was also risky, us working together – we'd be living and working in each other's pockets – not to mention how Jake had never done this exact line of work before. But I knew he was more than qualified for the job, and he quickly proved me right. As it happened, spending more time together didn't pose any problems at all. Maybe all those weeks reluctantly sharing an office had prepared us well for the dynamic, or maybe we were both too loved-up to be apart. Because we really are loved-up.

After his birthday party and the long, hot night that followed it, Jake and I returned to his flat and stayed there talking until the sun came up on Monday and he went to work. When he returned from work that night, I had dinner waiting for him as well as an eager readiness to answer any more questions he had. Our evenings followed the exact same pattern for the rest of the week until Saturday when we stayed in bed all day communicating in many wordless ways and then on Sunday, Jake and I went to spend the day with Mom and Roxana. The following week when we went up to Birmingham, Jake and I walked around the corner to knock on my childhood friend Dev's house. Despite my body being a barrel of nerves, Jake and I had been welcomed warmly and it took no time at all before we were drinking tea and playing Nintendo with his kids, including my godson, Jaden who kicked all of our asses. We followed this routine almost to the letter for a month or so until I took Jake back to LA with me so he could meet Cassie and we could finalise the world tour plans.

It was both jarring and therapeutic having Jake in California with me. On one hand, I had feared having him there would blur my old and new lives in ways I wouldn't make sense of. Likewise, I didn't feel completely comfortable with him meeting people who had known me back when I was a very different person. And then there was the proximity to the desert, Michelle, and Gee. An irrational, illogical part of me was almost worried this closeness would infiltrate Jake and tarnish his opinion of me in one way or another. But after letting these fears come and go, I was able to make space for the healing aspect of being in LA with Jake. I got to experience his excitement at a new city, one I had also been thrilled to discover for the first time many years ago. And I got to stand proudly by his side as various friends and acquaintances met him and instantly warmed to him. After a few days, it really did feel like the beginning of a new chapter. It was also good for planning the tour.

Although, at first, he described Cassie as a "terrifying Miss Trunchbull type of woman", over the course of several meetings they became firm friends whose primary shared interests quickly came to include taking the piss out of me and also agreeing they would hide all my black clothing on the world tour so I would have to wear some colour, something that scared me more than I would like to admit.

But still, that couldn't stop me smiling. I feel like I haven't stopped smiling since Jake and I kissed outside Clapham Manor House nearly four months ago.

After our LA trip, Jake worked out his notice at Status while I started doing a few warm-up gigs to promote the tour up and down the UK. Once Jake had left his flat and job, he then officially started as my tour manager and together we travelled through most of Northwest Europe doing more gigs and club nights for a few weeks. After a deliberately planned night in Dublin, we spent a week with Marty and Jenna, whose growing baby bump had to endure Jake singing most of Wham!'s Greatest Hits to it. After that, we returned to London for a short time while I got my Hoxton apartment ready to rent. Jake also had a proper farewell party with his friends, which was a modest affair in a Mayfair pub's function room and there was absolutely no dancing or lip-synching by me, much to Lionel and Luigi's disappointment.

We took a week off to spend Christmas in Edinburgh with Malcolm and Carol, which was exactly the slower-paced rest we both needed before we boarded a flight to Sydney two days ago. It was also what Jake needed, to spend quality time with his father who revealed he's started doing cognitive behavioural therapy, and I even managed to persuade him and Carol to join me on some of my meditation sessions.

The next eight months will see us travel most of Asia, North America, South America and Europe on this world tour that I am more excited about than I expected. This is thanks in large part to Jake accompanying me but it's also because I've created a set that will honour my roots and my father's memory. Gone are the EDM remixes I once used to do and instead I will be focusing on playing the seventies and eighties disco and soul my father loved so much. I've remixed my old releases to have this same flavour and I'm bringing nearly half of my personal vinyl collection on the tour with me. The rest of the records are now lovingly displayed on the unit in my living room and my new tenants have my full permission to enjoy them as much as they choose.

While Jake still has a way to go with his debt, he continues to pay off a decent chunk each month, helped considerably by the fact he no longer has to pay rent or many living expenses, something I insisted on as soon as he agreed to be my tour manager. More than a few times I've considered paying off the remaining balance for him and one time, I was seconds away from voicing the suggestion, but in the next breath, I sensed that Jake would refuse it even if I offered. And I don't want to offer. Me paying off his debt wouldn't bring him the affirming mood boosts he enjoys each time the number drops. Me paying off his debt wouldn't give him the self-esteem-enhancing pride that he feels when he puts a little extra cash aside into savings that he regularly tells me he wants to spend on our first home together. Me paying off his debt would present more problems than it solves.

Not that it's all been easy. It hasn't been. Jake has had many wobbles along the way including a few pairs of shoes that he grumblingly took back a few days later of his own accord. Despite us being with them last week, since the party he's also not had the regular contact he wanted with his father and when he finds himself having to call him more often than Malcolm calls him, sometimes Jake drifts off inside himself and it takes a little encouragement to bring him back to the surface. And other times, whenever they have spoken, the conversations have been so stilted and one-sided that Jake can't move on from them until he's had a big cry on my shoulder. It feels a little insensitive to say this but those are the moments I treasure most and I always, always tell Jake how grateful I am that he gives me the privilege of being there to look after him.

I am slowly getting better at showing Jake the same vulnerability.

A month ago, I finally heard from Michelle. It was off the back of an interview I did with The Guardian, the only piece of public press I have done about my comeback tour. In it, I talked openly about RemiX, and about what it cost me, emotionally and to a certain extent, financially. I didn't mention Gee or Michelle's names and it was a condition of the interview that the article also didn't refer to any other individuals, but there was enough noise surrounding the publication that it wouldn't have taken people much to piece it all together. Indeed, Michelle read enough about herself in the article that she felt motivated to contact me after over two years of silence. Her email was scornful and it detailed just how disappointed she was in me, and just how much I had betrayed her and Gee. She also told me how much I had now "muddied my waters", tainting "the purity" I attained when I was part of RemiX. It stung at first. I felt old familiar stirrings of panic mixing with the dreaded fear of letting down someone I used to care about. But then I glanced up from my laptop and watched Jake cooking me dinner while shaking his perfect backside to Sister Sledge's *Thinking of You* and I deleted the email and let it go.

  The hardest day we've had together was on a windy autumn day in November: my dad's birthday. I'd been feeling the build-up to the day for almost a week, and I hadn't uttered a word to Jake about how I was feeling, choosing instead to try and push through the way I woke up with a heavy weight on my chest and how any moment of silence invited that deep, dark self-disgust that had kept me company since the day I found out he had died. And I didn't tell Jake about it. I didn't share how awful I felt. I didn't even tell him when it was the day that should have been my father's 76th birthday. I didn't tell him until I was pushing food he'd lovingly made around a plate and staring at the wall of the London apartment we were renting for a few weeks. Jake had kicked me under the table and insisted I talk to him or he would take my credit card to Selfridges and ruin my perfect credit score. When I'd opened my mouth to tell him it was Baba's birthday, only sobs fell out.

  After a few minutes of crying at the table, Jake dragged me to the bathroom where he ran me a bath and put on his own playlist of choice, which was anything but chilled-out music. I continued crying as I lay in a sweetly fragranced bubble bath with Britney Spears playing on a Bluetooth speaker near my ear and Jake holding my hand while sitting on the closed toilet. It had taken me a few more hours to really voice why I felt so bad, to admit how disgusted I felt with a previous version of me, but I did share some of those feelings and mercifully, gratefully, Jake had stayed by my side the whole time.

  I hope Jake is always by my side.

  "You know I do wonder what Steveo is up to these days." Jake is looking back outside at the view.

  "Steveo?"

  Using air quotes, he explains, "The 'straight' man I was stupidly hooking up with when I was living here. He had a wife in Melbourne and swore he was straight but nevertheless had a terrible habit of rogering me senseless."

"I happen to think that's my best habit of all. After meditation, of course."

Jake laughs and it's my favourite song. "God, I'm so glad you're funny these days," he says. "No way we would have lasted this long if you weren't."

I smile at my boyfriend. "So what do you think Steveo is up to?"

"I really don't know. But I'd like to think he's living his best gay or bisexual life, or just being whoever he wants to be. Life's not exactly easy when you're living a lie."

I nod before moving to stand behind Jake again, my arms wrapping around his chest this time.

"That was what, sixteen years ago, you say?" I ask and in my mind I pinpoint the year and start to scroll back through my memories.

"Sixteen years to the day. I remember that new year so vividly. We were at a club night in the hotel I worked at. I left it too late to get tickets for something more exciting. I can't remember who was playing but it wasn't terrible. Besides, that night I was all preoccupied with Steveo. Or rather, I was preoccupied with trying to get *un*-preoccupied with him. I actually dumped him that night, and I was all ready to stop messing around with unavailable men for good, but somehow a few weeks later he broke me down. And spoiler alert, he wasn't the last unavailable man I slept with."

"We've all done things we regret," I say and bend my neck to kiss the skin I find just above the collar on Jake's shirt. "The key is to not be consumed with that regret."

"Yes, Guru Rami," he says and then when I don't say anything, he adds, "Too soon?"

I smile into his skin. "Not too soon." I drop my voice. "I just prefer Daddy."

"Yeah, you do," Jake says rocking back into me again.

"Wait, you said you were in a hotel nightclub for New Year's Eve sixteen years ago?" I ask as a half-formed memory flashes into my brain.

"Harbour North Hotel, where I worked. It has a nightclub on the top floor. Or it used to. Maybe it's gone now, I don't know…"

I freeze and Jake's voice drifts into background noise.

"Sixteen years ago," I say again, more to buy me a little memory-searching time.

It can't have been. Surely not.

"Yes, why?"

I close my eyes and inhale the scent of my man. Could I really have had all this sixteen years ago? Could life have been so very, very different?

"No reason," I say quietly.

"We should get going." He taps my arm, but I don't let him go.

"Jake."

"Yeah?" he replies, leaning back against me once more. I stand strong and take his weight.

"We should go shopping tomorrow."

"Rami, that's not exactly a good idea for me," he says in a quiet voice. "Australia is not a cheap country."

"No, *I* want to take *you* shopping," I clarify.

"Oh, finally! You're going to be the Sugar Daddy I need! It's taken you long enough to realise that's what I've wanted all this time," Jake jokes, and I know he's only teasing because as he turns his head so I can see his pout, I see it clashes with the love that swims in his eyes.

I laugh softly. "No, I just want to buy you some shoes."

"Shoes?"

"Yes, some really beautiful shiny shoes."

"I like shiny shoes," he says and I hear the smile in his voice.

"I know you do." I lift my head so I can look over Jake's shoulders and outside, searching the night sky to once again give thanks to the moon for guiding me to where I was always supposed to be.

THE END

THANK YOU!

Thank you so much for reading this ARC of The Moon Also Rises.

Here are your links for leaving a review:

Goodreads: https://geni.us/TheMoonGoodreads

Amazon: https://geni.us/TheMoonAlsoRisesBook

If you want to share the book or your review on social media, please use the hashtag #TheMoonAlsoRisesBook.

GET YOUR FREE BONUS SCENES!

Want more of Jake and Rami? Would you like to know what happened immediately after Jake's birthday party in that hotel suite Rami confidently booked? Then sign up at the link below to receive three chapters of bonus scenes!

https://francesmthompson.eo.page/themoonalsorises

And if you want to stay in this world and you haven't already done so, you can read Jenna and Marty's love story in Five Sunsets, and you can also read the spicy festive novella, Christmas Sunrise, which takes place the Christmas before The Moon Also Rises begins and it also features four-way POV. Maeve's book is coming in 2023 so keep your eyes open for that!

Author's Note

When I first considered making Jake's biggest challenge credit card debt, I didn't exactly feel inspired. Debt and money and our relationship with these things is hardly exciting or sexy, however, there was also something in that in itself that intrigued me. Why do we find it so hard to talk about money publicly? Why do so many people live with debt and yet don't talk about it in a way that could potentially rid them from the burdensome shame that comes with it? And then there are the questions that are more urgent and pressing and yet even more buried; Why do we live in a world where debt is so common, and poverty on the increase? Why do we not try and change our systems and our institutions and our governments so that we no longer live in a world where debt is unavoidable and often the only way some people can survive?

These are big questions and certainly not ones I tried to answer in this book, however, I do hope I highlighted how for many people shame is a true stumbling block for helping them confront and manage their debt or relationship with money. I also hope I highlighted how removing that shame is something we all play a role in. If we can all think about debt in a different way – as a product of our corrupt and broken capitalistic world - we can help reduce the stigma that has many people stuck in their situations unnecessarily. I don't have a perfect relationship with money, and I highly doubt any of us do, but writing this book has helped me have more empathy for those who have debt or shopping addictions or similar struggles, and likewise, it has made me more determined to do more with how I act, vote and communicate, to make our world a better place where poverty is eradicated and people are taught to nurture a healthy relationship with money from their earliest years.

Resources that have helped me with my own relationship with money and also when researching this book include, but are not limited to @myfrugalyear on Instagram, @rainchq on Instagram and Martin Lewis, the Money-Saving Expert.

It was my plan to donate a small percentage of sales from this book to a charity that helps those experiencing chronic problems with debt, however, while I was writing The Moon Also Rises another cause demanded my attention and efforts. The uprising in Iran is a long overdue bloody and brave fight for freedom by the people of Iran, led predominantly by the women and youth of the country. It first came to the world's attention in mid-September 2022 with the killing of twenty-two-year-old Mahsa Amini while in police custody. She was arrested for not wearing her hijab and for also reportedly wearing skinny jeans.

While I had already created Radia and Roxie for this book before this tragic event, there was something suddenly haunting about my two young British-Iranian women – one a proud hijabi and the other a skinny-jean wearing, piercing-sporting student who doesn't wear the hijab – having and enjoying their freedom to proudly and loudly be queer and neurodiverse respectively. I deliberately chose not to include the protests in The Moon Also Rises' narrative in order to not have the mention be flippant and perfunctory, but there's no doubt in my mind Radia and Roxie would have been at the front of any protests in solidarity with the women of Iran in either Birmingham or London.

As for the current situation in Iran, at the time of writing this, it continues. There have been strikes, walk-outs, demonstrations and large- and small-scale protests for the subsequent two months and the efforts show no signs of abating despite countless arrests and over two hundred lives being lost in the struggles. In fact, there are increasing reports that more beatings and death sentences are being dished out to protestors. It is highly likely more lives will be lost as the efforts continue and we are possibly a long, terrifying way off knowing how peace and democracy will come to Iran.

This is why the people of Iran desperately need our support to maintain momentum and continue to fight for their freedom. It's for that reason that 0.50c of each book sale will go to United 4 Iran https://united4iran.org/.

Acknowledgements

The more books I write, the more people there seem to be to thank, but I wouldn't want it any other way.

To my editor Sophia, THANK YOU! It was such a pleasure to work with you again and for The Moon Also Rises to benefit from your eagle eye, fantastic suggestions and heartfelt encouragement throughout. I can't wait to work with you again on Maeve's book.

My thanks to Sam who provided a thorough sensitivity read that also caught some editorial wobbles. You were the first to really fall for Rami and Jake and your enthusiasm for them carried me through the tough final stages of getting this book into the world.

Thanks also to Alexis, Eryn, and Fadwa who provided additional sensitivity reads and helped this book be as affirming as possible for all the identities and communities it touches.

Again, thanks goes to Crystal, my proofreader, who always does so much more in terms of catching any other errors or oversights. Always so grateful for you!

Thanks also to Lee-Anne for sanity proofing this book at a stage when every single word I read is blurry.

A big thank you to Teju for the cover art and design. I love how you captured exactly what I wanted and I still squeal a little whenever I see Jake's face in the illustrations. Can't wait to see what magic you reveal for Maeve's book.

Thank you again to M Designs for the final cover design and additional formatting help. You always step in whenever I need you and I will be forever grateful for that.

My thanks are owed to Rebecca who not only did an authenticity read for the Brummie characters but also provided much needed excitement for this book when I was close to the end of my wits getting it ready. Your Whatsapps and emojis gave me a truly much needed boost!

Thanks again to all of my ARC readers who found me after Five Sunsets or who came back for me after taking a chance with that book. I will never take any of you for granted and am forever grateful for your reviews and support.

Credit and thanks to Amanda Montel and her book Cultish for helping me understand that cults are not just obscure orgy-focused religious organisations or authoritarian institutions that indulge in satanic rituals. In fact, our daily lives are filled with "cultish" groups, interactions and branding, and while this is terrifying this did help me realise that Rami's experience of a cult didn't need to be overtly extreme to be deeply damaging and dangerous.

Now to thanking people who support me when I am away from my laptop. My never-ending thanks go to my good, good friends Rhi and Kristen. Thank you for supporting me on- and offline, for having my boys over and for having my back as I navigate the hardest few months of my life. Things would be so much harder without you down the road and I am incredibly grateful for you.

Thank you to my best ones, Beth and Cat. You are my biggest supporters and I will always, always love you.

My endless thanks and hugest hugs to Jenny, my friend who "just gets it" and will never get rid of me. You have saved me these last few months and I am forever in awe of your strength and sense of humour. I love you.

To my parents, thank you. Yes, this is another book I don't recommend you read, but it is another book that is only possible because of the love and self-confidence you instilled in me at a young age.

To my kids, O and JJ, I love you and I hope you are proud of Mummy for writing another book. I have no idea who you will end up loving when you're older, but I hope they fill your life with the best things in life, like good playlists and kisses in the moonlight.

To Mark, my love and life partner. THANK YOU. You have literally carried me at times in the last few months and I will never take the way you care for me for granted. I hope the future is easier for us both but please know that every love story I write is dedicated to you.

About the Author

Originally from UK, Frances M. Thompson (she/her) lives in Amsterdam, the Netherlands, with her partner and two young children. Please call her Frankie if you ever cross her path because nobody calls her Frances unless she's in trouble or you work for the tax authorities.

The author of three short story collections, a book of poems called Lover Mother Other and the London Killing series of suspense thrillers, Frankie is also the author of steamy contemporary romances and runs the semi-successful, but oft neglected travel and lifestyle blog, As the Bird flies. All of Frankie's books feature Bi+ main characters because that's what she needed more of growing up.

When not reading or writing, Frankie can be found dancing in her kitchen, cycling around Amsterdam, faffing with her many house plants, swearing her way through freezing open water swims, and squeezing in as many sunny or snowy holidays as she can.

Follow Frankie on Instagram or TikTok as @francesmthompson, or on Twitter as @FranceMTAuthor. You can find Frankie and all her books on Goodreads and Amazon, and you can listen to the playlists for her books on Spotify under her username "frankiebird".

Keep in touch with Frances M. Thompson:

Join my newsletter: https://geni.us/FiveSunsetsSignUp
Join my ARC team here: https://forms.gle/YyHUwesEhPprZ8D58
Frances on Goodreads: https://geni.us/FMThompsonGoodreads
TikTok (@francesmthompson): https://geni.us/FMTTikTok
Instagram (@francesmthompson): https://geni.us/FMTInstagram
Twitter (@FrancesMTAuthor): https://geni.us/FMTTwitter

Books by Frances M. Thompson:

Too Many Stars to Count (Sun, Moon & Stars #3) – Coming in 2023

Butterflies (Birds and Butterflies #2) – Coming 2023

The Way We Were (London Killing Thriller #3) – Coming 2023

The Moon Also Rises (Sun, Moon & Stars #2)

Christmas Sunrise (Sun, Moon & Stars 1.5)

Hummingbird (Birds and Butterflies #1)

Five Sunsets (Sun, Moon & Stars #1)

The Weaker Sex (London Killing Thriller #2)

The Wait (London Killing Thriller #1)

Lover Mother Other (Poetry)

Nine Women: Short Stories

London Eyes: Short Stories

Shy Feet: Short Stories About Travel

Printed in Great Britain
by Amazon